BECKY ALBERTALLI
& AISHA SAEED

YES
NO
MAYBE
SO

BALZER + BRAY

An Imprint of HarperCollinsPublishers

Also by
BECKY ALBERTALLI
Simon vs. the Homo Sapiens Agenda
The Upside of Unrequited
Leah on the Offbeat
What If It's Us (with Adam Silvera)
Love, Creekwood: A Simonverse Novella

Also by
AISHA SAEED
Amal Unbound
Written in the Stars
Aladdin: Far from Agrabah
Once Upon an Eid: Stories of Hope and Joy by 15 Muslim Voices
(coedited with S. K. Ali)

Balzer + Bray is an imprint of HarperCollins Publishers.

Yes No Maybe So
Copyright © 2020 by Becky Albertalli and Aisha Saeed
www.epicreads.com

Library of Congress Control Number: 2019950097
ISBN 978-0-06-293703-2 (paperback)
ISBN 978-0-06-297776-2 (int.)
ISBN 978-0-06-298379-4 (special edition)

Typography by Chris Kwon
20 21 22 23 24   PC/BRR   10 9 8 7 6 5 4 3 2 1
❖
First paperback edition, 2020

For Stacey, Lucy, and Jon, with gratitude

CHAPTER ONE
JAMIE

"Oranges don't have nipples," says Sophie.

I park our cart by the display pyramid, pointedly ignoring her. You could say there's a part of me that doesn't want to discuss nipples with my twelve-year-old sister in the Target produce section. And that part of me. Is all of me.

"They're tangelos," Sophie adds. "*Tangelos* have—"

"Good for tangelos." I tear a plastic bag off the roll. "Look. The sooner we get everything, the sooner we can leave."

Which isn't a diss on Target. No way. Target's the best. It's kind of my personal wonderland. But it's hard to catch that anything-could-happen, big-box-general-merchandise vibe when I'm here as my cousin's errand boy. Gabe is the assistant campaign manager for a special election in our district, and he never seems to run out of random jobs for Sophie and me. This morning he texted us a snack list for his volunteers: oranges, grapes, chocolate, pizza bagels, Nutri-Grain bars, water bottles. NO APPLES. NO PRETZELS. All caps, in true Gabe fashion. Apparently, crunchy foods and political phone banking don't mix.

"Still think they look nipply," Sophie mutters as I reach for a few tangelos near the top of the pyramid. I like the ones that are so bright, they look photoshopped, as if someone cranked up the color saturation. I grab a few more, because Gabe's expecting at least ten volunteers tonight.

"Why does he even want oranges?" Sophie asks. "Like, why pick the messiest fruit?"

"Scurvy prevention," I start to say—but two girls step through the automatic doors, and I lose my train of thought completely.

Listen, I'm not the guy who can't function when a cute girl walks by. I'm really not. For one thing, that would imply I was a functional person to begin with. Also, the issue isn't that they're cute.

I mean. They *are* cute. Around my age, dressed for Georgia summer air-conditioning in zipped-up hoodies and jeans. The shorter one—white, with square-framed glasses and brown spiral curls—gestures emphatically with both hands as they approach the carts. But it's her friend who keeps catching my eye. She's South Asian, I think, with wide brown eyes and wavy dark hair. She nods and grins at something her friend says.

There's just something so familiar about her. I swear, we've met before.

She looks up, suddenly, like she senses me staring.

And my brain stalls out.

Yup. Yup. Okay. She's definitely looking at me.

My friend Drew would know what to do here. Eye contact with a cute girl. A girl I'm pretty sure I know from somewhere, which means there's a built-in conversation topic. And we're in Target, the definition of my comfort zone. If there's even such a thing as a comfort zone when cute girls are involved.

Dude, just talk to her. I swear to God, it's not that deep. I wonder how many times Drew's said that to me. *Eye contact. Chin up. Smile. Walk over.*

"Okay, Mr. Heart Eyes." Sophie nudges me. "I can't tell which girl you're looking at."

I turn quickly back to the tangelo display, cheeks burning as I grab one from the bottom of the pyramid.

And everything comes crashing down.

First the pyramid trembles—followed by the *thwack thwack thwack* of oranges raining to the floor. I turn to Sophie, who claps both hands over her mouth and stares back at me. *Everyone's* staring at me. A mom pushing her baby in a cart. The guy manning the bakery. A kid, pausing mid-tantrum near the packaged cookie display.

Of course, the two girls are front and center. They stand frozen by their cart, with matching uh-oh expressions.

Thwack thwack thwack. And again. Without pause.

And.

Thwack.

The last tangelo falls.

"I'm—"

"A cartoon character," Sophie finishes.

"Okay. Yeah. I can fix this." I squat down right where I'm standing, and start passing tangelos up to Sophie. "You take these."

I tuck a few more into the crook of my arm and attempt to stand, but I drop a bunch of them before I'm even upright. "Crap." I bend to grab them, which sends a few more tumbling down, rolling toward the apple display—which you'd think wouldn't happen with tangelos. Shouldn't the nipples keep them from rolling? I scoot on my knees toward the apple display, hoping nothing slid too far under, when someone clears his throat loudly.

"Okeydokey, my dude, let's keep you away from the apples."

I look up to find a clean-cut guy in a red polo shirt and a Target name tag. *Kevin.*

I scramble up, immediately squishing a tangelo beneath my sneaker. "Sorry! I'm sorry."

4

"Hey," Sophie says. "Jamie, look at me." She's holding her phone up.

"Are you filming me?"

"Just a little Boomerang," she says. She turns to Kevin, the employee. "Meet my brother, Butterfingers von Klutz-owitz."

"I'll help you clean this," I say quickly.

"Nah, you're totally fine. I got this," says Kevin.

Sophie peers down at her phone. "How do you send stuff to BuzzFeed?"

Out of the corner of my eye, a flicker of movement: the girls in hoodies veering quickly down a side aisle.

Getting the hell away from me, I guess.

I don't blame them one bit.

Twenty minutes later, Sophie and I park at the Jordan Rossum state senate campaign satellite headquarters—technically the side annex of Fawkes and Horntail, a new-age bookstore on Roswell Road. Not exactly the Georgia State Capitol building, or even the Coverdell Building across the street, where Mom works for State Senator Jim Mathews from the Thirty-Third District. The whole state capitol complex looks plucked from DC, with its columns and balconies and giant arched windows. They've got security teams at the entrances, like an airport, and once you're in, it's all heavy wooden doors and people in suits and fidgety groups of kids on field trips.

And those bright, gleaming Coverdell Building bathrooms.

I know *all* about those bathrooms.

No suits or security teams at Fawkes and Horntail. I cut straight to the side-access door, hoisting two dozen bottles of water, while Sophie trails behind me balancing the snack bags. We're here so much, we don't even bother knocking.

"Hey, bagels," greets Hannah, the assistant field coordinator. She means us, not the snacks. There's a bagel chain in Atlanta called Goldberg's, and since we're Jamie and Sophie Goldberg, people sometimes . . . yeah. But Hannah's cool, so I don't mind it. She's a rising junior at Spelman, but she's staying with her mom in the suburbs this summer, just to be near the campaign office.

She looks up from her desk, which is stacked high with canvassing flyers—the ones Gabe calls *walk pieces*. "Is this for the phone bankers tonight? Y'all are the best snack team ever."

"It was mostly me," Sophie says, handing her the snack bags. "I'm like the snack team captain."

Hannah, halfway across the room with the snacks, looks back over her shoulder and laughs.

"Except I drove," I mutter. "I pushed the cart, carried all the water—"

"But it was my idea." Sophie jabs me with her elbow and smiles brightly.

"Mom literally made us."

"Okay, well I'm the one who *didn't* knock over a display, so."

Hannah walks back over and settles into her desk. "Hey, y'all are coming tomorrow night, right?"

"Oh, believe me," Sophie says. "We'll be there."

Mom never lets us miss Rossum campaign events these days. Lucky us. They're all the same: people milling around with plastic cups, making overly familiar eye contact. Me forgetting everyone's names the moment I hear them. And then everyone gets super extra when Rossum arrives. People laugh louder, angle toward him, sidle nearer to ask for selfies. Rossum always seems a little startled by the whole thing. Not in a bad way. More like in a *who me* kind of way. It's his first time running for office, so I guess he's not used to all that attention.

But the thing about Rossum is that he's amazing with people. I mean, his platform's great too—he's super progressive, and he's always talking about raising the minimum wage. But a lot of it's just the way he speaks. He can give you goose bumps, or make you laugh, or make you feel purposeful and clear. I always think about the people who shake the world with their words. Patrick Henry, Sojourner Truth, John F. Kennedy, Martin Luther King. I know

Rossum's just a guy running for state senate. But he makes it all feel huge. He makes this race feel like a *moment*, a brand-new dot on Georgia's timeline. He makes you feel like you're watching history change.

I can't imagine being able to do that.

Tomorrow's event is an interfaith outreach dinner at a local mosque, which means Mom's extra excited. We aren't the most observant Jews in the world, but she lives for this kind of religious community-building stuff.

"Should be fun," says Hannah, opening her laptop. But then she stops short, glancing back up at us. "Oh, right, you need snack reimbursement, don't you? Gabe's in the VIP room. I'll grab him."

The VIP room? A supply closet.

Hannah emerges moments later, followed by Gabe, who's wearing a crisp blue button-down shirt, with a picture of Jordan Rossum's face stickered onto his chest. People sometimes say Sophie and I look like Gabe, since he's tall and has brown hair and hazel-green eyes. But he's got bigger lips and archier eyebrows and a weird sprouting pseudo-beard he's always working on. And he's twenty-three, which is a solid six years older than me. So I don't really see it.

Gabe clasps his hands and grins. "I was wondering when I'd see your faces around here."

"We were here on Monday," Sophie says.

"And Sunday," I add.

He's unfazed. "You've been missing out on some sweet canvassing action. You should sign up for a slot. Or maybe you could swing by for phone banking tonight? It's gonna be lit." He pitches his voice high when he says it, tilting his palms up like he's about to raise the roof. I sneak a glance at Sophie, who seems caught between laughing and choking.

"So are you in?" Gabe asks. "Rossum needs you."

This time, I glance down at my feet. I want to help Gabe, but I'm not a phone-banking kind of person. Envelope stuffing? Absolutely. Postcards? Even better. I've even sent out what Gabe calls "peer to peer" text messages, though anyone old enough to vote is, by definition, not my peer.

Of course, the thing that throws me the most is canvassing. I'm not exactly great at talking to strangers. And I don't just mean cute girl strangers. It's everyone. I get really in my head about it. And thoughts never seem to travel smoothly between my brain and my mouth. I'm not like Sophie, who can walk into any room, befriend anyone, join any conversation. It's not even something she tries to do. Sophie's just fundamentally not self-conscious. Like, she farted on the school bus once in fifth grade, and was downright giddy about it afterward. Being embarrassed didn't even occur to her. If it were me, I'd have shriveled up on the spot.

Maybe some people are just destined to always say the wrong thing. Or *no* thing, because half the time, I just stammer and blush and can barely form words. But hey, better that than the alternative . . . which, as I now know, involves phlegm, a touch of vomit, and State Senator Mathews's black oxford shoes.

Let's just say I'm not the master of persuasion you want on the front lines of your political campaign. I'm not a history changer.

"I don't know." I shake my head. "I'm just—"

"It's super easy," Gabe says, clapping me on the shoulder. "Just follow the script. Why don't I put you down for phone banking tonight, and we'll find you a canvassing slot while you're here."

"Um—"

"We have Hebrew school," Sophie says.

"Oh, sweet. Big J, I didn't know you were still taking Hebrew."

"I'm not—"

Sophie cuts her eyes toward me, lips pursed—the patented Sophie Goldberg STFU Jamie Face. "Jamie *is* taking Hebrew," she says loudly. "Because he needs a refresher so he can quiz me on my haftorah portion."

I nod really fast. "Haftorah. Yup."

"Dang," Gabe says. "That's a good brother."

"He is. And I'm a good sister," Sophie says, smacking my arm. "An extremely good sister. Too good."

I glance at her sideways. "You have your moments," I say.

★   ★   ★

Karma, though. Wow. Sophie may have been lying about Hebrew school tonight, but from the moment we step through the kitchen door, it's clear: we're in bat mitzvah planning hell. My mom and grandma are huddled at the kitchen table in front of Mom's laptop—I mean, that's not the weird part. Grandma's always here. She moved in with us when I was nine, right after my grandpa died. And the huddled-over-a-laptop part's not weird either, since Mom and Grandma are both big-time tech geeks. Mom runs campaign analytics sometimes for Senator Mathews, and obviously Grandma is our resident social media queen.

But the fact that Mom's working from home in a bathrobe at four in the afternoon is concerning, as is the way Boomer, Grandma's mastiff, is pacing nervously around the table. Not to mention the fact that the table itself looks like a paper apocalypse, strewn with centerpiece mock-ups, printed spreadsheets, washi tape, binders, and tiny envelopes. I'd say there's a zero percent chance I'm making it out of the kitchen tonight without a stack of place cards to fold.

Sophie dives in. "New RSVPs!"

"Soph, let Grandma pull up the spreadsheet first," Mom says, reaching for a large binder. "Also, I need you to look at this floor plan so we can think about the flow. We'll mostly be in the ballroom, with the dance floor there, tables here, and we have two options for the buffet. One, we can stick it on the side, near the—"

"Tessa Andrews accepts with pleasure." Sophie slams a card down happily. "Oh. Hell. Yes."

"Sophie, don't cuss," says Mom.

Sophie tilts her head. "I don't really think of hell as a cuss word, though."

"It's a gateway cuss," I say, settling in beside Mom. Boomer parks his chin in my lap, leaning in for a head scratch.

"Here, I've got the spreadsheet pulled up," says Grandma.

"Sophie, are you listening?" says Mom. "Now, the other option for the buffet is this bonus room at the back of the venue. But is it weird having the food that close to the restrooms?"

I shrug. "At least it's convenient."

"Jamie! Don't be gross," Sophie says.

"Oh my God, for handwashing!"

Mom rubs her temples. "I'd like us to utilize the space, since we'll be paying for it anyway, but—"

"Hey." Sophie perks up. "What about a teen room?" Mom narrows her eyes, but Sophie raises a finger. "Hear me out. It's a thing. You've got the adults, all of your friends, family—you all get the nice party in the ballroom, right? And then we get our own super chill smaller party in the other room. Nothing fancy."

"That's ridiculous," says Mom. "Why wouldn't you want to be with family?"

"I'm just concerned about some of the music being a bit much for the old people, you know? This way, y'all can play 'Shout' or whatever in here." She pokes the middle of the ballroom on the floor plan. "And then *we* can have Travis Scott . . . and everyone's happy."

"Travis Scott. Now, isn't that Stormi's dad?" says Grandma.

"We're not having two separate parties," says Mom.

"Then why'd you ask my opinion?" says Sophie. "Why am I even here?"

"Why am *I* even here?" I mutter to Boomer, who gazes back at me solemnly.

I mean, let's be real. Mom didn't even want my input when it was my own bar mitzvah. I didn't even get to pick my own theme. I wanted historical timelines. Mom made me do Around the World, with chocolate passports for favors.

I guess it ended up being sort of cool—in an ironic way, since I've only been to one other country. My dad's been living for years as an expat in Utrecht, so Sophie and I spend a few weeks in the Netherlands each summer. Other than that, we don't talk to him much. It's hard to explain, but when he's physically present, he's *present*—he takes off work when we visit and everything. But he's not really a phone guy or a text guy, and he's barely an email guy. And he's only been back to the States a handful of times since the divorce. I doubt he'll come to Sophie's bat mitzvah, especially with it scheduled so close to our summer trip. He skipped mine, though he did mail me a congratulatory box of authentic Dutch stroopwafels. I didn't have the heart to tell him they sell the exact same brand at Kroger.

"—Jamie's toast," my mom says.

I jolt upright, startling Boomer. "My what?"

"You're giving the pre-challah toast at the reception. And the hamotzi, of course."

"No I'm not." My stomach drops.

"Come on, it will be good for you." Mom ruffles my hair. "Great speaking practice, and pretty stress-free, right? It's just family and Sophie's friends."

"You want me to give a speech in front of a room full of middle schoolers."

"Is that really so intimidating?" asks Mom. "You're going to be a senior. They're not even freshmen."

"Um." I shake my head. "That sounds like hell."

"Jamie, don't gateway cuss," says Sophie.

Grandma smiles gently. "Why don't you think about it, bubalah? It's not all middle schoolers. Drew will be there, Felipe and his fellow will be there, your cousins will be there."

"No." Mom rests her hand on my shoulder. "We're not doing the negotiation thing. Jamie can step out of his comfort zone for Sophie. She's his sister!"

"Yeah, I'm your sister," chimes Sophie.

"This isn't a normal brother thing! Where are you even getting this? If anything, you should be giving the toast."

"Andrea Jacobs's sister gave a toast," Sophie says. "And Michael Gerson's brother, and Elsie Feinstein's brother, though I guess he just said mazel tov and then belched into the microphone. Don't do that. Hey, maybe you could do your toast in verse?"

I stand abruptly. "I'm leaving."

"Jamie, don't be dramatic," says Mom. "This is a good opportunity for you."

I don't respond. I don't even look back.

I can't. I'm sorry. No offense to Sophie. Trust me, I'd love to be the awesome brother who can get up there and be just the right balance of sentimental and funny. I want to charm all her friends and say all the right things. Sophie probably deserves a brother like that. But the thought of standing in front of a packed ballroom, trying to form words and not choke or have a coughing fit or burn the whole banquet hall down . . . It's impossible. It's a job for some other Jamie, and unfortunately, I'm just me.

CHAPTER TWO
MAYA

Sara is on a mission. And since I'm her best friend, I am all in. But forty-five minutes into our treasure hunt we've come up empty. The object of our conquest? A trash can. And no, I do not mean this metaphorically. We are literally on a hunt for a receptacle for garbage.

"It's got to be here somewhere . . . ," Sara mutters. "They had three in stock when Jenna called to check this morning."

I stifle a yawn as people dart past us, pushing red shopping carts.

"I thought you were going with the other stuff you texted me last week," I tell her.

"Yeah, but then Jenna found a great theme here that goes with our dorm layout. This is the only thing we're missing."

"I still don't get it." I glance at her. "I mean, it's a trash can."

"Correction, it's the *perfect* trash can, Maya." Sara's eyes sparkle. "It's got a vintage feel. You'll see!"

I smile and nod, but the truth is, even if we've combed over the storage section three times, I'm just happy I get to be here with her. Between her babysitting gigs, swim coaching at the Y, and working at Skeeter's custard shop, she's as busy this summer as she was all senior year. I haven't even had a chance to tell her everything that's been happening at home. Just thinking about it now makes my stomach knot up. Because right at this moment, my dad is packing his things into cardboard boxes.

I rummage in my purse for my phone; my fingers slide over my passport. It arrived yesterday. Pulling it out, a fresh burst of sadness washes over me. We were supposed to leave for Italy after Ramadan ended, two days after Eid. But right after I turned in my passport application, the trip was canceled and, along with it, it turned out, so was my parents' marriage. I glance at my picture. I think there's some kind of rule that photos in stamp-sized squares must come out terribly. As evidence, I would present: my driver's license, my YMCA card, and now my new passport, where I look like a very stern woodpecker. But *how* I look in this photo feels like a silly thing to even think about, considering everything that's happened.

"It's not that bad," Sara says, looking over my shoulder.

"But not that great."

"It's a passport photo." She pokes me. "It'll get you where you need to go."

I bite my lip. Sara was the first person I wanted to tell about my parents, but she's been so busy. I haven't been able to find the right time. But . . .

"So." I look at her. "I'd been meaning to tell you. Italy got canceled. I think—"

"Are you serious?" Sara whirls around to face me. "You won't believe this. I just got a text this morning from a family who needs a part-time summer babysitter! I felt so bad, because I'm too busy, but I could connect you guys? Jessie's mom is super tapped into the network, so this could be your in."

I blink at the unexpected pivot. It's true. I'd been hoping to break into the ridiculously intricate local babysitting network since forever, but she didn't even pause to ask *why* Italy was canceled. I should rewind and tell her, but she's so amped up right now. And I haven't seen her in so long. . . .

"If it's in the mornings, I can," I finally say. My mom works from home until noon most days, so I can borrow her car.

"Jessie is the sweetest toddler you'll ever meet." Sara jots off a text and puts her phone away. "I don't even know what I'd do here without you," she tells me. "Finding this trash can is like playing a game of Where's Waldo. It could be shelved in so many categories. Kitchen. Bath. Storage . . ."

"I'm kind of shocked you're not working," I say.

"I know," she says. "They shut down the pool because of a plumbing issue, so all my classes have to be rescheduled. I can't believe I have a whole day to myself."

"Maybe we can grab dinner after I open fast?" I suggest. That way we can sit down and finally have a real conversation. Just the thought of talking to Sara about my parents makes me feel a tiny bit better. I don't think there's anything she can possibly say to make me laugh and move on from it, like she normally does when I vent to her. But if anyone can find the humor in my family imploding, it's Sara.

"Mellow Mushroom for old times' sake? We haven't done that in forever."

"Three weeks and two days," I tell her. "Not that I'm counting or anything."

"Sorry." She glances at me sheepishly.

"No big deal. We still have the rest of the summer."

Come fall, she's going to the University of Georgia. I try not to think too much about the fact that Athens is a solid two hours in traffic. And this is Atlanta, so there's *always* traffic.

"Oh yeah, about that." She bites her lip. "I'm not sure about August anymore."

"What do you mean?"

"Jenna is taking summer session two, and her girl-friend—Ashley—is a manager at Avid Bookshop. I just did a Skype interview with them this morning."

"You're leaving sooner than August?" I stare at her.

"Maybe. I don't even know if they'll hire me. Ashley said they got a ton of applications. But if I get the job, you've basically hit the lottery, Maya." She winks. "I bet they have a sweet employee discount on books. You know I'll hook you up."

This isn't a big deal. She was leaving anyway. But she was so busy all senior year—I hoped this summer, we'd finally find pockets of time to catch up. The disappointment stings. This is the downside to being best friends with someone a school year ahead of you.

"Oh my God." Sara glances down at her phone. "Jenna found *another* guy she's positive is 'the one' for me." She holds it out to show me. A boy with a shaggy surfer cut grins back.

"He's cute," I say.

"I haven't even moved yet, and she's already on the look-out." She groans.

"It's about time you got back out there. I think it'll be fun."

Sara hasn't dated anyone since she broke up with her long-term boyfriend, Amari, last year.

"Fun, huh? Okay. I'll tell her to keep an eye out for you too, then!"

"Sara." I bump her with my shoulder.

"Think about it." She grins. "We could even do double dates!"

"Right—that's definitely happening." I roll my eyes.

Here's the thing. Muslims fall all over the spectrum on dating and relationships—kind of what happens when there's over a billion of us—but my parents? They're not cool about me dating in high school. They're not as strict as Lyla's parents, who said she can't hang out with boys, period, but my parents have always said relationships are sacred. They don't think it's a good idea to date just to date, without the potential for a long-term future together. It's not something I really talk about, since it's kind of weird to announce that sort of thing when you're seventeen years old. Sara's the only one who knows, and she thinks that it's bonkers I go along with it—but I actually see where they're coming from on this. Relationships are complicated, and right now there's too much stuff changing in my life for me to think about adding anything like that to the mix. So the truth is, unless Mr. Darcy from *Pride and Prejudice* shows up at my door with flowers announcing his eternal devotion, count me out.

"There it is!" Sara shrieks just then. We're in the "back to school" section. Shelves of cute lamps and alarm clocks frame the space. Five different twin beds are stacked next to each other, outfitted with different patterned sheets, blankets, and throw pillows.

Sara rushes over, scoops up a metal trash can, and gently places it into our shopping cart, like it's a fragile work of art. She snaps a photo and texts it. "I don't know why I didn't check here first. It's the last one too!"

"Awesome." I smile, trying my best to look supportive. But just how excited am I supposed to be about a trash can?

"Jenna texted me to check out the curtains." She pushes the shopping cart along with one hand while glancing down at her phone. I hurry to keep up.

"Still going with sky blue and cream?"

"Yep." She nods. "Let me know if you see anything cute."

I walk along with her as she browses the curtains and then the rugs. She texts Jenna photos along the way. It's like we're hanging out with Jenna too. Which is fine. Really.

We're about to turn into the next aisle when I pause.

"Love muffin straight ahead," I say.

Sara looks up with a start. Her eyes widen.

It's Kevin Mullen from school. He's walking down the main aisle toward us, sipping an iced coffee. In school, he wears loafers, jeans, and preppy button-down shirts, always untucked. But right now, he's in full Target uniform, with practical sneakers, khaki pants, and a bright red T-shirt. I've known Kevin since seventh grade and it's probably statistically impossible not to like him, since he's the chillest and nicest guy around. Even when he was fourteen, sporting

22

the most extreme bowl cut known to man—everyone let it fly without a snicker. We'd gotten to know each other better this past semester when we got assigned to do a presentation on the First Amendment. He'd even come along with Sara and me to Menchie's for frozen yogurt twice. I'm not saying we were friends exactly, but we were on our way. Of course everything fell apart when he brought Sara a basket of her favorite chocolate muffins two months ago and confessed his long-standing crush on her. When Sara told him she didn't feel the same way, he handled it in trademark Kevin style—said it was a bummer, but he understood—but it hasn't been the same. And Sara's been avoiding him anytime she sees him coming. We slipped by him pretty handily when he was cleaning up an orange spill, but it's too late to duck now. He's spotted us.

"Hey, guys." He walks over. Sara quickly glances down at her phone.

"I didn't know you worked here," I say.

"Assistant manager." He taps his badge. "And let me tell you, it has been a day."

"Yeah. What's the deal?" I say as a woman grazes me with her cart. "It's like the migration of the wildebeests."

"It's the Summer Trifecta," Kevin says. "Fourth of July sales plus swim clearance and then an early-bird back-to-school special. It'll be a zoo until August." He looks at Sara and blushes a little. "So, you're leaving soon, right? UGA?"

"Yes." Sara smiles politely.

"I hope they recruit me next year," he says. "Their basketball game is pretty strong."

"It is." Sara brightens, the awkwardness magically vanishing. "You should definitely take a tour and see if you like it."

"Nah, as long as their scholarship game is strong, I'm there."

Sara launches into a speech about the glory that is the University of Georgia and the wonder that is Athens. I suppress a laugh. I mean, don't get me wrong, UGA has a great veterinary medicine program, so I'm all in if I get accepted there one day—but Sara's love for that school is next level. I'm glazing over when I get a text message.

Mom: Where are you?

Maya: At Target helping Sara with some errands.

Mom: When will you be done?

Maya: We're almost wrapping up.

Mom: Pick up some red and blue plates and napkins for the iftar while you're there so we have extra. And come home soon. We need to have a family meeting.

I shove the phone back in my purse. I don't want to have another meeting about this. I want to pretend it isn't happening at all.

We say goodbye to Kevin, and I grab the plates and napkins my mother requested.

"That wasn't so bad," Sara says, glancing back at Kevin's retreating figure.

"Good," I say, slightly relieved. "Also, please tell me you're free tomorrow. I could use some company at the campaign iftar. The food's going to be really good."

"Babysitting," she says. "Sorry."

I'm about to suggest we head to Perimeter Mall before dinner this evening, when her phone buzzes. Glancing down at it, her expression falls.

"Jenna change her mind on the color scheme?" I ask her.

"It's Lucas." She winces. "He fractured his wrist. He needs me to cover his shift at Skeeter's tonight."

"What?" My voice goes two octaves too high. "Can't they find someone else?"

"It's my turn to cover. I'm so sorry, Maya, I really wanted to catch up." She glances at her phone. "I think I'm off Friday evening. I can check with Hen's mom to see if she needs me to sit or not and let you know?"

I shrug. I'm not going to be a big baby about the fact that my best friend has to try and pencil me in like a dentist appointment. It's not like she's leaving soon and I won't see her again except for holidays. Yeah.

I do not want to talk about this.

If you asked me to choose between sitting on this

25

ottoman across from my parents or sticking my hand in a bee's nest, I'm not saying I'd go for the bee's nest, but I would definitely need to think about it.

My parents are pretty cool people, and normally I like hanging out with them. And sitting across from each other in the family room isn't unusual, especially during Ramadan, when we're trying to kill the last few hours before it's time to open fast by playing a game of Spot It! or Uno or Pandemic (my dad is a major nerd).

But there are no board games out right now. We aren't hanging out.

This is a family meeting to sort out the details about how we are not going to be a family anymore. I'm still reeling from the announcement. When they told me Dad was moving out. That it was for the best. That they wished it didn't have to be this way. They normally ask for my feedback on the type of flowers to plant around the mailbox in the spring, or what color to paint the dining room—but breaking up our family unit as we know it was something they didn't bother to run by me.

It shouldn't have come as a complete shock. I'd heard the arguments since the middle of junior year. I saw the unmade guest bed the last few months. I just thought they'd get over it, whatever *it* was. We're a family. Families fight. Families make up and move on. It didn't hit me until now that moving on could mean something else entirely.

"Maya?"

They watch me expectantly.

"The movers are coming tomorrow," my mother says. "In the afternoon."

"The leasing office is still trying to find the spare key," my father says. "I'll get it to you as soon as I have it."

"Do you have any questions for us?" my mother says.

"About?" I glance at them.

"This . . ." My mother gestures to the half-packed moving boxes around us. "Anything on your mind?"

"It's a little too late for that, isn't it?"

"We just want to make sure you're okay," my father says. "Whatever you want to say, we're here."

"Did you figure out the time frame yet?" I clear my throat. "For the trial separation?"

Trial separation. The words themselves sound heavy—I think of courtrooms and unsmiling judges with wooden gavels.

"We still don't know. We're going to have to take it as it comes," my mother says.

"But what does that mean?"

"The apartment lease is month to month," my father says.

"I still don't get why you had to do this now. During Ramadan."

"I know. But Ramadan felt like the right time," my mother says. "We're supposed to be reflecting on ourselves anyhow. Hopefully time apart can help us recharge and focus on what to do next."

"So, end of Ramadan then." Twelve days to go. That isn't so bad.

"We're not sure," my father says gently. "*Maybe* that's all the time we'll need, but it might be longer."

My cat, Willow, walks past me just then—she rubs her body against my leg before heading toward the kitchen. My phone buzzes.

Sara: Whoops sorry, Jessie's grandma is going to cover their sitting needs. I'll keep you in the loop if anyone else reaches out.

"Could you put the phone down?" my mother asks. "We know this is a big change."

"Thanks for the alert."

"Maya." My mother sighs.

"Do you have any ideas on how to fill up your extra time this summer?" my father says. "I found a couple of day camps with open spots. There's a really interesting robotics one at Mercer. And a dance camp by your mom's work still has two openings."

Dance camp? Robotics? I stare at him.

"I called the humane society," I say. "They're good on volunteers for now but said to check back next month. Sara might be able to get me a sitting gig in the mornings." I look at my mother. "That way you'll have the car back in time for work."

"I was going to talk to you about that," my mother says. "My work schedule is shifting the next few weeks. Chris assigned me a really messy case that's going to trial. I'm going to have to go into the office each day until it settles down."

"Are you fucking kidding me?" I blurt out.

"Maya, language," my mother says.

"Crap. I mean . . . sorry." I wince. Ramadan isn't just about not eating from before sunup to sundown. We're supposed to be patient—the best versions of ourselves we can be. But this is . . . flocking unbelievable.

"How am I even getting to Dad's apartment, then?"

"Door to door, it's only four minutes away, and—"

"Four minutes by *driving*," I correct him.

"I'll set you up with a rideshare app," he says. "Honestly, it's so close by, it's barely moving out."

No such thing as barely moving out, I want to say. Moving out is moving out. And what about Willow? She freaks if we move a houseplant to the other end of the room. Am I going to cart her back and forth to two different houses in random people's cars? But I can't get the words out, because tears threaten to spring to my eyes.

They look at me from where they sit on the ironically

named love seat. What do they want? Absolution? Tears? All *I* want is to run as far as I can out of here and never look back.

Because the truth is, it's not just Willow who doesn't like change. I literally got twitchy when my favorite yogurt company rebranded to a bigger font. When my hairdresser accidentally cut off three inches more than usual, I wore it in a bun until it grew back out. Let's just say I'm not exactly the most adaptable person in the world.

But I don't mention that. I don't even move. I just stare at the coffee table and try my best not to cry, because I'm legitimately terrified that if I start, I might never stop.

Because this?

This fucking sucks.

CHAPTER THREE
JAMIE

"Knock knock," Grandma says, instead of just knocking, which I used to think was a funny Grandma quirk. Now I know it's because she always has her hands full of food or dog or both.

I sit up in bed, yawning. "Morning."

But she doesn't come in—she just cracks the door. "Now, take your time, lovey, but just so you know, there's breakfast in the kitchen."

"Um. Thanks." I rub my eyes. "Are you—"

The door clicks shut, and she's gone. I yawn again, tugging my phone out of the charger. Per usual, I've missed a mile of texts on last night's group chat. I peek at the most recent one, from Felipe. **Nine o'clock tomorrow it is.** 😭 **I cannot emphasize enough how much you owe me for this. I** scroll back to find a whole series of negotiations—namely, Drew explaining the absolute exquisite hotness of a long-distance runner named Beth and making a hard pitch for early morning wingman backup at our school's track.

I glance at the time—8:15. Normally I'm kind of weird about texting back this early. Not because I'm worried about waking anyone—Drew and Felipe sleep through texts, thunderstorms, sirens, pretty much anything. But there's something fundamentally uncool about being the first texter in the group chat. Which I am. Every single morning. I'm like that guy who shows up to keg parties at the exact time listed on the evite. Or I would be, if I got invited to keg parties.

But there's no point trying to convince Drew and Felipe I'm suddenly a rage-all-night-sleep-till-noon kind of party animal. I text back a thumbs-up. And then I run through the full repertoire: shower, teeth, mouthwash, deodorant, fresh clothes, everything. I don't know if I'm a good wingman, but I'm a hygienic wingman.

By the time I reach the kitchen, Mom and Grandma are camped out in their usual chairs, nursing coffee. Boomer jumps up from his spot near Grandma's feet as soon as he sees me.

"Good morning, sunshine!" Grandma hits me with the shoulder-squeeze, cheek-kiss combo. "Look at you, all dressed. Let me get your breakfast out of the warming drawer. Where are you off to?"

"I'm supposed to help Drew flirt with some runner girl."

"Isn't he dating that girl from Steak 'n Shake?" Mom looks up from her news app.

"They were just hooking up. It wasn't really . . ." I trail off, watching Grandma bustle over to the oven, Boomer zipping along beside her. I narrow my eyes. "Okay, why am I getting a special home-cooked breakfast? What happened?"

"Well." Grandma turns around, smiling warmly. She's holding a plate stacked high with challah toast. "You were so upset yesterday about having to give the pre-challah toast, I thought . . ." She peers down at the plate, eyes glinting behind her red-framed glasses. I follow her gaze, and then groan.

"It's challah toast!" she says. "Get it?"

"Oh, I get it."

"Too soon?"

"Way too soon." I take a giant bite—it's slightly crispy, with no raisins, and it's perfectly buttered. "Okay, food toast is good," I admit. "Speech toast is not good."

"You'll be great, bubalah. I have no doubt."

"I have doubt. Doubts. Plural. Lots of doubts."

"Jamie, you have to stop doing that." Mom looks up again. "It's a self-fulfilling prophecy. You're so convinced you're going to screw up, you end up sabotaging yourself with that negative self-talk."

"It's not negative self-talk if it's true."

33

"It's not—"

"Mom. I'm a catastrophically terrible speaker. That is an objective fact."

Grandma pats my shoulder.

Mom frowns. "Sweetie, is this about the interview? You have to let that go. I know it sucked. No one's pretending it didn't. But you're still getting to work in politics. It's just a different side of the experience."

"You're missing the point."

I think she thinks I'm bitter. Or that I resent having to make spreadsheets and run errands for my cousin all summer, rather than marching up and down marble staircases in the state capitol. But it's not the lack of marble staircases that depresses me. And I don't mind the errands. I mean, that's what I'd have been doing for Senator Mathews anyway.

It's more the I-suck factor. The I-couldn't-even-make-nepotism-work-for-me factor. The a-sitting-state-senator-created-an-internship-just-for-me-and-I-totally-choked factor.

I mean, I literally choked. I don't know how to explain this without being gross, but a lump of phlegm lodged in my throat, and I panicked, which made me start gagging, and then that turned to puking, and I spent about an hour in the bathroom, and needless to say, I did not get the job.

Which doesn't exactly bode well for my half-baked dream of running for office one day. Let's face it. Some people are meant to change history. And some people are meant to change out of their vomity interview clothes.

"You just have to keep practicing," Mom continues. "Speaking to strangers is a skill. It's like a muscle, you know? You keep exercising it, and you'll see. One day it's going to be second nature. It'll feel just like talking to Drew and Felipe."

I scratch Boomer's ears. "Right."

"You can even work on it tonight at the Rossum event. What if you made it your goal to chat with five people? Just casual everyday stuff, quick and painless. Or even just one good conversation. It would be such a great step for you."

"Does Siri count as people?"

"No, Siri doesn't count." She smiles wryly. "You have a clean button-down shirt, right?"

"I was gonna wear a dirty one. With no buttons."

"Very funny."

What's actually funny is that Mom thinks I don't know by now what to wear to these things. I've been to more than two dozen Rossum events. Which she should know—she's the one who forces me to go to every single one of them, even when she can't make it.

Grandma ruffles my hair. "It won't be so bad. I'll pop in for the first bit. We'll hang out. We'll mingle."

I hate that word. *Mingle*. I mean, the word itself is fine; I just hate the concept. When has anyone in the history of earth ever made a meaningful connection while mingling? It's like, hey, let's have only the worst parts of a conversation—the approach, the small talk, the trying-to-figure-out-when-and-how-to-disengage part. It's not that I dislike being around people. I just wish we could skip to the sitting-in-comfortable-silence part, or the inside-jokes part, or even the we-both-love-*The-Office*-so-let's-overanalyze-it part.

"You should invite Felipe and Drew," Grandma suggests.

"Highly doubt they'd come to a campaign event."

"Never hurts to ask," Grandma says. "Which reminds me . . ." She stands and crosses over to the counter, and Boomer leaps up, ready to follow her to the end of the earth. But all she does is pluck her phone out of her purse, setting it before me on the table. "What do you know about adding links to Instagram Stories?"

"I've never done it," I say, taking her phone. "I'm sure I can figure it out."

"Can you? Thank you so much, lovey. I swear, being verified is a whole new world."

I tap into the app, biting back a smile. Grandma's blue check mark arrived two weeks ago, and she humblebrags about it at every opportunity. It's the only time I've ever seen Sophie visibly impressed by a family accomplishment.

I mean, the last thing any of us expected was for Grandma's Instagram to go viral. She started it after Grandpa died, mostly to take pictures of her and Boomer visiting Grandpa's favorite local spots. But then *Creative Loafing* did a feature on her, which led to a few YouTuber shout-outs. I wouldn't say she's famous or anything, but lots of local people know about her, at least in Brookhaven and the northern suburbs. Of course, Gabe just has to milk every bit of Grandma's notoriety to get attention for the campaign. I don't think Grandma minds too much—she's a big-time Democrat—but still. When Gabe named our seventy-five-year-old grandma as an official campaign social media surrogate, he pretty much sealed my fate as unofficial campaign tech support.

There's a Story sitting in Grandma's drafts—just a still-frame shot of Boomer wearing a custom Jordan Rossum bandanna, with a caption about tonight's event. "Are you trying to attach the event page or the donation link?"

"Ooh." Grandma leans forward. "The event page, but then let's do another one with the donation link." She sits up straight, cocking her finger at me. "I like the way you think."

I figure out the link stuff pretty easily, and hand it back to her. "This is one hundred percent the real reason you made me breakfast, isn't it?"

"Not a hundred percent," she says. "Fifty percent? Sure. Seventy-five percent? Probably."

I shake my head, smiling.

"You'll see," Grandma says. "When you're my age on Instagram—"

"I don't even have Instagram now."

"I didn't either when I was your age," she says, shrugging.

Naturally, I beat Drew and Felipe to the track, so I hang back near the bleachers, trying to look like I belong there. It's so strange being at school in the middle of the summer. I know some of the sports teams practice here all year round, but that's never been my scene. Nothing about this is my scene. There's a group of cheerleaders warming up on the football field, and at least a dozen runners circling the track at all different speeds. I sneak a glance at them, trying to guess which one's Beth. I don't recognize a single person here. Which probably tells you everything you need to know about my own athleticism.

Drew and Felipe finally show up around 9:15, looking puffy-eyed and half asleep. Felipe greets me with a half-hearted fist bump, but Drew scans the track and turns back to us, crestfallen. "She's not here."

"Beth?"

"I can't believe it." Drew shakes his head.

Felipe yawns. "Maybe she's running late."

I snicker, which earns me curious looks from both of them. "*Running* late," I say. "Get it? Because she's a runner?"

Felipe shoots me finger guns. "Goldberg, bringing the dad jokes."

"Uh, no." I scoff. "That's a grandma joke."

"I don't know if that's something to brag about."

Drew ignores us. "Their practice started at seven. How is she not here?"

I follow his gaze to the runners, a couple of whom have stopped for water near the far goalpost. I don't blame them. It's eighty degrees out already, maybe more. I mean, I'm breaking a sweat, and I'm barely even moving.

"I think . . . I'm going back to bed," Felipe announces.

"Oh hell no." Drew's blue eyes narrow. "We've got to investigate. Come on."

He takes off at a sprint, and Felipe and I shrug and jog after him. But I'm panting before we're even fully past the bleachers, and Felipe's an even bigger disaster. "Nope," he says breathlessly. "We're not doing this."

"Literally . . . can't . . . ," I huff, stopping short. Felipe stops too, gripping his thighs and breathing heavily.

Drew circles back around to meet us. "Wow. You guys are terrible wingmen."

"No, we're terrible runners," says Felipe. "That is a completely unrelated skill set to wingman ability. No wingman should have to wing in these conditions."

"A true wingman must wing in *all* conditions." Drew runs a hand through his hair, making it stick up in places. "Snow, hail, hurricanes . . ."

"You're thinking of the postal service," I say.

Drew shoots us one last disdainful look before jetting off

toward the goalpost to catch up with the track girls. I follow Felipe onto the edge of the football field, sinking cross-legged onto the grass beside him. "So." I lean back on my hands. "Do we think Drew's going to hold out for Beth, or end up with a different girl's number?"

Felipe snorts. "It's fifty-fifty."

I uncross my legs and let myself fall backward on the grass. Closing my eyes makes it feel like we're in some big, empty field, miles away from every other human on earth. The noise fades in my brain. No bat mitzvah speeches, no failed interviews, no tumbling produce displays.

But a sudden burst of laughter from the cheerleaders knocks me back to earth. I sit up hastily, cheeks burning.

Felipe eyes me. "You think they're laughing at you?"

"No. I don't know."

"Man. Your brain." He shakes his head. "Why would they be laughing at you? What are you doing that they could possibly be making fun of right now?"

I stare at my feet and don't answer.

"No, seriously. Walk me through it. Why are these cheerleaders making fun of you?"

"Because." I shrug. "I don't know."

Because I didn't even finish a lap around the track before I had to lie down. Because I'm sweating. Because my shirt's riding up. Because I'm too awkward to function.

"Because I'm this." I gesture vaguely to my entire self.

"You are straight-up paranoid about girls, I swear."

"I'm just . . . rightfully cautious."

"Why? Because of what happened at the Snow Ball?" Felipe raises his eyebrows. "Dude, that was four years ago."

"Three and a half." And it's not like anyone's forgotten.

In retrospect, it was a terrible idea. I mean, eighth-grade dances are a terrible idea in general, but asking Brianne Henke to dance was *next-level* terrible. And of course I have this awful, almost photographically detailed memory of the moment itself—everything from the paper snowflakes dangling over the dance floor to the tight little smiles flicking across Brianne's friends' faces. Brianne looked at me and said, "Hi, Jamie," without the slightest shred of enthusiasm. Without any inflection at all, really. But I took a deep breath anyway, and forced myself to go through with it.

I asked her to slow dance. Except my mouth didn't say *slow dance*. It said *slowmance*.

"It wasn't even that bad." Felipe laughs. "It was iconic."

I roll my eyes. "Right. Iconic."

So iconic that the concept of slowmance became a Thing. Among the jock bros, mostly. They morphed it into every part of speech too, like slowmantic and slowmantify. Once I heard someone's mom say it. People literally petitioned for A Night of Slowmance to be our homecoming theme last year, and were pissed when the seniors overruled it.

"Listen," Felipe says, "if that's your most embarrassing moment—"

"It's not."

That would be the fifth-grade presidential reception, when I called former president Carter a penis farmer.

I grasp desperately for a subject change.

"Hey," I blurt. "Any chance you're up for an insanely boring campaign dinner tonight?"

Felipe grins. "Wow. That is a compelling pitch. *Insanely boring*—"

"Did I say insanely boring? I meant amazing. Insanely amazing and fun and . . . amazingly insanely fun."

"No way. Nolan and I both have tonight off, so we're watching the *Christmas Prince* sequel."

I look at him. "It's June."

"It's always Christmas in Aldovia."

I mean, I get it. Felipe's been working all summer, ringing up self-serve frozen yogurt at Menchie's. It's for college money. He qualifies for the HOPE Scholarship, but the thought of books and housing expenses has him scrambling to take as many hours as possible. And his boyfriend, Nolan, works a lot too, which means their hangout time this summer is vanishingly rare. I know there's no way I'd be going to this campaign event if the alternative was spending time with my girlfriend. I guess it's pretty lucky for Gabe that girlfriends are so far from my reality, it's laughable.

Felipe shrugs. "Maybe Drew will be down?"

"Ehh. I'm not expecting much." I glance back at the goalposts, where Drew's talking animatedly to a red-cheeked girl with a messy blond bun. "It's for Rossum, so."

"Ah." Felipe nods. "Got it."

Rossum campaign stuff is kind of a tough sell for Drew. Not because he's conservative. But his parents are—Newton sign in the yard and everything. Drew's already on thin ice from the time I dragged him to the campaign office and Gabe sent him off with a stack of Vote for Rossum post-cards. His parents found them tucked into the side pocket of his car door, and they . . . weren't exactly cool about it.

"I don't even know if I should ask him," I say.

I watch Drew smile at the girl, high-five her, and start jogging back to us.

A moment later, he plops down beside Felipe. "So. I'm an idiot."

Felipe pats his arm. "We know."

"No, seriously. Just talked to Beth's friend Annabel, and she says Beth works at Catch Air on Thursdays, which opens at ten, so Beth has to be there by nine, so, like, she *was* here, but only until eight. She left early."

"I am literally not following this at all, even a little bit." Felipe yawns.

"And I don't think they'll let you into Catch Air without a kid. So, my lads, we are firmly SOL today."

"Catch Air . . . ," I say slowly.

And it clicks. Catch Air. *That's* why the girl from Target looked so familiar. It isn't just that I've met her before. I spent half my childhood with her.

Maya Rehman. It's been almost ten years since I've seen her.

But her face hasn't changed at all. Same wavy hair, same giant eyes, and I bet she still has that dimple in her cheek when she talks. She's always looked kind of like a less pale, darker-haired Belle from *Beauty and the Beast*. But personality-wise, she was a total Mulan. Super badass, completely self-assured. She would climb anything, ride anything, stand up to anyone. I swear, running around Catch Air or the park with her made *me* braver. I mean, yeah, she was the Disney princess and I was basically the animal sidekick, but I kind of liked that. It's not like I ever wanted to be the prince.

I can't believe I actually saw Maya Rehman yesterday. Like, grown-up, real-life Maya Rehman. She's not even a month younger than me, so of course she'd be seventeen. But my brain doesn't know what to make of the time jump. It's like catching a glimpse of the future.

I should have talked to her.

Except—*right*. I was too busy exploding tangelos all over the produce section.

In front of her.

Because I'm me. And wow, do the hits keep coming.

CHAPTER FOUR
MAYA

Twenty more minutes until the sun sets and I can break my fast with a crispy fried samosa. Though to be honest, I'd eat just about everything on that table, including the fruit salad with the green apples and Auntie Samra's soggy pastry puffs. There's so much food today, the puffs are set up next to the bottled water on the poker table, where the overflow items go. I swerve around two toddlers chasing each other, sidestep a man setting down extra folding chairs, and casually position myself by the plates and forks. *Someone* has to be first in line, right?

Glancing around the masjid's gymnasium, I'm taken aback by just how many people are here today. It's always busy during Ramadan, but with the Atlanta Interfaith Alliance cohosting this iftar dinner with us, there are so many people milling around you'd think we were waiting for Taylor Swift to show up for an impromptu concert. Pastor Jones, Rabbi Levinson, and Imam Jackson are huddled over by the punch bowl. Bits of their conversation like *the defense is weak* and *fouls are how they get us* drift over to me, which means they're discussing their summer basketball league. Typical. My mom stands over by the entrance with some of her friends. They're chatting and playing it cool but they crane their necks every so often toward the entrance to see if our special guest has arrived. She was so distracted today, she didn't even remind me to wear the shalwar kamiz my nani mailed me from California—so I got away with jeans, a long-sleeved striped shirt, and my favorite pink scarf for prayers wrapped like an infinity scarf around my neck. I'd feel smug about this, except I know why she didn't notice my outfit choice—and there's nothing to smile about when it comes to that.

I was looking forward to coming here tonight. I knew Imam Jackson would be busy, but I hoped to run into him and talk a little about what's happening with my parents. Even if I couldn't, it would have been nice to at least absorb the calming energy of his presence—but it's not easy feeling calm or spiritual in a place that looks like a high school pep rally. The masjid invited both candidates, but Newton didn't even reply to the invite. Which is just as well, because the walls are papered with campaign posters saying *JULY*

9—VOTE ROSSUM—HE'S AWESOME!

Just the thing to get you in the Ramadan mood. I'm not saying I have anything against Rossum—but he's another white dude in Georgia running for office. What is there to get *this* excited about?

I check the wall clock by the entrance again. *Still* twenty minutes? The clock must be broken. My phone buzzes in my hip pocket.

Sara: I'm sitting for Lizzie on Tuesday and Charlie's mom needs me at the same time. He's a hardcore Elmo fan, so you'll have a lot to talk about.

Maya: Um, pretty sure you were a bigger Elmo stan than I ever was!

Sara: Ha! Fine we were both equal fangirls. Think you can cover?

Maya: I'll check! My mom's schedule is funky right now, but fingers crossed!

Sara: Cool let me know! Iftar going okay?

Maya: Meh. I'm hungry. 😋

Sara: Eat a samosa for me?

A word bubble, and then—

Sara: I miss you.

Tears spring to my eyes. I swallow.

Maya: I miss you too

Sara and I have been inseparable since we bonded over our mutual love of a certain red Muppet in our Montessori preschool. She was a bit busy her senior year with all the AP classes she was balancing, but now I realize that was just a taste of what's to come. I look around the room. Soon Sara will be gone, and this—being alone—will be the new normal.

My phone rings. My father's face—scrunched in horror from the Starbucks Unicorn drink I made him try years ago—pops in and out of my screen.

"Hey, you," he says when I answer the phone. "How's it going over there?"

"Oh, you know, the usual. Standing around waiting to eat."

"Senator-to-be there yet?"

"Nope. He's late. But everyone is crowded by the door to mob him as soon as he enters. 'Tis the season, right?"

"Someone sounds hangry."

"Everyone is a little hangry during Ramadan!" Though, now that I look around, no one really *looks* all that grumpy. Except me.

"You know you don't have to fast every single day," he says. "It's great you've been fasting since freshman year, but I didn't start full-time until I graduated high school."

"I *want* to fast, but I can't help it if medical science backs up the fact that not eating can make some people irritable."

"It makes *some* people very irritable."

"Funny. Are you on your way?" I ask him. "Mom

thinks the board meeting is going to run longer than usual tonight."

"That's why I was calling." His tone shifts; the laughter in his voice vanishes. "The movers are running late. I don't think I can make it. I'm sorry, bug."

All the air gets sucked out of the room. The words and noise and chatter surrounding me are probably still blasting at 100 decibels, but all I hear is one word: movers.

It's happening. Right now. It's not as if I didn't know it was coming. But it's like when you're at the doctor's office and they say they're going to draw your blood. You can get that on an abstract level, but when the needle comes down, the pain still manages to surprise you.

"Can Sara drop you off?"

"Sure." I don't bother to tell him Sara isn't here. I promise to pack him some biryani if there's any left and hang up.

Right this moment as I stand here, my father is erasing himself from our house.

I blink back tears. I haven't let myself cry about any of this. And I'm definitely not going to cry about it right now. Not here.

When I glance again at the clock, I pause. There's a boy standing on the other end of the iftar table, wearing a plaid button-down and khakis. Our eyes meet. He looks familiar. He smiles a little and takes a step back.

Right into one of the iftar tables.

The poker table wobbles, and then—it's like watching a slow-motion crash—the tray of pastry puffs and bottled water tumble onto the ground. I glance around. But everyone's so busy studying the empty doorway no one's noticed. I hurry over to survey the damage.

"I'm . . . I'm so sorry," the boy stammers.

"Don't worry, you're not the first person to do this," I tell him. "The poker table is notoriously wobbly."

"They're . . . they're ruined." He gestures to the puffy disks of pastry strewn on the ground.

"To be fair, they were kind of ruined from the start," I tell him. "Seriously, it's okay."

I prop the table back up while he disposes of the pastry puffs and then gathers water bottles in his arms.

"So . . . Maya, right?"

"What?" I look up at him.

"You don't remember me." He blushes. "Of course. I mean, it makes sense. It's probably been like a decade or something, other than . . . Yeah, anyway, I'm Jamie. From the Catch Air days."

"Oh. Right. Wow." I stare at him. Our moms were friends years ago; they'd tow us along to that indoor playground where we ran around and bounced on stuff while they drank coffee and caught up on life. That was ages ago, but I see it now—his hair darkened a bit and he's got half a foot on me, but he's still got those green eyes and the same awkward smile. "Sorry. It's been a while."

"So weird to see you here," he says.

"Why is it weird?" I smile a little. "I'm Muslim. This is a mosque near my house."

"No. Sorry. I didn't mean it was weird to see you *here*. Just that it was weird to see *you*. Good weird, though. Not bad weird! I go to a bunch of these campaign stops. You know this is his one hundred and thirtieth campaign stop of the election season? The most of any state candidate ever."

"This isn't a campaign stop," I tell him. "It's an iftar dinner. For Ramadan."

"Oh right, yeah, of course." He nods. "I've been to nearly thirty of his events and this is the nicest . . . dinner so far. The decorations are classy, but super festive too."

Red, white, and blue plastic tablecloths, wallpapered advertisements to vote for Rossum, and confetti center-pieces are classy and festive?

"Uh, thanks. Well, I gotta go help my mom with . . . something. It was nice seeing you again." I hurry away before he has a chance to respond. As much as I hate small talk in general, today in particular, small talk feels extra small.

"Who were you chatting with?" my mother asks when I approach her.

"No one. Can I borrow the car on Tuesday? Sara has a babysitting gig for me."

"Sorry." She shakes her head. "Next week is really busy. Depositions and filings all week."

"Fine, I'll just take a rideshare then," I tell her.

"That's for getting back and forth between our places," my mother says. "Those costs add up."

"Then it's probably time I get a car." I cross my arms.

"Maya," my mother sighs.

"I'm going to be stuck at home all summer. All our plans fell through. And *no*, I'm not going to dance or robotics camp, so don't even bring that up. How am I going to get anywhere?" I stare at her. "And Dad just called and said he's not coming tonight. You have a meeting after the event. How am I even getting home today? I'm completely stranded."

"Someone can give you a ride after the iftar ends, inshallah."

"If I had a car, this wouldn't be happening," I snap. "I'm seventeen."

"Cars are expensive. They require insurance and gas and maintenance. We're already overloaded with two places, two utility bills. With everything going on, it would be helpful if you could just take a break from arguing with me. At least just for this iftar."

"This isn't an iftar. It's a campaign stop."

"It *is* an iftar." My mother shoots me a look. "And I've been working around the clock to get it done just right.

The least *you* can do is not fume like this in front of every-one. And honestly, Maya, if—"

Before she can continue, the Rossum folks burst through the gymnasium doors across from us like an explosion of red, white, and blue confetti.

"There he is!" my mother exclaims. Her expression goes from frustrated to perky in a matter of half a second. Thank you, Jordan Rossum.

I recognize him immediately from his gray suit and yel-low tie, since we have his curly-haired, smiling face on a flyer taped to our fridge. My mom is such a diehard she has not one but *two* Rossum signs in our yard. Before she can take a step toward him, he's engulfed by a crowd.

I look up at the clock. Seven minutes to go.

"Alina?" a voice calls out over the din.

"Lauren?" My mother's eyes widen. A woman with light brown hair wearing a power suit zooms toward us and smooshes my mother into a big bear hug. Jamie's mom. She looks the same as ever; I recognize her instantly.

"What brings you here?" Lauren asks.

"I'm on the board for the mosque. We helped organize this. Did you join the interfaith alliance?"

"My nephew is Rossum's assistant campaign manager. I've been trying to make it to some of his events to support him." Lauren turns to me then and her eyes widen. "That can't be," she gasps. "Is it Maya?"

"It is." My mother pats my shoulder.

"How does this happen? How do they grow up so quickly? Look at my Jamie. He's taller than I am now." She glances back. "Jamie, come here and say hello."

"So *that's* who Maya was talking to," my mother exclaims.

I glance over at him. He hasn't noticed any of this. He's texting.

"Jamie!" his mother says louder. He looks up with a start and blinks, before coming over to join us.

"Jamie!" My mother leans over and hugs him. "How lovely you and Maya were already catching up. What grade are you in?"

"I'll be a senior this fall," he says.

"Of course, just like Maya." My mother nods.

"They're three and a half weeks apart, remember?" Lauren says.

"That's right!" My mother laughs and turns to me. "Lauren went into labor at the Caribou Coffee while we were getting our decaf lattes!"

"We promised we'd keep up those coffee dates."

"We did," my mother says. "At least for a while."

"But school."

"Jobs."

"And just like that the years slip by. Time is a trickster, I tell you."

I will never understand why adults find the passing of

time to be so unexpected. Time is literally what life is made of. But it's like a ritual; each time my mom chats with a friend or family member she hasn't seen in a while, they spend half the time talking about how fast time goes, and the other half promising to see each other soon, which they almost *never* do.

"This election feels like a family affair," Lauren tells my mother. "But I've been so busy planning Sophie's bat mitzvah, I haven't been able to help out as much as I'd like. Jamie's really stepped up—text banking and monitoring our social media analytics. He's a lifesaver. People are retweeting about the campaign, but volunteers are scarce."

"The national races get all the attention and volunteers." My mother nods.

Our mothers continue talking and I look back over at Jamie. It makes sense now that he looks so familiar, but I swear it's like I've seen him since then. I'm about to ask him which school he goes to when a loud voice interrupts us.

"How's everyone doing today?" A lanky guy with a clipboard approaches us. He's grinning so wide, I can see the fillings in the back of his mouth. He nods at Lauren and Jamie before fixing his attention on my mother and me.

"I'm Gabe," he says, extending his hand.

"Alina, nice to meet you." My mother shakes his hand. He's just a guy who works for the campaign, not even the candidate, and my mother is so excited, she looks like the physical embodiment of the heart eyes emoji.

"Can we count on your vote next month?" Gabe fishes out two brochures and hands me and my mother one. "We're getting enthusiastic feedback, but it all comes down to who comes out to vote."

"I'm not old enough to vote yet," I tell him.

"How old *are* you?" he asks.

"I'm seventeen."

"Well, seventeen-year-olds can knock!" he says brightly.

"What?"

"You can knock!" He pushes the clipboard toward me. "It's perfect, actually! We desperately need more canvassers to go door-to-door to spread the word about how awesome Rossum is. Studies show canvassing is the most effective way to get people to go to the polls."

"Oh, I would," I tell him. "But I don't have a car." A fact that, for the first time, makes me feel practically triumphant.

"But Jamie does!" Lauren exclaims.

What now?

Jamie looks up from his phone with a start.

"This works out great!" Lauren clasps her hands and turns to my mom. "I've been on Jamie to canvass for ages, but he's so shy about it. But they can do it together! It's perfect!"

I'm about to interrupt and tell them something, *anything*,

to stop this, but my mother joins in too.

"That's a great idea! Maya's summer is pretty open, and this will give them a chance to catch up some more. I'll drop her off at the campaign office tomorrow." She takes the clipboard to fill out my information.

"I know it sounds scary," Gabe says. "But after one or two houses, it's as easy as stuffing campaign mailers into envelopes—which you can also help us with!" He grins at me. "The headquarters aren't too far from here." He hands me a business card with an address. "See you Friday at three o'clock sharp for orientation?"

Before either of us can respond, he's marched off to the next unsuspecting sucker.

Lauren and my mother talk a little more, while I glare at my mother's profile. She acts like I'm not even there.

As soon as they're gone, I turn to my mother.

"Why did you volunteer me like that?" I explode.

"What's the problem? You have time, don't you? Plus, you need volunteer hours for school."

"Sara was going to see if she could take off that evening so we could hang out together. You know how busy she's been."

"Honey, you know how her plans always change and you end up sulking on the couch all night."

"No." I shake my head. "I don't want to go canvassing

with some random person."

"Random? He was your best friend before you could even talk."

"Friendships when you're still in diapers don't count! And now I have to knock on strangers' doors? Like I don't have enough to deal with?"

"Look." She takes a deep breath and closes her eyes. "I know how much you have to deal with. And I know change is difficult for you—I bet this is all landing extra heavy. But doing something positive will take your mind off things. It's just one day. If you don't like it, you never have to do it again."

"I'm not going."

"This wasn't a request." Her voice grows sharp. "Mom Card getting pulled, kiddo. You are going." Before I can say another word, Imam Jackson walks up to the podium at the front of the hall and clears his throat in the microphone. Everyone grows quiet.

"Asalamualaikum. Thank you for attending our seventh annual interfaith iftar," he says. "And what a special honor to have none other than Jordan Rossum with us. We will hear from him later this evening. In a few moments, the adhan will sound for evening prayers, which will conclude another day of fasting. Please join us in food and conversation as we remember, yet again, that there is far more that unites us than divides us."

Imam Jackson continues his talk as I glance around the room. After the frenetic energy that came with Rossum's arrival, everyone is standing quite still now, listening attentively. When he finishes, the adhan sounds from the loudspeakers. Rabbi Levinson and Pastor Jones pass out plates with dates for people to open their fasts. A line begins to form at the iftar table.

"Hey, Maya." Jamie approaches me. His hands are in his pockets. "I'm heading out after this meal. I'm happy to give you a ride home. I mean if you need one. I could drop you off. No problem."

"Um, no." I look at him. "I'm all set."

"Oh yeah, sure. Of course." He nods quickly. "Well, see you tomorrow."

I watch him walk away and think of my empty house. Sara, who will soon be two hours away. And now, a Friday knocking on strangers' doors.

Suddenly, I'm not so hungry.

CHAPTER FIVE
JAMIE

Maya's not even here yet, but I can't stop thinking about how the campaign office is going to look through her eyes. I've been in and out of this annex all summer. How have I never noticed the hellscape of empty coffee cups and half-eaten pizza bagels on Gabe's desk, or the weird eggy smell wafting up from the trash bin? No one would mistake the office for fancy, but I guess it seemed passable. Now I realize it's basically the room version of Gabe's beard—scraggly, unfinished, and kind of painful to look at.

Something tells me Maya won't exactly be blown away.

I can't believe she was at the Rossum dinner. Or at Target. How does that happen? How do you go nine years without seeing someone, and then run into them twice in the span of two days? It's like when you learn a new word, and suddenly it's everywhere.

I guess seeing her kind of threw me—though not in a bad way. Really, it was the opposite of a bad way. I don't believe in signs, but it's so weird. There I was, kicking myself for not talking to her at Target—and then there she was *again*. An unmissable second chance. For a split second, I actually thought mingling might not be such a terrible concept after all.

Until I made the mistake of actually speaking to her. Wow. I didn't think anything could come close to the Snow Ball, but this may have actually been worse. Who knew it was possible to squeeze so many painfully awkward moments into two five-minute interactions? Let's start with the fact that I knocked over a whole table of food and water bottles. Because of course I did. And I still feel stupid for offering her a ride. After all, we're practically strangers at this point. But when I heard her tell her mom she was stranded, not offering just felt mean.

Turns out, Maya would rather be stranded than ride with me.

Of course, there's no point worrying about what she thinks about me, or the campaign office, or anything. Frankly, I don't even know if she'll show up.

It's the first time I've ever been here with a real group of volunteers. I'm pretty good at popping in during off-hours when it's just Gabe and Hannah and sometimes their lead intern, Alison. And anyway, the canvassers usually start from the main office, out in Dunwoody. But now there are a dozen people here, mostly Hannah's friends from Spelman, plus a friendly-looking black woman with deep dimples and a pair of middle-aged white women in scarves and chunky jewelry. I know a dozen's not a particularly huge number of volunteers in the grand scheme of things, but quarters are so tight, people are crowded all the way to the stack of cardboard boxes and yard signs lining the back wall. Everyone's holding the manila envelopes Alison distributed when we walked in, but nothing's really happened yet, even though we're a few minutes past the start time.

I glance back toward the door. Still no Maya.

Though I guess I shouldn't judge her for being late when Gabe isn't even here yet. And sorry, but if *Gabe* doesn't show up, I'm bailing.

But right then, Gabe emerges from the side-entrance door, wearing a blindingly bright white T-shirt with Rossum's logo across the chest. He climbs onto a kick stool and cups his hands around his mouth, like he's doing crowd control. "Welcome, one and all, to volunteer orientation," Gabe announces. "Now holler at me if you're ready to have a *Rossum*ly awesome time. State District Forty is about to get hella canvassed, and I am *so* here for it." He pounds a fist in the air.

It's like watching your oldest, cringiest teacher try to win over the class with slang they googled during their planning period. And I'm pretty sure Gabe being only twenty-three makes it worse.

After a few minutes of Gabe booming a bunch of vaguely campaign-related words, Maya slinks in through the back. I wave tentatively, and she walks over. "I grabbed you an extra packet," I whisper.

"Thanks. And FYI, there are at least two car alarms going off in the parking lot right now."

"Gabe's greatest talent." I attempt a casual smile.

Maya's smile back is ninety percent grimace.

"Now I know this all may be a little out of your comfort zone," Gabe is saying. "So let's take a minute to emotionally prepare. Repeat after me. *We're awesome*."

"We're awesome," I mumble, with the rest of the volunteers. Maya looks skeptical.

"*Rossum is awesome*," Gabe says.

"Rossum is awesome."

"And we're about to kick some canv . . . ass!" Gabe claps. "Sweet. You guys can partner up, and then we'll turn it over to Hannah, who's going to walk us through the Door to Door app."

"Go, Hannah!" cheers the woman with dimples.

Hannah winks. "Thanks, Mom."

As soon as Gabe descends from his stool, he makes a beeline for Maya and me. "'Sup, Big J!" He fist-bumps me.

"Glad you could make it." He turns to Maya. "I've been trying to talk this guy into canvassing all summer. Should have known all I needed to do was bring in a few cute girls. Am I right?"

"Gabe, stop." I feel my cheeks burn. Maya looks unamused.

Gabe pats my shoulder. "I see our social media queen just got here." He juts his chin toward the back of the room. I glance back to find Grandma in the doorway, wearing a printed blouse, blazer, and her signature red glasses. She smiles at me and points to Gabe, curling her finger back to beckon him over. "Duty calls," Gabe says.

"Wow," Maya mutters as soon as he leaves. "How did Rossum find this guy?"

"Oh. Uh, Rossum went to Hebrew school with Gabe's sister Rachel, so I guess—"

"Nepotism. Great," she says. "Also, why are the campaign headquarters in a bookstore?"

"Well, they have a real office space in Dunwoody, so this is just a satellite location. Kind of an extra home base. Fawkes and Horntail usually does book clubs and stuff back here, but they're renting it to the campaign for a dollar per month."

"A dollar?"

"They really want Rossum to win."

Maya's expression softens a little. "Well, clearly, you're

Gabe's favorite volunteer." She lowers her voice, imitating him: "*I've been trying to talk this guy into canvassing all summer.*"

"Oh. Yeah. I'm not really his favorite. I'm more like . . . his cousin."

Maya's eyes widen. "Oh." She pauses. "Ohhhh."

I shrug, and glance back at Gabe—who's currently getting a smudge rubbed off his face by Grandma.

"Sorry," Maya says sheepishly.

I turn back to her. "You don't have to be sorry."

"Well, I'm sorry I was late."

"You didn't really miss much."

"We just knock on doors, right? Give them a flyer? Say 'Vote for Rossum, he's awesome'?"

"Well, there's a script, but Gabe said it's good if we use our own words. And then they want us to try to get people to commit to voting, and we mark down their response—definite yes, definite no, maybe—"

"So it's like those notes you pass in third grade."

I smile. "Will you go out with Jordan Rossum on July ninth? Circle yes, no, maybe so."

"So that's it?" Maya asks. "That's all the data they want for the app?"

"I mean, there are a few other options you can pick, but it's pretty self-explanatory. We can skip the app training if you want. I already have it downloaded."

"Okay—"

"Or you can download it yourself, if you want to split up the houses. Divide and conquer."

She shakes her head. "Let's just go together."

"Really?" I glance at her in surprise.

She opens her mouth to respond, but suddenly we're intercepted.

"Jamie! I'm so glad you're here." Grandma hooks her arm around my shoulders. "Now, I was just talking to Gabe, and he mentioned wanting to get a couple of shots and maybe a little video. Oh, and hello, dear. I don't think we've met. I'm Ruth."

"I'm Maya."

She extends her hand, but Grandma swoops in for the hug.

I guess the last time I hung out with Maya was before Grandma moved in with us. Which makes my friendship with Maya feel like something from another era.

"So nice to meet you, sweetheart," says Grandma. "Would you mind if I snap one of you two? Here, Jamie, grab one of those yard signs. Perfect. Now, Maya, why don't you take the other end." Grandma peers at us through her phone camera lens, while Maya and I awkwardly fake-smile. "Lovely. Let me just take one a little closer up, and . . . voilà! Flawless. Now, are you okay if I post this on our Instagram?" Grandma tilts the phone screen to show us the photo, and I nod.

Maya shrugs. "Sure."

"Fabulous." Grandma adjusts her glasses, blows us a kiss, and totters off to help two of the Spelman girls pick up an overturned box of campaign stickers.

Maya blinks, watching Grandma's retreating figure. "This campaign is a mess," she mutters.

Okay, it's one thing to insult Gabe, but coming for my grandma is another thing entirely. And the campaign? Funny how Maya's the expert, even though she hasn't stuffed a single envelope. Not to mention the fact that this is her first time setting foot in its headquarters. *And* she was late.

She sees me staring at her and narrows her eyes. "What?"

I should call her out. Tell her exactly who that woman who took our picture is, and why she's completely amazing. I'll think of the most scathingly perfect comment and fling it at Maya, and she'll spend the whole ride stunned and remorseful.

But by the time we reach my car, all my arguments dissolve on my tongue. I'm not exactly a scathing callout kind of guy. I'm not even a mildly confrontational kind of guy. I guess you could say I'm more of a food-as-a-peace-offering kind of guy.

I reach behind my seat, handing Maya a fresh bag of Goldfish I'd stowed away for later. "Here, help yourself."

She looks down at the bag, and then back up at me,

almost incredulously. "What is this?"

"Uh, Goldfish?" I'll just note for the record that the packaging of Goldfish crackers is not subtle. The bag literally says *Goldfish Baked Snack Crackers*. With a Goldfish cracker dotting the *i*. But, okay, maybe Maya shops exclusively at farmers' markets or something and legit doesn't recognize them. "They're like a snack cracker—"

Her mouth quirks. "I know what Goldfish are."

"They're cheddar," I add, digging into the bag for a handful.

"Jamie."

I look at her. "You . . . don't like Goldfish?"

She looks like she's about to burst out laughing. "Seriously? They're okay, I guess. But we were just at an iftar."

I nod slowly, trying to decode this.

"Jamie, I'm fasting. For Ramadan?"

"Ramadan! Right." My cheeks flush. "Crap. I'm so sorry. Here." I roll down the top of the Goldfish bag and fling it into the backseat, out of sight. "I can probably find a trash can when we get there. I'm so sorry. I keep forgetting Ramadan is all month. Our fasts are only one day—not that it's the same—wow. Okay, yeah. I'm shutting up. Oy. I'm sorry—"

"It's fine." Maya presses my arm, for just a split second. "You're fine. Just drive."

★   ★   ★

68

It's a ten-minute ride to our assigned neighborhood, but Maya doesn't say a word the whole way there. Hard to tell if she's listening to the NPR station my radio's stuck on, or just feeling as painfully tongue-tied as I am. But when I pull up and park along the curb, she sighs, pressing her hands to her cheeks.

"Are you okay?" I ask, startled. I've never seen Maya look quite so uneasy. "Are you nervous?"

"No."

"Oh—"

"I mean, yeah. Kind of. I don't know. I just don't want to do this." She slides her hands down, peering up at me. "Like, we don't even know if they're going to listen to us. Or they might be angry we're taking their time. They might hate Rossum. They might be total jerks in general. They might—"

"I know." I meet her eyes, for just a moment, but then I look away quickly. "But if it helps to know this, they're only having us knock for Democrats and Independents. Who can be jerks, yeah. But it's not like . . . you know."

"Yeah." She presses her lips together. "Yeah." For a minute, she stares moodily out the window.

Then, suddenly, she unbuckles her seat belt.

"Are we—"

"Come on, let's just get this over with. Okay? What house are we starting with?" She opens her door, stepping onto the curb.

I scramble out behind her, scrolling frantically through the app. "Okay. Uh. Two thirty-six. This brick one, right there with the—okay, yup, that one."

Already, she's halfway up the driveway.

So now I'm standing on a stranger's doorstep with my hand hovering over the doorbell. "You ready?"

Maya crosses her arms and nods. I ring the doorbell, and immediately, there's a frenzy of dogs yipping and footsteps and even muffled voices. But no one answers.

Maya and I exchange glances. "They're definitely in there," she says.

"Do you think they're ignoring us?"

"Looks like it."

"Maybe they're showering or something? In separate showers," I add quickly. "Not like a big group shower. Unless that's their thing, which is fine—"

"Come on." Maya grabs a walk piece and shoves it next to the doorknob. "We'll get the next house."

But we don't.

And we don't get the house after that either. Turns out, nobody's even answering their doors. And it's after six. I guarantee at least half these people are home. There are cars parked in almost every driveway. I keep marking everyone down as *not home*, but I feel gross about it. It's hard not to take it personally.

"I get it," Maya says as we approach the next house. "We're interrupting everyone's Friday evening. I hate when people knock on my door."

I glance up—there's a mezuzah on the door frame. "Yeah, they may be getting ready for Sha—wait, is someone coming?"

"Whaaat." Maya's jaw drops, just for a moment, but then she quickly collects herself, standing up straight. "Okay. Okay! It's happening."

The door creaks open, revealing an elderly white woman—at least a decade older than Grandma—wearing a blue quilted pajama shirt, jeans, and white sneakers. "Why, hello," she says. "Who do we have here?"

Maya springs into action, beaming so brightly, I almost stumble backward from the shock of it. It's the first time I've seen Maya smile all day. And okay, I'm not saying Maya's general face is heinous or anything. But when she's smiling? It's next-level not heinous. She's just so—

Yeah. I'm not going to go there. Literally no point in going there.

"Great. Hi!" Maya says. "I'm Maya, and this is Jamie, and we're here with the Jordan Rossum cam—"

"Well, isn't that a nice surprise. Y'all can come right on in. I'm Barbara." She turns, gesturing for us to follow.

Okay, so. Following old ladies into their houses? Not in our script. Not part of the game plan. And I don't want to say for sure that we're getting kidnapped, but I'm pretty sure we're getting kidnapped.

Maya and I exchange panicked glances.

I clear my throat. "Uh. We were just—"

"What are you waiting for? Come on in."

I look helplessly at Maya, who's clutching the stack of walk pieces like they might fly away. Actually, Maya looks like she wants to fly away with them. But Barbara's still standing in the foyer, expectantly.

I take a deep breath and cross the threshold.

"Now what can I get you? Lemonade? Sweet tea?"

Maya shakes her head. "I'm okay, thanks."

"Nothing? Well. I'll just make a little plate of cookies. Won't take me but a second. And you can just have a seat right there on that couch."

I settle in, and Maya sits beside me, so close to the edge that she's barely sitting at all. "This is like a fairy tale," she whispers. "But in a bad way."

"That's exactly what I was thinking."

"I think she's coming back. Okay, what's our—hi!" Maya's whole tone and expression shifts the minute Barbara walks back in, and I have to kind of marvel at that. I barely know how to be myself, and here she is turning into an entirely new person, mid-sentence.

"Now please help yourselves," Barbara says firmly, setting a plate of dusty-looking cookies in front of us. And of course my stomach growls enthusiastically, which pretty much locks me into taking one. I guess they don't look *that* dusty. I go for a vanilla-looking one with a Hershey's Kiss pressed into the middle, taking a tiny nibble off the edge. Maya looks on in horror, but the cookie isn't so bad. A little stale, but it's edible.

Barbara settles into an armchair, facing us, and Maya leans forward to hand her a walk piece. "Thank you so much for taking the time to speak with us," she says brightly. "Like I said, we're here with the Jordan Rossum campaign—"

"Oh, isn't he handsome," Barbara says, peering through her glasses at Rossum's headshot. She turns to me. "This young man looks quite a bit like you!"

"Uh . . . thank you?"

Okay, I'm pretty sure we just slipped into some strange alternate universe. I look like Rossum? I mean, we're both white Jews with dark hair, but that's about it. He's a candidate for the state senate, and I'm . . . me. I glance sideways at Maya, who's clearly trying very hard to keep a straight face. When I catch her eye, a grin breaks through, and she claps a hand over her mouth.

Barbara looks back and forth from Maya to me, smiling. "Well, aren't you two the cutest couple I ever saw."

Maya's hand falls. "Couple?"

"But here's my advice. You can take it from an old lady who knows a thing or two about relationships. Now, I'm not going to tell you to see other people, but don't be in a rush to settle down. Take your time and get to know each other before taking the final step."

Awesome. So much for me ever making eye contact with Maya again. Random ladies think we're dating? And not just dating. They think we're dating so seriously that we need to be cautioned against settling down. What?

I stare at my knees, cheeks burning.

Barbara keeps going. "But I think inter-race relationships are such a delight. I really do. You know, my grandson Joshua married the loveliest girl. Prisha. Her relatives traveled all the way from India for the wedding. Oh, it was absolutely wonderful. All of those beautiful traditions—I'm sure you know." She smiles at Maya, who looks frozen. "But here's—"

"Well." I clear my throat. "We'd, uh, love to tell you about Jordan Rossum, if that's okay."

"Sure!" Barbara glances down at the picture again. "What a sweet face. I swear, he looks barely old enough to drive."

"Um. Yeah." My eyes flick sideways to Maya. "He looks young, for sure. But Rossum has years of experience working for Georgians in our district at a local level. In fact—"

"Is he Jewish?" Barbara asks. "He looks Jewish! I wonder

if I know this young man's parents from shul. Remind me, what's his name again?"

"Jordan Rossum," I say. "R-O-S—"

"It's on the flyer," says Maya. "And actually, if you look at the flyer, there's lots of information about his platform. I know people are probably interested in his position on health care—"

"You know who he resembles? The Shapiros' eldest daughter. I'll have to ring up Nancy."

"Um. Great," I say, with a quick sideways glance at Maya. "So, uh, can we count on your vote on July ninth?"

Barbara looks me right in the eye. "Tell me this. Is he a Democrat?" I nod. "Well. In that case, you can tell this gentleman he's got my vote. No question about that."

I sneak one last glance at Maya—and this time she's smiling for real.

"Well, that was . . . something," Maya says as we wave goodbye to Barbara from the sidewalk. "I was pretty sure we were about to get Hansel and Gretel'd."

"Yeah, I kind of expected that cookie to start talking to me. Like the gingerbread guy from *Shrek*."

Maya laughs, which makes me feel slightly light-headed.

I look away quickly. "Also, I'm not sure if that was allowed?"

"If what was allowed?"

"Going into someone's home and eating their food?" I rub my forehead. "It might be an improper campaign contribution or something. Gabe is always talking about stuff like that. How they get you over the little things."

Maya looks amused. "Um, I think we're good."

"Well, at least she opened the door," I say. "And we got our first commitment to vote!"

And just like that, it hits me: we actually did it. *I* did it. I just talked to a total stranger, and I didn't choke or knock the table over or anything. And here I am living to tell about it.

I log the visit on my phone, and marking Barbara as a *definite yes* voter tugs happily at my heart. Maybe Gabe was right all along. Maybe this could really tip the scales. After all, you never know how things will go. Maybe Rossum will win by a single vote—Barbara's vote. Maybe Maya and I just flipped our district in a single afternoon.

Maybe we changed history.

I think it's the first time I've ever wished I could high-five myself. I would totally high-five Maya if I didn't think she'd find it weird and excessive. Something tells me she's not about to run a victory lap over a single voter commitment.

But then again, when I look up from my phone, Maya's outright grinning.

So maybe I should—

"Hey," I say slowly, trying to keep my voice from

jumping. "Um. If you ever want to do this again—"

Maya's smile fades. *Crap.* Okay.

"Or not," I say frantically. "Or, you know. You could canvass on your own, or with someone else. No worries. Or you could go with me again. If you want. No pressure. I just mean Gabe is always looking for volunteers. So I would go again . . . if you wanted to. Either way." I attempt a smile. "Yes, no, maybe so, right? Ha ha."

She presses her lips together. "Um—"

"Okay, wow, I'm putting you on the spot, and you're probably really busy, and I'm sorry. Seriously, no worries," I say. My whole face is burning. Pretty sure that's not supposed to happen when you're casually notifying someone about volunteering opportunities. I mean, Gabe *is* always looking for volunteers. I'm not making that up.

"I'm not . . ." She pulls her phone out, glances at the screen, and shoves it back into her pocket. "I don't know, Jamie."

"Okay." I smile slightly. "That sounds like a maybe so."

She smiles back, shaking her head slowly. And there's that heart-tug-high-five feeling in my chest all over again.

CHAPTER SIX
MAYA

It's Saturday.

My dad should be on the ottoman watching soccer. My mother should be jotting down the weekly grocery list. And all of us should be arguing about whose turn it is to fold the laundry.

But the television is off today. The ottoman is empty. And the light only just turned on in my parents' bedroom. Besides Willow crunching her food next to the fridge, the house is silent. I grip the book in my hands so tightly, my knuckles go white.

"Hey, honey." My mother walks up to me, wearing a white robe over her pj's, and yawns. I study her expression; does she also feel it's weird? This first weekend without my dad? Or is she relieved? Her face is unreadable.

"What do you have there?" She gestures to my book.

"*Saints and Misfits.*"

"Reading it again?" She smiles.

"It's a good one. I have a couple of holds ready for me at the library too."

"I'll swing by and get them on my way home from work Monday," she promises. "Any plans for today? The car is all yours if you need it."

"Sara said she might be free this afternoon."

"Oh, that'll be nice," my mother says. "You haven't had a chance to see too much of each other. How do you feel? With her leaving so soon?"

I look down at the counter.

"I don't even know how to process what life will look like without her."

"She'll still be part of your life," my mother says. "And she'll be home for holidays and vacation."

"But it won't be the same."

"I'm so sorry, Maya." She puts a hand on my shoulder. "This is a lot. So many things landing at once."

I blink back tears.

"How are you feeling? About . . . everything else?" she says gently.

I shrug. Like I got hit with a sledgehammer. That's how I feel. She knows that, doesn't she?

"I hate not knowing how long this will last."

"Me too," she says softly.

My phone buzzes. It's Shelby Yang from school.

Shelby: Mateo and Olivia are getting a group together to see the new Marvel movie. 8:20 p.m. showing. You in?

Maya: Oh, I'd love to, but today's a little tough. I'm so sorry! 😭

Shelby: You're the busiest person I know! Get you next time?

Maya: 🙏

I put the phone away.

"Was that Sara?" My mother nods to the phone.

"No, it was Shelby, something about a movie."

"That sounds fun. You should go."

"I hate sitting through a movie at the theater," I tell her. "I get so antsy."

"But it'd be nice to meet up with her, wouldn't it? You haven't seen her since the end of school. Maybe you could join them for a bite to eat after you open your fast?"

I shrug. Yes, Shelby is a friend. We grab lunch together during the school year and discuss the pros and cons of our favorite celebrity crushes of the moment (mine's been Jim Halpert from *The Office* for a solid year and counting). But she's a School Friend. Our relationship doesn't extend beyond campus boundaries. I'm not saying I'm antisocial or anything. I've got a bunch of acquaintances, like Kevin. It's just that I'm a quality over quantity kind of person. And my quantity has mostly always been Sara.

My phone buzzes.

It's Jamie. We exchanged numbers before we left the campaign offices.

Jamie: I had to share this.

I open the text. It's a GIF of a screaming gingerbread man from the *Shrek* movie, going into an oven.

"Oh my God. No." I cover my mouth and laugh.

"What's so funny?" my mother asks.

"Jamie sent me a GIF," I tell her. "At canvassing yesterday, there was this lady who offered us cookies à la Hansel and Gretel. I mean, she was actually pretty sweet, but we were a little creeped out at first."

"Sounds like canvassing wasn't too bad then?"

"It wasn't the worst thing on the planet."

"Think you'll go again?"

"Um, 'worst thing on the planet' is a very broad standard," I tell her. "Once was enough."

I look back down at the GIF and click my phone to find one to send back to him, when my mother clears her throat.

"I've been thinking about the car you've been wanting."

Say what? I slam the phone down on the table.

"I know with Sara leaving for school soon, and my work schedule picking up, it'll be trickier for you to get around than it was before . . ."

"Exactly," I tell her quickly. "And that way I can get myself to school this fall instead of needing you or Dad to drop me off. It'll save *you* time in the long run. And it doesn't have to be fancy or anything. I don't even care if the air-conditioning works."

"We'll have to see what we can afford. Between our student loans, mortgage, and your grandmother's health costs, we were pretty stretched as is—and with the double housing—for now, at least—it's just not as simple as you'd think."

She talked about the separate housing and said "for now."

Not *forever*. For. Now.

I cling to those two words like a life raft.

"So I was thinking," she continues. "Since you and Jamie had a good time canvassing yesterday, why not keep it up?"

"We need to have a serious conversation about what 'not the worst thing on the planet' means, Mom. It was okay, but not exactly the most exciting way to spend my summer."

"Well, be that as it may, here's my proposal: you keep up the canvassing and we'll think about getting you that car."

"After the election?"

"Yep," she says. "It's a win-win. You get your volunteer hours in for school, and you're not sitting around all summer waiting for Sara to call. And in exchange, you—"

"Get a car! I'll pay you back for it. Once I have the car, I can start working and—"

"You don't have to pay it back. The canvassing is the work."

"Then insurance and gas. You guys won't have to worry about a thing. And I promise I'll be super responsible."

"Of course you will, honey." My mother smiles. "Do we have a deal?"

"Yes!" I delete the GIF I was about to send. Instead I type: Think we could go canvassing for a few hours today?

A word bubble pops up instantly. And then—There's a four to six time slot. Want me to sign us up?

Meet you at the headquarters, I tell him.

I'll get Hansel and Gretel'd every day if I can finally have my own car.

The packet Gabe gave us this time sends us to a completely different type of neighborhood from the last one. The homes here are even more enormous, and the sprawling lawns mean each house is almost its own city block. We've been canvassing for a full thirty minutes but we've only made it to five houses. So far only two people opened their doors and took our flyers.

"Next one is about eight houses down that way." He squints and points up the road.

"That far?" I groan. Eight houses means we'll have to trudge at least one whole street over. "There's no Democrats or Independents in any of these houses close to us?"

"This looks like a pretty red neighborhood. Not sure we'll get Jewish ladies feeding us cookies here." He double-checks the paperwork before we continue on our way.

"How was that cookie yesterday?" I ask him. It was pretty brave of Jamie to take one for the team like that. Ill-advised, but brave. "No side effects?"

"It wasn't too bad. My grandma makes those cookies all the time. The thing with them is, if you don't seal them right away, they get stale within the hour. My grandma's taste way better than Barbara's, but hers were definitely edible." He puts his phone in his back pocket and glances at me. "You met her, actually. My grandmother. At the campaign headquarters . . ." His voice trails off and he looks away.

"Your grandmother?" I flush. "That was your *grand-mother*? Oh, wow. O-Okay." I stammer. "I didn't mean to . . ." My voice trails off. Did he notice me side-eyeing her?

"She's a social media surrogate for Rossum's campaign, but she has her own really popular Instagram account too. She's got a great eye for photos and captions and she can hashtag like a boss, but she has a hard time getting the filters and Stories features just right. I run tech support for her."

"Your grandmother has an account on there?"

"Yeah." He looks over at me. "It's called InstaGramm."

"I know what Instagram is," I tell him, trying to hide my irritation. This, after mansplaining Goldfish crackers to me yesterday?

"No, no," he says quickly. "I mean, that's not her handle, but that's how everyone knows her on Instagram. She's Insta. Gramm. Like Gramma."

"Oh, wow." I pause. "That's clever."

"She's a pretty big deal." He smiles. He's so clearly proud of her, it's kind of cute. "I don't know how she does it, but somehow her stuff always goes viral. She's got like ten thousand followers last time I checked." He pulls out his phone, clicks around on the screen, and holds it out to me. "She takes photos with her dog, Boomer. People are seriously obsessed with her. She's a local sensation."

I shield the phone from the sun's glare and scoot next to him to look at the photos. There's one of her cuddling Boomer at Piedmont Park. Grandma and Boomer are wearing matching Hawaiian shirts in the next one. I smile at one with her sipping a frappé at a local coffee shop, and Boomer photobombing. The next one makes me pause— it's an old-school photo. It's clearly her, because she's got some seriously fashionable frames on, but she's younger— maybe in her twenties—and she's next to a man with dark hair and a smile that looks like Jamie's. They're sitting on two matching Adirondack chairs with iced tea, gazing into each other's eyes.

"That's my grandpa." Jamie points to the man. "He died when I was nine—my grandma shares their photos for Throwback Thursdays."

"They're so cute."

"They really were. They'd been married over forty years, and they still used to hold hands all the time, completely lovestruck."

My parents used to be that way. Holding hands. Looking at each other from across a crowded room and smiling in a secret language even I couldn't decipher. I remember rolling my eyes when I'd walk into the kitchen early mornings before school and catch them standing next to each other, holding coffee mugs, heads pressed together as they took in the sunrise from our bay window. They made it eighteen years. They were happy for most of them. At least, I thought they were. I wish I knew why some people keep holding hands and why some people stop.

I'm not sure what the reason is, but the people in the next few houses we knock on actually open their doors. Five of them promise to vote in the special election, and one lady shrugs and says "maybe," which is better than staring at closed doors while the owners peek down at us from their upstairs windows. I would call that behavior a bit creepy, except we're the randos knocking on *their* doors.

When the person at the next house opens up, it takes a second to register that I actually *know* him. I'm not sure why that's so surprising. We're canvassing four miles from my house; it would probably be more weird *not* to run into someone I know, but it still throws me off guard.

"Kevin?" Jamie and I say at the same time. I look at Jamie. He knows him too?

"Maya?" He smiles at me and glances at Jamie. He's wearing an Atlanta Falcons jersey. "And Von Klutzowitz, right? What are you both doing here?"

Von what?

"Um, we're canvassing for the special election." Jamie blushes. "We're talking to voters about Jordan Rossum."

"Yep," I tell him. "Are your parents home, young man? We'd like to have a word with them."

"My mom is running errands, but I'm eighteen, thank you very much. How about you try to get *my* vote too?"

"You're a lost cause," I say.

"Wait? Why?" Jamie asks.

"Maya's right. Your words will be wasted on me." Kevin takes a flyer from me and holds it up. "Look at this slogan. Just look at it. Rossum is awesome? Cheesy much?"

"But you're not going to vote or not vote because of his campaign slogan, right?" Jamie asks.

"Jamie." I side-eye him. They must not know each other all that well if he's asking him to vote for Rossum. "This guy is as staunch a Republican as they come. Trust me, we had US history together."

"I'm more of a Libertarian now," Kevin protests. "But this race is getting ugly. I'm not sure I'll vote for anyone.

You know, if Newton wins, the GOP will have a veto-proof supermajority. They could pass any bill they want. So obviously, the trolls are out in full force against Rossum."

"What trolls?" I ask. "I haven't seen anything."

"You haven't heard of the Fifi-ing around town? It was on the news all last week."

"Fifi-ing?" Jamie and I say together.

"You know, that meme with Fifi the poodle holding a cup of tea to celebrate white supremacy or some shit."

"I've seen it," Jamie says. "It's all over the internet."

"It's not just online anymore," Kevin replies. "Some local trolls make these Fifi stickers, steal Rossum car magnets on people's cars, and stick the bumper sticker in its place."

"My mom's got those Rossum magnets on both our cars," Jamie says.

"I think I saw a dog like that on someone's car the other day . . ." My voice trails off.

"It's everywhere. And once those things get on your car, they *do not* come off. You can try to scrape them off, but then you're just going to damage your paint."

"Wow," I say slowly. "That's . . ."

"Fucked up." Kevin nods. "Exactly. I don't love this Rossum guy, okay? He hardly has any experience, and I'm not impressed with his debate skills. But bumper-stickering without consent is peak trolling. And I've heard the stickers going up around town have anti-Semitic messages." He tucks the flyer under his arm. "I'll give this to my mom when she gets back. You can put her down as a yes. She's definitely going to vote."

We thank him, and Jamie and I head back onto the sidewalk.

"How do you know Kevin Mullen?" I ask as we walk to the next house.

"He works at Target, the one over by the Publix, where the Staples used to be. I . . . uh, met him there a while back."

"I like that Target."

"It's basically the best place on earth."

I laugh, but he looks completely and utterly sincere. "Wait, seriously? I mean, there's Disney, the Grand Canyon, Iceland . . ."

"Maya, they hand out free cookies in the bakery! The sign says you have to be twelve, but no one bats an eye when I grab one. It's so great. I'd live there if I could."

"Well, you're on your way if Target employees recognize you on sight."

"I made a bit of an impression with Kevin," Jamie says bashfully.

"What happened?"

"Just a little mistake."

"Does it have anything to do with that Von Klutzowitz nickname?"

"It was a display of tangelos." Jamie winces. "I pulled one out and everything went tumbling."

"Wait." I slow down. "That was you? I was there that day!"

"Uh, yeah." He flushes. "I thought I saw you . . ."

"That was such a mess."

"In my defense, a pyramid display of citrus, which is famously *round*, is kind of an accident waiting to happen. Kevin was really nice about it, though." He looks at me sheepishly. "Kind of like how you were pretty understanding about the whole 'destroying food at a place where everyone's been fasting all day' incident."

"Trust me, if you'd tried the puffs, you'd know you did everyone a favor." I glance at my watch, surprised it's almost six o'clock.

"Good news," Jamie says. "We have only one house left to go, the one across the street." He nods to a gray stucco house.

"They're definitely home." I point to the opened garage and two cars parked inside.

"Now to see if they'll actually open the door," Jamie says. "I'm going to guess no."

"I'll go with yes."

"Loser gets the winner donuts on the way back!" He hops up the steps.

Still fasting, Jamie! I'm about to call out, just as he rings the doorbell. Seriously, though—first the Goldfish crackers in the car, and now this. I guess I could take the donuts to go if I win and eat them this evening. My stomach grumbles. Donuts sound *really* good right now.

But thoughts of fasting or donuts-to-go take a backseat when the door parts open. It's a man. He looks a bit older than my dad. He's balding and has on a blue T-shirt with a picture of a white swordfish across his belly.

He's staring at us.

More like glaring at us.

At me.

And just like that, all the lightness from moments earlier vanishes.

Jamie must feel it too. He hasn't said a word either.

"Well?" The man glances at both of us. "What do you want?"

"Oh, sorry." Jamie clears his throat. "Um. Are you . . ." He glances down at his paper and then back up at the man. "Are you Jonathon Hyde?"

"That's my landlord. Hasn't lived here in years. What do you want with him?"

"We're campaigning on behalf of Jordan Rossum. He's running for state senate in the special election," I say quickly. I've got the words down pat, I realize, since I can say them through my racing heart. "He's running on the promise of hope and change in our district, and every person who can come out to vote will make a difference. I have more information here if you'd like it." I hold out the flyer toward him.

He looks down at the flyer. He doesn't touch it.

"This guy's a *Democrat*, right?" He says it like it's a bad word, like it physically tastes bad on his tongue. "Does the fact that you two are here interrupting my day mean I'm renting from a Democrat?"

"Well, we're targeting Independents and Democrats," Jamie says in a hesitant voice. "Would you like a flyer to read over?"

He stares at us, his hand resting on the door. I glance at Jamie. Why is he waiting for a response? This guy is obviously not voting for Rossum. We can cross this house off the list with a resounding no and get on with our day.

"Look," the man finally says. "I don't mean to be offensive or nothing. I just tell it like it is. Do you really think you're going to get anyone around here to vote for your candidate when they've got *her* knocking on doors?" He raises a hairy finger and points it toward me.

He doesn't touch me.

He is a good two feet away on the other side of the door. But I feel punched.

"Think about it." He turns his attention to Jamie. "You really need to do a better job keeping this agenda hidden." He nods toward me. "Being politically correct is fine and all, but it won't get him votes. Not in this district. May want to pass that tip on to your Rossum person. We do want change out here, but not the kind he's promising."

Before either of us can say another word, the door slams in our faces.

Jamie looks exactly like a squirrel my mom almost hit when she was dropping me off super early to school last year. She had to slam the brakes, because even though the squirrel was pretty much looking death in the eye, it seemed like it was so scared it couldn't move.

I know people feel the way this guy does. But to say it to my face as casually as if he's discussing the weather? I've gotten racist stuff here and there, especially when I'm with my mom, who wears hijab. The mumbling as someone passes us, or a look by the cashier you know is saying something without saying it. I'm used to that. But this?

I have to get out of here. Before the man opens the door again. Before he does something worse. I study the door and breathe in. It's a deep mahogany, this door. I can see the grains of wood. The doorknob is faded brass, worn at the edges.

"Hey." Jamie's voice floats in and out. "Maya, can you hear me?"

I turn my head toward him. He's looking at me. How long has he been calling my name?

"You okay?" he asks.

I nod numbly. He gently takes me by the elbow, and to-gether we get off the stoop and step back onto the sidewalk.

"Listen," he says. "That guy . . . he was . . . he was a total monster. And you know what I think? I think we should . . ." He looks at me. He hesitates.

Oh God, Jamie, I think, biting my lip to push back the tears. *Please don't tell me you're planning to knock on this dude's door and try to say something on my behalf.* I'm pretty sure I can predict how a confrontation between him and that man would go.

But that's not what he says.

What he says next is something so unexpected, it's just the thing to shake me from my weirdly catatonic state.

"Target?"

"What?" I blink.

"It's on the way back to the campaign office," he says quickly. "Have you seen the patio section lately? It's got blue lights overhead and everything. It's like being at the weirdest garden party ever. Want to check it out?"

I look into his worried eyes. Anywhere that isn't here sounds really good right now.

"Yeah," I tell him. "Let's go."

CHAPTER SEVEN
JAMIE

I should have said something.

I keep replaying the moment in my head. The way that racist dude looked at Maya with death-ray eyes. The drop of spittle in the corner of his mouth. And the sound of the door slamming in our faces. The whole time the guy was speaking, it was like I'd stepped out of my brain. It felt like I was watching it all happen in a movie.

And then, afterward, the way Maya stared at that door without blinking. The sheer blankness of her expression made my stomach lurch. She was clearly as shocked as I was. More than shocked. She looked like the ground had given way beneath her.

This just wasn't supposed to happen.

That's the thought that plays on a loop in my brain, all

the way to Target.

"The Rossum campaign needs to update their system," I say at a red light on Roswell Road, glancing toward Maya.

She nods. "Yeah."

"That can't happen. It's ridiculous. We're in Sandy Springs, not, like, middle of nowhere Georgia. It's just not okay."

"Wouldn't have been okay in the middle of nowhere either," Maya says.

I blush. "Right."

The Target patio section is so underrated. I mean, yeah, Target's Wi-Fi is the worst, which would normally make me twitchy—and my phone doesn't even get cell service here. But when I'm in the patio section, it's like it doesn't even matter. It's my favorite place to sit and think.

"I don't know if you want to test out different chairs or anything," I tell Maya. "But I will say I'm kind of a patio expert these days."

"A patio expert?" She smiles.

"I mean, I know my way around the patio section, and I'll just leave it at that."

Maya peers up at me for a moment, still smiling, and I get this flutter in my stomach. "Okay," she says. "So if you're the *expert*, what chairs are the best?"

"Those two." I point, without hesitation, to a pair of cushioned chairs on display underneath a slatted wood awning. "And they're right near the blue lights, so."

"I see." Maya's eyes drift around the patio area, taking in the clusters of sample furniture, rows of barbecues on display, and bins of rolled-up outdoor rugs. "Yeah, I'm gonna need to test out all the options," she says.

I press my fist to my heart. "You don't trust me?"

"Not at all." She sinks into a nearby chair, nodding solemnly. "Hmm. Not bad."

"Yeah, but—"

"But the armrest is kind of iffy."

"Right? That's what I said! What's with the low armrests? Who wants low armrests?"

"Maybe we just have high arms?" Maya says, shrugging.

She slides onto a stack of cushioned porch chairs next— but by the time I settle onto the stack beside it, she's moved on to an Adirondack. Followed by a few patio dining chairs around tables, and then a couch, and then a tightly woven brown set with bright orange cushions. Every single time she sits down, she makes this face like she's judging a reality show competition and trying not to reveal the winner.

She pauses for an extra-long time in a double-cushioned wicker chair shaped like an egg. "Ooh, I like this one." But then she circles back around to the very first set of chairs, the cushioned ones under the slatted awning. "Okay, we have a winner."

"I told you!" I say, settling into the chair beside her. "You should have listened to me."

"Um, we both know the egg chair is the best. I just decided to pick a place where we could both sit. So, you're welcome."

I make a face at her. "You just can't let me be right."

"I'd let you be right," she says, "if you were actually right."

She grins, and I grin back, trying to ignore my quickening heartbeat. I feel strangely at home with her.

For a moment, neither of us speak.

"So," I say, finally—just as Maya says, "Well—"

"You go first," I say.

"No, you."

"Okay." I pause. "I was . . . I just wanted to see how you were feeling about . . . you know."

"The racist guy?"

"Yeah." I exhale. "Maya, I'm sorry I didn't—"

"You're fine. You were great. We were both in shock."

"Yeah, but I should have stuck up for you. Or I should have gone back in there and—"

"No way. Not a good idea." She tucks one leg onto the other, leaning toward me. "Never a good idea. Listen. What happened back there sucks, okay? I mean, no one's

98

ever done that to my face before, but it's not like what he said is anything out of the ordinary."

My jaw tightens. "That's—"

"I know. I know! It's not okay. It's ridiculously not okay. But Jamie, we live in the suburbs. In Georgia. I'm a Pakistani American Muslim. People get pissed when cashiers don't say 'Merry Christmas' here, you know?"

"Ugh. Yeah."

"It's not like being Muslim in New York City. Though, actually, that's probably not a cakewalk either. People can be awful. And it's been . . . kind of worse in the last few years. For obvious reasons."

The look on her face makes my stomach feel like it's free-falling. I don't think Maya and I have ever talked about the religion thing. How I'm Jewish and Maya's Muslim. I mean, how deep do six-year-olds really get on faith-related topics? I highly doubt we were comparing notes on Islamophobia or anti-Semitism at Catch Air. I don't even think I'd heard those words before.

Now it seems like those words are everywhere. Maybe because we're older. Or maybe because the world sucks more.

"I just hate this," I say.

This isn't how history's supposed to work. The timeline's not supposed to move backward.

"Me too," Maya says.

For a moment, we just look at each other.

"But we're going to make things better. I have to believe that," she says. "Remember the iftar? That whole community united around Rossum? There are lots of good people in our district."

"You sound like my grandma. She always says that there are at least two good people for every bad person in the world."

"I like that a lot." She smiles. "You're a real grandma's boy, aren't you?"

"Is that like a mama's boy?"

"It's like a mama's boy on steroids."

I tilt my head, biting back a smile. "I don't think mama's boys are known for using steroids."

"You would know."

"I thought I was a grandma's boy." Now I'm grinning for real. "Get your insults straight."

She grins back. "I'll keep practicing."

Time moves differently in Target. I'm not just saying that. It's an actual fact, confirmed by my mom. I swear, you can spend twenty minutes inside a Target, and two hours will pass outside in the real world.

And that's exactly what happens. It feels like fifteen minutes have gone by, thirty tops, when Maya jumps up and says, "Oh! It's going to be sunset."

Which—okay, I really love that. The way she says *sunset*, like a fairy-tale princess, not like, you know. Eight fifteen.

"I didn't make you miss dinner, did I?" I glance down at my phone, feeling a slight twinge of guilt. Mom's probably been texting me since six, but I've been in the Target no-cell-service zone. I look back up at Maya. "I can drop you off first and then drop off the packet. Or we can go to a drive-through on the way if you want."

She looks at me oddly.

"Right! It's Ramadan." I jump up. "You're breaking the fast and then having the special dinner. At sunset. Got it."

"And maybe next time we can canvass a little bit earlier."

"Next time?"

She laughs. "Why do you look so surprised?"

"Sorry. I just thought—I don't know." I sound so flustered that I wince. "I just figured after the racist guy, you probably don't want to canvass again."

"Well, I do."

"Really?" I look at her.

"Of course! We don't want the racist asshole guy to win, right?"

"He already did win. In 2016."

Maya laughs out loud. "Right. Well."

"But you're right," I say. "I mean, I get what you're saying. But . . . are you sure you're okay, after everything that happened today?"

"I just want a chance to fight back, you know? I don't want to let a guy like that scare me off. And then, obviously, if Rossum wins, there you go. We've proven him wrong."

"That's true. Rossum winning would be kind of like kicking that guy in the balls."

"With spiked stilettos," Maya adds, and then her eyes get huge. "He *has* to win."

Suddenly, I feel tongue-tied. "Yeah," I say finally.

"So we'll keep fighting."

"Yeah, definitely." I nod. "If you want, I can pick you up next time."

"Oh, awesome. Thanks," she says. "So . . . tomorrow?"

She's looking at me with the sweetest half smile, and I make a million promises to myself right on the spot. I'm going to be a badass. I won't freeze up. I don't care who opens the door. Even if it's literally Fifi the white supremacist dog meme. I don't care. I'm going to knock that cup of tea straight in its racist poodle face.

I look Maya right in the eye and smile back. "Tomorrow's perfect."

CHAPTER EIGHT
MAYA

"So, what do you think?" my dad asks.

We're standing in the apartment. *His* apartment. Unopened cardboard boxes line one side of the family room. The old futon that lived in our basement has made a comeback—it's propped against the other side of the wall like it's trying to be an official and proper sofa. Then I notice the folded-up blanket on the edge. The pillow.

Or maybe it's trying to be a bed.

I almost ask him if he's going to buy a table to eat on, but I stop myself. No need to fill this place up with furniture. This is temporary.

"They have valet trash." He clears his throat. "You put your garbage outside and someone gets it. Like magic. And the appliances are all brand-new and up-to-date."

He gestures toward the stainless-steel fridge, which apparently tells time. And the stainless-steel oven. That also tells time. I glance around at all the appliances blinking 11:15 a.m. at me.

"How was the ride? Did the app work okay?"

"Four minutes door-to-door, like you said. Ten minutes if you count waiting for the car to show up."

"Great. And oh!" His eyes light up. "I didn't even show you the best part of this place. I set up your room. You're going to love it."

"My room?"

"Yep." He grins. "Follow me."

I follow him down a carpeted hallway with cream-colored walls. He swings open a door with a dramatic flourish. When I step inside, I blink.

"It's . . . pink." I glance at the walls. There's a lavender bedspread. A poster of Zayn Malik eyes me from next to the window, and a gray kitten with a beanie hat grins above my bed.

"Yep." He smiles proudly. "And look at the posters. I couldn't find an exact match but it's pretty close, isn't it?"

"Exact match?"

"To your room back home."

My first instinct is to laugh. I mean, this room is definitely very Maya—circa five years ago. But the laughter fades in my throat when I look around and realize—he's right. It's a little fun house mirror-ish. But all of this stuff is up in my other room. I cringe at the Imagine Dragons poster next to the closet. That was my intense Haris Divan phase. He taught my Sunday school Seerah class when I was twelve and always wore Imagine Dragons T-shirts, so somehow *I* became a fan for the three months he taught us. It's weird to wrap my head around the fact that I didn't recognize my own bedroom decor. All these things have been up for so long, I stopped noticing.

My father has the I-hope-I-didn't-screw-this-up look on his face right now.

"Thanks, Dad." I hug him. "It looks . . . terrifyingly identical."

"I know this is hard enough as is for you," my father says. "I wanted to make sure your personal space at my place was as comfortable as it could be."

His place. Suddenly, my heart feels so heavy, I can't breathe. How can the two people I love most in the world not love each other anymore?

"I miss you," I whisper.

"I'm four minutes away, silly," he says. But his voice is tight. He understands what I mean.

The phone rings just then. My dad glances down. "Gotta take this, bug," he says. "On call this weekend. Why don't you get settled into your room?"

He heads to the kitchen with the phone balanced on his

shoulder. I glance up at the poster above my bed. I swear, that kitty is winking at me. I snap a picture and text it to Sara.

Maya: My new art aesthetic, courtesy of my father. Do you see all the fun you're missing out on? #SaveMe

I check the screen, waiting for the three dots to appear like they normally do. But they don't. It's never been a problem before to have only one close friend, but I feel the scarcity now.

My phone buzzes then. But it's not Sara.

Jamie: Two minutes away. 😎

"Jamie's on his way," I tell my dad as I walk past him.

"Have fun canvassing." He covers the mouthpiece with his hand. "Home in time for iftar?"

"Does pho sound good?" I ask.

"Pho is always good."

I kiss his cheek and head down to the curb. Jamie's still not here yet. I lean against the stone exterior of the building and pull out my phone. I have to admit, I was a bit skeptical, but the truth of the matter is, InstaGramm is the absolute best.

There's a new photo posted. I stifle a laugh. This one is too much. She's lying down on the grass with her arms spread wide, Boomer licking her face, and the Valencia filter is on full force. The caption says: *Help! I've fallen and I can't get up.*

It's too cute for words.

Jamie's faded green Subaru pulls up just then. His

phone, balanced in the cup holder, flashes and buzzes when I get in.

"Do you need to get that?" I gesture to the phone.

"No." He glances down. "It's just my friend Drew. I was supposed to get together with him this afternoon."

"Oh, well, I mean, if you had plans . . ."

"It's fine. He's just going to be gaming, and I'm seeing him later anyway."

"Gaming? Like video games?"

"Mostly *Fortnite*, lately. He and some other guys from school are planning a marathon today. I forgot." He sighs.

"A gaming marathon? You sit around in a darkened room and stare at a screen all day?"

"Yeah—it's fun." He nods. "What's your favorite system?"

"I don't have a system," I tell him. "I don't think I've played a video game. Ever."

"What?" The car slows down as he glances at me. "That is . . . so sad."

"You know what else is sad? Listening to the best retirement options for government employees." I point to the radio station. "I'm down with NPR, but we're not the target demographic for this interview." I lean over to change the station, but nothing happens.

"Oh yeah, that," he says. "Sorry, it's stuck on NPR."

"Seriously?"

"This is my mom's old car. I think she listened to that

station so hard, poor old Alfie forgot any other station exists."

"Alfie?"

"The car," he says.

"I can use my dad's Spotify account. Do you have a cable? I can connect my phone."

"Sorry, Alfie's old-school. No USB capabilities. But if it's annoying, I could turn the radio off?"

"Nah." I sink back against the car seat. "Maybe I'll pick up some retirement tips. Can't start too early, right?"

We swing by the bookstore to pick up our canvassing packet, and Jamie enters an address from the top sheet into his phone. As we pull out of the parking lot, I glance down at the floor—there's a crinkled mailer by my feet.

"'Rossum believes in people,'" I read. "'He believes in you. This July, vote Rossum. He's awesome.'"

"Gabe came up with the wording for that himself," Jamie says. "He flipped when the main campaign headquarters approved it. Wait." He glances over at my expression. "What's wrong?"

"This flyer." I shake my head. "That slogan."

"Well, yeah, it's definitely cheesy."

"Not just that. What kind of ad *is* that? Vote for him because he's awesome? He doesn't even say what he stands for. It's like Kevin was saying. What do we really know about this guy?" I unlock my phone and google: *Jordan Rossum*. I'm a little embarrassed this is the first time it's occurred to me to look into the guy. I've been Team Rossum because my mom has heart eyes for him, he visited our masjid, and I get a car out of this canvassing gig. But is that enough?

"Says here he went to the Gallovin School," I read from his Wikipedia page. "So he's super privileged. That school costs like fifty thousand dollars a year or something."

"I think it's like twenty-three thousand, actually. . . ."

"College at Emory."

"Then he's lived in the Atlanta area his whole life. That's why he's so invested in the community."

"He's a former tennis player, but his professional dreams crashed after a knee injury. He loves volunteering, and . . ." I scroll down. "He interned two summers with Representative John Lewis."

"That last one is legit," Jamie says. "Lewis is my second-favorite congressional representative of all time."

I can't help but smile a little. "Who could you possibly love more than John Lewis?"

"Well, my number one was Barbara Jordan from Texas. She was *amazing*. Her speech from the 1976 Democratic National Convention will give you chills. I can play it for you if you want! It's online."

"Okay—"

"And she was the first Southern black woman elected to the House."

I glance at him. He's so pumped. It's like when my dad's sharing basketball stats for his favorite players. I don't think I know anyone our age into politics like Jamie. Or anyone of any age, really.

"That's great, Jamie," I say. "But she's not running. Rossum is. And yeah, maybe he interned for John Lewis, but it was an unpaid internship. He was probably getting coffee and filing papers."

"Maybe you're right," Jamie says as we pull over to the side of the road at our neighborhood for the afternoon. "But Rossum's got a great platform. He believes in a livable wage. He also wants to push for increased funding to public schools—people are really excited about that. He's got a strong track record for civil rights activism too."

"Maybe . . . ," I say. "But he's still brand-new at all of this."

"Well, check out Newton's deal," Jamie says. "Even if Rossum is brand-new, he's better than him."

I click over to the other candidate. The dude is literally smirking in his photo.

I scroll through his campaign promises:

End entitlements.

Protect the Second Amendment.

Safeguard religious freedoms.

I know about that last one. It's not my religious freedoms he's talking about.

I pause at the next Google search link.

"Oh man." I scroll through the article. "Newton favorited a Holocaust denier tweet a few months ago." I pause at the article from two days earlier. "Look at this. He's posing with that young Nazi guy that made headlines two weeks ago." I skim the article. "And a former grand wizard of the KKK endorsed him. Wow."

"What?!" Jamie looks at the screen. His jaw tightens.

"I mean, Rossum isn't perfect." I glance at him. "But at least he's not saying 'Give Nazis a chance.'"

We sit silently in the car for a few moments.

"In the Mario Bros. games there's the big bad—Bowser, who is this evil mega-turtle," Jamie finally says. "And they also have these Koopa Troopas—little turtles that are weirdly cute but completely evil. Bowser became president in 2016. But I guess I didn't really think about how it's not just about him—there's hundreds of Koopa Troopas everywhere to watch out for too."

"Thousands," I say grimly. "Not as flashy—but just as dangerous."

"It's weird to think about." Jamie turns to me. "But they were *always* there."

"They hid themselves a little better a while back. They knew they'd get roasted for saying any of their white supremacy bullshit, but, well—"

"Bowser became president."

"Exactly." I look down at my phone. "And now they're running for office and winning all over the country."

"Not Newton. Not here." Jamie shakes his head firmly. "We won't let him."

"Ready to knock on some doors?" I grin.

Maybe people who go to church on Sundays feel bad pretending they're not home, because nearly every door we knock on opens for us today. In just a matter of hours, we've been hugged by one grandfather, been offered water bottles by three different families, and helped someone retrieve their puppy who bounded out of the house when they opened the door. We also got eleven commitments to vote.

After we drop off our packets, Jamie clears his throat. "Want a quick overview of how gaming works? Target has a demo screen."

"I'm never going to be a gamer, Jamie."

"I'm not a gamer either, but you can't snark on a thing properly if you don't even know what it is."

"Good point." I laugh. "Let's go."

Mario Odyssey is the best gateway into gaming," Jamie explains once we're standing in front of the monitor. "It helps you get the best sense of the controllers."

He tells me where to turn and how to duck as Mario walks through a red sand valley. He sidesteps a ghost. He throws his pal Cappy in the air and it boomerangs back. I have to admit, this is fun.

"The graphics are kind of cool," I tell him.

"Kind of? Switch has the *best* graphics. Don't tell Drew and Felipe that, though. They're PlayStation all the way. But trust me, Switch is the best."

"Where are the Koopa Troopas?" I ask him. "I want to kick some turtle butt."

"That's the weird thing with *Mario Odyssey*," he says. "The Koopa Troopas are nice here."

I take a step closer to him and lean in conspiratorially.

"Maybe the evil ones got voted out."

He looks down at me, moving to speak, but before he can say anything, we're interrupted.

"Back from another day of canvassing?" We look up and see Kevin.

"We had a good day," Jamie says.

"Got eleven commitments to vote."

"Wow, that many people opened their door?" Kevin asks.

"Don't underestimate us." I grin. "We're pretty good at this."

"Clearly. Way to go, guys!"

"Thanks, Kev." He's not a Democrat, but he's definitely *not* a Koopa Troopa.

"Now I'm teaching Maya how a video game controller

works," says Jamie.

"Ugh, *Mario Odyssey*?" Kevin looks at the screen. "That's for kids."

"Kids?" Jamie looks at Kevin like he personally insulted InstaGramm. "Look at those graphics!"

"I'm actually pretty good!" I tell Kevin. "Look, I'm about to beat the Broodal!"

"Um." Kevin glances at the screen and then at Jamie. "Should I tell her or you want to?"

"Tell me what?" I pause the game.

"Well." Jamie scratches his head. "Okay. Fine. You're on assist mode."

"Assist mode?"

"Like when they put up blockers on the bowling lanes so you can't ever hit the gutter?" Kevin grins.

"It's just how the demo is set up," Jamie says quickly. "You're playing really well, though! I bet you'd have reached this stage even without the assist mode."

And with that, I'm done.

They continue talking about the graphics and the storage space on PlayStation versus Switch versus Xbox.

My phone buzzes, and I pull it out.

Sara: Noooo your dad did not do that! But in his defense, your cat phase WAS intense.

Maya: Excuse me, cats aren't a phase. They're a lifestyle.

Sara: LOL. Hey. Sorry about earlier. Was finishing up a swim lesson and then worked out. I think my sitting gig is coming through though. 😣 But I could FaceTime now if you're free.

I glance up just then and pause. Jamie's looking at me. His eyes meet mine. Something about the way he's gazing intently makes my stomach flutter.

"Hey," he says with a small smile. "Do you seriously have Wi-Fi on your phone right now?"

"What?"

"You looked like you were texting. That's so cool. I never get any service here."

"Yeah." I stare at him. "It's so cool."

Maya: Sorry. At Target with a friend right now.

Sara: A friend? 😮

Maya: Stop it!

Sara: I thought I was your only friend.

I glance at Jamie before looking back down at my phone.

Maya: Branching out I guess.

Sara: Better not replace me!

I look at the screen. She's going to think I'm joking when I say this, but I'm so not.

Maya: No way. You're my best friend. Always and forever. No replacements in that department.

Three dots.

Sara: Same here <3 But, glad you're expanding your circle.

I glance at Jamie.

Maya: Yeah. Me too.

CHAPTER NINE
JAMIE

Mom's a rage machine this morning. "Unbelievable." She waves her phone around. "Jamie, as soon as this is over, I'm taking a three-year nap. I've never seen such gross incompetence in my entire life. I swear to God."

I shove a spoonful of Trix in my mouth, trying not to laugh. I mean. For someone planning a sacred religious rite of passage, Mom does a whole lot of swearing to God. Though, to be fair, the DJ for Sophie's bat mitzvah did just announce he's breaking his contract to be on *The Bachelorette*.

"If it was a family emergency? Fine. Understandable. But this schmuck's going to pull out less than three weeks before the bat mitzvah, and for this nonsense?"

"Maybe he'll come out of the limo wearing glow-in-the-dark bracelets and holding an inflatable guitar."

She stops pacing abruptly to point at me. "That's not funny."

"*Tune in July sixth, for the most dramatic hamotzi in Bachelor Nation history . . .*"

"How do you know this much about *The Bachelorette*?"

"It's a good show."

"Well, I'm glad you're a fan, but now I'm going to have to rearrange my whole day to deal with this. And then—oh no. Jamie, are you canvassing today?"

"No, not till this weekend," I tell her.

Mom exhales. "Good. I've got a meeting with the caterer this afternoon, so I need you to take your sister to Hebrew school—"

"But Felipe and Drew were going to—"

"Jamie, please." Mom presses her hand to her temple. "Help me out here. I know it's hard, sweetheart, and you've been so great. I hate to ask, but with this curveball from the DJ . . ."

Jewish mom guilt for the win. You'd think I'd be immune to it by now, but I swear, it's like a virus. Every time I built up my defenses, Mom introduces a new strain.

"I can take her."

Mom softens. "Thanks, sweetie." She ruffles my hair. "Three thirty at The Temple, okay? I can pick her up afterward. I'm just so glad it's not one of your canvassing days." She smiles. "By the way, I hear that's going well."

"Yeah, it's been pretty cool. We got like eleven people on Sunday."

"Alina says you and Maya are getting along."

I flip my phone facedown abruptly. "What did she say?"

Mom glances at my phone, smiling slightly. "Nothing in particular. She just mentioned Maya seemed to be enjoying the process. I'm just so glad, Jamie." She pats my shoulder. "I think all this speaking practice is really going to help you prepare for your toast. And once you conquer that, the sky's the limit. I know you used to talk about running for office one day . . ."

My stomach drops. I guess a part of me was hoping Mom would be so impressed by all my canvassing that she'd give me a pass on the bat mitzvah. But nope. She's like the mouse from those picture books. You give her a cookie, and she wants milk. I bust my butt doing spreadsheets for Rossum, and she wants me to canvass. I canvass, and somehow that's practice for speaking in front of hundreds of people. And apparently the next step is me running for office, because we all know that would be a chill and vomit-free situation.

I mean, can you imagine me trying to give one of those mega-inspirational mic-drop Rossum speeches? Sure, I could drop a microphone. Because my palms would be sweating too much to hold it. And if I actually managed to choke any words out, I'd be a gaffe machine. Seriously, I wouldn't just lose my election. I would call it an erection.

And *then* I'd lose.

But the worst part is, Mom's not entirely off base. It's not like she's pulling this political stuff out of thin air. Do I still daydream sometimes about running for office? Yeah. Have I ever typed out *Rep. Jamie Goldberg (D-GA)*, just to see it in print? Maybe.

Sophie says I'm secretly, and I quote, "a power-hungry mofo." But it doesn't have anything to do with power. At least not power for its own sake.

I want to be a history changer. I want to help draw the timeline.

And I know—*I know*—you don't have to be a politician to do that. There are a million ways to change the world quietly. No charisma necessary. No need to be the charming, bright-eyed candidate working the room at campaign events. No need to give some showstopper speech on the Congress floor. I'm not that guy. I don't have to be that guy.

I want to be that guy, though.

I'd rather be him than me.

I wait until Mom's gone before flipping my phone back over, which probably looks extremely shady. But I swear it's not like that. It's just that Maya *finally* accepted my Instagram follow request, and even with my mom there, I had to sneak in a quick scroll. But now that she's in the living room looking for a DJ who won't be journeying to find love this month, I can finally take a real look.

I tap back into Instagram, where Maya's page is already open, arranged into the standard stacks of squares. It's not the kind of account with a careful, planned aesthetic, or even a general tone and mood like Grandma's InstaGramm. It's really just Maya's life. There's a selfie with sunglasses, a close-up of a raggedy, well-loved Elmo doll, and, scrolling back a little, a bunch of pictures with the curly-haired friend I saw her with at Target. Her friend Sara, I now know. And there's even a close-up of one of the Rossum walk pieces we've been distributing, posted Sunday afternoon—which means I must have been right there when she posted it. The caption says, *awesome Rossum day*.

I can't help but smile when I read that.

But my favorite picture—the one I keep coming back to—is this black-and-white close-up selfie. Just Maya's face. Her dark hair hangs past her cheeks, wavy and long enough to fall out of frame. She's smiling slightly with her mouth closed. But her eyes have this glint—not like she's mad. More like she's silently teasing someone.

It's, uh. Not a bad look.

Then, out of the blue, as if I conjured her with my own thoughts—she texts me.

That's never happened before. I mean, we've texted. But unless you count the initial This is Maya Rehman text from when we first exchanged numbers, I've always been the one to initiate contact. But this? This is an actual, spontaneous, non-logistical Maya text, popping onto my phone screen like it's the most normal thing in the world. I almost drop my spoon.

InstaGramm followed me!! And before I can even respond, there's a second text: Okay I know it's because she's your grandma and I met her etc, but also I'm kind of fangirling???

I set my phone down on the table.

So here's the thing. Technically, Maya never accepted my Instagram follow request. That's because technically, I don't have an Instagram. I just don't see the point of it, since I myself am not particularly Instagram-worthy. And if there's something I want to look at, I just pop into Grandma's account.

Which is . . . basically what I did this morning with Maya.

So she clearly thinks I'm Grandma. An honest mistake, seeing as I'm logged in as, well, Grandma. But it's not like she would have denied my follow request if I'd followed her as myself. You don't block your social media from someone you're already texting—that's just backward. Anyway, I'm almost positive Maya said her mom is the one who made her stay on private in the first place.

I feel a little guilty, though. It's almost like I snuck past her privacy settings under false pretenses. I guess I could tell her right now that it's me . . . but that feels awful too. I don't want to rain on her followed-by-a-local-celebrity parade. And after the iffy first impression Maya had, it's clear she's now one hundred percent Team Grandma.

So I suck it up and write back: NICE.

And then I make Grandma's account like a few of Maya's pictures, because hey, Grandma *would* like Maya's pictures if she saw them.

But I don't click the heart on the black-and-white one. Not even from Grandma.

I'm just so painfully bad at anything girl-related. I don't even know how to talk to them. I suppose I can technically form words around most of them.

But I don't know how to do any of the other stuff.

Like that thing certain guys do where they tease a girl just the right amount. Or when the guy touches a girl's arm in this very particular way, where it's not a big deal, but it IS a big deal.

Drew's always telling me not to stress about it. To just trust my instincts and let things play out. But that really only works if you have good instincts. And I can't let things play out because there's no *thing* to play out. They just don't get it. Drew's a huge flirt, but never in a serious way. And even though Felipe's pretty guarded about boys, he stepped up big-time when Nolan entered the picture. I'm talking grand-gesture scavenger-hunt-promposal big-time. Meanwhile, I send one *Shrek* GIF, and days later, I'm *still* feeling like I came on way too strong.

I don't even know where I'd turn for real advice on this stuff. Grandma, I guess—though her advice would be about communication and "opening your heart" and not about certain very physical sensations that happen when I look at a particular black-and-white picture.

Maybe it's time for me to log out.

Sophie has a plan.

I mean, she pretty much always has a plan. When I was twelve, I don't even think my brain had switched on yet, and here's Sophie, forging schemes twice every day before breakfast.

"Here's my thing about the teen room," she says, settling deeper into the passenger seat. "It actually simplifies so many things. You'll have more space in the ballroom—"

"Oh, you're still stuck on this?"

"I'm not *stuck*," she says—and I don't even need to glance away from the road to know she's rolling her eyes. "I'm just thinking out loud. Okay, so it also allows the lighting to be more customized to your guests' needs. Right? Soft evening lights for the oldsters, dark mood lighting for the youth. Maybe a little bit of multicolored LED crystal ball strobe if we're feeling fancy. And don't say those words sound like drug names."

"I didn't say anything—"

"You were thinking it. And your predictability is a discussion for another day. But going back to the lighting . . ."

I tune in and out. It's not that Sophie's boring. But between the GPS on my phone and NPR droning in the background, I've missed a solid few minutes of her declaration.

". . . Spin the Bottle, Seven Minutes in Heaven, right?"

"Wait, what?" The light's red at 17th Street, so I can finally look at her face.

"Jamie, they're games."

"I know what they *are*. I just didn't know you were playing them."

"I never said I was." She sniffs. "I'm just saying, these are the kinds of things that would be possible in a teen room. You just don't know that, because you probably spent every weekend of seventh grade partying with people's parents. You know that's how they get you, right?"

I make the left onto Peachtree. "I don't think it's that diabolical, Soph. People are just trying to celebrate their kids."

"I'm just saying. And even if Mom says no to the teen room, eighth grade is going to be totally different. Tessa said she's having a no-parents birthday party this year, so yeah. We're doing Spin the Bottle, we're doing Seven Minutes in

Heaven, we're doing Suck and Blow—"

"Excuse me?"

"With a playing card. Jamie, you're so innocent. Anyway, the other thing . . ."

But suddenly, something from the radio catches my attention. A name. "Imam Shaheed Jackson, from the Brookhaven Community Mosque, here with us today to discuss . . ."

I turn the volume up. "What is this?" Sophie asks.

"NPR."

"Well, obviously—"

"I want to hear this. I think this guy was at the Jordan Rossum iftar."

And for the rest of the ride to The Temple, Sophie and I don't speak. We just listen.

"A new bill," says Tammy Adrian, who's hosting the segment, "introduced this morning by Republican state representative Ian Holden, calls for a partial ban on head and facial coverings while participating in certain public activities—including driving a car. Imam Jackson, thanks for coming on *Real Talk*. Tell me, what could legislation like this mean for the Muslim community here in Georgia?"

"Thank you, Tammy, for having me on. I think we're still absorbing the implications of a bill like this. But what we do know is this: this bill is unnecessary. It is based in fear. And it's yet another attempt by Republican lawmakers to limit the freedom of Muslim citizens to participate in the full range of daily life in this state and in this country."

"Proponents of the bill—like state senate candidate Asa Newton, who tried unsuccessfully to push through a bill like this when he was a congressman years ago—argue this is not about any particular faith—it's a safety measure barring facial and head coverings for all people. How would you respond to that?"

"We can pretend this bill doesn't target Muslims, but we all saw that the language of the proposed bill, which was published this morning, uses the pronoun *she* exclusively. This law is designed to impact women wearing facial and head coverings."

"Holden's spokesperson did issue a statement saying it was a typo and nothing more."

"More like something they forgot to hide before the bill was released."

"It does indeed raise some questions about its intent," says Tammy. "And what listeners may not know is that H.B. 28 is actually modeled after an existing bill that was introduced in the 1950s to protect Georgians from the Ku Klux Klan. But Holden's proposed bill broadens the restrictions so they now disproportionately affect Muslim women. Newton was unsuccessful in passing the bill in the nineties, but he's hopeful it may gain momentum now due to our current political climate."

Sophie's voice is soft. "That's awful."

"Yeah." I exhale. "Wow."

". . . seen a spike in hate crimes," Imam Jackson is saying. "And what a bill like this does—it flips the narrative. The reality is, here in Georgia, Muslim women are the victims of hate crimes. But they are not the aggressors. And yet the result of a bill like this . . ."

"Jamie, you're about to pass The Temple."

"Oh." I make an abrupt right turn.

". . . Doyle is a pragmatic Republican governor, and he's stated he intends to veto H.B. 28. So the passage of this bill will depend on whether the GOP can override Doyle's veto with supermajorities in both the House and the Senate. Since the GOP recently flipped the Thirty-Fourth Senate District, they just need to keep the Fortieth District red to get their supermajority," Tammy is saying. "This is the seat recently vacated by Republican John Graham, who was elected to the US House of Representatives in a special election this February. Democratic candidate Jordan Rossum has already released a statement condemning this bill as an affront to the dignity and religious freedom of the Muslim community here in Georgia."

"He's absolutely right," Imam Jackson says. "And these are the conversations we need to be having. What do we mean when we say we honor religious liberty? Who are we picturing in our minds at that moment?"

"It raises the stakes immensely for the upcoming special election," Tammy says.

I park in the side lot of The Temple, staring straight ahead through the windshield. "Maya's mom wears hijab."

Sophie's still curled up in the passenger seat, clutching her Hebrew school tote bag. "Everything's going to be fine. People aren't going to vote for Newton. He's so racist."

I laugh humorlessly. "Right."

Sophie hugs me before she leaves, which is unusual, but suddenly I'm barely thinking of Sophie at all. Still parked by The Temple, I tug my phone out of its car charger. Before I can talk myself out of it, I text Maya. Just heard about the bill. You okay?

She writes back immediately: Um. Not really.

And then, a moment later: Hey, are you doing anything right now? Maybe you could come over or something.

I'm so busy entering her address into my GPS, I almost forget to write back.

CHAPTER TEN
MAYA

Mom picks up on the first ring.

"I'm walking into a meeting. Everything okay?"

"No," I tell her. "It most definitely isn't."

"What happened? I'll tell Chris I need to duck out. I'll be home in twenty."

"No! The bill. Didn't you hear about the law they're trying to pass?"

"Oh, that." She exhales. "Yes, I know about it."

"Well? Aren't you upset?"

"Of course I am. It's infuriating."

"What are we going to do about it?"

"You *are* doing something. You're canvassing."

"Knocking on doors? This can't wait until the election! We have to handle it now."

"The board is meeting tonight to discuss next steps."

"I'll tell you the first step. Tell Newton to go fuck himself."

"Maya. Language."

"Sh—shoot." I wince. "It's just that he's such a racist . . . armhole."

"I promise I'll keep you posted," my mother says. "But trust me, we'll make him sorry. They will *not* get away with it."

I smile at the fire in her voice. *No one's* telling her what she can and can't wear.

"How're things over there?" my mother asks. "The apartment shaping up okay?"

I stop smiling.

"It's fine."

"What's the plan for iftar tonight?"

"Dad's picking up pho after work."

"Yum. Pho Dai Loi?"

"Yep." I straighten. "I could tell him to pick up an extra order."

"I don't think that's a good idea."

"It's Ramadan. Who wants to eat alone?"

"Aw, sweetie, you're so thoughtful. But I won't be by myself. We're having that emergency board meeting tonight." She pauses. "And now I *really* have to step into this meeting. Call you back after I'm done?"

"Sure."

"Love you, Maya Papaya."

"Love you too."

We hang up and I look down at my phone's wallpaper photo. It's us three cheesing it up in front of the Grand Canyon last year. That was the summer we decided bunny ears were peak hilarity. Things were good on that trip. I'd have noticed if they weren't.

I wish I knew how their time apart to reflect and focus was going. They definitely don't talk to me about it. But considering she can't comprehend having a shared family meal together, it can't be going all that well.

Which sucks.

My phone buzzes. It's Sara. A selfie with her eyes wide, holding up a scoop of something green and colorful. Beneath it a text: Presented without comment: Froot Loop custard.

Maya: The face you're making is comment enough.

Sara: This should be illegal.

I text her a barf emoji just as Jamie's name flashes up:

Jamie: Almost there.

I flush. I was so upset by the proposed bill that when he texted me, I instinctively told him to come over, but now after talking to my mom and seeing our Grand Canyon picture, there's this weird hollowness inside me I can't shake. I unlock my phone to tell him it's not a good time when there's a knock.

Too late.

"Hey," Jamie says when I open the door. He's in jeans and a T-shirt, his hands stuffed in his pockets. He looks at me with such genuine concern, I'm suddenly so relieved he's here.

I part the door and gesture for him to come inside.

"I heard the news," he says. "I thought I was misunder-standing it at first . . ."

"Me too," I tell him. "My friend Lyla texted a bunch of us to turn on WPBA, which was so weird, until I heard Imam Jackson talking . . . it feels *too* real now."

"He did a great job," Jamie says. "The way he called them out was perfect."

"It's ridiculous. Women are problematic if they show too much skin and problematic if they don't show enough?"

"What people wear is their own business," Jamie says. "If I want to wear a tiara every single day of the year, who is anyone to tell me I can't? I mean . . ." He pauses. "Not that I plan to wear one, but . . ."

"I would legit love if you wore a tiara every single day of the year. I'd pay to see that actually." I laugh despite myself.

Jamie smiles—and then his eyes widen. I follow his gaze toward the window overlooking the street outside.

"Is that seriously a Krispy Kreme donut shop?" He walks over to the window. He's admiring it like it's the Taj Mahal.

"It sure is."

"That's amazing."

"Yeah. Amazing."

"I'm serious. Anytime they have the fresh donuts ready to go, with this prime real estate location, you're literally the first person to see that red light go on."

"Good point."

Turning away from the window, he glances around the family room.

"Are your parents minimalists?" he asks.

"Minimalists?"

"Oh, I just noticed that there's not much furniture or decorations here. My mom read that Marie Kondo book last year and it was *intense*, but when she tried to donate Boomer's bed, my grandma staged an intervention."

I look around the bare room. It's a very good thing my dad hasn't started furnishing this place and settling in—but the emptiness is chilling.

"This isn't really my house." I sit down on the futon. "I mean, it is. I guess. This is my dad's place. For now. My parents are having a trial separation."

This is the first time I've told anyone. I thought it'd be Sara who'd know first.

Jamie sits next to me.

"That must be really difficult," he says.

"One minute everything is business as usual. And then, it all changes."

"Trial separation sounds like they're figuring it out? So they *could* get back together?"

"Maybe. I knew they weren't getting along, but they dropped it on me out of nowhere. We had a whole trip to Italy planned—a cottage in Tuscany. I was about to tell them about this pasta-making class walkable from us, and they told me the trip—and their marriage—was canceled."

"I'm so sorry, Maya."

"And I *hate* being in limbo, waiting to see what they decide. Why do they get *all* the say in something that affects me too? At this point, honestly, if they want to get divorced, fine. I'd rather just know. This waiting?" My voice breaks. "It sucks. I hate change, Jamie. I fucking hate it. But if everything's going to change, let's just get it over with, so I can start getting used to the new normal."

"You okay?" he asks softly.

It's a polite question. He *has* to ask, right? But something about how he says it—the way he's looking at me—

"No." Tears slip down my cheeks. I couldn't stop them if I tried. "I'm really tired."

He hesitates before scooting closer to me.

"Can I hug you?" he asks softly.

I nod. He puts his arms around me. I rest my head in the crook of his neck. He smells like lemons and mint. For the first time in a long time, I don't feel alone.

★   ★   ★

I tell him more. About the Talk. The movers.

". . . and now we're here. In this shoebox apartment. He keeps trying to be perky about it. But how am I supposed to pretend everything is great? There's literally nothing I can do except ride it out."

"It sucks to feel helpless," he says.

"Exactly." I wipe my tears against my sweatshirt and look up at him. "You're a good listener, you know that?"

"Thanks. It's the talking that trips me up."

"Some people suck at both." I smile at him a little. "So you've won half the battle."

We sit side by side in comfortable silence.

"Anything I can do to cheer you up?" he asks.

"Yeah, but I'm pretty sure my dad doesn't have any tiaras lying around." I smile at him.

"I know a place that might."

"Honestly? You know what'll really make me happy? Googling Holden's face. That way if I ever run into him, I can give him a piece of my mind. Wouldn't that be so awesome? To just watch his smug smile disappear."

Jamie's about to say something, but then he pauses.

"What if you could?"

"What do you mean?"

He pulls out his phone and starts typing furiously.

"What are you doing?" I ask him.

"I don't know why I didn't think of it earlier. But

Holden's got a legislative director—" His face is animated. "They're the one who probably green-lit this whole idea. What if you got an appointment to actually *give* them a piece of your mind?"

"How do you know all this?"

"My mom works for Jim Mathews in the Thirty-Third District," he says. "She has to fill in sometimes for the legislative director. She always vents to us about the obnoxious people who come through to complain about whatever policies he has or hasn't come up with yet."

"So I'd be the obnoxious person in this scenario?"

"Yep!" He holds up the phone. A woman with dark brown hair in a bob wearing a topaz necklace smiles back at me. "Jennifer Dickers. Should I make an appointment?"

I can't believe it's as easy as making an appointment. I could actually sit down and explain to this woman why this bill is misplaced and harmful. Still, the thought is intimidating.

"Is it off the MARTA? I have a rideshare app, but it's technically for getting back and forth from my place to here."

"I can drive you there. And"—he hesitates—"I could go in with you to talk to her . . . if you want."

"You'd do that?" Jamie's never struck me as a confrontational sort of guy. But he nods and smiles. "You really think they'd talk to high schoolers?"

"You mean will they talk to someone whose community is directly affected by the law they're proposing?" Jamie says. "You have every right to give them a piece of your mind."

"Okay, I'm in," I tell him. "Let's make them sorry they ever said yes to this bull . . . shop plan."

"Bullshop? Is that kind of like 'fork you'? Like on *The Good Place*?"

"Well, yeah—but also, I'm trying not to curse during Ramadan. Just go with it."

"Okay, yep, we'll call them on their bullshop so fast they won't know what flunking hit them."

At this, I start giggling.

And then we're both laughing.

And somehow, my heart isn't hurting quite as much anymore.

CHAPTER ELEVEN
JAMIE

I wake up Thursday morning to a string of texts from Maya.

Ugh I can't sleep!!! Too nervous

I can't believe we actually have to talk to this woman, I saw she was on Hannity?? 🤮

Am trying to decide what to wear. Like I need something that says I'm a professional but also fuck you

*fuzz you 😬

SO TIRED

What does a legislative director even do?? Like did she make up the policy or is she the mouthpiece of the policy

BOTH ARE HORRIBLE, SHE IS A KOOPA TROOPA NO MAT- TER WHAT but I want to know

Why can't I sleep??? Ugh it's light out already WHYYYY

Well I guess I'll see you soon 😭

By the time I pull into Maya's driveway, she's waiting on her front stoop in a button-down dress and cardigan. She slides into Alfie's passenger seat, her smile cut short by a yawn. "You made it! Jamie, meet Mom's house." She gestures sleepily toward the stucco facade.

"You weren't kidding when you said it's close to your dad's."

"It literally takes longer waiting for the car than the actual rides back and forth."

"I bet those fares add up, huh," I say, slowly backing toward the street. "You should think about asking your parents for a car."

Maya looks at me with an expression I can't decipher.

"Er. Anyway," I say, feeling suddenly tongue-tied. "I got you something." I tap one of the twin iced coffees resting side by side in the cup holders. "Since you were up all night. It's probably going to be a little strong. I skipped the milk and everything obviously, but don't worry. I got the same for myself. Ramadan solidarity, right?"

"Jamie, I can't have this."

"Wait, really?" I glance sideways.

She looks exasperated.

"I thought . . . Google said—"

"Did you read past the first entry?"

"But . . . it's black coffee!"

"I don't do coffee on Ramadan." She crosses her arms. "I don't even do *water*. I eat suhoor way before the sun is up and then I eat after the sun sets. That's it."

There's this quicksand feeling in my stomach. As always, I'm a disaster. As always, I've managed to screw up everything I touch. I guess I thought things were sort of good with Maya. Not in a romantic agenda kind of way. I don't know. I'm just happy we're friends. Or we were, until my bull-in-a-china-shop self ruined everything.

"Sorry," I say.

She presses her lips together and turns to look out the window.

State Representative Holden's district office is in this nondescript brick building, really close to my house. It's nothing like the state capitol. This place looks more like a strip mall where you'd stop for an emergency pee break on your way up Roswell Road.

I park, reaching into the backseat to root around for my messenger bag—a little excessive to transport a single stack of index cards, maybe, but it's the most briefcase-y thing I could find.

"Hey," Maya says when I resurface. "I'm sorry."

I look at her. "What?"

"I know you meant well. It's just . . ." She rubs her forehead. "Sometimes, people who aren't Muslim try to push food on me during Ramadan, like I'm starving myself or something. I mean, I *do* get hungry, but I still enjoy fasting. It usually brings me an inner peace I don't get to experience outside of Ramadan. But you were just trying to be thoughtful. I shouldn't have lashed out at you."

"Oh." I blink. "No, you're fine."

"I think I'm just nervous," she says. "About the meeting."

I am too—and I'm definitely not loving the about-to-interview-with-Senator-Mathews feeling in my stomach. But I'd rather die than tell Maya that. For one thing, I don't want to make her more nervous. And frankly, between the tangelos and the pastry puffs, Maya's witnessed quite enough of my showstoppers, thank you very much. I'm not exactly dying to fill her in on the rest of them.

Most of all, I don't want to say the wrong thing again.

But as stonily silent as she was in the car, Maya's more than making up for it in the parking lot. "Don't you think it's weird they had a cancellation, like, right before we called? It seems shady." She glances up at the faded trim around the building's entrance. "This is totally a trap. Hansel and Gretel all over again."

I laugh nervously. "I hope not."

"Okay, we can't tell them we're seventeen. I don't want them not taking us seriously because we can't vote yet. And we give your address, since you're a constituent. Maybe they'll actually listen to you."

Maya's in the next district over for the state House of Representatives. She was really smug about it until she realized her rep is another middle-aged white Republican guy who looks exactly like Holden.

"What if we see Holden?" Her eyes widen.

"I'm guessing he's at the capitol."

"Ugh, he's probably there working on the next big racist bill."

We take an elevator to the third floor, and the moment the doors open, I see it: *Suite 3250: Office of Georgia Representative Ian Holden.*

Maya looks at the wooden office door beside it, biting her lip. "Should we knock?"

"I guess so?" I clutch my messenger bag.

Maya knocks, tentatively.

"Come on in!" says a woman's cheerful voice, slightly muffled by the door.

We step in to find a small waiting room, not so different from my dentist's office. Three reception chairs line the back wall of the room, with a small end table in the corner and two more chairs along the side wall. Centered above them are a few Georgia-centric posters: an old-timey view of Peachtree Street, and, weirdly, the exact same St. Simons Island lighthouse illustration we have framed in our living room. On the other side of the room, there's a large reception desk, staffed by a blond woman who looks barely older than we are. "How can I help y'all?"

I step up to the desk, feeling shaky and light-headed. I can't believe we're actually doing this. We're about to walk into a legit private meeting with an elected official's legislative director. For a moment, I just stand there, staring at the small sign propped up on the desk, featuring an illustrated graphic of a cell phone in a no-smoking sign. *Thank you for respecting our no-recording policy.*

"Well, I'm Kristin, and it's *so* nice to meet y'all. Are you—"

"Here for a meeting," I say quickly, jolting back to earth. "Jamie Goldberg and Maya Rehman, meeting with Ms. Dickers at ten thirty."

"Yup! Got you down right here," Kristin says. "Ms. Dickers is just wrapping up a meeting. Can I get y'all any snacks? Anything to drink?"

"No, thank you," I say. Maya just shakes her head and walks straight to the back of the room, perching stiffly on the edge of one of the chairs.

"You okay?" I settle into the chair beside her.

"Fine." She exhales. "She's nice." Maya juts her chin at Kristin, who's now laughing sweetly into the receiver of her office phone. But the look on Maya's face tells me she's thinking the exact same thing I am: If Kristin were truly nice, how could she justify working for someone like Holden?

Every moment that passes in this waiting room makes Maya more jittery. "She's ten minutes late," Maya whispers. "Is that normal?"

"I think so?" I glance up at Kristin, who smiles warmly from behind the desk. "I guess the other meeting went over."

It's almost eleven by the time someone finally emerges from a door near Kristin's desk. Another staffer, maybe? He's a baby-faced white guy who looks like he walked straight off a yacht. He talks to Kristin for a moment, and Kristin gestures us over. "All right," she says brightly. "Ms. Dickers is ready for you."

The guy staffer doesn't introduce himself, but he leads us down a short hallway, into a small, windowless meeting room furnished with a table and chairs. "She'll be right with you," he says, shutting us in.

"So now we wait again?" Maya groans.

I open my bag, pulling out the notecards. "Maybe we should look over our talking points?"

"You're sure we're allowed to bring notes?" Maya asks.

"I mean." I glance down at the cards, suddenly not so sure at all. "I think so? It's not like an exam."

"It feels like an exam," she mutters.

The door swings open, revealing a woman in a blazer and a patterned neck scarf, carrying a short stack of papers. Ms. Dickers seems around my mom's age, maybe a little older, and she's actually super polished, but in a weirdly dated way, like an old headshot. "Jennifer Dickers," she says, smiling brightly. She shakes each of our hands before settling in across from us. "Y'all look so young, my goodness. How can I help you?"

Deep breath. "Thank you for meeting with us." I sound so stiff and rehearsed. I'm already cringing. "I'm Jamie Goldberg, and this is Maya Rehman, and we're here . . ." My voice starts to shake, but I swallow and start over. "We're here to discuss—"

She glances down at her papers. "I see you have concerns about H.B. 28."

"Yes." Another deep breath. "Georgia H.B. 28, regarding the partial ban on face and head coverings." I peek at my first notecard. "If it's okay, I'm going to paraphrase Imam Jackson from the Brookhaven Community Mosque."

I sense Maya straightening beside me.

Ms. Dickers looks amused. "You go right ahead."

I try to breathe through the tightness in my chest—I swear, it feels like I just ran up three flights of stairs. "Imam Jackson said that given the language of this bill, we can see its intention is to limit the freedom of Muslim citizens in daily life."

"Oh my." Ms. Dickers clasps her hands. "Now that's quite an assumption. H.B. 28 doesn't mention anything about Muslims."

I nod quickly. "But it's implied. And the pronouns used—"

"I'm certainly not seeing how it's implied. The purpose of H.B. 28 is actually to protect citizens as they participate in daily life."

Maya jumps in. "How would this bill protect citizens?"

Ms. Dickers smiles. "Well, in fact, this law is based on an existing—"

"We know, the KKK unmasking law," Maya says impatiently. "But why would you expand the restrictions to include driving? And why does the bill's language use female pronouns?"

"Congressman Holden is a believer in revisiting legislation and making sure it maintains its relevance. At the time of the initial law, the KKK was a threat—"

"They still are!" Maya lets out a blunt, disbelieving laugh. "Are you kidding me? The KKK literally endorsed Newton in the special election senate race."

Ms. Dickers raises her eyebrows. "Well, I haven't heard anything about that. And I'm certainly not sure what this has to do with H.B. 28. But you can rest assured, Congressman Holden is an expert on issues related to security, and constituent safety is his utmost priority. In times of crisis, I'm sure all innocent citizens understand the need for more transparency to protect our communities."

"But what does that have to do with facial and head coverings?" I ask.

"Well," Ms. Dickers says, "given recent advances in weapon technology, it's entirely conceivable that a would-be attacker could carry an explosive on his or her person that's small enough to fit beneath a standard bandanna or face mask."

"But that's not real," I say. "That's never happened."

"And I pray to God it never will," says Ms. Dickers.

"So you're basing your policy on random far-fetched hypotheticals," I blurt. I can feel Maya's eyes landing on me in surprise.

"Our policy is based on the best interests of our constituents," says Ms. Dickers.

"Not all your constituents," Maya says. "Some of Holden's constituents wear hijab! You know that, right?"

"Of course, and Congressman Holden is proud to represent people from all faiths."

"If he supports banning hijab, he's not representing my community!"

"Oh my." Ms. Dickers's mouth curves upward at the corners. "It's sweet of you to be so concerned, but I'm not sure how this affects you, precisely."

"What does that mean?"

"Well, I can't help but notice you don't wear hijab."

"You're kidding me, right?" Maya grips the edge of the table. "You're surprised I'm opposed to this? Because I don't wear hijab? I don't even—you realize whatever I wear or don't wear is *my* business, but it still affects me—and my mom wears hijab and she—"

"Oh, I see. Well, you'll be thrilled to know that this bill is for her safety as well. These guidelines let our neighbors know women like your mom have nothing to hide. Our research shows that greater transparency leads to fewer religiously motivated attacks."

Maya inhales so sharply, I can almost feel it.

"You're blaming hate crimes on the victim!" I say, flushing. "Your logic implies that wearing a hijab—a religious garment—means you're hiding something. Are you serious right now?"

"Yessir, Congressman Holden and I are serious about protecting our constituents."

Maya's eyes flash. "What do you think my mom is hiding under her hijab?"

"I hear you," Ms. Dickers says, smiling gently at Maya. "And it breaks my heart that a few bad apples make it necessary for us to take certain steps—"

There's an abrupt knock—which turns out to be the preppy guy staffer. "Pardon," he says. "Ms. Dickers, your eleven fifteen is here."

"Already?" She smiles widely at me first, and then at Maya. "Well, time just flies, doesn't it? Thank y'all so much for taking the time to stop by and share your concerns."

Maya shakes her head. "But—"

"Blaine will walk you out to the waiting room. You two have a wonderful day, now!" She waggles her fingers, and then steps past Yacht Club Blaine, who lingers in the doorway, barely sparing us a glance. When I meet Maya's eyes, she looks as bewildered as I feel. Thirty seconds ago, we were in the middle of a meeting. Now we're being escorted out by a guy who looks like he was born inside a Brooks Brothers.

"How'd it go?" Kristin asks cheerfully, but we barely acknowledge her. I just stumble out to the hallway behind Maya, my heart in overdrive. Maya turns to me, looking like she's this close to bursting, but she doesn't say a word until we're in the elevator.

Then she explodes. "What a *monster*. A few bad apples. She actually went there." She combs her hands through her hair, almost aggressively. "And the way she was just smiling the whole time, totally calm. So evil!"

"Yeah." I blink. "I felt like I was losing my mind—"

"Right! The gaslighting. And they just create their own totally warped reality. The bandanna thing. What?" Her hands fly to her temples. "She's seriously trying to sell this like it has nothing to do with their raging Islamophobia!"

"And then the victim-blaming—"

"Oh my God, don't get me started. She's an awful person.

149

Like, these are *terrible* people." The doors open, and Maya practically jumps out of the elevator, like she can't leave this place soon enough. "I mean, that *sucked*." She meets my eyes. "But you. Jamie, wow."

I blush. "What?"

"I was like, whoaaaa, Jamie. Call her out. You were *amazing*."

"Amazing?" I gape at her.

"Okay, so explain the supermajority thing. If Rossum wins, there's no supermajority? And they need that to pass this bill? What even is a supermajority?"

"It's when one party has two-thirds or more of the seats," I say. "Republicans have had that in the Georgia House for forever, and now Rossum's our last hope to block it in the senate."

Amazing. I was *amazing*. Is she serious?

"And they need a supermajority to pass H.B. 28?" Maya asks.

"Yes, because Governor Doyle says he'll veto it—"

Maya's face whips toward me. "Wait, really? He's a Republican."

"I think he basically doesn't want to piss off the film industry, you know? He mostly cares about the optics. But yeah, the thing with the supermajority is that a Republican supermajority in both houses can—"

"Override a veto," Maya says. "Got it." She stares glumly

out toward the parking lot. "We really need Rossum to win, huh?"

"Yeah," I say. "We do."

There's nothing sadder than coming back down to earth after you shoot your shot and fail. Even the backtrack through the parking lot makes me ache. We've barely spent an hour here, so we're walking by the same parked cars we passed on our way in. But the whole world feels like it's gone gray since then. We came in so hopeful. It's strange to even realize that, because at the time, I mostly felt terrified. But I think some tiny part of me thought this meeting could make a real difference. Maybe we'd say the perfect thing. Maybe hearing it from us in person would make Dickers see things differently. And then she'd convince Holden to strike the bill, and he'd issue a public apology, and then we'd end up on Upworthy or one of those inspirational videos Mom's always sending me from her suburban resistance Facebook groups.

Now I just feel depleted.

When we reach Alfie, I don't even notice the bumper at first. Not until I hear Maya's soft gasp. "No." She grabs my arm. "Jamie."

My eyes track down to the bottom right bumper, normally home to a circular blue Rossum logo. Mom's actually the one who talked Gabe into doing car magnets instead of just bumper stickers, so local Dems could flip each other's magnets upside down in parking lots. "It's a wink wink, I see you," she'd insisted. "It shows solidarity." And I have to admit, I'd get a tiny thrill every time we'd step out of Publix or Target to find our magnet flipped. It felt like an underground high five. Like we were part of something secret and important.

But now. Even with the midday sun glinting off Alfie's rear, it's plainly visible.

The magnet's gone.

And in its place is a sticker of a crudely illustrated, stark white, smiling poodle, with humanoid fingers making the alt-right "okay" sign. It's holding a white teacup too, branded with the number 88. I've seen this image hundreds of times on computer and phone screens, in countless variations—Fifi with the word *cuck* in a speech bubble, Fifi in a MAGA hat, Fifi transposed over a photo of Auschwitz.

But seeing it in real life is different. On a car. On *my* car.

Suddenly, all I can hear is Dickers's voice saying *religiously motivated attacks*.

But whoever did this probably doesn't know I'm Jewish. And anyway, no one's really anti-Semitic around here.

Right?

I glance quickly around the parking lot, a sudden chill coursing through me. What if whoever did this is still here? What if they're watching us right now?

"Jamie?" Maya says tentatively. I look back at her with a start. "You okay?"

I nod.

"You're not saying anything."

"I'm sorry."

"Don't apologize. I'm just worried," she says. And then she hugs me, sending my heart leaping into my throat. So I hug her back, pulling her closer.

"Whatever troll did this," she murmurs into my shoulder, "can go fuck himself."

"Fuck him," I say, the word heavy and strange on my tongue.

"There you go," Maya says, hugging me harder.

CHAPTER TWELVE
MAYA

It's not that I didn't think Jamie could get mad. I've just never witnessed it before.

Irritated—maybe.

Frustrated—sure.

Terrified squirrel? On a daily basis.

But this—his cheeks flushed, jaw clenched, kneeling in front of Alfie's bumper, scraping at the sticker with a flimsy plastic knife he dug out of the car? This is new.

The air is muggy, the humidity so thick you can almost taste it. Dark clouds hang heavy and low. It's comforting when the outside world reflects how you feel on the inside.

"Any luck?" I ask him.

"Kevin was right. These stickers are impossible to remove."

I dig around in my bag. There's an old mint, a Sharpie, a few coins, and a nail file.

"This might work?" I kneel next to him with the file. "It might scratch up the bumper, though."

"I don't care. I want this off."

The nail file adds a few marks on Alfie, but the sticker won't budge. The poodle eyes us like she knew we'd never get her off but it was amusing to watch us try. I glance at all the office windows surrounding us. The dog is a meme. But whoever did this is real. Are *they* watching right now? A shiver runs through me.

"Let's go get some Goo Gone," I tell him. "We used that when my baby cousin made a sticker collage on our kitchen window. I'll Sharpie over it for now."

"It won't work. It's one of those glossy stickers."

He's right; the black ink I've colored on it is already smearing from the humidity.

"Maybe it'll hold on long enough to pull out of the parking lot. If that jerk is watching us, they won't get the satisfaction of seeing us drive off with it visible."

"Good point," Jamie says grimly.

We get in the car. I can't believe this day. I knew Dickers wouldn't agree with us. It's not like I thought she'd hear our arguments and slap a hand to her forehead and exclaim,

"I work for a racist bigot and I'm quitting to join the Peace Corps" or anything. But the gaslighting was awful—how she used our words against us and smiled like she does this every day for sport. Which, maybe she does. And now, this.

"How you doing?" I ask Jamie.

"The meme looked obnoxious online," he says. "But seeing it on *my* car . . ."

"It felt like an attack?"

"Exactly. Were they watching us when we parked? Was it . . . was it aimed at me?"

"They're doing it to anyone with Rossum stickers," I tell him. "But I get why it feels aimed at you. I mean . . . it kind of was . . ." I trail off. Wow, way to make him feel better, Maya. Yep, it was in fact personal against you and who you are. But Jamie glances at me and nods, his jaw a little less clenched.

"You think someone on Holden's staff did it? We *were* in their parking lot."

"Maybe Kristin? That smiley routine has to be an act. Look who she works for."

"It's probably a team of people," Jamie says. "And using a dog for your racist mascot? How low is that? Why not use a cat? It makes no sense."

"Wait. Why a cat?"

"I just meant dogs are the symbol of unconditional love.

Cats are a little more standoffish and aloof."

"They aren't aloof! They have standards!"

He glances at me sheepishly.

"You have a cat, don't you?"

"Willow is definitively selective." I nod. "But she'd claw the face off any garbage racist in two seconds flat."

"Sounds like she'd get along with Boomer. He's as fierce as a squeaky toy, but if anyone looks at Grandma sideways, he'll make them pee their pants in two seconds flat."

"I think I'd like Boomer."

"You really would." And for the first time today, Jamie smiles.

We pick up the Goo Gone and get in the car just as a light rain begins to drizzle down. Jamie's looking out the window, lost in his thoughts. Again. I'm pretty sure I prefer angry Jamie to this downcast Jamie I see right now. I shift in my seat. He always knows what to say or do to make me feel better. I wish I could figure out how to do the same for him.

"You know what we should do?" I say. "We should go canvassing."

"In the rain?" He glances at me. "Plus, it's the middle of the day."

"It's just a drizzle. Maybe they have open slots in a

retirement community or something? This is how we stick it to them, isn't it? Dickers? The Fifi troll? We hand Newton *and* Holden their asses."

"Yeah!" His expression shifts. "You know what? That's exactly what we should do." He turns on his blinker and pulls into a shopping plaza. "I'll text Gabe to see if there are any slots."

When he picks up the phone, his expression drops.

"What's wrong?"

"Surprise, surprise." He leans against the driver's seat. "I'm urgently needed to assist with bat mitzvah planning— or more like bat mitzvah chauffeuring and delivering. Apparently, Mom ran out of sticky notes while mapping out the seating arrangements for the fiftieth time. Oh, and washi tape. There's always some sort of washi tape crisis going on. I need to get some before I come home, because otherwise the world might literally end." He sighs. "Do you mind a quick trip to stock up?"

"Not at all. Whose bat mitzvah?"

"My sister, Sophie's. My mom talks about it from the time we wake up until we go to bed. It's like this bat mitzvah is the most important thing to happen in the history of the planet. *And*." His cheeks flush. "She wants me to do a toast! A toast! I don't do toasts! I don't do public speaking. I mean, has she met me?"

"You'll be fantastic," I tell him. "You're so great at

canvassing. You have the whole script memorized."

"That's different . . . we're just stating facts about the candidate that someone else wrote for us. For this toast, I have to be funny and interesting and say the exact right thing to a crowd of over a hundred people. And when am I supposed to actually have time to think and work on this speech? My house is Rossum is awesome rah-rah-rah and bat mitzvah brouhaha all the time, and Sophie talking over my mom, and my mom talking over my grandma, and Boomer throwing in his two cents whenever he can get a word in? It's utter chaos."

"A noisy house sounds nice," I tell him. "My house is pin-drop silent lately. Not that it was ever a carnival, but since the trial separation, it's eerily quiet. It wouldn't bother me as much if Sara was around, but she's busy lately. And I'm pretty sure my parents won't be cool with me racking up hundreds of dollars taking rideshares around anywhere I want. It can be really isolating, I guess."

"I'm always happy to give you a ride," he says. "It doesn't just have to be for canvassing."

"Thanks." I smile at him.

"The secret to getting a car is you don't try to get them to buy *you* one, you convince *them* to get a new car. Point out every single ding super casually, like 'oh, that scratch on the fender isn't *too* obvious' until they can't unsee it, and then they'll buy one for themselves and give you their old one."

"Good advice." I shift uncomfortably in my seat.

A car.

I almost forgot that's what the canvassing was all about. Don't get me wrong, a car will be amazing, but what we're doing now—it's about more than just that.

The truth is, a car is the furthest thing from my mind.

CHAPTER THIRTEEN
JAMIE

"Hi, sweetie," Mom says when I walk through the door. She and Grandma are sitting side by side at the kitchen table, staring at their laptops, while Gabe hovers behind them, iced coffee in hand. I guess that means we're working on campaign stuff, not bat mitzvah stuff. Everything's so chaotic, I swear I can't even tell these days.

Boomer runs up to greet me, teeth clenched proudly around his favorite stuffed mallard duck, Mr. Droolsworth.

"Hey." I pat his head, swallowing. "So, something—"

But Gabe cuts me off, pointing fiercely at Grandma's screen. "Okay, *that*. That's what pisses me off. I don't know what it will take to get through to these people. Oh, it's just a special election! It's just the state senate! I can sit this one out! Well, you know who's not sitting this one out?" He throws his palms up. "Republicans. Those mofos show up every goddamn time."

Grandma frowns at the screen. "This doesn't help. Did you read the memo from the secretary of state's office? Van Kamp's removing four polling places in DeKalb County, and he's canceling early in-person voting."

I blink. "He can do that?"

"Apparently," says Grandma. "Which means—"

Gabe slams his hand down on the table so hard, Boomer drops his mallard with a start. "Which means Dems need to step it up! The problem is, no one's excited about this race. It's not glamorous, it's not sexy."

"Well, the supermajority issue is complicated," says Grandma.

"Exactly!" Gabe exclaims. "How many people understand supermajorities? Where are the soundbites from that? Do we do a local celebrity video? I don't know! Dallas Austin, Ludacris—no one's replying to my DMs. How do we convince people there's something at stake?"

"H.B. 28 is at stake!" It comes out louder than I mean it to. I blush, lowering my voice. "Is the campaign going to talk about that?"

"Sure," Gabe says, "but that doesn't affect most people. I don't even think people are necessarily following the story. It's just not a crisp narrative, so it's tricky to use that."

"Use it?" My jaw drops. I picture Alina at the campaign

iftar in her patterned hijab and dark jeans. I know Gabe doesn't mean to sound so flippant. He's just talking about how to get voters invested. But it feels like Gabe sees Maya's mom as someone he could potentially hold up for sympathy. Or worse, like he's glancing at her, shrugging, and saying, *Meh. Not important enough.*

"Jamie, my man. It's all about the narrative. You know that."

Mom looks up, suddenly, from her laptop. "Jamie, did you get the sticky notes?"

"Yup. And the washi tape." I hand her the bag, settling into the chair beside her. Boomer reclaims Mr. Droolsworth and zips under the table to sink his head in my lap—I scratch his ears, glancing back up at Mom. "So. Um. Something happened today—"

"Oh!" Gabe sets his coffee down. "Big J, we need to talk about yard signs."

I shake my head. "Okay, but—"

"No buts, Big J. We gotta pull together here, okay?" He pats my shoulder. "All hands on deck."

Grandma smiles up at me. "You look nice, bubalah. Was it a special occasion?"

I peer down at Boomer, who sets his mallard gently onto my lap. "Um—"

"Boom, don't you dare put Mr. Droolsworth on Jamie's date pants," scolds Grandma.

I freeze. "Date pants?"

Mom looks up from her laptop for real this time, clasping her hands. "You had a date? Oh, wow! With Maya?"

"No!" My head feels like it's spinning. "No, I had . . . a meeting."

"A meeting?" says Grandma.

I nod slowly, eyes glued to my hands. "Uh. Maya and I met with Congressman Holden's legislative director. About H.B. 28."

Everyone falls silent—and when I look up, they're all staring at me. Mom, Grandma, Gabe, even Boomer.

Mom's the first to speak. "You two just went in for a policy meeting?"

"Well, we scheduled it first."

"No, I figured." Mom smiles slightly.

I narrow my eyes. "Why are you all looking at me like that?"

"Sweetheart, we're impressed," says Grandma.

"Really impressed." Mom tilts her head. "How did it go?"

Suddenly, it feels like I'm under a spotlight—but not in a bad way. Which is wild. I honestly didn't know under-a-spotlight could ever feel good, or even okay. At least for me. Maybe this is what it's like to be a congressman. Or Sophie. I can't imagine ever basking in attention the way she does, but I have to admit, the way everyone's looking at me right now doesn't exactly suck. Just like it didn't suck when Maya called me amazing.

But you. Jamie, wow.

I sit up straighter. "It wasn't great." And just like that, the whole story tumbles out. Kristin's disarming kindness in the waiting room. The way Dickers almost chuckled when I asked to quote Imam Jackson. Her sugary-sweet accent, and the way she twisted everything we said to sound almost—*almost*—reasonable. *Safety. Transparency.* It was the weirdest split-brain sort of feeling. In one moment, the racism seemed so viscerally obvious. But a moment later, I'd feel like I was going crazy for even thinking that.

"Yeah. They always do that," Mom says, frowning.

"It was so frustrating." I exhale. "I don't get why she even took our meeting. Why do they bother taking meetings at all?"

"Because that's how democracy works," Mom says. "They're elected to represent us, and they have a responsibility to listen to our feedback."

I laugh humorlessly. "Dickers definitely wasn't listening."

"Maybe not. Sometimes they don't, which is so frustrating, I know." Mom reaches out to ruffle my hair. "But the fact that you tried. You showed up—Jamie, that's incredible."

My cheeks flush. "Thanks. It just feels pointless."

"I promise it's not pointless. Maybe you planted a seed. Who knows? And even if not, it's the fight that's important.

I'm so proud of you and Maya." Mom smiles. "Try not to be too discouraged."

"Yeah, well." I shrug. "Kind of hard not to be discouraged when we walked out of the meeting and found my car had been Fifi'd."

Gabe sits up straighter.

"Fifi'd?" Mom purses her lips.

"The poodle meme."

"Sounds kind of familiar . . ."

"It's on the internet," says Grandma. "Those alt-right Nazi dingbats use it to intimidate Jewish journalists on Twitter. But someone's been stickering cars around here too. I'm sure you've seen it. I'll pull up a Google image."

I sigh. "Or just look at Alfie's bumper. It won't come off. We tried to cover it in Sharpie, but you can still see it. Hopefully the Goo Gone will help."

Mom stares at me, wide-eyed. "Someone targeted you? A Nazi?"

Grandma squeezes my hand. "It's been happening quite a bit."

"Oh yeah," Gabe says brightly. "It's all over the district. They're going after Rossum supporters, anyone with a magnet or bumper sticker. Big J, we gotta get a photo of you with that sticker."

"With me?" I look at him. "Why?"

"Because we're not going to take this sitting down." Gabe's cheeks flush. "Gram, get this down. *Local Nazis Vandalize Car of Rossum Assistant Campaign Manager's Seventeen-Year-Old Cousin.*" He punches the air. "We're gonna go viral with this."

My stomach sinks. "You want *me* to go viral?"

"Hell yes!" Gabe says. "This is exactly the narrative we need to wake up all those Dems who were planning to sit this election out."

I stare down at Boomer's head. "Okay . . . you don't need to interview me or anything, right?"

"Absolutely not," Mom says loudly. "Gabe, you can't attach Jamie's name to this."

"How about something anonymous," Grandma suggests, "like *Local Nazi Vandalizes Teenager's Car.*"

"No!" Gabe says. "No, you're missing the point. The fact that he's my cousin—that's the game changer. That's what makes it personal. Like the Rossum campaign is under attack. What? Oh no! How do we stop the bad guys? Guess we should donate! Guess we should VOTE!"

Mom stands abruptly. "So you're just going to put your Jewish cousin out there as a target for these Nazi monsters? Jamie Goldberg? You think the name Goldberg isn't going to attract their attention?"

"You don't get it. The local guy is just going after Rossum

supporters." Gabe shakes his head. "It's not a Jew thing."

"Your grandmother *just* said Fifi is used to target Jewish journalists—"

"On Twitter!" Gabe says. "Jamie doesn't even have a Twitter."

"Well, now we know there's a Nazi prowling around Sandy Springs. At least one, who knows how many! I don't want Jamie's name out there."

"But the narrative—"

"Screw your narrative!" Mom smacks her hands down on the chair back.

"Okay, let's all calm down and think about this rationally—"

Grandma raises her eyebrows at Gabe. "Bubalah, should we try dialing back the condescension?"

He glances down at her sheepishly. "I just want to make sure we're considering all the angles here."

Mom shakes her head firmly. "You are not putting my Jewish son's name on the internet in this capacity. You're not going to make your cousin a target for Nazis. That's final."

"Hello! I'm Jewish too!" He turns to Grandma. "Don't you think—"

"She's right," Grandma says.

"Oh, come *on*—"

"Lovey, listen to what your aunt is saying. We have to

step back for a moment and realize our experience may be a little different here. You, me, your aunt Lauren—we walk through the world with the last name Miller, and people don't automatically associate that with being—"

"Jewish. I get it! But look, I'm putting myself out there too," Gabe says. "I'm saying Jamie's my cousin. You want me to be clear in the post that I'm Jewish? No problem."

"I'm just saying we owe it to Jamie to hear his perspective."

My perspective. I don't have a perspective. How could I? I've never felt threatened because of my last name. Never. I mean, yeah, everyone's always known I'm Jewish. It's the first thing people know about me when they hear my name. But no one's ever made that seem dangerous.

Except . . . maybe the danger's been there the whole time, like a sleeping Voldemort everyone knew to be on quiet alert for.

Everyone but me.

Or maybe a part of me knew. Not intellectually, not a kind of knowing I could put into words. But there's this nervous prickle I get reading certain news articles. Or when I saw Fifi smiling up from Alfie's bumper. It's not so much like someone pulling the floor out from under you. More like someone tugging the floor sideways, just a little. Just to remind you they can. But how do I even compare that to what Maya must feel? Pretty sure Maya hasn't had a solid floor to stand on for years. I think a lot of people haven't.

I mean, in the face of something like H.B. 28, does a symbolic cartoon poodle even matter?

"We're not doing the perspective dance," Mom says, rounding on Gabe. "I'm Jamie's mom, and I say it's not happening. It's a done deal."

Gabe sputters. "Well, excuse me for trying to give the Dems a reason to give a shit about this random local election in the middle of July." Gabe glares back and forth at them. "If I can't even make my own family care—"

"I care," I say quietly.

"So what? You can't even vote."

I want to scream. I've been canvassing. I've addressed postcards. I've gone to campaign events and run errands and I woke up early to plead with a racist in a neck scarf.

I *do* care. Kind of a lot.

And I wish—for the eleventy billionth time—that I were a mic-drop kind of person. The kind of person who harnesses words and stacks them together. Someone like Rossum. Maybe Gabe would listen to me then. I'd make him listen. I'd make *everyone* listen.

But then something inside me deflates. I rub my forehead, peering up at Gabe. "I can do yard signs, okay?"

"Okay, sweet," he says, perking up. "We'll get you hooked up tomorrow morning."

"Isn't it supposed to be like a million degrees tomorrow?"

"So wear sunscreen," says Gabe. "We really can't go another day. Newton's got the whole district postered. We gotta step up. You got it under control?"

"I—"

"You care about Rossum winning, right?"

"Of course I—"

"Great. I'll text Hannah and Alison—they'll have the signs ready for you to pick up by eight thirty. And before I forget, let me snap a quick pic of Fifi on your car."

Mom's jaw drops. "Excuse me? We agreed—"

"No names mentioned. Just hanging on to it in case we can fold it into some kind of narrative later." Gabe grins. "It's bound to happen to someone else soon, right?"

Grandma and Mom exchange glances, and even Boomer sighs.

CHAPTER FOURTEEN
MAYA

It's still dark out as I finish up my cereal and OJ.

My dad, aka Mr. Morning Person, is all about making an elaborate suhoor spread to start off a full day of fasting. He always woke up an hour before my mom and me to make coffee, whip up omelets, fry turkey bacon, and chop up fruit.

But he's not here. My mother is nursing a microwaved cup of tea and moving some leftovers around her plate, and I'm looking down at some soggy Cheerios.

I used to get annoyed with my dad's nonstop chatter so early in the morning. It should be illegal to have spoken conversation before the sun is up—but now that he's not here, I'd give literally anything for a 4:00 a.m. rundown of our weekend plans.

"Are you really canvassing again *today*, on a weekday?" my mother asks. "I thought I misread the Google calendar this morning."

"We were," I tell her. "But Gabe needs us to put up signs and posters around town."

"I'm impressed. You're going above and beyond." She pauses. "And is there anything we need to talk about?"

"Like what?"

"Jamie and you . . . the two of you have become close, haven't you?"

I look up at her. She's looking at me meaningfully.

"Yeah, we're close." I roll my eyes. "And how close am I to a car now?"

"After the special election, we'll talk about it," my mother promises. "By the way, we still have ten minutes until suhoor ends." My mother glances at the oven clock. "Sure you don't want a little of my chai? I made too much."

"No caffeine. I'm crashing as soon as I finish praying."

"I miss those days." My mother takes a sip of tea. "But starting my day now means I can get done sooner and come home early to nap."

"Except you never do," I tell her.

"This case is eating up way more time than I thought." She sighs. "But it'll calm down after the trial."

"Imam Jackson hasn't announced if Eid is Sunday or

Monday. You'll take time off if it's Monday, right?"

"It's been so cloudy lately, I doubt they'll see the moon to call Eid earlier. I'm betting Monday. I'll take off either way, but I hope it falls on Sunday."

"How's Eid going to work?" I swallow. "You know, with Dad . . ."

"We're both going to the masjid for Eid prayers," my mother says. "You'll go with whoever you stayed with the night before, and we'll all be there for the potluck brunch. Maybe you and I could go out for manicures after, and then you and your dad could get dinner in the evening?"

"With Ramadan ending soon . . . what's the status of the separation?" I ask her.

"We're working on it."

"But you had a chance to focus and reflect, didn't you?"

"Maya, it's not that simple."

"It's not that complicated either." I stare at her. "How can you just have no timeline?"

"Because things like this aren't neat and organized." She looks at me. "I wish I could give you an idea of what exactly to expect. But some things, you just have to walk through to know where they will lead."

"But what *happened*?" I burst out. "How can you undo everything and not even tell me why?"

"Honey, there's no big secret. You were there. You know. You heard the fighting. . . ."

"You and I fight all the time," I tell her. "Fighting means you stop being a family?"

"It's complicated." My mother's eyes are fixed on her teacup now. "I know you want more details. Explanations. I wish I could give you an answer that would satisfy you, but I can't. We need time to reflect and figure things out. That's all I can say. When we know what the future holds, you'll be the first person we tell, okay?"

It's not okay. But I'm too tired to argue anymore.

Jamie picks me up at eleven o'clock sharp. He smiles when I get in the car, and I'm relieved he doesn't look as upset as he did yesterday.

"Want to canvass after we're done putting up the yard signs?" I ask him.

"Well, first check out how many he wants us to get up around town." He nods to the backseat.

I glance back. It's impossible to even see the cars behind us—the signs are stacked up to the car roof.

"The trunk is full too."

"Gabe . . ."

"Yep."

Turns out putting up yard signs isn't *that* bad. It's hot and definitely muggy, but it feels good to mix it up a little.

"This is the last stop," Jamie says, a few hours later. We've papered every legal spot in Brookhaven and Sandy Springs, and stuck yard signs at every intersection. "It's the grassy area across the street from Blackburn Park."

Just as in all the other places, Newton's beat us. Twenty of his signs litter the grass.

"I want to yank them out and throw them in the dumpster," I say.

But we don't. We angle our signs so they mostly cover his signs. A few people honk and wave as we put them in.

"All done," he says as he sticks in the last of the signs.

"That wasn't too bad," I say. "Hot. But not awful."

We duck under the awning of the strip mall to get a break from the sun as we head toward the car. Just then, I hear a familiar voice.

"Maya?"

It's Sara. She's standing halfway in the door of Skeeter's custard shop. We walked by, and I didn't even notice it.

"Sara! Hey!" My voice sounds a little too loud. Which makes no sense. Why am I surprised to see her working, of all things? I nod to Jamie. "This is Sara," I tell him.

"Hi." Jamie extends his hand. "I'm Jamie."

Sara glances at his outstretched hand and grins at me before shaking it.

"*Great* to meet you, Jamie."

The shop is empty. We follow her inside and sit down at a plastic round table.

"I know Maya's fasting, but do you want anything?" she

asks Jamie. "We have a great Froot Loop custard that . . ."

"Sara!" I side-eye her. "That's just mean."

"Ha." She leans over and gives me a hug. "Only kidding. How about the strawberry custard? New flavor. On the house."

"No, thanks," Jamie says.

The doorbell chimes, and two mothers lugging four kids between them stumble into the shop.

"Give me a second," Sara mouths, and heads back behind the counter to help them.

"You should take Sara up on her offer," I tell him. "Everything here is delicious. I don't mind if you eat around me."

"Solidarity." He thumps the table. "We can try it later once you've broken your fast."

"You've come a long way from pushing Goldfish at me."

"Yeah." He blushes. "Sorry about that."

I laugh. He looks so cute when he's embarrassed.

"Have you been thinking any more about the toast?" I ask him.

"No." He winces. "Or maybe, all the time. Every minute of the day? Something like that."

"When do you have to give the speech?"

"In fifteen days, four hours, and twenty minutes. I mean, not that I'm counting or anything."

"That's so far away. You have more than enough time to come up with something."

"It's just that every idea I have is terrible."

"You're overthinking it. I've been to a few bat mitzvahs. The speeches aren't that complicated. Tell Sophie you're proud of her, thank people for coming, and tell a joke or share a funny story."

"But how do I know what's a funny story and what's traumatic? What if I share a funny story about Sophie, but it ends up making her mad? And what if I make a joke and nobody laughs—it's just crickets?"

"You can always run it by your sister first. And if you make a bad joke, so what? It happens."

"It happens to me way too much."

I pull out my phone.

"There are thousands of bat mitzvah and bar mitzvah toasts online." I show him my search results. "Just look through them for examples or frameworks. Here's one. It says 'funny bar mitzvah speech' and it's got a ton of views."

The video opens with a guy in a three-piece suit standing in front of a cake table. He's telling the crowd how proud he is of his brother and his amazing accomplishments. He takes a sip of water, but before he can say anything else his eyes widen, and he starts coughing. Or choking? I can't tell. He spits water all over the cake and flings his hands toward the audience. The glass flies into the air, knocking out a woman in the front row.

"Um . . ." I pause the video. "Well, *that* wasn't what I

thought it would be."

Jamie looks green.

"Well, on the bright side, you'll definitely do better than this guy?"

"So you think."

"Don't bring water up with you," I say. "We learned something today."

"Sorry about that." Sara walks over to us. "Lucas is still out after the wrist fracture, and I'm the only one on shift. What are you both up to?"

"Putting up yard signs," I tell her.

"For what? Concert coming to town?"

She's joking, right? But she's looking at me expectantly.

"Rossum," I tell her. "The special election coming up in a few weeks?"

"Oh, that." She wrinkles her nose.

"You don't like him?" Jamie asks.

"Oh, *of course* I do. He's awesome, right?" She glances at me and smiles a little and rolls her eyes.

I shift in my seat. I can't blame her sarcasm. I know what she means. Yes, he is another white, cis, straight dude running for office. But—

"He's better than Newton," I tell her.

"Voting for the best of two bad choices still means you're stuck with a bad choice."

"I get that, but this is different. Newton is evil. He's why

H.B. 28 is on the table in the first place. He masterminded it years ago."

"H.B. what?"

"House Bill 28," I say slowly. "You know, the racist bill?"

Sara shakes her head.

"It's the one with—"

But before I can say anything else, the front door chimes. A troop of tweens in cheerleading outfits march inside.

"To be continued," Sara says apologetically. "Jamie, it was so nice to meet you. Come back for a custard with Maya once Ramadan is over."

"Sara's nice," Jamie says.

"Yeah." My phone buzzes. A text from Sara.

I can see why you're canvassing now. He's cute.

I look up at her. She winks at me and slips her phone in her pocket. And then she's back to work, scooping and handing out tiny spoon-sized custard samples. It's like I'm gone, even though I'm sitting right here.

We head out to the car, mapping out our day tomorrow. I think about what Sara texted to me. She doesn't get it. I mean, yes. Jamie is cute, but if Sara thinks I'm doing all of this just to hang out with a good-looking boy, and not because my community is in imminent danger—how far apart are we drifting?

CHAPTER FIFTEEN
JAMIE

I wake up with yesterday running through my head like a film reel. But it's not the usual cringe-by-cringe replay. This is a legit sun-soaked montage. I picture Maya with a stack of Rossum signs up to her chin. Maya, looking so at home in my passenger seat. Maya's dimple deepening as she smiled across the table at Skeeter's.

Maya, who texted me four times overnight.

Which isn't a big deal. And I'm pretty sure a normal person would just read the texts and be done with them. As opposed to staring at the ceiling, trying to put off reading them as long as possible, for no real reason. I guess it's kind of like how Sophie will go for weeks before reading the last chapter of a book. The longer you put good things off, the longer they're there waiting for you. And texts from Maya are good things. They are very good things.

I'm not looking, not looking, not looking—

I yank my phone from my charger.

Maya: Oh no!! Really sorry, I need a rain check on canvassing. Already started prepping the biryani for the Eid potluck, and my mom keeps getting emails from clients and forgetting about pots on the stove, it's a mess

Okay, so maybe not *all* texts are good things. But I keep reading.

She literally gets so many work emails at 5:00 on a Saturday morning, is this what being an adult is going to be like???

Anyway, I have to stay and keep the house from burning down 💪

Sorry Jamie! Maybe later this week?

I smile down at my phone. Kind of wild how seeing my own name written out by Maya can make me forget my disappointment completely. I know it's just a text. But there's something about the way it sounds in my head when I read it.

I write back.

Happy almost Eid! Are you excited to eat again during the day?

And even though her last text is time-stamped 5:30 a.m., she replies immediately.

Maya: YOU HAVE NO IDEA.

Already planning the menu.

Jamie: For the potluck?

Maya: No, for my life!! Okay, thoughts for my first post-Eid donut meal, are we thinking Dunkin or Krispy Kreme?

Jamie: Is this a serious question??

Maya: Hahahaha good point, Krispy Kreme it is

OMG AND THE 7 LAYER CHOCOLATE CAKE AT CAFE INTERMEZZO

I have a NEED

Jamie: Ooh, sounds really good!

Maya: You haven't tried it?! Jamie. You are missing out.

Jamie: Apparently!

Maya: Okay it's like beyond chocolatey, and HUGE. Like remember when the kid from Matilda had to eat the whole cake and we're supposed to feel bad for him but you and I were so confused, like why is he struggling with this? He is living the dream!

Jamie: Bruce Bogtrotter!!! Lucky jerk

Maya: This cake is like THAT. Super dense, not spongy, and that icing omfg

Okay I need to stop talking about this, I'm getting hungry!
😭 😭 😭

I smile even harder, typing Bruce Bogtrotter's name into the GIF menu bar. But before I can press search, my bedroom door swings open.

"Jamie! It's an emergency." Sophie practically skids

across my floor, flanked by her friends Maddie and Andrea.

My heart drops. "Wait—is everything—"

Sophie cuts me off. "Okay, so Tessa and Paige are meeting at Perimeter Mall at eleven thirty, and Grandma's out somewhere with Gabe, and I don't want to ask Mom, because she'll rope me into her mason jar washi tape thing."

I just stare at Sophie, heart still pounding. "That's your emergency?"

All three of the girls nod cheerfully.

"You need me to come with you to the mall?"

"What?" Sophie wrinkles her nose. "No, we need a ride."

Maddie and Andrea giggle, and my cheeks go warm. Awesome. Sophie barges into my room uninvited, pretty much implying someone *died*, and somehow she's acting like it's sad pathetic Jamie trying to bust in on their mall trip. Which, frankly, sounds like actual torture, and not something I'd ever willingly do. But of course I'm now being laughed at by tweens, which is definitely making me flash back to middle school. And flash forward to the inevitable trauma of the bat mitzvah toast. Double the fun.

"So can you drive us?" Sophie asks.

I glance down at my slept-in T-shirt and mesh gym shorts. "Right this second?"

"Well, we have to be there at eleven thirty," Sophie says matter-of-factly, "because Tessa likes this guy Daniel who works at Sbarro on Saturdays, and his shift starts at eleven, but we can't show up right at the beginning of his shift, or it will be really obvious. But everything gets really busy with the lunch crowd at noon, so it really has to be eleven thirty!"

"And all of you need to be there to help Tessa flirt with this guy." I look from Sophie to Maddie to Andrea.

"Exactly," says Sophie.

"How old is this guy anyway?"

"Fifteen," says Andrea.

I raise my eyebrows. "And Tessa's twelve?"

"She's thirteen," says Sophie, "and Daniel thinks she's fourteen, so—"

"That doesn't make it better!"

Sophie frowns. "Don't be judgmental."

I grimace. "If I were to drive you—*if*—what time would you need to be picked up?"

"Oh my God, Jamie, you're the best!" Sophie bounces on the balls of her feet. "Maybe two? But you have to stay at the mall while we're there. You know I'm not allowed to hang out there alone."

I gape at her. "Okay, you *just* said—"

"So we really have to leave in five minutes," Sophie says, shrugging. "You better get dressed fast."

Five minutes into our eight-minute car ride, and I officially know how I'll die.

It will be death by bat mitzvah toast. The first recorded case of someone's heart actually combusting from mortification. And I do mean *recorded*, because we all know Sophie's friends are going to film it. You're welcome, choking YouTube kid—future me is going to make you look like John F. Kennedy.

Because groups of middle school girls? Are as terrifying as I remembered. More terrifying, even. And they ask so many questions.

"Jamie, did you go to Riverview?" Maddie asks as I pull onto Ashford Dunwoody.

"Yeah—"

"Did you have Ms. Williams?"

"Or Ms. Finnigan?" chimes Andrea.

"I don't . . . think so."

"Okay, so what's better?" Maddie leans forward. "Eighth grade or ninth grade?"

"Neither," I say, and Maddie and Andrea both burst out laughing.

"You're so funny, Jamie."

"Sophie, you're so lucky," says Andrea. "My sister never even talks to me. She's obsessed with her phone."

"Jamie's so nice," Maddie adds, like I'm not sitting directly in front of her.

"I know." Sophie smiles smugly at me from the passenger

seat. "I trained him well."

"Do you have a girlfriend?" asks Maddie.

"Um—"

"Oh my God," Andrea says. "I found out who Vanessa hooked up with!"

"Seriously? Who?" Sophie's seat belt strains as she whirls around to face them. And just like that, I'm blissfully forgotten, in favor of a very detailed discussion of Vanessa's hookup with someone's hot cousin. I just tune it out, easing Alfie through the parking deck.

The second I park, all three girls leap from the car like it's on fire. By the time I turn off the engine, they're halfway to the mall entrance.

I lean back against my seat, just happy to be alone.

Until it occurs to me that I'm now stuck at the mall for two and a half hours. One hundred and fifty minutes. Is it weird that I could easily make that much time pass in Target, but I don't even know how to kill half an hour here? The closest movie theater isn't really walking distance, and even GameStop's kind of meh when you're not there to spend a gift card. Honestly, everything's meh compared to the day I thought I'd be having—canvassing with Maya, maybe hitting up the patio section afterward . . .

I tap into my text chain with Maya, realizing with a start that I never pressed send on that Bruce Bogtrotter GIF this morning. So I send it now. I mean, Bruce Bogtrotter is always relevant.

Eid goals. How's the potluck prep going?

No reply, no ellipses. I shove my phone in my pocket so I won't obsess over it.

But then a second later, I pull it out again, and tap into my group text with the guys. Not that there's any chance Drew and Felipe are going to drop what they're doing to race to the mall. I should have texted them before I left. But I guess there's no harm in putting feelers out.

Stuck at Perimeter with Sophie, anyone want to join me?

Just as I'm about to pocket my phone again, Felipe writes back.

Felipe: lol 😂 We're already here! We're bothering Nolan, he's working

Jamie: wow, everyone's hanging out, guess my invitation got lost in the mail

Felipe: Uh hello, what happened to mr sorry I can't hang I'm canvassing today

Drew: With maaaaya

Felipe: 🧑🏿

Drew: sorry not sorry dude 😂

Felipe: Come hang, we're just @ Disney store

The mall is always super hectic on Saturdays, packed with stroller-pushing parents and clusters of Sophie-clone tweens. When I step through the Mickey-shaped Disney

Store entrance, there's Nolan at the checkout counter, ringing up a set of giant plastic Elsa and Anna dolls for a father and daughter.

Nolan smiles and waves when he sees me. I've always liked Nolan, even before he and Felipe started dating. He's preppy-looking, but not in a frat bro way like that intern from Dickers's office. Nolan's really polite too, so parents always love him. Even Drew's über-Republican parents claim to love Nolan, just like they love Felipe. I can't ever wrap my head around that. How can you love your son's gay friends, but dick them over every time you vote?

There's still a line at Nolan's counter, so I don't want to bother him, but he points his chin toward Drew and Felipe at the back of the store. Turns out, they're camped out near the stuffed animal display, arguing over whether Anastasia counts as a Disney princess.

I jump right in. "She does now! Because of the Disney-Fox merger."

"Nope. Doesn't count. Disney princess is like a specific thing." Felipe cranes his neck, peering over my shoulder. "Hold that thought. I'm gonna go check on Nolan."

Drew waves him off with a Pumbaa doll's stiff front leg. Then he turns back to me, shrugging. "So Maya ditched you."

"For Eid. She has a potluck coming up, so she's helping her mom cook."

"Eid's sort of like Muslim Christmas, right?" Drew asks.

"Does that mean I get to say Easter is like Christian Passover?"

"Okay, wiseass," Drew says. "I just mean it's a big deal and you send holiday cards and stuff, right?"

"I guess so? It's the end of Ramadan." I make a mental note to google Eid again, even though I *might* have spent an hour or two falling down that rabbit hole already. Maybe I'm being a little extra, but I don't really care. All I know is there's no way I'm making even one more Ramadan-related faux pas.

Drew's looking at me with this curious half smile. "So, you're really—"

"Hey, what did I miss?" Felipe asks, suddenly reappearing. "Nolan's still slammed."

"Jamie's just bringing me up to speed on his girlfriend."

I smack Drew's arm. "Not my girlfriend, dodo."

Felipe smiles. "But you're working on it, right?"

I blush. "We're just doing campaign stuff together."

Drew laughs. "Felipe, remember when you and Nolan were 'just doing a history project together'?"

"I do remember that." Felipe beams.

"Okay, we're done here."

Felipe side-hugs me. "We're just teasing you. I think it's cool that you're doing this stuff for Rossum."

"Me too." Drew nods firmly. He pauses, suddenly fixing his gaze somewhere over my shoulder. "Why are those baby princesses staring at me?"

"They know their father," says Felipe.

"NO," Drew says, pointing at the dolls. "I disown each and every one of you creepy fuckers."

My eyes drift back to the stuffed animal display, landing on a big stuffed poodle. It looks so much like Fifi, it makes my stomach twist.

I turn back to Drew and Felipe. "Did I tell you guys someone put a Fifi poodle meme bumper sticker on Alfie?"

Felipe's face falls. "Really?"

I nod. "Thursday, right when we were coming out of a meeting with Holden's legislative director. I have no idea who did it."

"Shit," says Drew.

"Yeah, it was pretty bad. Hard to get off too."

"I hear you," Drew says, making a face. "I had to get all my mom's Hilton Head stickers off before they sold their car, and it was such a bitch. You know they make stuff for that—you just have to rub it on there—"

"I know. I got some. I took care of it." My heartbeat quickens. "You know, Hilton Head bumper stickers and white supremacist memes aren't really the same thing."

Both Drew and Felipe turn to look at me, startled. To be

honest, I think I startled myself. I guess I don't usually speak up about the stuff that annoys me. I just swallow it back.

"We know it's not the same," Felipe says slowly.

My cheeks go warm. "I'm just saying, someone literally put an anti-Semitic symbol *on my car.*"

Felipe shakes his head. "That's so gross."

"People are assholes," says Drew.

I look at him. "It's not just a random asshole, though. It's been happening to a lot of Rossum supporters. They took our magnet too."

"Can't you get Gabe to give you another one?" Drew asks.

"You're missing the point."

"Look, I get it." Drew flips his palms up. "But you got the sticker off, right? You have the hookup for a new magnet. No harm, no foul."

"It's an anti-Semitic meme! In real life! I don't know if Newton's people are trying to intimidate Rossum's people, or—"

"Do you actually think it's Newton's campaign behind it?" asks Drew. "Don't get me wrong, Newton's an asshole. But it sounds more like a random troll trying to get a rise out of you—"

"So I should just—"

Drew cuts me off. "You have nothing to gain from getting upset. You're just letting him win."

I open my mouth, and then close it again. Wow.

"You okay?" Felipe asks.

I stare wordlessly back at him, head spinning. They don't get it. Drew especially doesn't get it. Fifi may not be a big thing, but it feels like part of a bigger thing. And I know Drew isn't trying to gaslight me on purpose, like Dickers, but I have that same weird prickle I had stepping out of that meeting. Like I'm going crazy. Like everything I say or think or feel is an overreaction.

Sometimes I honestly think Maya's the only one in the world who understands.

Though clearly the guys think I have some kind of ulterior motive. That this all comes down to me trying to make Maya my girlfriend.

Right.

I'm tired of that too. Maybe I just want to spend time with someone who actually gives a crap, for once. Unlike my so-called friends, who literally couldn't be less invested.

Even as I think it, I know I'm being unfair. After all, there's nothing quite like the futility of being seventeen in an election year. And from a strictly logical perspective, Drew's right. I have nothing to gain from getting upset. My anger won't get Rossum elected, won't make H.B. 28 go away, won't stop a single troll from trolling.

I mean, two weeks ago, I wasn't so different from Drew and Felipe. I wanted Rossum to win, obviously. And yeah,

I was putting in hours at the campaign office. But I certainly wouldn't have canvassed if Mom hadn't forced me.

Now it feels like I can't canvass enough. I really feel that.

It's like living with fire in my chest. Maybe it was Fifi. Or Dickers. Or H.B. 28. I don't know what sparked it, but suddenly everything's different. Everything feels huge and momentous and terrifyingly real.

And I can't seem to push it to the background. I can't put the fire out.

I don't think I want to put the fire out.

CHAPTER SIXTEEN
MAYA

My dad bought a bed.

It's just a bed.

But it's a bed.

A bed.

If you say it enough times, *bed bed bed bed bed*, the word squishes and compresses and retracts until it doesn't even mean anything at all.

Except this bed in my dad's apartment means everything.

Today is Eid. Ramadan is officially over. We need to head to the masjid for prayers, but I'm stuck at this spot in the hallway looking at the comforter spread over a queen bed in my father's bedroom. I missed it when I came over last night. Walked right by it. Now I can't unsee it, even if I wanted to.

My mother dispelled any fantasy I had of Eid being some kind of magic countdown that would reset my parents back to *happily married* . . . but this bed. This bed means this separation isn't ending anytime soon.

"Got coffees in to-go cups because we're running a little late," my dad calls out. "Almost ready?"

I swallow the brick wedged in my throat and join him.

As if on cue, Tammy Adrian starts talking H.B. 28 as soon as we get in the car. The pushback has been surprisingly vocal, she explains. But the GOP majority in the state House of Representatives is determined to push ahead and bring it to a vote, maybe even before the special election.

"Annnnd that's enough of that." My dad switches to a music channel.

"Put it back! We need to know what's going on."

"It's Eid," he says. "We get one day to take a break from it."

"We can't take days off. This is urgent."

"Days off are as important as days on, bug. You have to recharge or you burn out. And your mom and the other board members are scheduling a sit-down with Holden's people sometime next week."

"She better be careful. Dickers is awful."

"Dickers?"

"Holden's legislative director. I met her last week. She was the absolute worst."

"You *went* to Holden's legislative director?" My father glances at me. "Subhanallah. That's amazing."

"It would have been more amazing if she hadn't gaslit us the entire time."

"But you did it. That's something. I'm really proud of you, bug."

"I guess. I just hate feeling like no matter what I do, it's not enough."

"No one person can fix it all," my father says. "All our actions are little drops that collect into a groundswell for change. It's the only way most change happens. Ordinary people doing everything they can. You're doing that, Maya. I'm so proud of you."

"Thanks, Dad."

"I want to hear more about this meeting. I'm popping into the office to wrap up a few patient charts while you and your mother do your manicures, but I'll get you around six for dinner. You choose the spot. Oh, and before I forget—" He pops open the glove compartment and hands me a card. "Your Eidi. Spend it wisely."

"Thanks, Dad." I lean over and give him a hug.

I'm in line for the breakfast buffet after prayers when my mother finds me.

"There you are!" She hugs me tight. "Eid Mubarak, sweetie!"

It's surreal to have our Eid hug here. She always wakes me up each Eid with a big hug—and even though it felt a little past its prime by the time I was thirteen, it's so linked to Eid mornings, the whole day felt a little off-kilter without it.

I was so conflicted last night about who to stay with. On one hand, I wanted to be home. Willow goes on food strikes anytime I go to my dad's—and all my stuff is at home—but I also figured this would be a tougher day for my dad, since he's the one alone in a brand-new place with hardly any furniture.

Well, he has a bed now. So there's that.

"What time's our manicure?" I ask her. "I was thinking maybe we could spring for foot massages too?"

"About that." Her face falls. "You know that trial coming up? My client needs to meet this afternoon. Last-minute complications. I have to go in for a little while."

Complications. Complicated. My mother really likes plays on that word.

"I'm sorry." She takes in my crestfallen expression. "This case has been taking up so much of my time, but it's over soon. Rain check," she promises. "And after it's over, we'll make a whole spa day and splurge on foot massages too. Sound like a plan?"

I nod and tell her it's fine just as a board member walks over to steal her away for "a second."

My phone buzzes. It's probably Sara. She always remembers Eid.

But it's not Sara. It's Jamie.

I click the text.

There's a GIF of a dancing gingerbread man and the words: Eid Mubarak! Happy eating day!

Lol, thanks! I reply.

I glance around the masjid. My father's getting seconds. My mother is huddled up chatting with her fellow board members. Lyla Iqbal and a couple of other girls are over by the drinks—but I'm just not in the mood to mingle. I look down at my phone.

Maya: Want to hang out? I'm at the mosque but I can head over to wherever you are.

A word bubble pops up immediately, and then—

Jamie: I'll come to you! On my way!

I press a thumbs-up to the text, and scroll down until I find my last exchange with Sara. It's beneath messages from my mom, dad, and even Shelby, who had a new movie she wanted to group hang at. Our last text exchange was three days ago. Three days is three years in Maya-Sara time.

It is what it is. But it doesn't make it suck any less.

I take a quick selfie by the buffet and post it on Instagram with the caption *Eid Mubarak!*

I can't blame Sara if she didn't think of it first thing in the morning. But she lives on Instagram, so this little nudge should remind her, in case she forgot. Which I'm sure she didn't.

Alfie pulls up in the parking lot just then.

"Thanks for picking me up," I tell Jamie once I get in. "My afternoon plans fell through, and I didn't want to sit around in an empty house until dinner."

"It was perfect timing," he says. "I have to take Sophie to her Hebrew tutor at noon, but I'm free until then." He glances at me. "I bet today's kind of tough. A first holiday without your parents in one house."

"It's weird. And depressing. Want to go see if there's any open canvassing hours?"

"Canvassing? It's Eid! You're supposed to celebrate it, right?"

"I'm not feeling too celebratory, I guess."

"Well, you can fake it till you make it! Let's go get a bite to eat somewhere. Didn't you say something about a chocolate cake at Intermezzo?"

"Hmm." I smile and lean back in the seat. "That cake is *amazing*, but it's too early for that right now . . . ditto Farm Burger . . . I know." I straighten. "How about Skeeter's? Let's get those strawberry custards Sara mentioned."

"Your wish is my command." He nods, and we pull out of the parking lot.

★   ★   ★

I'm not saying I picked Skeeter's because I hoped I might run into Sara, but I can't pretend I don't feel a touch disappointed when it's Lucas who greets us instead.

We order our custards—Jamie insists I top mine off with sprinkles for celebration purposes—and settle outside on the front patio.

"Sara was right." Jamie's eyes widen as he takes another bite. "This custard is amazing."

"And you were right, the sprinkles do make it taste better. Though it feels a little weird to eat in the middle of the day."

"Oh!" He stands up just then. "I almost forgot."

Before I can respond, he's hurrying over to Alfie in the parking lot. He pops open the trunk and then walks back, holding a glittery gift bag—green and white tissue paper poking out the edges.

"Here you go! Happy Eid!"

"You got me a gift!" I take the bag from him. "Jamie, that is so sweet."

Glancing in, I pull out—

Goldfish crackers. It's a gift bag stuffed full of Goldfish cracker bags. I do my best not to laugh, but this guy and Goldfish . . .

"I was thinking about it," he says. "I know you aren't the biggest fan of them. That's totally understandable. Some parents go overboard packing them with every meal. It's important to space out snacks, even good ones. But these are the best of the bunch. There's extra cheddar, white cheddar, and my personal favorite, *rainbow* Goldfish."

"Jamie, they're basically all the same thing."

"Yeah, right." He laughs. But then he glances at me and pauses. "Wait. Are you serious? You know they have Oreo-flavored Goldfish, right? Are you saying even those taste the same?"

"Well, obviously the Oreo ones are different, but the rest of them are similar. It's just marketing."

He looks like that kid in kindergarten who I accidentally let slip to that Santa wasn't real.

"No way. This calls for a taste test. But we'll need to get some regular Goldfish crackers to do it right."

"We can't just use the ones here?"

"It's important to have a neutral one to cleanse the palate between taste tests. We'll get some before canvassing tomorrow."

"Sounds good." I smile.

I settle into the couch after Jamie drops me back home. Willow hops in my lap. I flip on *The Office*—my go-to show I've seen so many times, I know most of the dialogue by heart at this point. It's the ultimate comfort viewing.

I pull out my phone as the theme music opens, and scroll through my feed. Four likes on my Eid selfie. A comment from my aunt Jameela in Philadelphia about how big I'm getting.

Nothing from Sara.

I click the home feed. And then I freeze.

It's a post from Sara. A repost of Jenna's, actually. The time stamp says it was posted forty-five minutes ago.

It's a photo of their dorm room, all set up with cream curtains, a fluffy pastel-blue rug, and lights strung around the windows. The metal trash can is there too. The caption reads, *Check out my dorm, thanks to the amazing artistic eye of my bestie and future roomie, Jenna!*

It's like I've been physically punched.

I screenshot the photo and text Sara.

Nice dorm room. Loving the BFF lingo.

Sara responds quicker than she has in weeks.

Ha. I'm still as much of a cheeseball as I ever was. Isn't the room great?!

My finger hovers over the phone's keyboard. I want to ask her why, if she's on Instagram right now, she hasn't even so much as liked my Eid photo? I want to tell her why the term *bestie* cuts straight to my heart. Best is quantifiable. It means someone is better than all the rest.

Jenna is her bestie.

Where does that leave me?

Part of me wants to ask her if she's free. But I can't bring myself to hear that she's busy.

The room is great, I tell her. I put the phone down and rub Willow's ears. On-screen, Michael Scott is explaining why he's the best boss ever. Jim deadpans into the camera. Like he's wondering what on earth is happening and how did he end up here.

Today, I completely understand.

CHAPTER SEVENTEEN
JAMIE

Hi, everyone. Thank you all for being here. I just want to take a minute to say mazel tov to my amazing sister—

Delete.

Jewish tradition says Sophie's an adult now, but I'll always think of Sophie as the little girl who peed on the floor so often—

Delete. Sophie would kill me.

When Sophie was six, she replaced an entire carton of eggs with Barbie heads, and I screamed so loud—

Yikes.

I don't know how YouTube makes it seem so effortless—or where everyone's finding these troves of funny, sentimental childhood stories. No joke: all my memories make Sophie and me look like complete weirdos. Even the ones that seem funny in my head just sound tragic when I try to write them out.

Remember when Sophie called me da-da for a year because she forgot I wasn't her dad? Delete. Delete. Delete.

I stare listlessly at my Notes app—it's so blank, it's taunting me.

I can't do this. I roll onto my stomach, checking the clock on my phone. Time's been moving so slowly all morning. I just want it to be three o'clock, so I can pick Maya up for Goldfish and then canvassing. And *maybe*—

Well. We'll see if I'm brave enough.

I log into Grandma's Instagram to sneak a peek at Maya's profile. I really like her last picture—a selfie from yesterday near a buffet table, captioned *Eid Mubarak*. She just looks so goofy and cute with her lips pressed together and her eyes gazing upward. It's weird, but I almost wish I could comment. And not as Grandma.

Maybe I should bite the bullet and get my own Instagram.

I tap into my camera app and flip it to selfie cam, studying my face. I look . . . okay. I think? My hair's thankfully at that just-right semi-overgrown stage—note to self: avoid haircuts. And Mom and Grandma say my summer freckles are cute, so who knows?

I'm going to ask her. This doesn't have to be a big deal. Not a Brianne Henke slowmance situation. Just a casual, friendly invitation.

So . . . any interest in going to cafe intermezzo after canvassing for the inaugural post-Eid chocolate cake?

Cool. We're cool. Staying calm. Even though there
are ellipses, which means Maya's literally typing right this
second. Probably just trying to think of the nicest way to
say *eww no, never*. God. She'll probably cancel Target and
canvassing too, just to drive the message home. I bet—

Intermezzo sounds perfect!!

Wow. Okay, *wow*. She just—

But before I can fully process it, there's Grandma.
"Knock knock!"

I play it chill. Like a regular Jamie. As opposed to a Jamie
who just successfully invited Maya to Café Intermezzo
tonight. Not that it's a date. But Café Intermezzo—I mean,
it's *Café Intermezzo*. That's literally where my parents met.
And, okay, my parents aren't exactly relationship goals. But
still. Café Intermezzo's about as close to a date as a non–date
can get.

Unless Maya thinks it's a date?

Hahahahahahaha. Yeah right. Like that would even
occur to Maya. Pretty sure *Jamie* and *dating* are two mutu-
ally exclusive concepts. To Maya and literally everyone
else.

"Jamie? My goodness, you're not still sleeping, are you?"
Grandma says through the door. "It's almost noon!"

"I'm up! Sorry. Come on in."

She opens the door, peering at me from the doorway. "Aren't you supposed to be canvassing today?"

"You're going canvassing?" yells Sophie from the hallway, careening past her, into my room. "When?"

"Not until four. Picking up Maya at three, though—we're going to Target first to grab some Goldfish. We're doing a taste test."

"Perfect." Sophie clasps her hands. "Mom's leaving work early today to finish the chalkboard sign, and she's out of control. I'm texting her right now that I'm coming with you guys. Ha!"

I narrow my eyes. "Shouldn't you be studying your Torah portion?"

"Nope!"

"Or something . . ."

"Nope! I'm all yours and Maya's."

"Lucky us," I say, sighing. But Sophie just grins.

Of course, Sophie's in full chatterbox mode, talking nonstop all the way to Target. And it's even worse when we get there.

"You should have seen his face," Sophie says as we make our way through the home decor. "He was trying so hard to pick them up, but they kept dropping. It was raining tangelos. Hold on, I think I have the Boomerang saved."

"Can we not—"

"Oh, hey! Here's the Snapchat filter that makes Jamie look like Rachel Maddow."

"Sophie!"

"I thought you loved Rachel Maddow!" She shoots me a guilty sidelong glance. "Maya, he *loves* Rachel Maddow. He and Mom used to watch her show every single night, and like, *take notes*, and discuss it, and—"

"I'm going to go shrivel up and die now," I say.

Maya laughs. "I think it's cute!" She hugs me quickly, before veering off to look at a stuffed unicorn wall mount. "What is this supposed to be—a hunting trophy?"

Sophie gasps. "Who would hunt unicorns? I love unicorns!"

"She does," I tell Maya. "A lot."

"At least I know they're not real." Sophie pats my arm.

"Excuse me, Siberian unicorns *were* real," I say. "They're just extinct."

Maya grins up at me. "Interesting."

Sophie lets Maya drift a few feet ahead, and then leans toward me, beaming. "She's totally flirting with you."

"Shh!"

She pats my shoulder. "Don't worry, I got this. Gonna go probe for info." I watch as Sophie sidles up to Maya near the table lamps, gesturing slyly to a Ryan Gosling look-alike in a crisp button-down. "Ooh," Sophie says, just loud enough for me to overhear. "He's cute. Maya, what's your type?"

Then Sophie—I could *murder* her—turns and winks at me over her shoulder.

Thank God Maya doesn't notice. "No way," she murmurs. "Too fancy. And why isn't he wearing socks? Who wears shoes like that with no socks?"

Sophie laughs. "Right?"

Well well well. Looks like Ryan Gosling's little brother should have thought harder about his footwear. You know who always wears socks? Jamie Goldberg. I'm just saying.

Sophie's going in deeper now, probing for what kind of guys Maya *does* like, if she likes guys. I can't tell if Maya's flustered or amused. I guess it's nice that Sophie's trying, but if she really wanted to help, she could just . . . not be a third wheel.

Sophie's like that, though. She's always calling me out for being too innocent, or insisting that I should have a girlfriend. But I don't think she actually cares about me *having* a girlfriend. She just wants to *find* me a girlfriend. She wants to captain the ship. And God forbid she miss a single moment of that doomed voyage.

By the time we swing by the campaign office, my brain's entirely elsewhere. And during canvassing, I can barely remember my own name, much less Rossum's platform and credentials. But Maya's as sharp as ever, and even Sophie seems to have a surprisingly detailed grasp on the issues.

Not going to lie. My sister amazes me sometimes.

But I still have to find a way to ditch her before Intermezzo. I mean, I don't even want to mention Intermezzo out loud, because I know Maya will invite Sophie to join us. Either that, or Sophie will straight-up invite herself. And it's *Sophie*—if I ask her to go home, she'll be even more dead set on sticking around. So I can't just give her a reason to leave. She has to think it's her own idea.

I wait until Maya's a few yards away, tucking a walk piece behind someone's doorknob.

"Hey, Soph? I had a thought."

"Is it about you having a crush on M—"

"Shh!" I glare at Sophie, cheeks burning. Maya's coming up the driveway behind her. "It's about the teen room," I add quickly. "I thought of another angle you could try with Mom."

Sophie eyes me. "I'm listening."

"What if you agreed to have a chaperone?"

"That's literally the opposite of the point."

"Yeah, but what if you got to pick the chaperone," I say quickly. "Someone really chill. How old is Andrea's sister? Talia, right? Isn't she a sophomore?"

Sophie nods slowly. "Talia never looks up from her phone. Ever."

"You should see if Mom will pay her to come. Extra hands on deck, right?"

"Jamie, you're . . . kind of a genius?"

"Why is Jamie a genius?" Maya asks. "I mean, no question, he is one."

She pokes my arm—and my brain dissolves on the spot.

Genius. I mean, I can barely blink and breathe at the same time, but sure. "I'm not—"

"I need to talk to Mom," Sophie interrupts. "Jamie, drive me home. And don't take Roswell Road, it's almost six. Maya, put our address in Waze."

And just like that, I'm blinking and breathing and grinning my face off. All at once.

Maya spends the whole ride to Intermezzo gushing about chocolate cake—but the moment we step inside, she goes silent.

The hostess leads us to our table, handing us menus. Maya plops into her seat, cupping her chin in one hand and staring vaguely at the dessert display.

I settle in across from her, trying to act as normal as possible. Which isn't the easiest thing to do at Café Intermezzo. The room is softly candlelit, crowded with small round tables, each barely big enough for two people. Waiters and waitresses weave through tight quarters with mug-laden trays, and there's a buzzy drone of quiet conversation all around us.

Maya's still quiet.

I pause. "Everything okay?"

"Oh! Yeah." She looks up, startled, smiling faintly. "Sorry. Zoned out."

"You're totally fine."

"No, I'm just." She makes a face I can't quite decipher. "It's weird. I've always come here with Sara."

"Oh." I hesitate. "Do you want to go—"

"No! Not at all," Maya says quickly. "I'll come back with her another time. It just made me realize how little I see her lately. It's been really hard with her schedule. She's so busy with work, and now she might be leaving early for UGA if she gets this job she applied for." She pauses for a moment, staring at the candle in the center of our table. "I guess I feel like I'm being replaced?" she says finally. "Sara has this friend—her roommate, Jenna, and all summer, Sara's been so focused on her. I mean, I barely see her anyway, but when I do, every other word out of her mouth is *Jenna*. And then yesterday—this is really embarrassing, but I was waiting all day for Sara to say Happy Eid, because she always does—she *always* remembers. But she never did, and then I checked Instagram, and—" Maya looks up at me suddenly, her expression abashed. "I'm so sorry, Jamie. You don't need to listen to my stupid friend drama."

"It's not stupid. I'd be really upset if I were in your

position. Maybe you should tell her how you feel."

"Maybe. It's so confusing. This is why I want to be a veterinarian. Animals are way less complicated."

"It's true. People suck. Who needs them?"

"Exactly." She glances sideways and smiles a little. "But people watching *is* pretty fun. Especially here."

I follow her gaze—a man and woman have just been seated at the next table over. Maya leans in conspiratorially.

"You realize basically *everyone* is having a first date here, right?" she whispers. "This is like Atlanta's first date factory."

"I know! My parents actually had their first date here. Not *here*. The Buckhead one."

Maya's eyes flare wide, for just a split second.

And I'm an idiot. *Wow.* I'm an absolute, next-level, record-shattering idiot. Who does this? Who brings a girl to his parents' first date spot? *And then tells her it was his parents' first date spot?*

"Right." Maya bites her lip.

Lip biting. The universal gesture of freaked-out people who are trying not to hurt the feelings of the person who freaked them out. I mean, *of course* she's freaked out. How could she not be? I basically just proposed marriage and offered to father her children. I stare at my hands, pulse quickening. I might as well—

"Can I ask you a question?" Maya asks.

"Um. Sure. Yes!"

She hesitates. "I was just wondering . . . you never really talk about your dad."

"My dad?" I look up, startled.

"Or not. We don't have to talk about it," she says quickly.

"No, it's fine." My heartbeat slows back to normal. I meet her eyes, and she just looks curious.

Not freaked out.

I can't believe she's not freaked out.

"I don't mind talking about him," I say finally. "I just don't talk to him that much. My parents divorced when I was six. You probably don't remember my dad—he used to work a lot, even before he left. He lives in the Netherlands now. Sophie and I go out there for a few weeks every summer."

"I didn't know that. Are you seeing him this summer?"

I nod. "End of July. He's not coming to the bat mitzvah. He says he's saving vacation days so he can take off work when we're out there."

Maya looks stricken. "Wait, aren't bat mitzvahs really important? He's just not coming?"

"He didn't come to mine either. He didn't have a bar mitzvah as a kid, so I don't think he sees it as a big deal." I shrug. "He's, like, super involved when we're out there, though. He borrows bikes for us, and we go into town every day and eat at pancake restaurants. He knows everyone. He's kind of like Sophie—he'll talk to anyone. Mom says she always thought he'd run for office one day. She says he's *too* charming. He's like a politician without the politics."

Maya laughs. "I can't figure out if that's a compliment."

I smile a little. "I doubt she means it as one."

Funny how I can know that, and still wish she'd say it about me. *Too charming.*

Maya's smile falters. "But that must be hard, with him not coming home much."

"I mean. Utrecht is his home."

"God, this whole time, you've been listening to me whine about my dad moving five minutes up the road—"

"What? Maya, no—this stuff with your parents . . . it's not trivial. You're not whining."

"I feel bad that I didn't realize, though." Her eyes look almost liquid in the candlelight. "Do you miss him?"

"Not really?" I blush. "That sounds awful. Sorry. No, I do . . . kind of. But it's been over a decade, and I'm really used to it. I still see him every year, and we do Skype sometimes. I mean, I guess I feel weird about it every now and then, but I don't miss him like I miss my grandpa."

Maya reaches out, almost like she's going to touch my hand—but suddenly, the waitress appears. "What can I get you two?"

I look at Maya. "The seven-layer, right?"

Maya turns to the waitress. "Can we get two slices of the seven-layer cake? And also, if you don't mind bringing the check . . ."

"No prob." Our waitress smiles like it's nothing, but I have to admit, I'm thrown. We just ordered, and Maya's asking for the check? She already has an exit strategy?

The waitress leaves, and Maya looks at me. "Sorry." Her dimple flickers. "It's just, they can be *so* slow here. Sara and I always ask for the check right away. And it's more crowded than I expected for a Tuesday." She eyes a hipster-looking man and woman seated at a high-top table near the wall.

"First daters." I smile. "What do we think they're talking about?"

Maya watches them for a moment, and then cups her chin in her hand again. "Okay, he's like, *seen any good movies lately?* And she's like, *no.*"

"Just—no?" I ask. "Nothing?"

"Nope. Look, she's no bullshit. Look at how she's sipping her drink."

"Okay." I nod slowly. "But now he's leaning forward. He's totally like, *well, bucko—*"

Maya laughs. "Bucko?"

I grin. "I don't know."

"Do you usually call girls you date Bucko?"

"I . . . don't usually date. So."

"Ah," says Maya.

"I'm really cool, I know."

"What? No, you are," Maya says, looking up at me earnestly. "Not everyone has to date in high school. I haven't."

"You haven't?"

"Well, I'm not—" She stops herself, mouth snapping shut. But then, a moment later, she shrugs. "I guess I don't really see the point of it."

"The point of dating?"

Maya nods. "It's so messy and unpredictable in high school. I can't tell you how many times my friend group at school has totally fractured because of a breakup. And there's *always* a breakup."

"I don't know. My friend Felipe has been with his boyfriend almost a year, and they seem pretty happy."

"I mean, there are exceptions. But let's be realistic. Even adults can't keep their shit together half the time. What are the odds that some random high school couple will? And that's assuming it's even a mutual thing to begin with! I've seen friendships totally ruined just because one person has a crush on the other."

"Oh." My stomach drops. "Right."

"No, seriously. You know Kevin, right? I've known him since middle school. We sat by each other in history class, and we even did a huge project together. He's a really good guy—"

"Even though he's a Republican?"

"Right?" Maya laughs. "Yeah, he's a legit non-racist conservative. He just likes to talk about economic policy and stuff. It was cool hanging out with him. He's really into video games, so he'd use all these gaming metaphors to explain stuff."

"Well, of course! He knows you're a gaming expert—"

"Excuse me." She grins. "I'm actually amazing on assist mode."

"Touché."

"Anyway, the point is, we were actually becoming friends. But then he started liking Sara, and she didn't like him back, and it's been so painfully awkward for all of us. Sara kept darting into empty classrooms to avoid him for the rest of the school year."

My mind is reeling. So Maya's never dated anyone. I can hardly wrap my head around that. She's so self-assured and funny and brave. And pretty. And I guess I kind of assumed she'd find my lack of experience to be this huge turnoff.

But now she's saying she doesn't see the point of dating, and I don't even know how to interpret that. Is she getting . . . some sort of vibe from me? Maybe this is her way of rejecting me without actually rejecting me. Like the whole

thing about unreciprocated crushes ruining friendships—
is that supposed to be some kind of gentle heads-up? An
emotional caution sign?

It occurs to me that it's been an agonizingly long time
since either of us has spoken.

Deep breath. "So . . . seen any good movies lately?"

"No." Maya smiles. "Bucko."

And just like that, the tension disappears. "Want to know
a secret?" I ask. "I don't even watch movies that much. They
feel so short, because I'm so used to bingeing TV shows."

Maya laughs. "Yes! I'm rewatching *The Office* now—"

"Wait, seriously?"

"Yes, seriously."

I just stare at her for a moment. "That is my favorite
show."

"Mine too!"

"What's your favorite season?" I ask.

"Duh," she says, "season two. All that Jim and Pam sex-
ual tension."

I smile. "Jim and Pam are the best."

"They're OTP," Maya says. "They're so cute and oblivi-
ous, and season two is so great, because Pam is so in love,
and she doesn't even realize it. I love them so much."

"Me too." I grin back.

"All right!" says our waitress. "Two slices of our

seven-layer chocolate cake. And the check." I blink up at her, startled.

"Ooh, thank you!" Maya says.

"No problem, sweetie. And I just have to say . . ." She looks from Maya to me, and back to Maya. "You two are the cutest couple, I swear. I'm so used to awkward first dates here. It's nice to see the real deal."

Maya's eyebrows shoot up.

I shove a bite of cake in my mouth so quickly, I almost choke.

CHAPTER EIGHTEEN
MAYA

I don't normally buy into miracles, but sign me up as a true believer now.

Because Sara is not working today.

I tie my hair up into a messy bun and glance at the phone again.

Hen's mom just canceled. No babysitting today! Pick you up at 1?

It's 12:30 and she hasn't followed up to cancel or postpone. Like I said, a genuine miracle.

My phone buzzes.

Jamie: I think I ate my entire lifetime supply of chocolate cake yesterday.

Maya: Aw, bummer. I was hoping we could go for seconds today.

Three dots blink and then—

Jamie: I was totally kidding. I'm hanging with my friends at my place, but we can go after?

Maya: Can't 😟 Meeting up with Sara 😳

Jamie: Whoa. So it's happening. The talk?

Maya: I think so?

Jamie: You got this, Maya! 💪

I press thumbs-up to his text and put the phone in my pocket. I'll talk to Sara. I will. But right now, I don't feel the tiniest bit upset. I'm just relieved to have a moment to hang out with her. To talk about our lives and fill her in on what's been happening with my parents and canvassing. Everything. Suddenly, I feel a rush of missing her so much it makes me ache.

I slip on my sandals in the foyer. Glancing up, my eyes land on my parents' framed wedding photo on the wall. It's been up there so long, I never notice it—but today it catches my eye. It's not a normal wedding photo with the couple posed like royalty wearing clichéd smiles. They're in front of a wedding cake. My mother is wearing a velvety red outfit with a gold tikka on her forehead. My dad's wearing a cream sherwani kurta with a matching turban on his head. They *do* look like royalty, but my mom has icing on her nose and chin, and my dad looks like someone slammed a meringue pie in his face. My mother's bent slightly at the waist, her hands on her hips, and even though it's a picture—you can almost see her shaking from laughter. My father looks down at her with the biggest smile I've ever seen.

The front door jangles and parts open. My mother steps inside and kicks her shoes off. She glances at me and startles.

"Hey, you." She leans over and kisses my cheek. "Heading out?"

"Yep. Home early?"

"Quick detour to pick up my laptop," she says. "Are you and Jamie going somewhere?"

"Sara's picking me up. We're going to get a bite to eat and hang out."

"About time!" My mother smiles.

"Why this picture?" I blurt out. She looks confused, and then follows where I'm pointing to their photo on the wall.

"What do you mean?" she asks.

"I was putting my shoes on, and I guess it hit me how random that photo is. Most people put up formal wedding shots, and you guys put the most ridiculous possible one on the wall. . . ." My voice trails off, and I glance at my mother. "Sorry. I shouldn't be talking about that right now, I guess . . ."

"I forgot that photo was up there."

I wonder if she'll reach over and yank it down. But she doesn't. She's looking at it quietly.

"I'm not an extrovert," my mother finally says. "And

between the guest list for both sides, we had over five hundred attendees. You know the term stage fright? Your father and I were seated on a stage, and I panicked and completely froze. Your dad said he knew how to help me get comfortable and asked me if I would trust him. At the cake cutting time, your father took a piece of cake and smooshed my bite on my nose. And, well, my defense mechanisms kicked in, and I smashed a whole slice in his face." She shook her head. "We couldn't stop laughing. Your grandparents were mortified."

"And you put that photo on the wall."

"We have a ton of stuffy wedding photos." She smiles a little. "But this one was my favorite. The unscripted part of the wedding, just about us. It made me the happiest."

"You guys met in college, right?"

"My sophomore year. His freshman year." She nods. "He asked if he could study at my table because the tables were all full at the library."

"Likely story."

"It worked." She smiles.

"So, it was love at first sight?"

"No." She wrinkles her nose. "You know your dad, he's such a chatterbox. But we were friends for a long time."

"When did things change?"

"I'm not sure. It wasn't one moment in particular. A

movie here, a meal there . . . and then before you know it . . ."

She's talking about my dad and smiling wistfully. *This* was the thread I needed to follow—trailing back to their past, to help them remember how it all began. To realize they can get back there again.

"What kind of restaurants did you like to go to on your dates?" Even if they don't have the exact same restaurant in Atlanta, I could figure out something equivalent and come up with a way to get them there—so they can stop "reflecting" and finally talk.

"We didn't really date. We hung out."

"Hanging out is dating, Mom."

"Most of the time we went out with friends."

"Group dating."

"I guess you could call it that," she says reluctantly. "I didn't see it that way."

"Why not?"

"Because we were keeping it halal." She eyes me. "You know, Maya, intimacy is for after marriage."

"TMI!" I fling my hands up. "I was just asking what your favorite restaurant was."

"I'm only saying," she presses. "Kissing and all the rest— those are sacred moments between a husband and wife. And since we're on the topic. It's one thing to date just to date, and another to pursue a relationship because you're seriously thinking of marriage."

I've heard this refrain since middle school. I get what she's saying, but . . .

"So, you have to want to marry the person in order to date?" I ask. "That's a lot of pressure when you're just getting to know the person."

"It's not that you *have* to marry them, but you should be thinking along those lines." She hesitates. "And that's why I've told you it's not a good idea to get into a relationship with anyone until you're in college. There's too much going on in high school to add one more thing to your plate."

"Isn't there plenty on people's plates in college too?"

She studies me for a second.

"Are you thinking about dating?"

"Me?" I stare at her.

She looks at me expectantly.

"How did this become about me? I was asking about your favorite restaurants to see if maybe you and Dad might want to have a talk at some point. Maybe go out for dinner—just to connect? You've been focusing and reflecting for weeks. A talk might be nice."

Way to show all your cards, Maya. I sigh.

"Oh, honey," she says. "We *are* talking."

"I never see you talk."

"We talk every week, during our therapy sessions."

Therapy sessions?

"And we meet with Imam Jackson weekly too. I *hate* that our issues have to affect you like this. We both hate it. So much."

They are talking.

All this time, they've been talking.

And my dad still bought a bed.

Settling down on the front steps to wait for Sara, I click on Instagram. The first picture in my feed is InstaGramm. Jamie's in this photo. It's the first time I've seen him on her feed. They're taking a selfie in front of a Rossum yard sign. The caption reads: *Behind every grandmother is a wonderful grandson. Meet the man behind the scenes—the Stories expert and filterer extraordinaire: Jamie. And look at those cheeks. Isn't he cute?*

I laugh. There's no denying Jamie is cute, but he's not toddler cute. The way his hair frames his forehead, his easy smile—you can't deny the guy is objectively good-looking. And the way the green of Jamie's eyes shifts depending on the day or the light or what he's wearing . . . Yesterday, under the glow of the dim lights at Intermezzo, they looked touched with a hint of honey. I smile a little. Last night was perfect.

But all my good feelings vanish when I see the next photo.

It's a selfie. Of Sara and Jenna. They're holding mugs with rainbow straws. The caption reads: *It's official—rainbows do make everything better.*

This isn't a repost. This isn't a throwback. The time stamp is yesterday. The geotag is Brookhaven. Three miles from my house.

Sara honks.

Numb, I get in the car.

"Hey, Maya." She grins at me. "Intermezzo for some cake?"

"I went there yesterday," I manage to say.

"Well, I'm kind of hungry for real food anyway. How about Mellow Mushroom? For old times' sake?"

"Okay."

She doesn't stop talking all the way to the restaurant. About how complicated it is to organize the things she's buying. How her mom wants to repurpose Sara's bedroom once she's gone so it can double as a sewing studio. Lucas trying to get out of every shift, using his arm as an excuse.

Old Sara would have noticed I haven't said anything in response. Old Sara would know something was wrong. But this isn't that Sara anymore.

Except for some men sitting at the bar watching ESPN pundits on television, the restaurant is empty. Sara gives the waitress our usual order of pizza with olives and a side of cheesy bread. This is a vintage Maya and Sara destination. We've been coming here since we were in fifth grade and our moms dropped us off for our Percy Jackson book club for two. But I don't feel nostalgic right now. The numbness from the car ride is wearing off. Something else, harder, is taking its space. I exhale and try to calm down. Jamie thought I should talk to her. He said it would keep building if I didn't. And that's what's happened, isn't it? The longer we go without talking, the worse things keep getting. I need to stop this avalanche.

But before I can say anything, Sara does.

"I'm *so* glad we're doing this." She leans across the table with a huge smile. "I wanted to tell you the news in person. I heard back from Avid. Guess what? I got the job!"

My mouth goes dry like sandpaper.

"Can you believe it? The competition was fierce, but Ashley fought for me, so I'm in! It's such a cute bookshop, and I'm so excited to only have one job!"

"When are you moving?"

"That's the thing." Her smile falls. "They need me ASAP. I'm going June twenty-eighth."

"That's . . . that's Friday."

"Can you believe it? I am *scrambling*. Thank *God* Jenna has summer session. My financial aid doesn't kick in until the fall so I didn't know what I was going to do if I couldn't crash in our place until then."

She's telling me about how financial aid and living arrangements work. How she might be able to add on a summer class if the school lets her. But I can't focus on any of it. I can't process the fact that our first real hangout of the summer is now also our last one.

"I'm sorry." She leans over and squeezes my hand. "This summer was intense. I wish we could've hung out more."

But you found time to hang out with Jenna.

Everything I was going to say flies out the window. My brain is a complete blank. Sara looks at me expectantly. I need to say something that won't end with me crying. I take a deep breath. Something neutral. Something safe.

"You'll come back to vote, though, right?" I ask her.

"What?"

"Vote." I clear my throat. "The special election is in less than two weeks. It's always low turnout for local elections. Every vote is going to count."

"Wow." She pulls back. "That's what you want to know? No congrats? No questions about my move? Thanks for being happy for me."

"Why do you need me to be happy for you?" I spit out. "You have Jenna, don't you?"

"What's *that* supposed to mean?"

"You were together." My voice cracks. "Yesterday. I saw the picture."

"Seriously? Is that what you're upset about? She was

driving through on her way up to Athens. We went to the coffee shop next door on my break."

"When's the last time you asked *me* to meet up with you during a break?"

"I'm sorry, but aren't you too busy '*canvassing*'?" She raises her fingers into air quotes.

"What are you trying to say?" My eyes narrow.

"You know exactly what I'm saying." She crosses her arms. "Don't act like you've been sitting around sobbing about me. You've been plenty distracted."

I get that she didn't understand what H.B. 28 was about. And it's fine that she didn't want to go knocking on doors— even I didn't want to until my mom pushed me into it. But to belittle everything we've been doing?

"Maybe some of us want to try to effect change around here. Maybe some of us care about things beyond ourselves. This election is important."

"If you think I'm wasting gas money to drive down here to vote for that smiling potato, you should take up stand-up comedy, because that's fucking hilarious."

"It's not funny!" I stare at her. "This election has huge stakes. How can you not get that?"

"I go to rallies and marches. I do my part, but I'm not participating in a corrupt system and pretending I deserve a cookie for it."

"How can you say that?" The men at the bar glance over

at us. I know I'm talking way too loudly. But I don't care. "They're going to ban hijab!" Sara looks surprised and I feel a tiny bit of satisfaction. "You didn't know. Why would you? You're too focused on yourself—and fucking *trash cans*—to notice what else is going on. You didn't text me to say Happy Eid or anything." I blink back tears. "I posted a photo on Instagram, since I know you live on there, but you didn't even like it. You're too busy with Jenna to notice anything or anyone else."

"I'm sorry I forgot about Eid, but I can't help it if I follow a thousand people on Instagram and you follow ten, Maya!" Sara exhales. "Do you know how impossible it is to be your friend? To be your *only* fucking friend? God forbid I have more than one person I'm close to. Most people do. Do you understand how much pressure it puts on me that you lean on me for all your emotional support?"

"Believe me, the message is loud and clear that I can't lean on you at all." Tears stream down my face now. "When my parents split this summer—I had no one to talk to. *No one.* You were always too busy."

"What . . ." Sara's eyes widen. She pauses as she digests this information. Then she shakes her head. "If you needed to talk about something, *anything*, all you had to do was tell me it was urgent, and I'd have made the time for you. But no." She glares at me. "You had to be all precious about it, and now you're acting like a martyr, like I chose not to be there for you when I didn't even *know.*"

"There was no time to tell you! You're always working."

"Gee, I'm sorry, Maya. I'm sorry my dad isn't a doctor who can fund my entire college education. I'm sorry I have to get scholarships and loans and even *then* have to save up so I can eat more than ramen noodles during college. Forgive me for trying to make a living for myself."

There is a long ugly silence. She leans against the seat and glances out the window. "Friday can't come soon enough," she mutters. "I can't wait to have friends who aren't such damn high schoolers."

I jump out of the booth, gulping down sobs. It's hard to breathe. I can barely see through my tears. I rush outside and lean against the side of the brick restaurant wall. Sara hasn't followed. Not that she would.

That's something old Sara would do.

I pull out my phone and try to keep my hands from trembling. *Acting like a martyr?* The words feel like needles cutting into me.

I have to get out of here.

But I'm not going home. I can't.

I open the rideshare app.

I type in Jamie's address.

CHAPTER NINETEEN
JAMIE

"Jamie, your roll," says Felipe, but I hardly hear him. I'm frozen, staring at the text on my screen.

Maya: I'm outside your house.

I scramble to my feet, leaving Felipe, Nolan, and Drew gaping at me from around the Catan board. "Everything okay?" Nolan asks.

"Maya's here."

Felipe's brows shoot up. "Right now?"

"I want to meet her!" says Drew.

I'm already halfway down the hall, my heart in overdrive. I just . . . can't believe this is happening. Maya's here? Other than last night's drive-by when we dropped Sophie off, I don't think she's been to my house in almost a decade.

I open my own front door.

And there she is on the doorstep, sobbing, clutching her elbows. The minute she sees me, she crumples. I rush outside, bumping the door shut behind me as I envelop her in a hug. "Hey. Hey." I rub her back as she sobs against my chest. "It's okay."

I swallow roughly. I've never seen Maya this upset. Not even after the Dickers meeting. She's crying so hard, she can't talk, can barely even catch her breath. But she pulls me in so tight, there's not an inch of space between us.

"I'm sorry," she says shakily. "Your friends are still here, aren't they?"

"What?" I draw back, just enough to see her face; she's gazing past me at Felipe's car in the driveway. "No—no, it's fine. They're just hanging out here. Maya."

She disentangles from the hug, breath still ragged. "We can talk later. I'm totally fine. I can just—"

I grab her hand. "Please don't leave. Just. Hold on." I crack the door open to peer inside—sure enough, the guys are camped in the entryway, looking way too intrigued. "Get Sophie to cover for me," I mutter to Felipe—and then I yank the door shut again, turning back to Maya. "They're fine, okay? They're just playing Settlers of Catan. Sophie's going to step in, and she'll probably win the whole game."

Maya wipes her eyes with one hand, but keeps the other hand in mine, lacing our fingers together. Which is—okay. Wow. *Wow.*

Except Maya's clearly heartbroken. There's nothing *wow* about that.

"Do you want to sit out here and talk? We could go on a walk. I could grab Boomer."

Maya shoots me a teary half smile. "Boomer the celebrity Insta-dog?"

"Boomer the influencer!" I make myself let go of her hand. "Okay, wait right here. I'll get him. Don't leave, okay?"

Maya nods. "I won't."

By the time I step back onto the stoop with Boomer, Maya's much more composed. She shoots me a wavering smile. "Hey."

"We're back! Maya, meet Boomer. Boomer, meet Maya."

Boomer decides to meet Maya very intimately. She steps back, with a startled laugh.

"Boomer, NO." I yank his leash back, cheeks burning. "Sorry. He's—uh. Friendly."

We set off down the street, Maya walking so close beside me, the backs of our hands keep brushing. It's strange just drifting through the neighborhood with Maya. I keep getting the urge to knock on doors.

"You sure this is okay?" Maya asks. "I don't want to pull you away from your game. I should have checked—"

"It's totally fine. I'm just glad you're here. What happened?"

For a moment, she's silent.

"It's okay," I say quickly. "You don't have to tell me if you don't want to. Whatever you want to talk about, I'm all yours." I blush. "All ears."

"Thanks, Jamie." She stares glumly at our street sign and sighs. "It's Sara."

"I thought so."

She nods. "We had the talk. I was pretty up front about all of it. I guess a part of me thought—maybe this is stupid, but I hoped it was this big misunderstanding, and she'd feel so bad for hurting me, but we'd talk through it, and everything would be fine."

I glance sideways at Maya. "But it wasn't fine."

"No." Her voice sounds choked all over again.

"I'm so sorry, Maya. I shouldn't have told you to—"

"No, no—it's not your fault! It needed to be said, really. It's been the elephant in the room for so long. But it was just *so* bad. It's like she didn't even care that I was hurt. She turned it all around, like I was the unreasonable one. Like I'm so immature—"

"What?" My jaw drops. "You're like the most mature person I know. You use a rideshare app to get around town!"

Maya laughs tearfully. "True, that's pretty mature of me."

"And you canvass, and we had that meeting with Dickers—that was mature of us. And you watch *The Office*.

It's a show about work! That's peak maturity."

"True!"

"And that is a *very* mature cat poster at your dad's house—"

"Shut up." She bumps me sideways, laughing for real now. I bump her back, trying not to grin.

But Maya's face falls. "I just don't know where to go from here. It's like she doesn't even want to be friends anymore. Just like that."

"How could she not want to be your friend?"

Maya shrugs. "She has Jenna."

"Well, fuck that."

"Jamie!" Maya gapes at me.

I smile sheepishly. "Fork that?"

"No, I liked the first one. I'm just shocked." She laughs, sounding startled—and then hugs me again. "Only you could say *fuck* and have it be the sweetest gesture ever."

Okay, I might be a terrible person. Maya's having the absolute worst day imaginable, and here I am, flooded with sunshine. It's not that I'm happy she's upset. I could never be. But I've never gotten to hold her hand like that, or *anything* close to the way it's been today.

"I think I just need a distraction," Maya says.

"A distraction. Hmm." I pause. "Look! A squirrel!" Boomer stiffens, tugging the leash taut. "Well, my distraction worked on Boomer."

Maya laughs. "What's InstaGramm working on? Mostly Rossum stuff right now, right?"

"Yeah, I think Gabe is pretty much monopolizing her time. Tomorrow he's actually going to photograph Rossum himself with Grandma and Boomer." I shrug. "Gabe is obsessed with trying to go viral."

Maya smiles down at Boomer. "Oh my God, you lucky dog. You get to meet Rossum?"

"He's already met him! Boomer's very well-connected."

"I would flip if I met him," Maya says. "I'm kicking myself that I didn't get an introduction at that mixer! I didn't really get it, you know? It was just a thing my mom made me go to."

I nod. "Same here."

"You haven't met Rossum?" Maya looks surprised.

"Sort of? He's mostly based at the Dunwoody office. And I've been to lots of his events, but I've never gone up and talked to him or anything."

"Do you think you would now?"

"I don't know. I'd be so tongue-tied."

"I think you'd be great," Maya says. "You're so much braver than you think you are."

I turn to see if she's messing with me, but her expression is completely sincere. I guess that's the thing about Maya. When she thinks or feels something, she says it. Which can be a little scary sometimes if she's pissed at you, or if you're a

Koopa Troopa like Dickers who needs to be called out. But Maya never lets the good stuff go unspoken either. There have been hundreds of moments where Maya's sweetness or cuteness or brilliance has struck me. I just never work up the nerve to say it out loud. But Maya always says it out loud.

And she's so casually convinced that I'm brave, I almost believe it.

"Well, that means a lot coming from you," I say.

Maya smiles, and I swear she holds my eyes a beat longer than usual. "Thanks."

For a moment, we just stand there smiling on the sidewalk, Boomer pacing ahead of us.

"So . . . do you think Sophie's ruined everyone at Catan yet?" I ask finally.

Maya laughs. "I love Sophie so much."

"Oh, the feeling is *very* mutual. She hasn't shut up about you since we finished canvassing."

"I remember when she was a baby!" Maya says. "Your mom let me hold her, and I went home and threw the biggest tantrum, demanding a little sister. I was so jealous of you. I just remember thinking she was *so* cute. And now she's this legit grown-up person, and she's actually really cool. She was so great at canvassing too!"

"Maybe you should give the bat mitzvah toast," I suggest.

"Nice try." Maya grins up at me. "I'll help you with it later, though."

We make our way back home, where the guys and Sophie have abandoned Catan in favor of *Bob's Burgers* and Goldfish crackers. Felipe and Nolan are on the love seat, while Drew and Sophie have claimed the couch, an economy carton of cheddar Goldfish stationed between them. Boomer dive-bombs into Sophie's lap as soon as I release him.

I hang back in the living room doorway with Maya, suddenly feeling like I'm under stage lights. "So. Uh. Guys, this is Maya. Maya, this is Felipe, Nolan, Drew, and you know Sophie."

Felipe jumps up to hug Maya, which seems to both startle and please her. Nolan peers over the back of the couch, smiling. "You're Jamie's canvassing partner, right?"

Drew snorts and grins. "Canvassing partner."

I ignore Drew, turning quickly to Nolan. "Yes!"

Maya eyes the Goldfish carton. "Are you guys obsessed with Goldfish too?"

"No," Felipe says. "It's just the official Goldberg house snack food. I'm more of a Cheeto Puff guy."

Nolan smiles. "You don't say."

"And I'm a cereal guy," says Drew.

Maya tilts her head. "You know you don't have to pick just one snack food, right?"

"But I'm a cereal monogamist," says Drew, throwing back a handful of Goldfish.

"Clearly not." Maya side-eyes him.

Drew beams up at me, not-so-subtly mouthing, "I like her."

"Well, it was really cool to finally meet you guys," Maya says. "Sorry I was such a mess—"

I shake my head. "You weren't—"

"I should probably head out."

"No!" Drew jumps up, flinging the Goldfish box at Sophie. "Nope. We were just leaving, right?"

"Yup." Felipe and Nolan stand and hold hands.

Drew turns to Maya. "You should stick around to keep Jamie company."

"Definitely," says Felipe.

"Indubitably," says Nolan.

Sophie narrows her eyes at Nolan. "You got that from a Bitmoji."

Maya turns to face me.

"You should stay!" I say. "If you want to. You don't have to. But you totally could. That would be great. Unless you—"

Drew smacks my arm to shut me up.

"Okay, cool," Maya says.

"Sweet. We'll just head on out, then," says Drew. "Let you two have some alone time."

Wow. I don't know if I want to choke Drew or hug him. Maybe both.

But. Alone time. With Maya. In my house, which contains my room, which contains my—okay, I'm not going to think about beds. That would be absurd. No point in thinking about beds or alone or Maya or alone with Maya in beds or—

"Yay, I love alone time!" says Sophie. "Should we move to your room, Jamie?"

We end up working on the toast—which I thought would be torture, but isn't. Sophie sinks backward onto my bed, already bubbling with ideas for how I can sing her praises. "Tell the one about when I put Saran wrap over the toilet."

"Why would I possibly tell that story in public?"

Maya grins, leaning into my yellow wingback chair. "You could always just tell it right now."

"Oh my God," Sophie says. "It was a mess. It, like, *caught* his pee—"

"Soph, you do not want to bring up the subject of pee," I say warningly. "Trust me."

"Do you have two full sets of Harry Potter?" asks Maya, peering at my bookcase.

"Of course. Hardcovers and paperbacks."

She looks around. "I love your room. It's so *you*. Is your wallpaper border . . . a timeline?"

"Of US history." I nod.

She picks up a framed picture from my desk. "And that must be your grandpa."

I smile. "Yup."

"My friend Maddie says our grandpa was hot when he was younger. And I was like, *okay, but he looks exactly like Jamie*, and Maddie was like, *I know*." Sophie sits up straight, her eyes practically shooting off sparks. "So, Maya, what do you think? Hot grandpa?"

"Hey," I say loudly, pointing over Maya's shoulder. "Want to see me at the fifth-grade presidential reception? It's the one in the shiny frame."

Eleven-year-old me, in a button-down shirt, tie, and cardigan, smiling next to a propped-up photo of the Carter Center. Could be worse, right? I mean, Felipe had to play Eisenhower in a bald wig. So there's that.

"Jamie. Oh my God." Maya presses her hand to her heart.

Sophie looks at me. "Wasn't that the time you called President Carter a pe—"

"OKAY. Sophie. I think Boomer needs you."

Sophie is unmoved. "Nah, he's fine. Mom just got home. Maya, want to see Jamie's official bar mitzvah photo?"

I shoot her an especially vicious are-you-serious-right-now face.

Sophie widens her eyes and does an unmistakable just-trust-me nod.

"Are you asking if I'm up for more adorable vintage Jamie Goldberg photos?" Maya says, beaming. "Um, obviously."

My phone buzzes with a text, and I glance at it quickly.

Sophie: See? Adorable.

Adorable. Great. Like a puppy. Or a gnome. No one passionately makes out with *adorable*. And even if that weren't the case, let's be real. My bar mitzvah picture? Is about as adorable as Mr. Droolsworth, Boomer's chewed-up stuffed mallard.

I glare at Sophie, who saunters toward the door, entirely unfazed. Maya jumps up to follow her—but then she pauses, glancing sheepishly back at me. "I should head back home after this, huh?"

"What? No, you don't have to—"

"My mom's probably wondering where I am. This has been so nice, Jamie." She meets my eyes. "Thank you."

"At least let me drive you."

"I can totally use my app. It's fine!"

"Are you kidding?"

"Maya, come on!" Sophie calls from the hallway.

Okay, if Maya thought the presidential reception was awkward, she clearly hasn't seen the "cool casual" super-enlarged portrait Mom had matted in advance for guests to sign at my bar mitzvah. It hangs framed over our dining room table, my metallic-smiling face surrounded by scrawled Sharpie messages and misspelled "congrags" and "mazzle tovs."

Maya studies it like she's in a museum, the corners of her

mouth twisting upward. "That is some outfit."

"Right?" Sophie giggles. "I love the polo shirt with the gym shorts."

"Business on top, party on the bottom." I blush. "That was my look in seventh grade."

Maya sighs. "Wow. I so wish I'd gone to this."

"Is that Maya?" Mom calls from the kitchen. A moment later, she pops her head in the doorway. "Hi!"

"Hi." Maya smiles. "Sorry! You're probably about to have dinner. I was just heading out."

"No rush whatsoever. Stay for dinner!" Mom says.

"I should head home."

"Do you need a ride?" Mom asks.

"Oh. Well. Jamie said he'd take me, but—"

Mom laughs. "That's who I was going to volunteer. It's so good to see you, sweetie. Are you canvassing again soon?"

Maya nods. "Thursday, right?"

"Ooh," chimes Sophie. "I could do Thursday."

Mom shakes her head. "You have tutoring."

"What? No, that's—"

"I scheduled you an extra day. On Thursday. Jamie and Maya are going to have to go by themselves." The second Maya looks away, Mom shoots me a wink.

And there you have it: my new crowning achievement.

I'm pretty sure my mom is my wingwoman now.

247

CHAPTER TWENTY
MAYA

When I check my phone, there are three texts. One from Jamie that he's on his way. Another from my mom. She's wondering if I'm staying with my dad tonight. Shelby messaged that the movie selections this week are unappealing—if anyone wants to meet up for laser tag tonight, she'll organize.

Zero texts from Sara.

Not that I expected one. But she's leaving soon. She might already be gone. I'm tempted to send her a quick message. Just to reach out. But I don't know what I'll do if she doesn't reach back.

Jamie pulls up. He waves. Suddenly I feel a little self-conscious as I get in the car. Maybe it's post-embarrassment syndrome from barging into his house with snot and tears all over my face.

"Any luck with the toast?" I ask him.

"Not yet. Been so busy with other stuff, I haven't had a chance to draft anything."

"Yeah." I flush. "Me crashing your hangout with your friends definitely didn't help."

"Crash away," Jamie says. "My friends loved you."

"Even with our conflicting snack philosophies?"

"Can you believe it? Only thing is, next time you'll have to play Catan with us."

"I've never tried that game, but I'm up for it."

I know Jamie complains about how loud and messy his house can get, but I love that about his place. All the different corkboards up with plans for the bat mitzvah resting against the kitchen counter. Rolls of washi tape on the table. The sofa filled with friends and Goldfish crackers. His house isn't chaotic. It's perfect.

The campaign office is busier than usual today. In addition to the ladies in batik scarves and the usual handful of college folks, there's two moms wearing babies in carriers, and a bunch of people my parents' age reading pamphlets and glancing around nervously.

"Newbies," Jamie whispers.

"Totally." I smile.

You'd think Gabe would be doing cartwheels at all the fresh new faces to pontificate to, but instead, he's sucking down an iced coffee and he looks . . . agitated.

He rattles off the usual speech about canvassing, and lets them know Hannah will help troubleshoot the Door to Door app. I wait for him to conclude with his patented "rah rah rah, Rossum is awesome" portion of the speech, but he's more solemn today.

"Folks," he says, setting down his coffee. "I cannot stress to you how important it is to make these final days count." He clasps his hands. "We need to get as many doors in as we can. We must make sure every registered Democrat votes. We need every Independent in our district to get their butts in the voting booth too. This is a fight to the finish, people—we have to show the other side"—he raises his hands—"that we have claws!"

Everyone blinks at this. An older woman raises her hand.

"My app is showing more houses assigned than usual."

"Darn right." Gabe nods. "We need to hit as many doors as possible."

"How many doors exactly?" asks someone.

"It's not too many. Each of you has about two hundred homes."

The crowd collectively gasps. One of the women with the baby carriers raises her hand.

"I'm sorry, but that is a *lot* of houses," she says. "I was planning for a two-hour commitment."

"I have to take my son to soccer practice," a man says.

"My mom has physical therapy at four," another chimes in.

"My baby will need to go down for a nap by noon. . . ."

The crowd murmurs quietly.

"You people are unbelievable!" Gabe shouts. His face reddens. "Your baby can nap after the election! Yes. It's a lot of work. But we need Rossum to win! Is that what you all want? Or only if it's *convenient* for you?"

He stalks off and slams the VIP supply closet shut behind him.

I glance at Jamie. What just happened?

Hannah clears her throat and hurries to the front of the room.

"Hey, y'all." She smiles brightly. "We're just so super excited to be in the home stretch for Rossum! Let's aim for one hundred doors, and if you can't do that, just do as many as you can. Whatever you accomplish today is amazing. We'll sync the data we collect from the app when you return." She glances at the supply closet. "And Gabe and I both want you to know we appreciate you volunteering your time, and we know how valuable it is. Don't forget to grab water bottles on your way out. It's a hot one today! We'll have pizza waiting for you as a thank-you when you return."

The crowd relaxes a bit. Everyone starts filing out of the room.

"Hannah to the rescue," I say.

"That could have gone *really* badly," Jamie agrees.

We walk over to the VIP supply closet. Jamie taps the door and peeks in. Gabe is pacing the cramped area and looking down at his phone. His forehead is coated with sweat.

"You okay, Gabe?" Jamie says.

"That was kind of rough out there," I add.

"Too tough?" He looks up at us. "I should go out there and say something." He moves to hurry out, but Jamie reaches out and stops him.

"Hannah took care of it," he says. "What is with you? Your face is red. Do I need to take you to urgent care?"

"No." Gabe wipes his sweaty forehead with his arm. "The VIP room doesn't get good ventilation, that's all. It's just. This campaign. We're in the last gasps—fundraising isn't going as well as we hoped. I reached out to every Atlanta celebrity, and only two responded with donations. I just don't get it."

"A lot of people showed up today," I tell him.

"Twenty-four people is nothing," Gabe snaps. "We need quadruple times quadruple that if we want to actually hit every door." He massages his temples. "I don't know what to do. Every angle feels futile. There's no traction with ads. People glaze over. Ditto yard signs. What we need is for something to go *viral*. Do you know that two of our folks got Fifi'd while canvassing? I pitched it to every local station, no one picked it up! They said they covered it a few weeks ago. So what? I'm *handing you content*, people!"

"Yeah," I say slowly. "That sucks. That people got Fifi'd."

"Fifi's messaging is the problem." Gabe paces the room. "It's all, pardon the pun, dog whistles—anti-Semitic stuff no one except for people in the know would get. Does any ordinary person know the 88 on her cup stands for Heil Hitler? Or the okay sign she's doing while holding her teacup is another anti-Semitic nod? Now, if it had a swastika, everyone would be all over it."

"Gabe." I look at him. "Are you saying you wish it had a swastika?"

"Look." He lowers his voice. "I know it's not PC. But it would help move the needle for Rossum to win. I'm just being honest."

"You're honestly being the worst," Jamie interrupts.

"No need to be condescending, Big J." Gabe frowns at him.

"You're asking for a swastika on a teacup. Do you hear yourself?"

"This isn't about me. I'm trying to get Rossum this election."

"But sooner or later this election will be over," Jamie says. "And when it's behind you, you'll still have to be you. Make sure you'll be able to live with yourself when it's done."

Jamie turns and walks out. I glance at Gabe.

"He's right," I tell him before I follow Jamie to the car.

"You okay?" I ask him when we get back inside.

I thought he'd be freaking out. But Jamie is grinning.

"I'm great," he replies. "Can you believe I got him to shut up for a second?"

"I'm not sure I've seen Gabe without a comeback before." I wipe the perspiration off my forehead. "Hannah's right, though—it is really hot today. Can we swing by to get some iced coffee?"

"I need a palate cleanser after that too," Jamie agrees. "Sometimes, I can't believe that guy is my cousin. I mean—he's not usually *this* ridiculous. The problem with Fifi is they're not actual swastikas?"

"Dog whistles are worse, because they're designed for maximum plausible deniability."

"Exactly! People can throw up their hands and say, 'What do you mean the 88 is anti-Semitic?'" Jamie says. "'I just like that number. Am I not allowed to have a favorite number?' Or, 'Hey, it's an okay sign. It's just me saying all is cool—why would you think it's bigoted? You're overreacting.'"

"Gaslighting is way worse," I agree.

We pull up and order our coffees. He hands me mine and I take a sip.

"Oh, yum. I've missed iced coffees." I glance at him again. "Sorry again about that time I nearly bit your head off for getting me one."

"I get it. I mean, I should have gone past the first Google search page."

"I think I was just stressed about Dickers," I say. "That woman probably has a PhD in dog whistles."

"As crappy as that went, I don't regret going."

"Me either."

We park by the neighborhood sign for the street we're about to canvass. But neither of us gets out. I glance out the window. There are no clouds in the sky. The sun is blazing so hot, steam rises from the concrete.

"Gabe's speech knocked all my enthusiasm out of canvassing. We're not doing it for *Gabe*," I say. "But still . . ."

"No." Jamie nods. "I get it."

Jamie puts the car in park as Lois Reitzes finishes up an interview with local author Laurel Snyder.

"Next up," Lois says, "Tammy Adrian, with a look at today's local headlines."

"Good afternoon, Atlanta listeners, Tammy Adrian here with your local news updates. First up is H.B. 28."

Both of us fall silent.

"Asa Newton announced yesterday at a fundraising event that passing H.B. 28 will be his first order of business in office. Whether the law passes constitutional muster, however, may be a matter decided in the courts if it's passed. Meanwhile, the Atlanta Symphony Orchestra just celebrated its . . ."

Jamie clicks off the radio.

"Speaking of coded assholes." I sigh. "Holden and Newton are literally the worst."

Two kids bike past us. Jamie glances at them, and then he looks at me.

"What if we don't canvass today?" he asks.

"Really?"

"Let's do something about this bill. Maybe we can figure out how to get a rally set up at the capitol or something."

"Don't we need to get permits for that?"

"Oh, right." His face falls. "That'll probably take a long time to get through."

We sit quietly for a few seconds.

"What about informational flyers?" I say. "That's more important anyway, because so many people aren't aware of H.B. 28. NPR is covering it, but Sara didn't know the bill existed."

"We could print them out and stick them on people's mailboxes."

"And hand them out at restaurants and shops!"

"Should we get a notebook and brainstorm?" he asks.

"To Target it is." I smile.

* * *

The patio section is all ours today. We load up on two notebooks, a pack of colored pens, and a little more coffee, before settling into a little couch that fits both of us perfectly. Jamie's T-shirt brushes against my bare arm.

"It has to be catchy," I tell him. "The slogan. Something to roll off the tongue, like Nike's *Just do it* or *The few, the proud, the Marines.*"

"Or *Break me off a piece of that Kit Kat bar.*"

"Yeah." I look at him. "Like that."

"I got it!" he says. "How about *Love, not hate. Say no to H.B. 28.*"

"Jamie! That's genius! It makes a good rally cry too!"

We doodle talking points and sketch out ideas on how to design it. The hours slip by until Jamie gets a buzz on his phone.

"That's my alarm reminder," he says reluctantly. "My mom made me promise this morning to swing by and get some confetti before dinner tonight."

I glance at the clock with a start. We've just spent five hours here. That's got to be some sort of record for a Target hang. After a crappy few days, it feels good to have done something positive today.

I flip on the TV that night and settle into the sofa with the notebook we were working in. My mom's door is closed, the lights are off.

New Ninja Warrior today, my dad texts me. **I'll save it to watch with you tomorrow.**

I send him back a heart eyes emoji. Our favorite show to watch together, rooting for every single person and getting choked up at all the emotional personal stories.

My thoughts drift to Jamie. It was probably just the welcome reprieve of air-conditioning on this absurdly hot day, but curling up with him at Target was the happiest I've felt in so long. I wonder what Jamie is doing right now. Is he watching a movie with his friends? Drafting his toast?

I load up *The Office* on my TV and glance back at my notebook. I love the slogan *Love, not hate. Say no to H.B. 28*, but we need another piece. I just have to figure out what it is. . . .

I glance at the television. Michael Scott is sharing the downsides of depression and deciding if he'll jump off the roof onto a bouncy castle below, before Pam and Darryl stop him.

"I saved a life today," Michael says solemnly into the camera. "My own."

And that's when it hits me. The perfect slogan.

I pull out my phone and call Jamie.

He picks up immediately.

"Hello?" he says in a hushed voice.

"Oh," I falter. "I didn't mean to wake you up. I'll call back tomorrow."

"No, no . . . one sec." I hear some noise in the background, and then a door shutting. "Sorry," he says. "I was just watching TV. No one calls me, really."

"Yeah." I blush. "Same here. I got so excited because I had this idea for our flyer."

"Cool! What were you thinking?"

"Everyone likes to think of themselves as a hero, right? So, what if we have in big print on the bottom of the flyer: 'It takes thirty seconds to be a hero—call your state senator today.' And then we have a phone number. So we have a message, but also an action item."

"That's brilliant," Jamie says. "I can't believe you came up with that out of nowhere. I'll fiddle around with the design tomorrow."

"I was watching *The Office*," I admit. "Michael Scott gave me inspiration. I'm not sure how I feel about that."

"I'm watching *The Office* too!" he says. "Which episode?"

"The one where he talks about depression on the roof?"

"I was about to start season two again. The one where he does the Dundies."

"I love that one!" I exclaim. "Hold up, let me switch over."

The intro music starts up on his end as it plays on my end too. I settle back onto the couch.

"This guy cannot read the room. Literally no one wants

to do these awards," Jamie says.

"Well, Dwight does," I respond. "Look, he's the musical accompaniment to the award night."

"Dwight is the worst," Jamie says.

"By worst you mean the best, right?"

"Of course." Jamie laughs.

We watch the episode together, my phone pressed against my ear. I've never seen this show with anyone. I know he's at his house three miles away, but if I close my eyes, it's like he's sitting on the couch next to me.

The next episode autoplays. And then the one after that. I sink further back into the couch, the phone tucked against my ear. *We should probably get some sleep*, I want to say. Jamie yawns on the other end. But even as my eyes grow heavier, as Jamie's hot takes get softer and softer, I don't hang up.

Jamie doesn't either.

CHAPTER TWENTY-ONE
JAMIE

I wake up in a contented fog, phone still pressed to my cheek. The battery's totally dead. But when I plug it in, Maya's name pops onto my screen.

Incoming call. 8 hours. 25 minutes.

I fell asleep watching TV with Maya. Which is . . . kind of the most romantic thing that's ever happened to me.

I mean, yeah, it was technically just a phone call. But there's something nice about that too. No pressure or weirdness or worrying about where my hands go. Just our voices and Dunder Mifflin in the background and Maya's soft laughter in my ear. We'd started drifting off after the third or fourth episode, waking ourselves up only enough to migrate to our bedrooms. But we didn't hang up.

For eight hours and twenty-five minutes.

Probably only six hours of that were actual sleep. I'm definitely having trouble keeping my eyes open. To be fair, it's barely seven in the morning, but going back to bed is pointless.

Is there such a thing as being too hazy and happy to sleep?

Turns out, everyone's awake but Sophie. Mom's at the kitchen table in her work clothes, frowning at her laptop while she sips from a mug. But Grandma's pacing all around the kitchen, opening and closing drawers, and stepping over Boomer, who's gnawing on Mr. Droolsworth in the middle of the floor. "I love that boy, but my goodness." Grandma clenches her fists. "Wants me to cross-post, do more videos, message more celebrities. DM Oprah—can you imagine?"

Mom chuckles without looking up.

"And he's texting me thirty times a day. Driving me batty."

I pour a mug of coffee, grabbing a bagel from the bread box before settling in next to Mom at the table. "Are you talking about Gabe?"

"I swear, bubalah. I'm this close to blocking him."

"He was really intense at the campaign office yesterday. I guess he's pretty stressed about the election."

"Oh, I know." Grandma joins us at the table. "Don't mind me. I'm just being a grouch."

"No, you're totally right. He needs to chill."

Grandma rubs my arm. "How are you doing, sweetheart? So, you were at the campaign office yesterday? Good for you."

Mom looks up from her laptop, meeting my eyes. "I really am so impressed, Jamie. All this canvassing."

"Well, we didn't actually knock on any doors yesterday," I admit. "But we will! Right now we're working on flyers to push back against H.B. 28. Maya came up with the whole concept—it's pretty brilliant. We're FaceTiming tonight to finalize the design, and then we're meeting at Target tomorrow to start handing them out."

"Oh, wow," Grandma says. "At Target? Are you sure that's allowed?"

"It's worth a try. We're starting small," I add quickly. "Just local places. But eventually we want to hand them out at Emory, Tech, Georgia State, and Kennesaw. We really just want to educate people. And Maya was thinking—"

I catch Mom smiling.

"What?"

Mom's eyebrows shoot up. "Nothing."

I pause. "Anyway, we're hoping to put more pressure on people to make phone calls. No one ever calls state legislators, so if we flood their phones, that could really have an impact. I may even shout it out at Sophie's reception during the toast."

"Jamie."

"Actually, we could bring flyers to the reception! *And* I could mention it in the toast. We could do both."

Mom and Grandma exchange quick glances.

"Jamie," Mom says slowly. "I'm glad you're resisting the bill, and frankly, I'm glad you're thinking about the toast—but are you sure your sister's bat mitzvah is the right moment for that?"

"Why not? There will be a hundred and fifty people there! I'll have a captive audience. I can shout out the Rossum campaign too, and remind everyone about the election date. And even Sophie's friends can make phone calls—"

"Jamie, no." Mom presses her lips together. "That wouldn't be appropriate. You're a cohost of this event. And it's about Sophie, not politics."

My cheeks flush. "But H.B. 28 isn't about politics! That's the hijab bill. It's a human rights issue. You can't just pretend this stuff doesn't exist because we're at a party. The election is three days after Sophie's bat mitzvah!"

"I get it! I do. H.B. 28 is completely vile," Mom says, nodding. "But sweetie, there will be other opportunities to protest. Your sister's bat mitzvah isn't just a party. It's a really important moment for her—"

"But—"

"End of discussion," Mom says. She turns back to her laptop.

I set my mug down with a clank and stand so abruptly, I

startle Boomer. I can't remember the last time I've been this furious at my mom.

"End of discussion? Seriously? You're the one who goes on and on about political action, and how important the Rossum race is. You're the one who made me canvass in the first place! So, what, it's important to care, but only sometimes?"

"That's not fair. Jamie, you have to remember, we're hosting—"

"Really?" I fake gasp. "We're hosting a bat mitzvah? Wow, it must have slipped my notice. Guess I haven't run any errands recently—"

"Sweetheart." Grandma sets a hand on my shoulder.

Mom looks up at me, stunned. "Jamie, what is this? Talking back? That's not like you."

My chest tightens. "I'm not—"

"Maybe Gabe isn't the only one who needs to chill out a little," says Mom.

"You think I'm like *Gabe*?"

"No, Jamie." She snaps her laptop shut. "This isn't worth fighting over, honey. We're all on the same team here. I know it's been a lot, and you're under tons of pressure. Maybe you should take some time off from canvassing."

"Time off from canvassing? The election is in eleven days!"

"I know, I know." Mom peers at me. "But Jamie, I've

never seen you this upset. Yes, it's an important election, but you have to take care of yourself too. It's just not sustainable otherwise. Why don't you and Maya have a fun, normal date instead—"

"What are you talking about?" I gape at her. "Maya and I aren't dating."

Mom flips her palms up defensively. "Okay. I just thought, since you guys have been spending so much time together—"

"Oh my *God*. Can we not?"

I storm back to my room, yanking my phone from my charger, before collapsing into my desk chair. This is bullshit. Utter bullshit. Mom spends all her time trying to get me to speak up and be more assertive, but the minute I do, she can't handle it. It's ridiculous. And then she has the nerve to say I sound like *Gabe*—

Okay, maybe I do sound like Gabe. A *little*. But maybe Gabe is right! Not about Fifi—that was gross—but the fact that people only want to support Rossum when it's convenient? That's legit. Oh, sure, let's canvass . . . when we have time. Resist white supremacy—as long as it doesn't interfere with our super chill weekend. I'm not saying I'm perfect. I'm as guilty as anyone. But at least I'm trying.

And the Maya thing? Mom *knows* she's not my girlfriend. Maya doesn't believe in dating. And even if she did, there's no way she sees me that way. We're friends. *Canvassing partners*, like Nolan said. We're canvassing friends who sometimes vent to each other about stuff.

The worst part is, I can't even vent to Maya about this. *Hey, Maya, my mom thinks you're my girlfriend. Bet you're totally cool with that.* I mean, for all I know, Mom's going around telling people that. People like Alina, which means—yup. Maya probably thinks *I think* we're dating. Wow. That'll be a fun conversation. Can't wait to find out what it feels like to be unambiguously rejected by the girl I'm completely—

Yeah. Anyway.

A lump settles in my throat, thick and heavy. To think that an hour ago, I was sure I'd never stop smiling.

I open my laptop, blinking fast. I need a distraction. Like the H.B. 28 flyers. I could work on the flyers. Which are hardly a distraction, at least not from Maya.

Then again, nothing is.

By eleven, I've tried every font, every color, every layout. I have no idea which ones look good, or if *any* of them look good. All I know is that Maya hasn't texted me, Grandma hasn't knocked, Sophie's still sleeping, and Mom—

I don't want to talk to my mom.

I feel like I'm going to explode all over again.

This calls for the group text. I tap into iMessage, fingers flying over my keyboard.

Jamie: I'm so pissed at my mom

sflskjfghlkszjdhfglkjhsdlkj

Drew: whoa. what's up

Jamie: I swear, I'm so

ARGHGGGGGG

like she's so dismissive of the stuff I'm doing with H.B. 28

even the Rossum stuff!!!

Drew: huh really? I thought that was her idea

Jamie: It WAS

but apparently I'm supposed to turn all of that off and focus

on the bat mitzvah

like I'm incapable of doing both!!

Drew: sorry dude, that sucks!

Felipe: Sorry I'm at work, customers just left, who gets fro yo

at eleven??? Okay catching up now

Oh man, Jamie, I'm sorry. Maybe she's just stressed about

the bat mitzvah?

Jamie: she doesn't have to be so condescending though!

She was implying I was only doing it as a way to get closer to

maya. She was like, just go on a normal date

Drew: ohhhhhh shit 💀

okay so not gonna lie, we thought the same thing at first BUT

we get that you're for real with this stuff.

I stare at my laptop screen. So that's what everyone
thinks. All this work—the canvassing, the flyers. It's all to
get closer to Maya.

I mean, do I like seeing Maya? Yes. Is it fun to work

on this stuff with her? Yes. Do I have a crush on her? Yes. Okay? But that's not why I'm doing this. That's like saying I don't care—about the campaign, about H.B. 28, about Islamophobia and anti-Semitism and bigotry or *anything*. And the idea that I would use all of that to somehow trick Maya into falling for me. Like it's even possible to trick someone into falling for you!

I reread Drew's text, and—yeah. I need to calm down. Drew's saying he knows I'm for real now.

So why does it feel like he's saying the opposite?

Maybe Drew's not actually the one questioning my sincerity.

I shake my head, squeezing my eyes shut for a moment, before turning back to the screen.

Drew: though maya is reeeeealllly cute bro

Jamie: that doesn't mean we're dating!!

Felipe: You should ask her out

Jamie: that's not the point!! The point is that my mom totally trivialized my work when she said that!

Drew: okay but also

you should ask her out

Jamie: uh yeah, not doing that.

Felipe: Why not?

Jamie: remember the slowmance!!

Felipe: Hahahahaha, legendary, but Maya actually likes you! You know that, right?

Jamie: as a friend

Drew: uhhhh

Felipe: 😄

Jamie: what??

Felipe: Nothing. We just . . . did not get a friend vibe on Wednesday.

Um. WHAT?

I stare at the messages box, stunned. Not a friend vibe. And from Felipe too, who's way less likely to be joking.

Drew: dude, have you seen the way she looks at you?

Jamie: uh

Drew: okay, here's a question. When you're alone, does she touch your arm and stuff? Lean into you? things like that?

I think about Wednesday, when Maya was so upset about Sara. The way she collapsed into my arms and stayed there, and how she laced our fingers together when I grabbed her hand. But that doesn't count. She was upset. And I was comforting her!

But the way she kept drifting near me on the walk afterward was . . . kind of flirtatious, maybe? And the tiny couch she picked at Target yesterday was definitely built for physical contact. Unless that was unintentional. Probably unintentional. Definitely.

Felipe: She texts you a lot right??

Jamie: yeah

she actually called me yesterday

For eight hours and twenty-five minutes.

Drew: DUDE

like on the phone?

Jamie: well at first it was about a protest idea

Drew: uh, she could have texted that shit. She likes you

But she can't. There's no way. Unless—

Maybe? *Maybe?* I mean, Drew and Felipe are probably just trying to make me feel like less of a loser. But then again, they've always been brutally honest about my lack of game. So.

Maybe?

Felipe: Is she going to the bat mitzvah?

Drew: oooh good call

Jamie: I don't think so—haven't brought it up

with maya OR with my mom

Felipe: Well I think your mom just made it clear that she approves haha

You should invite her! see what she says

Jamie: I don't know

I can picture it. Maya wincing. Maya biting her lip. *Oh. Jamie, I don't want to give you the wrong impression. I really love us as friends.* Maya patting my arm. *I think you're a really great guy and everything, but . . .*

Drew: Don't overthink it!! just be casual.

Jamie: okay! Sheesh

Give me a minute

Maybe if I did it over text. Kept it really casual. I mean, it would make the bat mitzvah a million times more bearable having her there. After all, Felipe and Nolan have each other, and God knows Drew will be busy hitting on my cousin Rachel. And the thought of dancing with Maya, hanging out with her all night, maybe sneaking off somewhere to be alone—and if she *does* like me—NOT that she does.

Okay. No big deal. Gonna just—

Jamie: Hey, I meant to ask you

Do you want to come with me to Sophie's bat mitzvah?

WITH ME? With me with me with me with me. Seriously? Why am I like this?

Ellipses. Maya's typing. Okay.

God. Why did I say *with me*? Why?

Maya: Oh!

More ellipses.

Shit.

Okay, I can't do this.

Jamie: Was just thinking we could pass out flyers and stuff!

Cool. Just like Mom expressly forbade. Awesome. This is going *great*.

Maya: Are you sure? I don't want to mess up the numbers or anything!

Oh, right, the flyers!! That makes sense

Jamie: You wouldn't be messing up anything! You should come

Maya: Okay! That sounds awesome. Thanks, Jamie!!

I lean back in my chair, pressing my hands over my eyes, just breathing. Wow.

I mean, I did it!

Sort of.

Drew: did you ask her???

what did she say

Jamie: she said

Felipe: The suspense!!

Jamie: she said sounds awesome ☺

Drew: SHIT

Felipe: What did I tell you!!

Jamie: as friends though! Not a date.

Not a date. Definitely, definitely not a date.

Drew: we'll see 😉

CHAPTER TWENTY-TWO
MAYA

"Busy day?" my dad asks. He's making coffee and scrambling eggs. "You're up way too early for summer vacation."

"It's ten in the morning." I glance at the clock.

"At your age, I hibernated until lunchtime."

"I can't imagine you sleeping in. You're such a morning person."

"It's your fault." He takes a sip of coffee. "When you were a baby you woke up every morning at five. Screaming. As if there was some important meeting you urgently needed to be at. Ever since then, I get up at five and hit the gym. You sleep trained me pretty good."

"Sorry about that."

"Don't be! Look at these guns." He flexes his arms.

"You are ridiculous." I roll my eyes and laugh.

"Canvassing with Jamie today?"

"We're doing something different." I pull up the flyer Jamie and I designed and formatted. We were up late last night FaceTiming and figuring it all out.

My dad squints at the screen. "*Love, not hate. Say no to H.B. 28. . . . It takes thirty seconds to be a hero. Call your state senator today!*"

"The second part was me, the first part was Jamie."

"Wow, Maya. When your mom offered a car in exchange for canvassing, I figured you'd follow in your dad's footsteps and do the bare minimum to seal the deal, but you've gone above and beyond."

"Yeah." I shift in my seat. "It's not *just* about the car anymore. . . ."

"I'm proud of you, bug." He kisses my forehead.

My dad heads off to work, and I wander to my bedroom. Sitting on the edge of the bed, I reread the text from yesterday where Jamie invited me to Sophie's bat mitzvah. For a split second, I felt goose bumps. He asked if I wanted to go *with him* to the bat mitzvah. His plus-one. Which—we hang out all the time, but being an official date for his sister's bat mitzvah—what does that mean, exactly? I had no idea how I'd explain it to my mom (and way to go, Maya, for defining *all* hangouts as dating). But it's not a date. Jamie made that very clear.

So, dilemma solved.

Whatever it is, I'm excited about Sophie's bat mitzvah. I really like her, and plus I'll get to hear Jamie's toast in person. I spent the evening googling gift ideas for a bat mitzvah. Some people give money in multiples of eighteen because it symbolizes life—but it feels so impersonal to give cash. And then what to wear? I went to a few when I was twelve, but I'm sure fashion standards have changed. Also, according to my research, you can show up in jeans at some bat mitzvahs, and some have people wearing full ball gowns.

Jamie hands me my invitation when he picks me up that afternoon.

"An official invite!" I squeal, opening the envelope quickly. "Look at this." I trace my hands along the embossing. "It's so fancy, like a wedding card."

"My mom has no chill."

"So that means this will be a fancy event, right? I should dress up?"

"That's up to you," Jamie reassures me. "You can wear whatever you want."

"I'm not showing up in my pj's. Any guidance at all on what to wear?"

"I'm wearing a suit and tie, if that helps."

"Suit and tie isn't my aesthetic." I shoot him a look. "I just wanted some ideas. I don't want to show up looking completely ridiculous."

"You couldn't look ridiculous if you tried."

I meet his gaze, expecting a half grin, but he's looking at me with such utter sincerity, I suddenly feel shy.

"I printed out the flyers." He clears his throat. "They're at your feet."

I pull up the cardboard box. Opening it, my eyes widen.

"How many are in here?"

"Three hundred. To get us started."

"These are in full color! This must have cost a fortune."

"It's my house printer."

"Your mom was cool with that?"

"I figure all the unpaid labor for this bat mitzvah is worth at least a pack of ink cartridges."

I look at the freshly printed flyers. They looked nice on the computer, but holding them in my hands, it feels real.

"I can't wait to show these to Kevin. He'll love them."

"Yeah." Jamie glances at me. "My grandma was saying we might not be allowed to just hand them out at Target, though."

"Maybe most people can't, but we have inside connections." I grin.

Kevin is at customer service helping someone with a lamp when we walk in. He nods to us as he finishes up her return, and then waves us over.

"Hello, my dudes!" he exclaims. "Welcome to casa

Target. Returning that box?"

"Hey, Kev." I open the lid and hand him a flyer. "No. Actually, had a question for you. A favor. We want to hand these flyers out to get the word to customers about this bill. It's set to be passed after the election. But we want to squash the narrative they're trying to build before it gains steam."

Kevin reads it. He frowns.

"This is so messed up!" he says. "I've never even heard about it."

"Exactly!" I say. "That's why we need to get the word out."

"Definitely. This is straight-up racist."

"Thanks, Kevin." I feel a rush of relief. "We were thinking we could maybe park ourselves somewhere, by the patio section or the dorm room displays, and hand them out."

"Oh." He shakes his head. "Sorry, Maya. That's going to be a solid no."

"What do you mean? You said this bill is messed up."

"It is. I'll call this number on my next break. Who doesn't want to be a hero? But you can't campaign here. Customers want to buy their hand towels and head on to the next thing, you know?"

"It's not campaigning," I tell him. "It's handing out a flyer."

"Well, it sort of *is* campaigning when there are two sides you can take, and one side wants this policy, and one doesn't," Kevin says.

"Taking sides?" I repeat. "This is a fucking racist policy. There's only one side to take—the *right* side."

"Whoa." Kevin holds his hands up. "I'm on your side here. There's no need to raise your voice."

Raise my voice?

"That's the whole problem these days," he continues. "Everyone is in this constant state of outrage. How are you going to build bridges between both sides when everyone's so angry, they won't listen?"

"There's no two sides to this," Jamie says.

"You say that, my dude. But there *are*. That's why there's so much anger."

"Well, *Kevin*." I grit my teeth. "I'm sorry I'm not speaking to you politely. But I'm not sure how to be upbeat when the other *side* says your mere existence is a problem to be outlawed. First headwear. Then what? Where will it end? When will it be okay for me to raise my voice?"

"I wasn't thinking of all that, but—"

"Of course you weren't," I tell him. "None of it affects you. This world is set up for *you*—and the rest of us? We have to be *nice* while people tell us they'll arrest us for what we wear."

I grab the box of flyers and storm out. Jamie hurries to catch up.

"You okay?" he asks.

"He's unbelievable." I exhale. "Fine. Maybe handing out flyers there was a long shot, but the nerve of him. Both siding it?"

"I know," Jamie says. He puts an arm around me. I bite my lip to fight back tears.

"I can't believe I yelled at Kevin," I say softly.

"The way he looked at you, I don't think *Kevin* believed that someone yelled at Kevin."

I laugh a little at that. But it's true. There are a few people at school I could reasonably see myself getting into it with. Never Kevin.

Jamie's phone chimes. He glances down.

"My grandma," he says. "She's at that new restaurant that just opened up, Scavino's. The owner bought all the servers optional Rossum gear to wear for work until the special election. She wanted to do some Stories about it for Instagram and maybe a live thing too. . . ." He hesitates. "Want to come with?"

"Are you serious? I get to meet InstaGramm?"

"You met her before."

"Oh yeah." I flush. "Sorry about that."

"You can make it up to me by coming along." He grins. "These photo shoots can go on for a minute. I love my grandmother, but she gets into full diva mode. On the upside, though—" He points at our box of flyers. "She can sweet-talk people into doing anything. I bet she'll get those flyers up and around for us."

"I'm all in," I tell him.

Grandma's diva side shows up before Jamie exits the parking lot.

"Jamie, dear," she says through his phone's speaker. "I could use a good cup of herbal tea. Can you be a darling and pick up some chamomile? Bon Glaze carries the brand I like. And swing by the house for my red scarf? It'll really make the photo pop with the color and lighting they have here."

We load up with the necessary accessories and drink, and meet up with her at the restaurant parking lot.

"Maya, sweetie!" Grandma approaches me. Boomer trots alongside her.

"Hello . . ." I falter. Should I say Ms. Miller? Mrs. Miller? Grandma? Ruth? But before I can think too long, she's smooshed me into a huge hug.

"What an absolute pleasure to see you again. Jamie just goes on and on and on about you. He just—"

"Here's your tea, Grandma," Jamie interrupts.

"Look at this darling." Grandma kisses Jamie's cheek. "He's just wonderful, isn't he?"

"He really is." I smile at him. Jamie has turned a delightful shade of radish.

"Grandma, do you think we could put up the flyers here?" Jamie asks.

"Of course." His grandma nods. "They have the cutest little corkboard up on the wall with all sorts of resistance stuff. I'm sure they'd be thrilled."

"Do you want to start with some exterior shots of the building?" Jamie asks.

"First let's go in and interview Devon and Chris while the restaurant's a little quiet. They're the sweetest couple you've ever seen." Grandma clicks a few buttons on her phone and hands it to him. "And then after the video . . ."

She pauses. She's looking at something just over my shoulder.

"Grandma?" Jamie says.

"Hold my tea, sweetie." She thrusts the cup into my hand.

Before we can say another word, Grandma is marching past us, Boomer fast at her heels.

"Hey, you! Yes, you!" she shouts. "Think I don't know what you're doing?"

"What is going on?" I glance at Jamie. "Is this . . . is this part of the process or something?"

"No, definitely not . . ."

We turn around. And then we see.

Someone's on their knees in the parking lot. And next

282

to him on the ground is a stack of bumper stickers. Fifi stickers.

"I asked you a question," Jamie's grandma says loudly. "Just what do you think you're doing?"

The guy looks stunned for a moment, but recovers quickly. He holds a bumper sticker defiantly in his hands and smirks.

"You need to mind your own business, old lady."

Boomer growls. The smirk vanishes pretty quickly.

"Is that how you speak to people, Nicholas Jacob Wilson?" Grandma asks. At this, the boy startles. "Oh yes, I know who you are. Your grandmother is always showing off your photos at Jazzercise. She goes on and on about what a hardworking boy you are. Is this the kind of work you're doing? Vandalizing people's property?"

Nicholas stands up slowly.

"Wait," he says. "Listen. It's just a prank."

"Terrorizing people is a prank? Including my own family, for that matter. You have some nerve, young man. When your grandmother finds out . . ."

"No, please," he cries out. All the carefully manicured cool is gone. He looks like a ten-year-old, caught red-handed with a cookie before dinner. "Don't tell my grandma. Please."

"Give me one good reason why I wouldn't?"

He doesn't respond. His lower lip trembles. Is he about to cry?

"I just have one more semester till graduation," he says shakily. "Please. She'll cut me off."

Jamie's grandmother crosses her arms, but before she can say another word, he starts to cry. It starts off like a leaky trickle, but before I can even blink—he's sobbing. About how this will ruin everything. How no one can find out.

"Is this real life?" I whisper.

I glance over at Jamie for the first time.

He is holding Grandma's phone. He's . . .

"Are you recording this??"

Jamie's jaw is tight.

"Instagram Live just got a whole lot more interesting," he says.

CHAPTER TWENTY-THREE
JAMIE

Stepping into the campaign office on Sunday is like stepping into an alternate universe. For a moment, Maya and I just stand frozen in the doorway, gobsmacked. Gabe had mentioned we should come in through the front of the bookstore today. But I didn't realize that was because we'd now *taken over* the front of the bookstore. And the back. And the extra event space near the side window.

"Seriously, where did all these people come from?" Maya whispers.

I peer around the room—which is so packed with earnest-looking college kids, you'd think this was an Apple Store. I spot Hannah near a display of scented candles, brandishing her phone for a large huddle of volunteers. Meanwhile, Alison the intern is sorting through printed address lists, looking frantic. But for all the bustle and chaos, there's this thrum of hopefulness in the air. I pause, taking it all in— the buzzing conversation, people clustered between rows of bookshelves, the ABBA album blaring in the background. I haven't felt this sort of electricity since Jordan Rossum himself burst into the iftar.

"I think there are more than forty people here," Maya says, sounding awed. "Remember when half the volunteers were related to either Gabe or Hannah?"

I laugh. "To be fair, Hannah's mom works for the Democratic Party."

"But still." Maya grins.

Gabe pops his head out of the annex, and his whole face lights up when he sees us. The next thing I know, he's springing toward us like an excited puppy. "The heroes of the hour!" He hugs me, and then Maya. "Listen. You two? Are game changers." He whirls around to beckon over a few nearby volunteers. "Guys, this is my little cousin Jamie and his best bro, Maya!"

Best bro. Bro? I mean, after dealing with Mom and the guys, I guess it's a relief that someone out there doesn't assume Maya and I are dating. Not that I mind the assumption. I just mind the idea of all those conversations leaking back to Maya. But then again . . . *bro*? How should I interpret that? Drew and Felipe saw some kind of vibe between us, but now I wonder if that's even real. Because if Gabe thinks we're *bros*—

"—the ones who filmed the Instagram Live and exposed the fuck out of that troll," Gabe declares.

"Oh. Wow!" says one of the volunteers, an East Asian girl in a Rossum shirt. "That was amazing. It has over a million views now, right?"

I blush. "It was all Grandma—"

Gabe thumps my back. "Give yourself some credit, Big J. Remember, if it's not on film, it didn't happen. You two are the reason for all of this." He gestures broadly around the room. "You know, we've had a threefold increase in volunteer turnout since the Fifi video went live?"

Maya's eyebrows shoot up. "Really? Wow—"

"Bustle, Mashable, BuzzFeed, Upworthy." Gabe counts them off on his fingers. "The *AJC* piece goes live tomorrow, and we've got Hannah's write-up in the *North Fulton Neighbor*. *Pod Save America* wants to interview Grandma. What did I tell you about building a narrative? Now you've got Newton, the official candidate of sniveling racists. But if you'd rather have a sweet little Nazi-crushing grandma? Booyah! Welcome to Team Rossum. We're going viral, baby!"

We all laugh, and Gabe pantomimes a mic dropping— for himself. But I can't even muster up a proper eye roll.

It's almost like . . . Gabe is actually making sense, for once. I mean, it feels funny to be happy about anything related to Fifi, but I can't deny the palpable energy in the room today. And for a local election? The tiny satellite office? It's nothing short of incredible.

Gabe turns to Maya and me. "Let me get the new guys started really quick. You two, don't go anywhere. Grandma's on her way, and we'll start filming as soon as we clear everyone else out. It's gonna be so hype. Reclaiming Fifi from the dark side!" He fist-bumps each of us.

Maya watches Gabe herd his group of volunteers toward the back room. "Wow. I can't believe he actually did it. He managed to go viral."

"Right? It's pretty wild," I say. "Plus, the ACLU just did an email blast asking its members to donate and canvass. The campaign has pulled in more donation money in the last twenty-four hours than all of this year, total. And Hannah said the Georgia Democratic Party is planning to fund a whole TV ad campaign!"

"Holy shit. Rossum may actually have a shot."

"He really might." I glimpse Alison, balancing a stack of folders almost higher than her head.

As soon as the volunteers file out, Hannah makes her way toward us. "Hey! Glad I caught you guys before your video thing." She clasps her hands. "So, my mom's organizing volunteers to be poll observers on election day. Can I sign you two up for a shift? It's pretty chill, and the training is super simple. You basically just hang around the polling place and make sure nothing shady happens."

"Oh," I say. I glance sideways at Maya, who smiles and shrugs.

"Sounds good to me," Maya says. "Maybe we can get a slot together."

"Definitely."

"Awesome!" Hannah says. "Adding you to my list. Election Protection Squad for the win." She high-fives both of us. "Thank you guys so much, seriously. For everything."

Maya and I exchange grins, and I'm basically a human hot air balloon. Warm and buoyant and bright. I mean, our video actually changed the course of the campaign. It did that. *We* did that. And if we changed the course of the campaign, maybe we'll change the outcome of the election.

Which would change history. Just a little slice of it, but still.

Not to mention the full-circle perfection of spending election day with Maya. It's honestly hard to believe I ever stepped foot in this office without her. Or that I used to dread coming here. I mean, my stomach would drop every time I pulled into the parking lot. I'd have to brace myself for small talk, even just with Hannah and Alison. And then there was Gabe, forever wanting more. Make more phone calls. Knock on more doors. Be less Jamie.

Everything's different now.

Yeah, Gabe is still all kinds of annoying, and the campaign's a haphazard mess. There's still small talk. I'm still awful at it.

But when Maya's here, every bit of it feels like home.

Half an hour later, Grandma's completely taken over. "Gabe, sweetheart, can you push that desk right in front of the backdrop? Good. And a few inches to the left. Thank you, lovey. Oh, I wish we had natural light in here." She unfolds her tripod, planting it a few feet in front of Hannah's now-pristine desk. With a sheet of heavy white fabric hanging behind it, it looks a little like the makeshift doll photography studio Sophie made in our basement at age nine. But when Grandma lets me peek at the setup through her phone screen, it looks surprisingly professional—a noticeable level up from the usual Rossum campaign content.

"You guys made a script, right?" Gabe asks as soon as we're settled in behind the desk. He props up a slightly enlarged card stock picture of Fifi between us, and I try not to look too closely at it. "But don't feel like you can't ad-lib. I want this to feel fun, spontaneous, hip—you feel me?" He does jazz hands.

Maya's eyes widen. "Okay."

"Just make sure you hit all the beats we talked about.

And don't forget to tie it back to Rossum. Let's keep that Fifi momentum going. We need people to be fired up."

"Just have fun with it." Grandma smiles from behind the tripod. "This is just the cutest idea ever. I love that you two thought of it."

"Right?" Gabe says. "The more Fifi, the better."

"That's . . . not exactly our message," Maya says.

"Just make sure you mention Rossum. And smile!" Gabe walks backward, tapping the corners of his mouth with his fingertips.

"Jamie, dear, move a little closer to Maya. Great. Now, try to project your voices as much as you can." Grandma peers at us through her phone camera. "And remember, we can go back and edit later, so don't worry if you need to repeat something—"

"But keep in mind," Gabe interjects, "the fewer mistakes, the less time we have to spend editing, and the sooner we can get this up."

"We'll be fine." Grandma pats Gabe's shoulder. "So we'll start with our intro, but let's pause for a second before moving on to the washi tape. Gabe will keep filming straight on, and Maya, I'll come around and zoom in over your shoulder. Sound good?"

I nod.

"Works for me," Maya says.

"Great!" Grandma smiles. "I'll count down with my fingers."

She holds up three, and then two, and then one—and we're off.

By five, Maya and I are tucked into our new favorite Target patio chair—the egg-shaped wicker love seat Maya once said was too small for two. I guess it's big enough now.

Maya's scrolling through the latest batch of polling data on her phone. I still can't believe she gets Wi-Fi here.

"Everything's still favoring Newton." She puffs her cheeks out and sighs.

"But look. This poll's from the twenty-eighth. That's before Nicholas Wilson went viral. Maybe that will be the turning point?"

"Yeah, maybe." She taps into Instagram, and her whole face brightens. "Hey, our video's live!"

"On the Rossum page or Grandma's?"

"Both. And apparently YouTube too." She scoots closer, tilting her phone toward me. For a minute, I can hardly speak, or even breathe. Every single inch of my left side is pressed against Maya's right.

"I'm scared to watch," says Maya. "I love the caption, though. Fifi Gets Flipped!"

"Grandma does love a good hashtag."

Maya grins. "You ready?" I nod, and she presses play.

A title screen flashes: *Fifi Gets Flipped.*

Video Maya smiles. *"Hi, I'm Maya."*

"And I'm Jamie."

"I sound so nervous," I murmur.

Maya hugs me sideways. "You sound great."

"—when you get Fifi'd," Video Maya is saying. Then Fifi's face flashes across the screen, accompanied by Halloween music.

Maya laughs. "Wow."

"For those who don't know," Video Me explains, *"Fifi is a meme popularized online in white supremacist, alt-right circles."*

Video Maya chimes in. *"But recently, local trolls have taken Fifi offline and onto the streets of Brookhaven and Sandy Springs."*

The screen cuts to a montage of Fifi stickers on cars, including Alfie—culminating in a clip of Grandma bearing down on Nicholas Wilson in the Scavino's parking lot.

Video Me nods solemnly. *"Our team of grandmas is working day and night to keep our streets Fifi-free—"*

"But just in case, we have a little hack to flip your Fifi nightmare into a resistance icon. Jamie, the washi tape." Video Maya removes the Fifi picture from its display. *"Let's start with the teacup. If you look closely, you'll see we've got an 88 here on the cup, and Fifi's holding the cup with an okay sign. Yikes. These are both major anti-Semitic dog whistles."*

I lean toward Maya. "We missed the chance for a good

dog pun here, didn't we?"

Maya rolls her eyes, smiling.

"*But with a few strategically placed strips of rainbow washi tape . . .*"

"I can't believe Mom's washi tape obsession came in so handy," I say.

The camera zooms in on a time-lapse demonstration of our hands covering the entire teacup with rainbow tape.

"*Fifi could look cool wearing a pink pussy hat, don't you think?*" says Video Me.

"*I most certainly do,*" agrees Video Maya—followed by another hyper-speed washi tape montage. "*And there you have it. Objective proof that cats are better than dogs.*"

Video Me shoots Maya a quick but obvious side-eye.

"Oh my God, Jamie. Your face there." Maya beams at me. "This video actually turned out really cute!"

I look at Maya on-screen. "Yeah."

"*—but remember,*" Video Maya is saying. "*The very best way to flip Fifi? Donate. Canvass. And most importantly, show up and vote for Jordan Rossum on July ninth.*"

Video Me turns to Maya and smiles. "*Jordan Rossum, for Georgia state senate, District Forty. Vote for Rossum, he's awesome!*" A Rossum campaign logo flashes, and then the video starts to replay.

I look at Maya. "That wasn't so bad, right?"

"Not at all! We did great." She leans forward, scrolling down. "Whoa, there are already more than four hundred views."

I peer at the screen over her shoulder. "And almost a hundred comments!"

"Don't read them," Maya says quickly.

I laugh. "What?"

"Cardinal rule of the internet, right? Never read the comments."

"You're not curious to know what they say?"

"Of course I'm curious," Maya says. "But trust me, it's not worth it. One shitty comment can ruin your whole mood like *that*."

"Do you think they're mostly bad?" I glance at Maya's screen, where the video's still auto-replaying.

"Not *mostly*, unless the trolls find it. But there's going to be at least a little bit of hate. Maybe not directed toward you, but definitely toward me—"

"No way. You're a total pro. Look!"

"Doesn't matter. It's called being a woman on the internet, *especially* a brown woman. And my brain just fixates for days on the bad ones."

"Oh." I frown. "Sorry. That really sucks."

"It is what it is." She shrugs.

I pause. "Want me to read you some of the good ones out

loud? Just so you can hear the nice stuff, without having to risk stumbling on any trolls?"

"Oh. Actually, yeah!" Maya nods. "I would love that."

"Okay! Let's see." I scroll down. "Lots of heart emojis, a few people saying *yassssss* . . . all right, here's one! Someone named Jacq with a *q* says: *this is such a cute, smart idea, I love it!*"

"Aww, thanks, Jacq with a *q*." Maya smiles.

"And someone named Granibella and a bunch of numbers says: *Rossum is awesome and so are Maya and Jamie!* And she put the hashtag! *FifiGetsFlipped*." I keep scrolling. "Okay, and Nancy Shapiro says . . . ohhhh. Wow."

Maya leans in. "What?"

"She says: *So proud of my grandson Jordan Isaac Rossum, vote for Rossum!!! Love, Grandma.*"

"That's his grandma?" Maya presses her heart. "That is so insanely cute."

"What can I say? Jewish grandmas are the best." I scroll further. "Okay, here's a good one: *lmao Jamie's side-eye is a MOOD.*"

"No kidding."

"And let's see. A bunch of people say they're voting for Rossum. And then someone named Anna with, like, fifty *n*'s says: *LOL Jamie's face when Maya mentioned cats.*"

Maya laughs. "Told you! That face was my favorite part of the whole video." She leans back, gazing contentedly at the chair's domed wicker roof. "Oh my God—did you see all the cat versus dog merch at Fawkes and Horntail? They had bag clips, they had socks . . ."

I nod distractedly, my eyes drifting back down to the comments section.

"Jamie, the washi tape" LOLOL

Find someone who looks at you the way Jamie looks at Maya at the 00:56 mark 😍

My cheeks flood with heat. You know what would be awesome right now? A trapdoor. To another dimension. Wow, Jamie. Good thing you're so subtle about liking Maya. It's not like total strangers can read it all over your face.

And the comment itself. No joke: if Maya read that, I'd die. I might actually die.

CHAPTER TWENTY-FOUR
MAYA

Jamie was wrong. Helping Grandma out with photo shoots isn't annoying. It's the absolute best.

We finished up a quick session with her and Boomer at a newly renovated park, and now we're working our way through all the shops in Town Brookhaven to drop off our H.B. 28 flyers. People light up when they see her. Everyone she asks gives us an enthusiastic yes.

Carmen's Cupcakes is no exception.

"Hello, dear, my name is Ruth Mill—" Grandma begins when she approaches the woman behind the register.

"I know who you are!" The woman hurries over to us. "You're InstaGramm!"

She's staring at Jamie's grandmother like Meryl Streep

herself swept in. Then she glances over at me and Jamie. Her eyes widen.

"Is that Jamie and Maya?"

I glance at Jamie. He looks as surprised as I do.

"I saw your video," she says. "The one about fixing the Fifi bumper stickers? I haven't gotten trolled, *thank God*, but I sent it to two of my friends who were hit. They loved you guys *so much*. Fifi gets flipped!" She pumps her fists.

"Fifi gets flipped," I manage to say. "I'm glad it was helpful."

It's *really* weird to be recognized. Is this what it's like for Jamie's grandma on a daily basis? Just like all the other shop owners, Carmen doesn't blink before agreeing to let us put out our flyers. She even promises to stick one on the front door, so everyone can see it when they come in.

"I was going to reach out to you," Carmen tells Jamie's grandma. "Scavino's resistance efforts really inspired me. I'm planning to hand out free coffee to anyone who comes in on election day with an 'I voted' sticker."

"That's wonderful!" Grandma exclaims. "Would you mind if I shared that information with my little online community? They'd be really appreciative."

Judging by Carmen's response, you'd think Grandma invited her to party on the moon. Carmen is a definite yes to the shout-out.

Grandma quickly switches into work mode. After taking approximately thirty minutes to decide which cupcake will complement the color scheme of the shop (strawberry cream), she's scoping out the store to find the perfect spot to set up the shot.

Okay, so maybe Jamie's right. She can be a bit extra.

I glance at the clock. We promised Hannah we'd come a little early for the canvassing session to drop off water bottles. I hope we won't be late.

"Maya dear, would you be interested in posing with me for this photo?" Jamie's grandmother asks. "I was thinking you could be on one side with a cupcake, and Jamie can be on my other side with a coffee cup."

"I'd love to!" I say.

Jamie and I stand on either side of Grandma.

"Cheese!" Carmen shouts out, and takes several photos.

Jamie's phone starts ringing mid-shoot. As soon as we're done, he pulls it out.

"Mom," he groans. "Be right back."

"By the way," I tell Grandma as she walks over to the table and picks up her purse, "thank you so much for following me. I nearly passed out when I saw the request on Instagram. I was going through a rough time, and it made me feel so much better."

"Hmm?" Grandma glances up at this and studies me for a second. She smiles. "You're an absolute sweetheart—you know that, right? And you've been so good to my Jamie. *For* Jamie. He's always been an easygoing kid, but he can really fall inside his head sometimes. Ever since you have been spending all this time together, he's just—"

"I'm back!" Jamie hurries over to us. "What'd I miss?"

"Your grandmother was just telling me how awesome I am, and how lucky you are that I'm your friend."

"That's right." Grandma laughs and pinches Jamie's cheek. He's crimson. It's so fun to make Jamie blush. It's almost a full-time hobby at this point.

"Almost a million and a half views on the Nicholas Wilson Fifi video," I tell them. We're in the car and on our way to the campaign headquarters.

"There were just over a million last night," Grandma says. "It's really catching on."

"Thanks to yours truly!" Jamie says.

"I'm glad it's started a conversation about trolling, but I'm not condoning this." Grandma shoots him a look. "You shouldn't use my account or post things without first informing me."

"But he did deserve it," I add from the backseat.

"Well, yes, that he did." Jamie's grandma smiles.

My phone blinks. A text from Shelby.

Just saw the video with you! You're so amazing! 😍

I feel a jolt of surprise—even though I shouldn't. The

video's up now, so of course people from school might have seen it.

Maya: Thanks so much!

Shelby: A few of us are going to the mall on Thursday. Let me know if you want to come too. It's been forever!

Maya: Oh, yeah. I'll check and get back to you!

She sends me kiss emojis, and I send her smiling ones back, and then I click over and scroll to our video. It has nowhere near a million hits, but seventy-five thousand views aren't bad. About five thousand percent more engagement than anything *I've* ever posted.

I click the hashtag, #FifiGetsFlipped.

"You won't believe this!" I exclaim. "Someone's made a CafePress shop with the Fifi hashtag! They have T-shirts, and mugs, and they even designed a sticker with Fifi wearing a rainbow hat and holding up a Rossum sign! All proceeds support the campaign."

"You see?" His grandma glances back at me and smiles. "Didn't I say a video was the best way to go about these things?"

"Yes. Grandma. You were right," Jamie replies.

"'Grandma, you were right' is quite possibly the best sentence in the English language," she says.

We pull into the canvassing office. There are even more cars than yesterday in the parking lot—we end up having to park by the acupuncturist next door. Stepping into the bookshop, we realize there are way more people too. Yesterday, the campaign had to move into the actual bookstore space; today they're practically filling it.

"Seventy people." I count again, just to be sure.

"Hey, you two!" A woman in athleisure wear and a ponytail walks over to us. "Your video was the cutest," she says. "And what he did to that poor sweet dog." She shakes her head. "I shared it with all the parents in the Ashford Park PTA—we figured if teenagers can wake up early in the summer to canvass, we can too."

After she leaves, Jamie leans in and whispers, "That's one more for Team Dog!"

"She just didn't want the dog to be racist! There's a difference!"

Before we can continue our debate, Gabe hurries over to us, coffee splashing out of his mug.

"Hey, guys! Check out this crowd."

"That's really great, Gabe," I say.

"You guys are two for two with viral Fifi videos." His eyes sparkle. "Nicholas Wilson is the gift that keeps on giving!"

Jamie and I glance at each other and sigh. Gabe.

"By the way, I need to ask you guys for a favor," says Gabe.

"What kind of favor?"

"Just a quick talk to the crowd. Nothing big."

"No way," Jamie says firmly. "Not ever."

"Great! You'll do awesome!" Gabe says. Before we can say anything more, he's hopped over to the front of the room and grabbed a microphone.

He starts off with the patented canvassing talk, thanking everyone for coming and explaining the packets.

"What does he want us to talk to them about?" Jamie whispers. He's flushed.

"Let's just leave," I whisper. "He can't ask us up if we're not here."

But before we can move, Gabe is pointing to us.

"Today, I'm passing the mic to Maya and Jamie—our canvassing experts—to share with you some of the dos and don'ts of knocking on doors."

I glance at Jamie. His color has shifted from red to green. I'm ninety percent convinced he's going to puke right now.

"Come on over, kids," Gabe says to us. "These two are our rockstar canvassers! They'll share their experiences, especially for any first-timers, as you prepare to hit the road."

"I am going to strangle Gabe," I mutter to Jamie.

But then I glance at the faces looking over at us. The college students fanning themselves with flyers. The moms with strollers. The senior citizens in velour jogging suits. Three women in hijab in the front row. I think of the man with the blue swordfish T-shirt I met on my second day canvassing. The way I froze up. The way I couldn't move.

"We got this," I tell Jamie. "We can do this."

I grab his hand, and together we walk up to the front of the room.

Everyone claps as I take the microphone. The crowd looks way larger standing from this angle. Gabe is in the back taking photos of us with his phone. I clear my throat and glance at Jamie. Judging from his expression, I'm definitely going to have to be the one who speaks first.

"Thank you so much for coming," I tell the crowd, trying my best not to let my nerves show. "As Gabe, um, just mentioned, we've done a bit of canvassing, and there are definitely some things I wish we'd known."

One of the women in hijab smiles at me and nods. I smile back at her. And then I begin to share.

Do knock on the door and give it a few beats before knocking again.

Don't knock more than twice; stick a flyer in and move on.

Do stick a flyer in the door or through the handle.

Don't put it in the mailbox. There's some sort of law against that.

"And hydrate," I tell everyone. "It's hot out there. And be careful of eating greasy or oily foods that can make you sluggish in the heat." I glance at Jamie and wink. "Like donuts."

Jamie straightens a bit at this.

"But Goldfish," I reassure the crowd, "are completely acceptable."

Jamie's looking less green. He's smiling.

"I have one." He edges closer to me. I hand him the mic.

"If you get tired while you're going, just stop," he tells people. "You've been assigned quite a few houses, and no one *reasonable* expects you to be able to hit them all."

"And if someone makes you uncomfortable—leave," I tell them. "You do not have to give them a flyer or any of your time. Trust your gut and go."

We offer a few more tips. Some people have questions. About footwear and knocking versus ringing doorbells. I'm stunned to realize we can comfortably answer all of them.

When we're finished, everyone claps.

"That wasn't so bad," Jamie says, once Hannah takes the stand to explain how to work the app. "Once you went after donuts, I realized I *had* to start talking."

"And did you see them clapping for us? I don't think anyone's ever clapped after Gabe spoke."

"Rolling their eyes, definitely, but not clapping. Never."

"I'm still going to strangle Gabe, though," I say.

"Oh, totally." He nods.

My phone buzzes. Glancing down, I blink. I have over one hundred notifications. Ever since our video about fixing the Fifi stickers got posted, I've been inundated with follow requests from people I don't even know.

"Terrific talk." A man approaches us. "You laid it out all so easily. And great to see you both in person. Fifi gets flipped!" He pumps his fists.

"Fifi gets flipped." We smile. It was one thing to say it in a room with just us and Jamie's grandma, but people listened. They cared. They showed up.

"I didn't know until your video that anyone was canvassing for this election," he continues. "Not a single person has come by my neighborhood."

"Where do you live?" Jamie asks.

"Hampton Hall. We've got hundreds of homes. Most of us are Democrats, but this election is more about letting people know it's happening in the first place."

"Let's see if it's on the canvassing list." I turn to Jamie. "If it isn't, we could just pop over. I mean, every vote counts."

"Hey, y'all!" Hannah interrupts us. "Can I speak with you both for a second?"

We excuse ourselves and turn to Hannah.

"The water bottles!" Jamie exclaims. "They're in the trunk. I totally forgot."

"No, it's not that." Hannah shakes her head. "Well, first thing, you guys were *amazing* up there. Old pros!"

"Thanks." Jamie is blushing again. But in the best possible way.

"And as old pros"—Hannah crosses her arms—"you know you have to stick to the canvassing road map, right? You can't go rogue like I just heard you both talking about."

"Rogue? It's knocking on doors," I reply. "His neighborhood has hundreds of homes, and they haven't been canvassed."

"I'm sure they're on our list."

"Can we check really quick?" I ask. "If they're not on there, we can just swing by."

"If the homes are not in the packets, we don't canvass them," says Hannah. "We have a system in place for a reason."

"If we just do a few neighborhoods on our own time, what's the harm?" Jamie asks.

"No," Hannah says firmly. "I'm sorry, but if you're going to be Rossum volunteers, you have to play by the Rossum rules."

The enthusiasm from moments earlier vanishes.

"I'm sorry," she says gently. "You both really are rockstars—but we don't want to risk affecting anything negatively by accident."

I watch Hannah walk over to another canvasser.

"That makes no sense," murmurs Jamie. "What's the

harm in knocking on a few extra doors?"

"Apparently it's against the rules to let Democrats know an election's coming up."

I grab our packet and walk out the side door. Kevin. Now Hannah. They're on our side—supposedly—but they have a funny way of showing it.

CHAPTER TWENTY-FIVE
JAMIE

I can't stop reading the comments.

I know I'm breaking the cardinal rule of the internet. But it's been three days since the Fifi Gets Flipped video, and the replies haven't stopped coming. And there's a whole new crop of them on the Carmen's Cupcakes picture, plus a new one Gabe posted on Grandma's account from our Canvassing 101 talk. It's kind of wild to see Rossum posts getting this much engagement. They used to get only a few hundred likes each, and even that was only when Grandma cross-posted them to InstaGramm. But the Nicholas Wilson video made everything explode.

Of course, it's not just the number of comments that's new. It's the fact that they're about Maya and me.

I ship these two so hard!!!!

Rossum should officiate their wedding lol

Aww I love this!!!! Definitely voting for Rossum, and thanks for the tips!

wow they want to kisssssssss

JAMIE, THE WASHI TAPE 😂 *I stan only Maya*

more maya and jamie content please!!!

I guess they're not *that* bad. Definitely a little creepy. But at least they haven't mentioned the way I looked at Maya at the end of that video. At least these new ones imply some kind of reciprocal interest, which is . . .

Well, for one thing, it's way less embarrassing.

And I guess I wouldn't mind knowing what makes people think Maya and I want to kisssssssssss. For research purposes. Obviously.

After all, if everyone sees it, maybe there really is something to see?

I tap into the nested comments under *I ship these two so hard!!!!* There are fifty-eight of them. Fifty-eight people weighing in on the issue with crying emojis and heart eyes and exclamation points. It makes my head spin.

"Jamie, it's starting!" Maya plops down beside me on my living room couch. Closer than usual. *Way* closer than usual. "You're so glued to your phone today."

I tap out of Instagram fast, shoving my phone in my pocket as *The Office*'s intro music rises. We've been working our way through the end of season two since we got back from canvassing this afternoon.

"'Conflict Resolution.' I'm so ready." Maya presses my arm.

So here's the thing. I don't want to read too much into a bunch of Instagram comments from strangers. But maybe it's not just that. After all, there were two drawn-out Maya hugs today during canvassing, not to mention a double high five after our first voter commitment. And not just any double high five. It was a lingering, finger-lacing double high five. Plus, ever since we got back to my place, there's been the sitting-with-no-space-between-us-on-the-couch thing . . . and now the arm press! That has to be a deliberate flirtatious gesture, right? So maybe the comments are right. Or maybe Maya's secretly reading them, and they're making her braver.

I think they're making *me* a little braver.

Maya's glued to the episode, and I'm doing my best to match her focus. Concentrating on *The Office* isn't usually a problem for me. But I can't stop thinking about the way Maya's thigh brushed against mine when she tucked her knees up onto the couch. On screen, Jim recounts all the pranks he's played on Dwight, and Maya winces.

"I have such mixed feelings," she says. "Like. On one hand, it's a *lot*. And some of the stuff he did to Dwight was pretty mean. I don't think it was harassment, per se, but was it punching down? I don't know." She leans in closer to me.

"But then again, it's *Jim*."

I sneak a peek at her face. "You're so starry-eyed right now."

Also, she's sitting. So. Close.

She sighs. "How could anyone *not* be starry-eyed over Jim? He's like Mr. Darcy from *Pride and Prejudice*. Universally swoon-worthy."

"What's so great about Jim?"

"Everything! He's just so cute. It's his confidence," Maya says, "and his sense of humor. He's so comfortable in his skin."

My stomach sinks.

Jim's literally nothing like me.

"I can't believe we're about to watch 'Casino Night.' This is the most romantic episode of any show on television, ever."

The most romantic episode of any show.

Most romantic.

I swear, sometimes I don't even know if Maya hears the things she says.

The episode starts, and I can't shake the feeling that something's shifted. Like the entire room is holding its breath.

"I always forget about Michael's two dates," Maya says, reaching for my hand. "I can barely watch this part. He's so cringy!"

So that's happening. Yup. Maya's holding my hand, and

not because either of us are upset. We are literally sitting here. Right now. Holding TV and watching hands.

Watching TV.

And holding hands.

I think my brain is short-circuiting.

She drops my hand, leaning forward, and suddenly she's a million miles away. Fully absorbed in the television. Probably doesn't even remember I'm back here.

But when Jim and Pam exchange smiles playing poker, Maya leans back abruptly. "The way they look at each other!"

The way they look at each other. It's just like the Instagram comment. The way I look at Maya. And how people seem to be rooting for us, in the same way Maya roots for Jim and Pam.

"God, Roy's so bad for her." Maya shakes her head. "Good riddance."

By the time Jim approaches Pam outside, I'm watching Maya more than I'm watching the screen. When Jim opens his mouth to speak, Maya makes a noise so high-pitched, it wakes up Boomer.

"Was that a squeak?"

"Shh." She swipes my arm, smiling.

"It was cute!"

She wrinkles her nose at me, then turns back to the screen. "Oh my God, he's about to do it." She presses her hands to her cheeks.

On screen, Jim tells Pam he's in love with her. Maya leans her head on my shoulder, sighing.

Her head.

On my shoulder. During a love confession. I'm just—

Okay, but how am I supposed to read this? Is this a friend thing? Is this what friends do? I've never had a close female friend before.

Her head's still on my shoulder, even though I'm the king of awkward, with my arm just hanging down stiffly.

God. Speaking of stiff—

I adjust the blankets, blushing furiously. Think of Asa Newton. Think of Ian Holden. Jennifer Dickers. Fifi. Fifi's humanoid hands—

Crisis averted.

Except Maya's head on my shoulder is a different sort of crisis entirely. My heart's hammering all around in my chest. I don't know what to do next. Should I put my arm around her? Is that what you do when someone puts her head on your shoulder during a love confession?

When the girl you're in love with puts her head on your shoulder.

During a love confession.

Everything's stopped working. My brain my heart my lungs. Have stopped working. I can't do this. I'm not a guy who can do this.

But.

I tuck my arm around Maya's shoulder.

And without missing a beat, she curls up closer to me. On screen, Pam sneaks into the office to call her mom. Maya's completely transfixed, biting her lip, hair falling loosely past her shoulders. So close to my hand.

Of course Maya has the softest hair in the world.

I run my fingers through it, tentatively. And then again, letting it thread between the tips of my fingers. And again.

She turns to look at me, smiling almost quizzically. And I lose my breath. I just.

Stop.

Breathing.

But she just turns back to the TV, nestling deeper into the crook of my arm.

I don't think I've ever been this completely, nonsensically happy in my whole entire life.

Of course, we've barely made it through the credits when Mom, Sophie, and Grandma burst in, talking a mile a minute about dress alterations. Maya lifts her head dazedly when they reach the living room. Mom raises her eyebrows, making me blush to my feet, but at least she and Grandma keep it moving.

Sophie, on the other hand, flings herself dramatically backward onto the love seat.

"I haaaaaaate going to the alterations place. Mom and Grandma are so embarrassing. I'm like, great, fine, it's perfect, but Grandma's like, let's try pinching it under the arm more. Grandma, let your armpits live! That should have taken five minutes, tops, but *no*."

Maya straightens. "Ooh. So you're wearing something custom-made?"

"No, it's from Nordstrom." Sophie rolls her eyes. "They're just obsessed with everything fitting exactly perfectly. Whereas I'm like, okay, can I zip it? And does it not fall off? Great. We're done here."

I lean toward Maya. "Don't let her convince you she's so chill about this. She tried on twelve dresses—"

"Uh, that's not a lot. Andrea tried on fifty-four dresses." Sophie smiles brightly at Maya. "I'm so glad you're coming, by the way!"

"Yes! I can't wait. Thank you so much for letting me crash it."

Sophie narrows her eyes. "Are you kidding? Pretty sure my brother's—"

I give her a death glare. If Sophie says *girlfriend*, I swear to God . . .

"—best friend is VIP material." Sophie shoots me a tiny smile.

Best friend. At first, Maya looks almost startled by the phrase, but then she turns to me and grins.

Kind of hard to know what to make of that. I mean, at this point, she really is my best friend. No question. But also . . . is that how Maya sees us? A pair of really touchy-feely best friends?

"Okay, Sophie, Jamie's no help," Maya says. "I need your advice about what to wear. It's kind of fancy, right?"

"Medium fancy. It's semiformal."

"Right." Maya furrows her brow. "So . . . not a ball gown, but not like a sundress, right? Should I wear a long dress to be safe?"

"Safe from what?" I ask.

"Oh God, you don't have to wear a long dress," says Sophie. "I mean, you can. But I'm not. Hold on. I can poll the squad." She pulls out her phone.

"Okay, thanks!" says Maya. "And for the service, I should go pretty conservative, right?"

"Yup, conservative," I say. "The goal is to dress as much like a Republican senator as possible—"

"Shut up." Maya covers my mouth. "Cardigan and skirt, right?"

"That works!" Sophie checks her phone. "Okay, FYI, everyone's wearing short dresses. And Jamie, Maddie wants me to tell you she'll see you at the bat mitzvah."

"Um. Okay."

Maya raises her eyebrows. "Sounds like Maddie has a crush."

"I think she's into some guy at the mall," I say.

Sophie rolls her eyes. "Ugh, no. That's Tessa. Did I tell you they're dating now?"

"Isn't he a lot older?"

"He's like a year and a half older, so not really, but . . . he's also kind of really skeevy?" Sophie wrinkles her nose.

"I can't believe you guys are already dating," says Maya.

"Well, I'm not." Sophie grimaces. "That's all Tessa."

"Weren't you actively trying to make this happen?" I turn to Maya. "She made me drive her to the mall, acted like it was this big emergency, all so she could be a wing-woman, and now—"

"It's called being a decent friend," says Sophie. "But I didn't actually think Tessa would be able to seal the deal. He's fifteen!"

"So your friends are all into older guys, huh," says Maya.

"Her friends are out of control." I shake my head slowly. "Now you know why I'm terrified of giving this toast."

When I get back from driving Maya home, Mom's parked on the living room couch, waiting for me. "Hey! Can we talk?"

I narrow my eyes. "Okay . . ."

"Don't look so scared." She pats the couch, beckoning for me to sit. "Just wanted to see how you were doing."

Translation: she saw me on the couch with Maya, and is now planning to make the next half hour of my life as excruciatingly awkward as possible. Pretty sure this is going to end with Mom saying the word *condom*. Can't wait to hit this exciting new low point.

I settle in cross-legged at the opposite end of the couch. "I'm good."

Mom doesn't say anything. She just looks at me with this gentle, searching expression. Which—wow—may actually be even worse than talking about condoms.

I rush to fill the silence. "Everything's good. The campaign is going really well. They've had at least three dozen volunteers every day this week. Maya and I did a shift in Dunwoody. It was good—"

"Great!" Mom says.

"Great," I repeat.

God. Why? Why are we doing this?

"I'm so glad you're having fun with this," Mom says, "and I really am so proud of you, Jamie. Canvassing a handful of times—that alone is incredible, but to have sustained that effort for so long now . . ."

"If we get Rossum elected, it's worth it."

"Right." Mom pauses. "Okay, here's the thing."

"Uh-oh."

"Nothing bad! You're not doing anything wrong, sweetie." She looks at me. "I just wanted to make sure you're going into this with eyes wide open. I'm scared you're getting your hopes up about Rossum."

"I'm not supposed to be hopeful?"

"No, of course you are! And there's a lot to be hopeful about, for sure. But . . . I guess I just want to make sure you understand that progress may not always happen as quickly as we want it to. Our district has been red for a very long time. Overwhelmingly so—"

"Are you following the polls, though? Yesterday, the *AJC* was showing Rossum behind by less than four percentage points, which is barely outside the margin of error. And you should see the momentum at headquarters. It was packed—"

"And that's great!" Mom smiles. "That's all so promising, and you never know. I just want to make sure you're emotionally prepared either way. No election is a guarantee."

"I *know* that."

"I don't mean to be discouraging. I think what you and Maya are doing is amazing. I love how invested you are. I just don't want you to get so invested that it breaks your heart."

So invested that it breaks my heart.

I try to push the thought from my brain before it even lands. Is it possible to be too invested in a candidate? Isn't that what you're supposed to do? Commit one hundred percent?

But maybe I really am on track for heartbreak.

Maybe the person I'm too invested in isn't Rossum.

"Jamie?" Mom asks.

"No, I know. I get it. I just think we have to believe it's

possible. Otherwise, what's the point?"

"Just remember," Mom says. "The fact that we even have a fighting chance is a win."

I smile faintly. "Okay, Mom."

She scoots closer, reaching out to pat my arm. "Anyway, I'm just happy you and Maya gave yourselves a night off for once."

Aha. There it is.

"You two looked pretty cozy," she adds.

"Mom, we're not—"

"I know you're not dating," she says quickly. "I just think it's good that you guys are also doing non-election-related things together. You should do more of that."

"Okay . . ."

"I'm serious! You should do something just for fun, like the aquarium, or the nature center, or even just dinner and a movie."

I blush. "It sure sounds like you think we're dating."

Mom laughs. "Well, I do think you guys would be cute together. Have you thought about asking her out?"

"*Mom.*"

"Just a suggestion! Sometimes we tend to build this stuff up, you know? And it doesn't have to be a huge deal. Would you want to date Maya?"

I laugh incredulously. "That doesn't matter. She has to want to."

"You're right," Mom says, "but I'm not asking if she wants to. That's for her to figure out. I'm asking if *you* want to."

"I guess."

"And does she know how you feel?"

She would if she read all those Instagram comments.

"I don't know," I say finally.

"Maybe you should spell it out for her."

I gape at Mom, horrified. "That's not—"

"Or just start simple, and invite her to something!"

"I have!" I shake my head. "Intermezzo, the bat mitzvah—"

"Oh!" Mom peers at my face for a moment, clearly biting back a smile. "Sophie mentioned Maya was coming, but I didn't realize she was your plus-one."

"Yup. Sure. Can we stop talking about this?"

I'm sorry, but it's ridiculous. Mom's here acting like this Maya thing is already a home run. How can she be so confident about that? And especially when she's so lukewarm about Rossum's chances! God knows what the polling data would say about my chances with Maya. Imagine if that were a thing.

Though. I guess it is kind of a thing. On Instagram.

Of course, the real problem is the fact that I've just told Mom that Maya's my plus-one to the bat mitzvah. Whereas Maya probably thinks she's my political accomplice.

And I have no idea which one's closer to the truth.

CHAPTER TWENTY-SIX
MAYA

The mall isn't the same without Sara.

The pagoda with the obnoxiously funky outerwear just looks like a sad stall with overpriced hats and scarves. Nordstrom, where we could spend an entire day trying on all the different high-heeled shoes, feels flooded with too many options. Even the Apple Store, where we'd check out the newest iPhones and iPads, looks like an ordinary electronics store today.

I'd debated asking Jamie to come with me, but this place is so "Maya and Sara" I didn't want to risk another sobbing, snotty-faced experience with witnesses. And I was right—memories lurk around every corner.

Focus, Maya. I'm on a mission: Buy a dress. Get Sophie a gift.

But the Fourth of July banners and sale signs are overwhelming, and even the smaller stores like Francesca's and Banana Republic feel dizzying with all the possibilities. If Sara were here, she'd pluck out the top five outfits. Where do I even begin?

I look at a dress hanging inside a store and pause. All those times Sara and I went shopping, it was me buying the outfits. Sara came along to help me decide. She jokingly called herself my "fashion consultant"—but why hadn't I ever stopped to consider why she never bought anything herself?

My phone buzzes.

Jamie: Hey, Maya! Cool if I put us down for some canvassing tomorrow? How's 11:00 a.m.? Would that possibly work for you?

I laugh at his weirdly formal tone.

Maya: Why yes, Jamie. It certainly does.

Jamie: Awesome! Pick you up at 10:45!

I walk through the food court. My stomach rumbles. I'm going to get something to eat and recalibrate.

"Maya!" a voice calls out just then. It's Nolan. He's getting up from a table right by me.

"You work at the Disney Store?" I glance at his name tag with mouse ears.

"If you ever want a stuffed animal or figurine, hit me up. I'll get you the employee discount."

"You don't sell formalwear there, do you?"

"If we did, it'd be covered in Mickey Mouse." He grins. "It's weird to see you out and about without Jamie. You have been inseparable all summer."

"I'm on a Jamie-related mission," I tell him. "I'm looking for an outfit for the bat mitzvah."

"Right! Felipe told me about that! Your first date."

"Oh! Um, no," I stammer. "We're not—"

"You guys are so cute together. Felipe and I met kind of the same way. We got assigned to do a school project, and then *boom*—it worked out perfectly."

"Oh, no. We're not . . . that's not us." My cheeks feel like they're burning. "I'm tagging along to the bat mitzvah to help spread the word about that racist H.B. 28 bill. And I mean—to support Sophie. And hear Jamie's toast." Maybe it's the way Nolan's smiling at me, but I can't seem to stop talking. "I'm serious. We got pushed into canvassing, and it was fun and important, so we're doing it but—" I feel myself flush. "I mean, you and Felipe really are perfect together; but—Jamie—that's not us."

"Right, okay." He nods.

But it doesn't look like he believes me.

We chat a bit more, before I hop on the escalator and head upstairs. It's so weird. First the waitress at Intermezzo. Now Nolan?

Jamie and I are just friends.

Aren't we?

I mean, he definitely looks at me in awe when I have Wi-Fi at Target. And he's a good listener, so he meets your gaze when you talk to him. But that's what friends do.

My mind wanders to when he invited me to Sophie's bat mitzvah. For five solid seconds, I thought he was asking me to go as his date. Fine. I can admit it: my heart *might* have skipped a beat at the thought of it. How I'd tell my mother. The objections she might have had to it. But it turned out it wasn't a date. He'd been very clear about that.

No. I shake my head. This is not the time to let Nolan get in my head.

Zara turns out to be a bust. Madewell is heavier into jeans than usual this season. The Anthropologie store looks warm and inviting when I pass by, though; it's also the last store before I make a full loop back to Nordstrom, where I started.

Stepping inside, my eyes are drawn to a teal dress hanging on a display dummy in the center of the store.

It's the first promising outfit I've seen.

"That dress looks great on you," the salesgirl says brightly when I step out of the fitting room. I study myself in the full-length mirror. She's supposed to say that, right? I wish I had someone I could actually ask, like Sara—she always told me the truth. I'm about to text my mother a photo when I see someone coming out of the changing room in front of me.

327

It's Shelby.

"Maya?" She's wearing a summery dress with a tag hanging off the shoulder strap, and looks as surprised to see me as I am her.

"Hey." I blink. "What are you doing here?" And then it dawns on me. The text she'd sent me about going to the mall . . . "Where's everyone else?" I glance around.

"Oh, they couldn't make it." She shrugs. "I came anyway, because I'm trying to find an outfit to wear to a Fourth of July barbecue my parents are dragging me to this afternoon. Hey, that dress looks really nice on you, by the way."

"You think?" I look at myself in the mirror. "I feel like it's bunching up a little at the waist?"

"Well, a little," Shelby agrees. "But the color is pretty."

"Yours is great too. I like the yellow."

"Too bad it was misplaced in the clearance section." She points to the tag. "I can't afford anything in the regular part of the store."

"I know what you mean. I have some money from a recent holiday, otherwise . . . ," I begin, but then I check the price. Two hundred and thirty-five dollars? For a dress?

"Well, make that two of us who can't afford anything in this store."

"They do have a good clearance section, though," Shelby says. "Want to check it out?"

Shelby leads me to a hideaway spot tucked in the back

of the store. There's a row of dresses hanging on one wall.

"Look!" She pulls one out. "The gray lace looks pretty!"

I check the tag. It's also seventy-five percent off.

I pull off a couple of other possibilities from the rack. Shelby hands me a pink one with flowers embroidered along the hem, and I help her pick out a couple of sundresses.

We try our clothes on in neighboring dressing rooms. Shelby ends up going with a short white one I helped her find. And it turns out, she was right about the gray lace dress—it's perfect.

I also find a great gift for Sophie in the other end of the store: a whitewashed crate and a journal decorated in unicorns.

"This is some fancy birthday you're going to," Shelby says.

"It's a bat mitzvah," I tell her. "My friend Jamie's little sister. I've been canvassing with him all summer for the special election, and he invited me to come along with him."

"I guess that's why you've been too busy to hang out this summer."

"I'm sorry about that." I glance at her. "It's been bonkers. . . ."

"I get it." She smiles a little. "Everyone's been busy. It's fine." She shrugs. "There's always something to do; besides, I can always drag my little brother along if I absolutely need someone to go with me."

She honestly looks like she means it. I take it so personally when Sara can't hang out with me, but Shelby just keeps on keeping on. Still, I pause and think of Sara and her myriad excuses. Just because Shelby is fine with it doesn't mean I don't owe her an apology.

"Seriously, Shelby. I should've texted you back. I assumed you had a whole crew coming, and you wouldn't notice if I was there or not, but that still wouldn't make it okay. I'm sorry."

She smiles. "Make it up by going axe throwing with me?"

"Axe throwing?"

"I was going to send a text out to some friends this week about it. Would you be up for it?"

"Isn't that dangerous?"

"It's amazing!" Shelby says. "My parents and I went last month. Best stress relief ever. If you're too busy, though, I get it."

"That sounds like fun," I tell her.

When she offers me a ride home, I say yes. It turns out, she lives a mile down the road from me. I get in the passenger seat, and we chat about school and our summers. I'm still stunned that not only did I go to the most Maya-Sara place in the universe and not cry, I'm leaving it smiling.

CHAPTER TWENTY-SEVEN
JAMIE

I shove my phone in my pocket as soon as Maya cracks open the passenger door. Barely 10:45 in the morning, and every organ in my body is cranked up a hundred.

Maya eyes me, equal parts suspicious and amused. "Who are you texting?"

I pause. "Sophie."

"Is she excited for tomorrow?" Maya clicks her seat belt, twisting around to face me. "I bet your mom's so stressed."

"Yeah, it's been intense. They're at the rehearsal right now, and there's a Shabbat dinner thing for the out-of-towners tonight. Oh, and Mom's freaking out, because we had to replace our DJ last minute, and the new one keeps mispronouncing 'Hava Nagila.'"

"Do you think it will be okay?" Maya asks. "I mean,

he'll be playing a prerecorded version of it, not singing it himself, right?"

"Oh, totally." I sneak a glance at my phone in the cup holder. "She's just looking for stuff to worry about."

"Well, it will all be over by Sunday. Then you can just go back to worrying about the election." She rubs her forehead. "I can't believe how stressful this is. We're not even really part of the campaign. How do people do this every election cycle? Why does anyone want to run for office?"

"I used to want to." The words slip out before I fully realize I'm saying them. "Run for Congress, I mean. I guess . . . I've thought about it."

Maya smiles faintly. "Really?"

"It's stupid. Can you imagine?" I laugh, rubbing the back of my neck. "Giving speeches all the time, trying to talk people into choosing me—"

"I'd choose you," she says.

"You would?"

"Of course." She nods emphatically. "You'd be an awesome congressman."

"I'm not exactly the politician type."

"So? I wish more politicians were like you. You'd be so great. You'd always vote with your conscience, you'd work twice as hard as everyone else, and, I mean, you'd actually listen to your constituents. That's huge." She pokes my arm. "What a game changer. You should totally do it."

She thinks—

I don't trust myself to speak. I just gaze at the road, head spinning. Maya thinks I should run for office one day. She said I'd be awesome. A game changer.

She said she'd *choose* me.

Which is ridiculous.

But maybe it's not.

By the time we pull into the campaign office, my stomach's churning with nerves. Maya peers around the almost empty lot, looking relieved. "Thank God. I really thought we weren't going to find parking last time."

"Right?" My voice can barely choke out one syllable without jumping.

Maya unclicks her seat belt, yawning. "Weird that Gabe wants us to canvass at eleven on a weekday. Is he sending us to an office complex?"

She starts to open the door, but I blurt, "Wait!"

Way too loudly. Maya raises her eyebrows at me, smiling.

"Let me just make sure . . . Gabe is ready for us." I pull out my phone.

"Since when do we make sure Gabe is ready for us?"

"I'm just . . ." I tilt my phone up, so she can't see what I'm texting. "You know."

Maya laughs, idly tapping into her own phone. "Why are you acting so shady?"

"I'm not."

She stares me down. "Are you up to something?"

"What would I be up to?" I glance quickly at the dashboard clock. *10:59. 10:59. 10:59.*

Neither of us speaks.

10:59. 10:59. 11:00.

"Okay!" I say quickly. "I think we can go in now."

"Okaaaaaay."

Maya's definitely side-eyeing me—but I'm pretty sure she's also biting back a smile. We hop out, and she follows me up the stairs to the side-access door. But just as I reach for the door, it bursts open.

"Hi, loveys!" Grandma bustles out the door, pausing only to hug us both. "Don't mind me! Just clearing out. I don't want to keep you! I know Jamie's been—"

"Getting ready for a canvassing day!" I shoot Grandma a pointed look. "A regular canvassing day."

Grandma's mouth snaps shut. "Well, look at the time! Past eleven. I better get home and walk that pup!"

"Pup." Maya laughs.

The campaign office looks empty at first glance, but I can hear low, murmuring voices coming from behind the white video backdrop.

I call out, "Hello?"

"Back here!" Gabe announces, stepping into view.

Maya looks at me questioningly. "Are we filming another video?"

"Not exactly," I say—but before I can finish, Jordan Rossum steps out from behind the backdrop. Maya's eyes flare wide, and she lets out a noise so faint and high-pitched, it almost makes her Jim and Pam squeaks seem gruff.

"Hi!" Rossum steps toward us, hand extended. "Maya and Jamie, right? I'm Jordan."

I shake his hand. A moment later, Maya unfreezes and does the same.

"Your Fifi Gets Flipped video was amazing. And Gabe tells me you're two of his top canvassers too. I can't tell you how much I appreciate it."

Maya stares at her hand, looking awestruck—and then back up at Rossum. "It's . . . so nice to meet you."

"Are you kidding? So nice to meet you," he says warmly. "You guys are rising seniors, right?"

Maya's eyes flick toward me, mouth falling open. I know exactly what she's thinking.

Rossum—*Jordan Rossum*—knows who we are.

Not going to lie—it really is pretty *wow*.

"Yup," I manage. "I—uh. I'm at Riverwild and Maya's at Stanley."

"Nice. I went to Gallovin, but I knew people from both at Hebrew school."

335

"That's so cool." Maya's voice comes out breathless. And when I sneak another sideways glance, she's twisting the ends of her hair between her fingertips.

She is, hands down, the cutest fangirl ever.

Gabe ambles over, collapsing a small tripod as he walks. "We just shot some sweet new video for the final social media push," he says. "It's Get Out the Vote time! GOTV, baby!"

Maya turns to Rossum. "How are you feeling?"

"Good! Definitely nervous." He half smiles, half grimaces. "It's my first time running for office. But the response has been incredible, and I've met so many awesome people. I feel really good."

"You got this, bro." Gabe pats his back. "Hey, let me steal my dude back for a sec. Gotta grab a few still shots to promote the vids."

The vids. Wow. Gabe is even more *Gabe* when he's trying to impress Rossum.

"Sorry!" Rossum smiles apologetically at Maya and me. "Should just take a second. Hold that thought."

They step back behind the cloth.

And the minute they're out of sight, Maya doubles over. "OH MY GOD," she mouths.

"Surprise!" I whisper. "I knew you wanted to meet him, so I got Gabe to—"

She flings her arms around me. "You're the best. Jamie! Is this real life?"

The look on her face makes me feel—I can't even describe it. It's like beating every level of every video game. And getting elected president of the universe. And being buried alive in puppies. All at once.

"I knew something was up," Maya whispers. "But God. I had no idea. And he's so sweet and down to earth! He really is awesome."

"I know! It's an accurate slogan."

She hugs me again, bouncing on the balls of her feet. "I can't believe we're meeting *Jordan Rossum*." She draws back slightly, meeting my eyes. "Thank you."

"Better than canvassing in an office complex?"

"Uh, yeah."

Maya looks at me, beaming—and there's this tug in my chest.

"Okay, we're back!" says Rossum, stepping around the backdrop again. Maya disentangles from the hug and clasps her hands together.

She's standing closer to me than before. So close, I can barely think straight.

"Sorry about that. It's so hard for me to get a good picture. I make the most awkward faces." Rossum demonstrates, stretching his lips into a panicked-looking smile.

Maya and I both laugh. I can tell she's totally charmed, and I don't blame her one bit. Rossum's the good kind of awkward—the cool, self-deprecating kind, with that sturdy, quiet nerd confidence. I'd give anything to be like that.

"So, what was your most memorable experience on the campaign trail?" asks Maya. She still looks slightly flustered, but she's starting to sound like herself again.

"Huh. Good question. Well . . ." Rossum turns to me. "Your grandmother brought me to an elderly Jewish singles mixer."

"To set you up?" Maya asks, looking delighted.

Rossum smiles, cheeks flushing. "Probably? I don't know. She told me it was a meet-and-greet for Jewish seniors, but . . ."

"Did you get any voter commitments?" I ask.

"Lots. And a couple of phone numbers."

Maya giggles. "Wow."

"What about you guys?" asks Rossum.

"You mean did we pick up any Jewish seniors?" Maya shoots back.

Rossum snorts. "That is definitely what I meant."

"Not yet." Maya nudges me. "Maybe your grandma can set me up with a bat mitzvah date."

Gabe grins. "Isn't Jamie—"

"So!" I say quickly, turning back to Rossum. "I was wondering . . . could we get a selfie?"

"Of course!" Rossum says. "Let's do it. Right here?"

Gabe's face brightens. "Actually, why don't I get some pictures of you three together for Insta!"

Soon, we're being ushered out the side by Gabe, who suddenly has very strong opinions about natural sunlight. "Right there. Brick wall. Great. Big J, you stay in the middle."

I look back at him, confused. "I'm not—"

"Not you. Other Big J. Bigger J."

Rossum leans toward me. "He calls you that too?"

I laugh. "Yup."

"Great. *Great.* Okay, everyone, look at me. And . . . smile!"

"Wait!" Maya bursts out of formation, jogging toward Gabe. "Will you take one with my phone?"

"Oh, good call," Rossum says. "If you post it on Instagram, tag me! Then I can follow you."

Maya looks like she might burst. "Oh! Okay, yeah!"

"Aww, cuz." Gabe smiles knowingly at me from behind his phone. "Bet you wish you had a 'gram!"

"I'm starting one," I say. Out loud, apparently.

Maya grins. "Oh, Jamie! That's awesome!"

Well, now I kind of have to, right? Because what could be a better inaugural picture than a shot with Maya—and Jordan freaking Rossum?

★　★　★

339

Ten minutes later, Gabe heads back inside to make phone calls—and Rossum heads out to his car. The minute he pulls out of the parking lot, Maya presses her hands to her mouth, letting out a muffled scream.

"Oh my God oh my God oh my God." She's bouncing again—almost dancing. "That just happened. Look." She waves her phone in front of my face. "Look how cute we are. Ahh! Okay, I'm texting you this."

My phone buzzes in my pocket. "Got it!"

Maya hugs me. "And it's about time you got on social media. Your grandma will be so happy. She told me you're too cute not to be on Instagram."

I nod. "Sounds like Grandma."

Maya smiles up at me. "Well, it's true."

There's a tiny, fluttery yank below my stomach. Is Maya . . . flirting with me?

Nope. No way. She's just comfortable calling me cute because we're so clearly, unambiguously platonic. After all, she was cosigning Grandma when she said it. So she probably means it in a grandma way.

"We have to take a selfie together too," she announces, "so you can post it on your account. That way, when you're a famous congressman, you'll remember me. I'll always be your first Instagram selfie."

I smile. "You really think I'd forget you?"

"Nah." She smiles back. "I won't let you."

The next thing I know, her face is smooshed against mine. I snap the picture, and then bring my phone back to show Maya.

"Okay, am I just in a good mood, or is this the greatest selfie ever taken?"

I grin. "I think you have a Rossum high."

"Oh, really?"

"Yup. Giddy, glowing, can't stop smiling." I look at her. "You have all the symptoms."

"Sounds serious," Maya says.

"It is." I nod. "I better document this." I hold my phone up in front of my face, camera-style. Maya leans back against the loading dock railing, and I swear, her eyes are shooting off sparks. She presses her hands to her cheeks, smiling hugely.

I sneak a peek at the photo, before looking back up at Maya.

She's so beautiful. Just ridiculously beautiful.

Maya wrinkles her nose. "Am I doing the eye thing?"

"The eye thing?"

She widens her eyes to demonstrate. "Like the big bullfrog eye thing. I don't know. I think I do it when I'm trying not to blink."

"You look perfect," I say.

Maya looks up at me. "Okay."

The air feels suddenly charged.

She clears her throat. "So, I guess we better get you home so you can set up your account."

"My account." I scratch my neck. "Should I follow Sophie? I'm kind of scared to follow Sophie."

"Definitely follow Sophie," she says, falling into step beside me. "But follow me first. Oh my God. Now you can actually see my pictures!"

I inhale quickly. "I have to tell you something."

"Oh yeah?" She smiles expectantly.

I stare at my feet. I don't have a clue how to begin. "Okay. I feel really stupid now, but remember when Grandma first followed you on Instagram?"

Maya nods slowly.

"That wasn't Grandma. That was me. In her account."

"Oh." Maya stops walking. "Okay."

"And I wanted to tell you, but you were so excited that she followed you, and I didn't want to take that away. But I should have told you anyway. Or not done it. I'm so sorry, Maya." My voice breaks, just barely. "You deserve to know who's actually following you."

"That's true." She frowns. "I mean, I knew you ran the account sometimes."

"Still."

She looks like she's debating what to say. But then, after a few moments, she meets my eyes. "Don't worry about it."

"Are you—"

"It's fine, I guess. I mean, don't, like, do it again—"

"I won't. I promise. From now on, I'm my own man on Instagram."

She looks up at me, with a hint of a smile. "I'm looking forward to that."

CHAPTER TWENTY-EIGHT
MAYA

Jamie's standing by the front door of Schwartz-Goldstein Hall, where the kiddush luncheon is taking place. He's chatting with his mother, Sophie, and Rabbi Levinson.

The bat mitzvah ceremony just ended, and everyone's pouring in for lunch. A huge table to the left is filled with bowls of fruit, platters of chicken salad, bagels, and lox.

I was nervous when my dad dropped me off this morning, but as soon as I stepped through the side doors of the temple, Jamie found me and got me a seat in the VIP section—right next to his grandmother. Watching the ceremony from the front row, seeing Sophie read from the Torah—the lights overhead glowing warm as Jamie and his mother looked on from where they stood on the bimah— joy permeated the room like a thing I could touch.

"Saved you a spot in line," I tell Jamie when he walks over to me.

"Thanks," he says. "Ugh, this tie." He tugs and grimaces. "It's so uncomfortable."

"It looks nice," I tell him.

"I'm just saying, accessories for your neck—this should not be a thing."

It throws me off a little, seeing him so formal. The crisp white shirt, the red tie . . . He looks so handsome. Mr. Darcy–level handsome. I think of Nolan and flush. I will keep *that* thought to myself.

"The flyers." I clear my throat. "I brought them with me."

"Oh, that." He looks at me. "My mom isn't letting me hand them out. She said it would take attention away from Sophie's big day, even though, you know, this is time sensitive, with actual liberties at stake. I'll try to work on her for the reception later, though. She's got to change her mind."

"She's got a point," I tell him. "It's like how you thought canvassing on Eid wasn't the best idea. Some days are meant to celebrate."

"But we can't just not hand them out. Can you imagine the number of calls flooding in if we got this to each person here?"

"Who said anything about not handing them out?" I ask him. "We can't *give* them to people directly, but maybe we could stick them in places where people can find them? If that's okay to do at a temple . . ."

"Like by the drinks table." He smiles slowly. "And the bathrooms have really wide counters, perfect for flyers. Maya, you're a genius."

"I'm not your political partner in crime for nothing, right?"

He hugs me. A jolt of electricity courses through me.

I look at him when we pull apart.

Did he feel it too?

Just then, we're interrupted by two tweens.

"Jamie!" one of them exclaims. She's wearing a floral sundress. "You look so *cute*."

"Uh, thanks, Maddie," Jamie says.

"Seriously. I almost didn't recognize you," the other one adds.

"Andrea's right. You should change your aesthetic." Maddie nods. "Suits all the way, all the time."

"Too bad no one wears suits outside of formal events," Andrea says.

"Set a trend, Jamie!" Maddie says. "If you just start wearing suits to school and to the mall, like it's no thing, maybe it'll catch on."

"Okay, um. This is my friend Maya." He nods to me quickly.

"Hi." I smile at them.

They give me a once-over.

346

"So, Jamie." Maddie turns back to him. "Did you see what Elsie was wearing? Red and yellow do *not* go together."

"And the white tights? Tragic. You should tell her," Andrea says. "That's what a real friend does. Gives their honest opinion."

"You're right," Maddie says. "*I'd* want to know."

"But even if the outfit doesn't work, she's already wearing it," I tell them. "Telling her will make her feel horrible, won't it?"

"Sometimes you have to be cruel to be kind," Andrea says.

"That's *such* a good point." Maddie nods somberly.

They say goodbye and hurry away.

"Wow." I glance at their retreating figures. "They just reminded me how royally middle school sucked."

"I wouldn't go back for any amount of money in the world," Jamie agrees.

We make plates for ourselves with bagels and cream cheese and fruit. Maddie and Andrea are now talking to someone in a red dress with a yellow cardigan. She's still smiling, so they haven't broken the news to her yet. Poor Elsie.

"Want to put the flyers out now?" Jamie asks me when we're done eating. "I'll print more for the party this evening."

We decide to divide and conquer. I put a handful on some round tables by a library, and Jamie charms the security folks into agreeing to let us put out flyers by the check-in counter. I set the last of the stack in the ladies' bathroom, and meet him in the hallway around the corner from the kiddush luncheon. Music and conversation waft down the hallway toward us.

His back is to me when I approach—he's taking a picture of a poster on the wall. Getting closer, I see it's a photo of a rabbi—Jacob Rothschild—and a quote he said in 1948: *We must do more than view with alarm the growing race hatred that threatens the South.*

"He said that over half a century ago," I say once I'm next to Jamie.

"Yeah . . ."

"I can't believe it." I shake my head. "There's this part of me that thinks if we work and resist long enough, we'll get to 'happily ever after,' but . . ."

"I know," Jamie says. "Things change slowly. Way too slowly, to be honest. But what's the alternative? Not like we can sit back and do nothing. We have to fight for change however we can."

I study Jamie's profile. I never thought about change as something to fight *for*—more like something I'm always fighting against. It's always the one thing that throws me completely off-kilter. And this summer has been a tidal wave of changes, one after the other, until it's felt like there's nothing left standing. But glancing now at Jamie, I smile a little. He's right. Sometimes, change can be good.

★   ★   ★

We wander out the side door of the temple. It's so quiet and peaceful out here. I take in the view from the parking lot. Sometimes all the traffic and congestion can make me forget just how pretty Atlanta is. Skyscrapers and leafy trees line the horizon—the morning sun feels warm, beating against our bodies. I sit down on Alfie's trunk. Jamie hops up next to me, our knees brushing together, and we sit in comfortable silence for a moment.

Jamie pulls out his phone after a little while and clicks a few buttons.

"Instagramming the poster?"

"Yeah." He glances at me and smiles. "I finally joined the modern world."

"The modern world welcomes you."

"Thanks for being one of my two followers," he says.

"Keep posting and you'll get as many as me!"

"Fifteen?"

"Exactly. Goals." I grin. "But seriously, I can't believe you posted the goofy one of me after meeting Rossum."

"You look so cute in it!"

"Ugh." I wince. "I look like such a fangirl."

"Nothing wrong with that. It *was* Rossum."

"Well, that's true." I nod. "After all the crap we've dealt with, it felt good to meet the person this is all about."

"I'm glad you liked it. And, hey, thanks for coming to the bat mitzvah."

"I wouldn't have missed it," I say. "Although Sophie's friends are intense."

"Right? And Maddie is just . . . the most intense."

"I told you. Maddie has a crush on you, that's all."

"No," he says quickly. "That's just how she is."

"Trust me. I know a crush when I see one."

Jamie flushes. I bump my shoulder against his and laugh. He's so cute, but I swear he doesn't know it.

"I'm traumatized by middle school," Jamie says. "I think even being middle school–adjacent gets me anxious."

"I don't think anyone looks back fondly on their middle school years."

"Sophie might. She's friends with everyone."

"That's impressive."

"She's fearless. She doesn't care what anyone thinks about her."

"Sounds like the exact opposite of how I was," I say.

"Are you kidding me? You were the one doing those killer Cirque du Soleil moves on the rotating twirly thing at Catch Air. Half the kids crowded around to watch you."

"Stop! I never did that!" I bat his elbow.

"You so did. I'm sure my mom has receipts on her phone. It was really cool."

"Well, even if I did that when I was five . . . middle school was different. It was mortifying. You know those yogurt squeezes you get from the store? My mom packed one for me on the first day of sixth grade, and somehow I squirted the entire tube on my face. Kids teased me about it all week."

"That's amateur hour." Jamie scoffs. "I asked a girl I had a crush on to slow dance with me at the Snow Ball, but I got so nervous I asked her to slowmance with me. People *still* bring it up."

"What's wrong with slowmance? That should be a word. It's like a slow romance. A way to let the romantic moments linger."

Jamie looks at me with an expression I don't recognize.

"What's wrong?" I reach over and squeeze his hand. "You okay?"

He doesn't respond, but I can see the way he's biting his lip and looking at me—a million thoughts are running through his mind.

"It's just," he finally says. "You're the only one who's heard that story and hasn't laughed."

"It's a sweet story, Jamie, and besides—you invented a word. How many people can say that?"

He meets my gaze. I hadn't noticed until now how close we're sitting together. My heart flutters. And then—

"Maya, I love you," he blurts out. "I mean . . . I'm *in* love with you. It's just. You're funny and smart and pretty, and I love—I love hanging out with you. And watching TV with you. And knocking on doors with you and falling asleep on the phone with you. You make me better and braver, and . . ."

He swallows. His eyes widen. "I'm so sorry. I shouldn't have blurted that out. I didn't mean to freak you out. I'm—"

"Jamie, it's okay. Breathe." I lace my fingers through his. "You didn't freak me out. I'm just . . ."

Now I'm the one who can't figure out the right words. Sara, Nolan, my parents—so many conversations swirl in my mind . . . there's so much I should be thinking about, but all I *feel* are Jamie's hands in mine, and the electricity coursing through me as I look into his green eyes. Jamie loves me. He is in love with me.

"Mint," I finally whisper.

"Mint?" He tilts his head.

"You always smell like mint. It's not bad. It's good . . . ," I trail off.

He smiles a little. "My mouthwash? I guess—"

I look into his eyes. The warmth of his hands. His lips, so close to mine. I inch closer until nothing separates us. He hesitates before leaning in.

He's going to kiss me.

It's like my body has decided to mute my brain. I close my eyes.

Jamie. Goldberg. Is. About. To. Kiss. Me.

And then—a high-pitched squealing shriek.

Instantly, we spring apart.

"What was that?" My heart races in my chest. The noise continues to blare in a pulsing beat. I know I'm not supposed to get intimate with anyone—but did God literally intervene on a kiss?

"Why is a car alarm going off?" Jamie glances around.

"Hey, guys!"

It's Gabe. He's heading toward us.

My knees are shaky. Did he see us?

"Looking all over for you, Jamie," he shouts over the noise. "Your mom wants to do family photos."

"Oh yeah, photos." Jamie clears his throat.

"They're right outside where the benches are. The photographer's paid by the hour, so chop-chop, little cuz." He slaps Jamie on the back. If he did see us, he shows no hint of it.

Jamie looks at Gabe and glances at me. He bites his lip.

"We'll talk more tonight," I tell him.

"Yeah?" He looks at me with a nervous smile.

I nod.

We trail behind Gabe through the side entrance, toward the luncheon hall. Maddie's leaning against a wall near the doorway, but she's so fixated on her phone, she doesn't even notice us walk past her.

Jamie extends his hand. A minute ago, I'd have taken it without a second's hesitation.

But it feels different now.

Everything does.

CHAPTER TWENTY-NINE
JAMIE

Felipe, Nolan, and Drew show up at six on the nose, wearing the same suits they wore to the ceremony. "Is your cousin Rachel here yet?" asks Drew, peeking past me, down the staircase.

I keep glancing at my texts. Nothing from Maya. Not a word since we left the kiddush luncheon. I'm so anxious to see her again, even the sight of her name stops me short.

I just wish I knew where I stood with her. I don't know what to make of what happened today in the parking lot.

Or what almost happened.

What *I think* almost happened.

Am I crazy to think Maya and I almost kissed? Obviously Gabe, being Gabe, had to show up and ruin it. But my brain keeps rewinding past that part, back to when Maya said I smelled like mint. When she shut her eyes and leaned forward, just barely. Maybe it was a platonic gesture that I just grossly misinterpreted? But . . . at that point, Maya already knew I was in love with her.

Am in love with her.

Because I told her.

I told Maya I'm in love with her. I made those words in my brain and I said them and Maya heard them and she didn't freak out.

I don't think she freaked out?

I mean, I almost *kissed* her.

And she almost kissed me back. I really think she would have kissed me. If not for Gabe.

Gabe. I can barely stand to look at him. He spent the whole family photo session grinning into his phone. I know that shouldn't piss me off. It probably means good news for Rossum. Still. It's like some kind of spell was broken the moment he showed up.

He probably has no idea what he ruined.

Sophie's friends start trickling in, leaving gift bags near the front table. The boys are all wearing literally the same ensemble: black jackets over white collared shirts, with blue ties. But the girls have all changed into shorter, tighter dresses, most of which basically look like tubes of fabric. Maddie shows up, looking tearful, and she and Sophie hug for about an hour. Then Maddie spends another hour hugging a wavy-haired blond girl—Tessa, as I now know from Instagram. And then she gets going *again* with Andrea—and even Andrea's sister. Apparently Sophie's reception is also a Maddie support group.

"Sophie looks so cute," Nolan says. "What a little peanut."

I nod, but I'm only half present. My eyes keep glancing back to the staircase.

Felipe prods my arm, smiling knowingly. "She'll be here."

"What? No, I'm just—"

My words fall away. Maya drifts up the staircase, carrying a wrapped gift and a tote bag, and my heart leaps into my throat.

She's dressed in pale gray lace, with delicate short sleeves. I'm pretty sure Drew's speaking to me, but I'm just—Maya's hair. It's shiny and straight, curling just barely at the ends. And her skin glows golden brown in the light of the reception hall.

Forget the toast. I legitimately don't know if I can get through the word *hi*. But I rush to meet her, leaving Drew hanging mid-sentence. I don't know if I should shake her hand or hug her, and if I hug her, should it be a quick friend hug? Or one of those century-long Maddie friend hugs? Or no hug? Do I keep it verbal? I mean, she said *talk*. Maybe she meant that literally. A nice, collegial, hands-free platonic talk.

She steps closer, close enough for me to really see her expression. I can't quite decipher it. She's not flustered—not exactly—but she's not exactly relaxed.

She shoots me a halting smile. "Hi."

"Hi." I'm trying not to stare. But her cheeks are so pink, and her eyes look extra Disney, and her face is closer than usual.

She's taller. Just barely. Maybe her shoes. She smells like flowers.

"You look so pretty," I say softly. "Your hair . . ."

She blushes, nervously fingering the ends. "Thanks—I . . . my friend Shelby has a hair straightener." Her eyes keep flicking down to my mouth. "You look amazing, Jamie. This whole place is amazing."

I glance back over my shoulder. "Yeah, the decorations came out really nice. Want to see the ballroom?"

She nods mutely, taking my hand.

But Drew, Felipe, and Nolan intercept us before we can even swing by the gift table. "Maya!" Drew hugs her.

"You look gorgeous," Felipe says. "Stunning."

Maya laughs and hugs them back, and suddenly everything's weirdly, maddeningly normal. Nolan whispers something in Maya's ear, and she elbows him. "Shut up!"

Felipe takes her hand to lead the way to our table. I have to admit: Mom knocked it out of the park with the reception space. The ceiling's strung with pastel paper candy necklace medallions, and a giant chalkboard out front reads *Sophie's Sweet Shop*. The table numbers are also on chalkboards, surrounded by washi-taped jars of lollipops, chocolate balls, and gummy bears. And there's a self-serve candy display in Sophie's after-dinner teen room.

Maya scoots her chair up close beside me. "What a great party theme."

"Aunt Lauren is an event-planning genius," says Rachel.

The ballroom fills slowly as people make their way to their tables. Sophie's holding court near the back, at a long, rectangular table with her friends. I turn to my group, trying to follow along as everyone argues about a serial killer stalker show they all binged last year. But Maya keeps sneaking glances at me, and I keep losing the thread.

"He has your last name." Felipe pats my shoulder cheerfully.

"Hmm?"

"The murderer."

I nod distractedly. "Great."

"Hey, guys!" I look up just as Mom leans over my shoulder. "I'm so glad you all could make it."

"Thanks for having me," says Maya.

"Are you kidding? I was hoping Jamie would bring you as his plus-one."

My plus-one. Mom had to go there—of course she did—and now my cheeks are practically blazing.

But Maya doesn't correct her.

She's just staring at me with this searching half smile.

Mom turns to me. "What do you say we give people twenty minutes or so to settle in? Then I'll do my welcome speech, and we can move into your toast and the challah."

Maya scoots closer as soon as Mom leaves. "Are you nervous?"

"Kind of."

"Okay. Come with me." She grabs her tote bag and tugs me up—and the next thing I know, she's leading me out of the ballroom. I follow dazedly, reeling from the fact that she's holding my hand.

"Where are we going?"

"You'll see. Come on." We head down the stairs toward the entrance, but instead of leaving the building, Maya takes a sharp left, opening a door off the main lobby. "I saw this on my way in. It's a coatroom."

"Where are all the coats?"

"Jamie, it's July." She laughs.

And then she shuts the door behind us and locks it.

Holy. Shit. Is she . . . about to kiss me? Are we about to kiss?

But—okay. The toast is in twenty minutes. Less than twenty minutes. Should I set a phone alarm or something?

Maya settles onto the floor, tugging me down beside her. "I brought you something."

I just look at her, stupefied.

"My mom told me this story about getting stage fright at her wedding. My dad calmed her down by smashing a piece of cake in her face. But," she adds quickly, "I don't want to ruin your face."

"You can ruin it."

She laughs. "No! You look so . . . nice. Really."

I look at her. "So do you."

I swear, every molecule of air in this room feels electric.

"So, I'm not going to smash it in your face," she says after a moment. She opens her tote bag, revealing a plastic take-out bag from Intermezzo. "But I did bring cake."

"I love cake," I say.

Love. Wow. That word just keeps tumbling out today, doesn't it?

Maya presses her lips together. For a moment, we're both silent.

"Should we . . . talk about earlier?" I ask.

Maya's brow knits.

"We don't have to," I add quickly. "Sorry. I shouldn't have brought it up. I'm—"

"Please don't apologize." She takes a deep breath. "You know, I haven't stopped thinking about what you said."

"I haven't either."

"Jamie. I—really like you." Maya stares at her knees. "So

much. I've been going crazy all day. I don't even know how to say this out loud."

I scoot closer. "You're doing great."

"Thanks." She smiles nervously. "This is just really new for me. You're my best friend. I'm not supposed to want to kiss my best friend."

"You want to kiss me?"

She smiles slightly. "Um. No. Maybe. Yes."

But the clouded look in her eyes stops me short. I meet her gaze. "You okay?"

She hesitates. "Yeah."

"You look worried."

"Yeah. I'm just . . . trying to figure out how this works. My parents . . ."

I nod slowly, trying to follow. Her parents?

"It's mostly my mom. She's kind of . . . I don't know. We're really close, though. I'm going to talk to her about this. Tonight." She nods resolutely. "I really think she'll understand."

My head's spinning. Maya thinks her mom will understand . . . understand what? That Maya wearing lace makes it hard for me to think straight? That I can't stop staring at her lips? How I'm so desperate to kiss her, it actually hurts?

"Anyway." Maya leans forward. "We better eat some of this cake. We have to be back up in, what, seven minutes?"

I smile. "And you're sure this will fix my stage fright, even without the cake smash?"

"I'll smash it where no one can see," she says, her eyes suddenly widening. "Oh my God, I don't mean—I just mean, like, under your sleeve or something."

"Under my sleeve?"

Maya takes my hand and rests it palm-up on hers. Then she pushes up my jacket sleeve and the shirtsleeve underneath. "Here we go." She runs her finger through icing, and traces a tiny chocolate heart onto my wrist. She looks up at me. "Cake smash."

And I stare dumbly at my wrist, barely breathing.

The minute Mom hands me the microphone, it hits me.

I'm about to speak. In front of one hundred and fifty people. Including Sophie's terrifying friends and State Senator Mathews and basically everyone I know.

And Maya. Who meets my eyes quickly, smiles, and taps her wrist.

I tap my own wrist, feeling suddenly calm. Well, not *calm*. But definitely calmer.

I clear my throat. "Hi." It comes out booming, and I startle. Everyone laughs warmly. I slide the volume down. "Sorry. Hi. I'm Jamie, Sophie's big brother, and I'm not really good at public speaking, and challah's really delicious, so I'm going to keep this short."

"Go, Jamie!" someone calls from the back of the room.

"Thanks, Andrea." There's a burst of giggling from one end of the teen table, but I tap my wrist and keep going. "I really wanted to get up here and mildly embarrass Sophie with a story from childhood. But, uh. Instead I'm going to tell you about the time Sophie invited herself to come knock on doors with me. For the Jordan Rossum campaign. So . . . yeah. I was pretty sure she just invited herself because Mom was being really intense about the decorations—which came out amazing, by the way. Shout-out to Mom."

A bunch of people cheer, and Mom grins up at me.

"Anyway, I expected her to be kind of whatever about the actual canvassing part, but in true Sophie fashion, she nailed it." I shake my head. "She didn't even have to look at the talking points. So, I brought it up later. Like, wow, Soph, your memory is amazing. And she was like, actually, I've been researching the candidates for weeks."

Sophie beams up at me.

"For weeks! She'd just been there quietly studying this stuff. Because she actually cares about it. It really floored me." I pause. "The truth is, it's a weird time to be coming of age. The world's really messy right now. And it's so hard to be twelve or thirteen or fifteen or seventeen, where you're old enough to get it, but . . . you can't vote. Maybe you can't drive. You can make phone calls and hang posters—which, by the way, you guys should all check the bathrooms. For some, uh . . . reading material. Sorry, Mom."

Mom's eyebrows shoot up. But she's smiling.

"Except nothing feels like enough. The bad stuff feels so big. It's easy to feel helpless." I turn back to Sophie, who's gazing earnestly back. "But Sophie's strength of purpose gives me hope. Soph, I'm really proud to be your brother."

Sophie wrinkles her nose, smiling faintly. Even from across the room, I can see her eyes are shining.

"Anyway. Uh. That's . . . oh, right! Baruch ata, Adonai Eloheinu, melech ha'olam, hamotzi lechem min ha'aretz. Amen. And now we eat!"

"I didn't know you knew Hebrew." Maya grins up at me on the dance floor. We're not really dancing together. I mean, we are. But it's all of us—the guys, Rachel. Even Gabe has temporarily unglued his eyes from his phone to join us. The DJ's been wooing my mom's friends since the first course ended, with "Take on Me," "Sugar, Sugar," and "Walking on Sunshine."

"Just the hamotzi," I say. "It's the only thing I remember. And *iparon*. That means pencil."

Maya laughs and touches my arm. "Noted."

I feel so fizzy and light, I swear I'm practically carbonated. How is this moment even real? I can't believe I'm here with Maya. I can't believe she wants to kiss me. I can't believe I survived Sophie's toast. More than survived it.

I think I actually kind of nailed it.

The DJ switches to a slow song—"Unchained Melody"—and I swear, the whole room can hear my heartbeat. It feels like everyone's watching me. Random Jewish ladies, family friends, strangers. *Definitely* Sophie's friends. That spotlight feeling.

Felipe and Nolan fall into an easy embrace, swaying to the tempo.

Maya smiles. "Want to slowmance?"

I just stare at her, trying to catch my breath. "Of course."

She steps closer, arms encircling my neck, and my hands fall to her waist. And suddenly, we're so close, our foreheads are practically touching. I breathe in the floral scent of her hair and try to hold on to every tiny detail of this moment. The way her face tilts toward mine, the paper medallions above us, the long sighing notes of music, the self-conscious lilt in Maya's voice.

"I feel like people are looking at us," she says. "Is that crazy?"

I laugh softly. "I've felt that all night."

"I think I'm just nervous." She bites her lip. "Sorry I was kind of incoherent in the coat closet. I'm not good at this. But I really . . . oh God, Gabe is looking at us. He's, like, *grinning*."

"I'm legit going to throttle him."

"It's not even just him. Everyone's watching us."

I nod. "At least now I get why Sophie was so dead set on a teen room."

Mom sidles up to us as the main course is served, planting a hand on my shoulder. "How are you guys holding up?" she asks.

"Great!" Maya says.

"Jamie, you were wonderful. I loved the toast—"

"Wait. Really?"

"Yes, really!" Mom laughs. "Look, you made the political stuff relevant. You were adorable up there. I'm just so proud of you. Both of you." She turns to Maya. "You guys have been working so hard this summer. I'd be shocked if you didn't get that car, Maya. Such a good idea. What a cool reward to work toward."

My brain skids to a stop. A *car*?

Maya looks frozen. She stares at her plate.

"And I guess it's safe to say canvassing turned out to be more fun than you expected. Win-win." Mom smiles, patting our shoulders, before moving on to greet Felipe.

Maya looks at me. "Jamie."

"So . . . your parents said they'd give you a car if you went canvassing with me." Her face falls. "Which is fine," I say quickly. "I get it. A car is a car—"

"No! Jamie. That's not why I canvassed. Okay, it kind of was at first, but—"

"You don't have to explain."

"No, I want to." She grabs my hand under the table, lacing our fingers together. "I mean, yeah, I wasn't really all in at first. It was something my mom roped me into doing. But then it started feeling more and more important, you know? With the racist guy and H.B. 28 and all the Koopa Troopas—"

"Yeah."

"I promise it wasn't just about the car." She squeezes my hand. "I started to feel like we were making a difference . . . and I like spending time with you. Obviously."

"So do I. I mean. Obviously."

"This is really hard," she says softly.

"What is?"

"Being in a room full of people. Not sneaking away to the coat closet again."

"Oh." I exhale. "No kidding."

Sophie's friends disappear to the teen room after dinner, but it feels like only moments before they're herded back in for the hora. Hands joined, feet moving forward-step, back-step, around and around in circles. I keep my hand locked with Maya's, feeling dizzy with joy. Like I'm threaded with something ancient, something larger than life. I feel so *Jewish*. I don't think anything's made me feel this wholly, utterly Jewish since Fifi. But this is the opposite of Fifi. The precise polar opposite.

The circles stall in place, and everyone steps back, clapping—everyone but a few of Mom's burliest family friends. The DJ brings out a chair, and Sophie clutches the bottom and shrieks when she's lifted. Then she comes down, and it's Mom's turn. Then it's mine. At my own bar mitzvah, all I could think about was how many people were down below. How many people were watching me. But now I only see Maya.

I run back to her as soon as my feet hit the ground. We hook elbows and dance in the center of the circle. "Jamie, I swear," she says, breathless from the movement. "Everyone's looking at us."

"Because we're—"

"Not because we're in the middle. Jamie. Look."

I peer around the circle as I dance, and my heart thumps hard in my chest. Maya's right. Sophie's friends are openly staring. And giggling. And holding up their phones. Maddie's glaring at Maya, looking close to tears all over again.

"Super weird, right?" Maya says. "It's not in my head."

"Definitely not."

Everyone switches partners, so I leap toward Sophie. "Why, hello," she says, linking our arms.

I cut straight to the point. "Why are your friends staring at us?"

I half expect her to deny it. Or say I'm imagining it. But she just shrugs and says plainly, "It's probably the picture."

My whole body goes cold. "The picture?"

We switch directions, still dancing, "Hava Nagila" still playing. I barely hear it.

"The one Maddie took of you and Maya kissing," Sophie says. "Gabe put it on Grandma's Instagram. And the Rossum account. I think it went kind of viral."

I stop short.

Kissing? But we didn't—we didn't kiss. Believe me, kissing Maya is pretty much all I've thought about for weeks. I would fucking know if it happened. But Maddie took a picture? Why the hell was Gabe looking at Maddie's pictures?

And it went—

No. No way.

I reach into my back pocket, hands shaking. Sophie eyes me nervously. "You okay?"

The hora circles have disbanded by now, and everyone's trailing back to their tables for dessert. But I'm frozen on the dance floor. "I don't understand."

I tap into Instagram. Grandma's account.

"Jamie, what's happening?" Maya rushes toward me. "Is everyone—"

Her voice falls away.

I stare dumbfounded at the screen.

It's us. On my car. In the temple parking lot. Our faces inches apart.

There's a caption: *We're feeling the love! And hey, don't forget to give Rossum his happily ever after on July ninth!*

It's been up for four hours. Twenty thousand likes. Over eight hundred comments.

Maya looks like she's about to throw up.

CHAPTER THIRTY
MAYA

This isn't happening. It can't be.

Jamie's searching for Gabe. To yell at him. To make him take the photo down.

Me? The same three words are running in my head on a loop: This. Isn't. Happening. It could be some sort of hallucinatory dream. I've had them before—fever dreams, where I show up to school pantsless and everyone laughs at me.

But this isn't a dream.

Jamie and I almost kissed.

Maddie took a photo.

Gabe shared it on the Rossum account.

The picture went viral.

Jamie deleted the one that got posted on his grandma's page, but it's on the official Jordan Rossum campaign feed, and a bunch of other places. The same photo over and over again, like endless infinity mirrors of us. The image is burned into my brain. Jamie and me sitting on his car. Our shoulders brushing against each other. Looking into each other's eyes. My hair obscures a bit of the image. You can't see we hadn't kissed. Judging from what everyone is saying, we may as well have.

With a trembling hand, I click on the campaign feed. I never look at comments. I know better. But I can't help it. When I start reading—my stomach drops. The comments under our picture churn into the four digits as I watch.

Yassss! 😊

True love can't be stopped! 😍

She straightened her hair! It looks nice!

He is CUTE.

More like awkward.

Awkward SEXY.

He could do better tbh.

No way—she's too hot for him.

Get a room.

Look at her skirt riding all the way up, im cringing

Each comment lands like a punch. Comments about my looks, my clothing. A couple of Islamophobic ones are in there too, because of course. I scroll down but I can't keep up—more comments pop up each second.

I pause at one comment: *I called it from the start, didn't I?*

Called it from the start?

My phone starts buzzing.

Text messages. Rania from Sunday school thinks Jamie's cute. Serene wants to know if I want to have a talk about faith and sex. Acquaintances I haven't seen since school ended are sending me shocked emojis. Heart eye emojis.

Kissing emojis.

The texts keep coming. A few are from Shelby—checking to make sure I'm all right. But so many are from numbers I don't even recognize.

I want to scream.

I want to punch a wall.

But I'm too nauseous to do much of anything—and now that's the least of my concerns, because the room has started spinning.

"Maya?" a voice calls out. It's Jamie. He's looking at me with unmasked worry. I don't know how long he's been standing there.

"You need to sit," he says. "You look like you're going to pass out."

I sit down numbly on a folding chair by the wall. I don't look at him. I can't.

"Gabe left," Jamie says. "I'll find him. I'm going to handle this." He kneels down in front of me. "Maya, please.

Say something."

But what is there to talk about?

He puts his hand gently on mine. I flinch. He quickly pulls it away.

"You have to breathe," he says gently. "You're literally going to faint."

"How can I breathe? How *could* he? And the comments." My eyes blur with tears. "The comments are *endless*—they won't stop . . . everyone saying things," I tell him. "The things they're saying about us . . . it's mortifying."

"People can be the worst. But you can't let it get to you like this, Maya. They've been saying stuff like that forever and . . ." His voice trails off.

"Forever?" I straighten.

Jamie bites his lip.

"What do you mean by that?" I look up at him.

"Nothing," he says quickly. "I didn't mean anything."

"Jamie."

"It's just. Well. You and I have been in so many photos for the campaign, and I guess, people just . . . had opinions. . . ."

I pull out my phone and click on InstaGramm's feed.

The Fifi Gets Flipped video.

Carmen's Cupcakes, with Jamie, Grandma, and me posing with large smiles.

The Canvassing 101 photo. I'm holding the mic and

side-eyeing Jamie with a smile.

Each and every photo, accompanied by hundreds of comments.

Her dimple is melt worthy.

They're totally going to hook up soon.

They'll have the cutest babies.

Comment after comment after comment.

About us.

"You *knew* people were talking about us like this?" I can't even look at him now. All this time, people were dissecting everything about us—making up a love story that didn't even exist—and he didn't say a single word about it to me. "Jamie. That day when you were reading comments that people left about our video. Were people saying stuff like this, even that day?"

"I don't know. I mean, does it matter?" Jamie blushes. "Who cares what they have to say?"

"It matters! Of course it matters! I can't believe I fell for it. I mean, it explains everything, doesn't it? Gabe didn't care about us doing a Canvassing 101. He was using us for clicks and comments." I stare at him. "And you knew."

"I didn't know *that*! I swear!" he insists. "These are just randos."

"Randos?" My voice trembles. "These are thousands of people analyzing everything about us. They have been. For *weeks*."

"But who cares, Maya?" he says. "I know it's mortifying. I get it. But it's not like these people know us or anything."

He's looking at me like I'm the one who needs to check myself.

"It makes sense you don't care." I wipe away tears. "I mean, you're the same person who pretended to be your grandmother online."

Jamie's eyes widen.

"You know I even thanked her for following me? How stupid do I feel now?"

"I shouldn't have followed you as InstaGramm," he says. "I messed up. I'm so sorry. But I was too mortified to share these comments people were saying. And we don't always share every single detail about everything with each other, do we? You didn't tell me *why* you were so into canvassing, did you? That it was just for a car—"

"Just for a car?" I stare at him. "Is that really what you think?"

"Well, it's true, isn't it? I mean, it's fine. I get it." He looks down at the ground. "But that was the reason you texted me to go canvassing again after the first time, wasn't it? Because you'd get a car out of it?"

I can't believe this is happening. Yes. It's true. For maybe *a minute* that was my motivation. But. If he honestly thinks all the work we did together—knocking on doors, drafting flyers, putting up yard signs, was for a stupid car . . . what more is there to say?

All our hangouts. Our conversations. It was meaningless. It was nothing.

I shut out of Instagram and click open my rideshare app. With a shaky hand, I type in my address and stand up.

"I'm going home. Tell Sophie I'm sorry I had to duck out early."

"You're leaving? No!" Jamie says quickly. "Let's talk this through, Maya."

The app chimes. A driver has been found. Felix. 4.8 stars. Four minutes away.

I walk out the door to the parking lot.

"Maya, wait!" He hurries after me. "Don't go like this. Please. We can't let all of this get in the way of how we feel about each other."

"How we feel about each other?" I whip around. "I can't date you, Jamie."

"Yeah, okay." He runs a hand through his hair. "That's fine. Dating is so old-fashioned anyway. No one *dates* anymore. . . ."

"I'm not talking semantics. I mean we can't be together like *that*. It's not going to happen. Ever."

"Oh." Jamie falls silent.

And just like that, seeing his crestfallen face, my anger vanishes into the air. All I feel is sadness, instead. I don't want to tell him. But it's not fair to him. And I've put it off for way too long. I have to tell him the truth.

"It's my parents, Jamie. I'm not allowed to date. I should have told you that from the start. I'm sorry."

"Your parents?" Jamie repeats. His expression shifts. And when he speaks now, his voice is harder. "Can't you own it at least?"

"What's that supposed to mean?"

"You're a senior," he spits out. "You're seventeen years old. If you don't want to be with me, don't hide behind your parents."

"You know I'm Muslim, don't you?"

"So, is it your parents?" he asks. "Or is it that you're Muslim? Make up your mind, Maya."

"It's both, Jamie! It's because of my parents, because we're Muslim. Dating is a little more complicated for me."

"We almost kissed!" His voice rises. "I told you I loved you. If Gabe hadn't burst in, you were going to kiss me back."

"Yes." I look down at the ground. "And it would have been a mistake."

"A mistake . . . ," he says softly. His eyes fill with tears.

"Jamie . . ." I move closer to him, just as headlights engulf us. A green Kia pulls up to the curb.

"I'm sorry," I tell him. "I'm sorry this is so complicated. . . ."

"But you see, it's not." A tear slips down his cheek. "You

either like me. Or you don't. It's really as simple as that."

"Jamie." I take his hand in mine. "This isn't how I wanted tonight to go. I'm not explaining myself well. . . ."

And for the first time ever—Jamie pulls away from me.

"You've explained well enough," he says evenly. "Safe drive home. And you should ask your parents for that car now. You've definitely earned it."

I get in the car. It pulls away and turns down the road. Jamie's figure grows smaller and smaller, until it's out of sight.

Until now I thought the word *heartbreak* was a cheesy poetic term—not an actual breaking that splinters down to the core of your being.

As the car pulls onto the highway, I sink my head into my hands.

Only now do I begin to cry.

CHAPTER THIRTY-ONE
JAMIE

I don't even know if I slept. I feel so bleary and strange, like my head's been stuffed with cotton.

It's all one giant blur. I barely remember getting home from the venue. There's a croissant on my nightstand—Grandma must have snuck in here before she left this morning. And Boomer's curled at the end of my bed. He hasn't left my side all night.

My whole face hurts from crying. I don't think I've cried like this in years, maybe not since Grandpa died. Everyone says crying's supposed to help. It's supposed to get rid of toxins or release endorphins or recharge you or *something*. But I don't feel recharged. I barely have the energy to lift my phone off my nightstand.

I've never gotten so many texts in my life. Texts from

Nolan, old camp friends, Felipe's sister, and this guy Peter from Academic Bowl. Thirty-six texts on the group chat with Drew and Felipe. Texts from literally everyone. Except Maya.

And they keep coming. A new one pops up from Alison, the campaign intern. **Whoa, you and Maya are on Buzzfeed!!!!** 😱 There's a link, but I don't even need to click it. The headline tells me everything I need to know. *These two teens fell in love working on a local Democratic campaign, and my heart is too full.* The preview photo is Maddie's picture. Of us.

I shove my phone back in its charger, flipping it facedown.

I just can't believe it's all over. Everything. Our campaign work, our friendship, and everything else I was stupid enough to hope for. I thought this would end like a movie. I honestly thought that. Awkward nerdy guy gets the dream girl. I mean, Maya said she wanted to kiss me. And her coatroom cake smash. Hands down, the sexiest moment of my entire life. I can hardly believe that was yesterday. Twelve hours ago. I still have icing on my wrist. Not the shape of a heart anymore—just a few smudges remaining. I guess it's fitting.

It's barely eight when Mom knocks on my door, but who cares? I've been up for hours.

"Hey. I've got leftover bagels." She sets a plate next to the untouched croissant on my nightstand, before nudging

Boomer off the bed and stealing his spot. "How are you feeling, sweetie?"

I groan into my pillow.

"Not your best night, huh?"

I mean, that's the crazy thing. Most of the night *was* good. It was incredible. The music, the hora, even the toast. And Maya. Who said she liked me. Who fit so perfectly under my chin on the dance floor.

One Instagram post ruined everything. Every single thing.

"Want to talk about it?" Mom asks.

I sit up slowly, rubbing my eyes. "Not really."

Everything was fine. It was *fine*.

Yeah, the picture was weird. Obviously, I wasn't cool with Maddie spying on us from the bushes, or wherever the hell she was, and Gabe putting it online was even worse. But Maya completely freaked out. I've never seen her go pale like that. She could barely speak at first. And the look on her face when she read the comments, like the idea of people knowing about us was too mortifying to stomach. Yeah. That felt great. Almost as great as when she said *it's not going to happen. Ever.* In the most matter-of-fact tone. Like I was supposed to have already understood that. Like it's obvious.

Cool. I guess I'm just delusional.

Mom scoots closer, resting her hands on my shoulders.

"Honey, talk to me."

I don't know what she wants me to say. That I'm broken? Shattered? That I should have known it was too good to be true? Maybe Maya felt something for me, but it obviously wasn't enough. If the situation were reversed, I'd have done anything to make it work. *Anything*. I would have toughed it out through any awkward conversation.

The way Mom's looking at me makes my throat clench. "Hey," she says, wrapping her arms around me tightly. "Hey."

She strokes my hair like she did when I was eight, which makes my eyes pool with tears all over again. When I finally speak, my voice comes out choked. "I'm in love with her."

"I know, sweetie."

"And I told her. Like you said. I told her how I felt." I catch my breath. "I've never said that before to anyone."

"And she didn't take it well?"

"I thought she did." I straighten up, wiping my eyes with the heels of my hands. "She said she liked me. And she seemed like she was nervous to tell her parents, but—I don't know. She didn't make it sound like that was going to be a dealbreaker." My throat clenches. "But then Gabe posted that picture, and everything just . . . collapsed."

"Okay, well, first of all, if it's any consolation, Gabe is in some deep shit with your grandmother. She's at the campaign office right now."

I wipe my eyes again. "Good."

"But listen. Jamie. The stuff with her parents . . . I have no idea what it would mean in Maya's family if she dated a guy who isn't Muslim. Or if she dated at all."

I shake my head. "If she knew she couldn't date a guy who isn't Muslim, why did she almost kiss me? You can't do that. It's fine if you can't date, or you don't want to date, or you don't want to date outside your religion. But if your best friend tells you he's in love with you, don't act like his girlfriend all night and come *this* close to kissing him, and then turn around and call it a mistake."

Mom just looks at me. "I'm so sorry, sweetie. I really am."

"It's whatever." I rub the last bit of chocolate off my wrist, flicking little specks of it onto my bedsheet. I'm too tired to care.

"It's *not* whatever," Mom says. "Listen. I've got to run out and grab those centerpieces back from the event planner, but I'll be around all afternoon. Let's do something special. You, me, and Sophie." She leans forward, pressing her hands to my cheeks. "We're going to get through this. I promise. And Jamie?"

I look up half-heartedly.

"You should be really proud of yourself," she says. "For everything. For your speech. For your advocacy work. And for having the guts to tell Maya how you feel. That was incredibly brave."

"I don't feel brave."

"I mean it. Jamie, I know you have this idea of yourself as this awkward kid who never knows what to say, who screws everything up—"

"Negative self-talk. I know."

Mom smiles wryly. "I won't get on your case about it. But can I ask you one question?"

"Okay."

"Why do you think you're so awkward?"

I furrow my brow. "What do you mean?"

"What's your evidence? What makes you such a screwup?"

"Um." I look up at her. "I mean . . . I vomited on your boss."

"Okay, but look at all the people you didn't vomit on."

I nod slowly. "That's a low bar for success."

"I'm just saying. This is your narrative. You get to pick the framing. Why does that one interview have to define you? Maybe it was just a shitty morning. Maybe you ate something weird for breakfast. Whatever! Look at everything you've accomplished since then. The canvassing, the videos, the toast. You know that toast was amazing, right?"

"Amazing? Yeah, right—"

"Hey, you're smiling." She pokes my cheek. "Because you know you killed it up there."

"Okay." I roll my eyes. "I killed it. I'm amazing. I'm an

amazing speaker who inspires the masses and hardly pukes on anyone. You happy?"

"You did," Mom says firmly. "And you are. And I am."

I don't want to cry again. I don't even think my eye muscles have enough strength left for round three. But a tear breaks free anyway.

"Love you, Mom." I swallow thickly.

She kisses my forehead. "Love you too."

She leaves, Boomer trotting out behind her, and my whole body deflates. But the moment I settle back onto my pillow, my phone buzzes. And then buzzes again. I tug it out of my charger, my heart lodged in my throat—

It's Grandma. Of course. Not that I thought . . .

Yeah.

Grandma: Hi, lovey! Just wanted to let you know that a certain picture is officially gone from Rossum's page! All I had to do was threaten to delete every single piece of Rossum content from my personal account, and your cousin was very reasonable about the whole thing. Apparently there's an election in two days he'd like to promote. Who knew? And I'm emailing Buzzfeed, Hypable, and Upworthy right now. 💪

I shove my phone under my pillow. God. The picture made it to Upworthy too? *Hypable*?

There's a knock. "Let me in." Sophie's morning voice, husky with sleep.

I sit up, cross-legged, yawning.

"It's open."

Sophie's in pajama pants and a tank top—half loosely curled bat mitzvah hair, half bedhead. There's an open cardboard box tucked under her arm.

"Dad sent stroopwafels," she says. "Global overnighted them. Probably cost a million euros. Here." She sets the box by my feet on the bed, and then plops down beside it. "I guess we should eat them. Or something."

"I do like stroopwafels." I grab two packs of them, handing one to Sophie, before sliding the box onto the floor. Sophie stares at it, glumly.

Okay. Got to rally. Sophie's clearly in that post–bat mitzvah slump. Which means she deserves a real big brother, not a catatonic mess.

"Do you feel any different?" I ask. "You're a woman now—"

"Shut up. What happened with Maya?"

My stomach drops. "We don't have to talk about that."

"Excuse me. I woke up at the ass crack of dawn the day after my bat mitzvah to bring you stroopwafels. The least you can do is fill me in. Mom won't tell me anything."

"There's not much to tell."

Sophie looks at me witheringly. "Oh, so you didn't spend the last hour of my party hiding in Mom's car?"

"I'm sorry. I didn't want to—"

"Jamie! It's fine. I'm just worried about you. I'm trying

to be a supportive sister here."

"That's not how it works. You're the little sister. I'm supposed to be the supportive one. And it was your night, which I ruined—"

"You didn't ruin anything." Sophie scoots closer. "*Shut up* and just tell me what happened."

"Okay, those are slightly contradictory demands—"

She pushes my arm. "So, you and Maya kissed."

"No! No, we didn't. It just looks like that."

"Fine. You almost kissed."

"And then somehow Maddie photographed us? I didn't even see her there."

"She feels awful," Sophie says. "She saw Gabe looking for you at the luncheon, so she followed him outside. She *really* likes you, Jamie."

"Then why would she want a picture of me with another girl?"

"I mean, I don't think she really thought it through. She just snapped it, and texted it to the squad—"

"And Gabe, apparently."

"Well, Gabe specifically asked for it," she says.

"And Maddie gave it to him."

"She didn't know he was going to turn it into a campaign ad!" Sophie tilts her palms up. "I'm telling you, she feels *so* bad."

"It's fine." I stare at my barely nibbled stroopwafel. "I

mean, it's *not* fine, and Maya's never going to speak to me again, ever. But that's Gabe's fault, not Maddie's."

Sophie's face falls. "You don't think Maya will come around?"

"Well, seeing as she said—and I quote—*it's not going to happen. Ever. . . .*"

Sophie's face falls. "Jamie, I'm so sorry."

"No, *I'm* sorry. It's the morning after your bat mitzvah. The last thing you need is my girl drama."

She sighs. "Girl drama is the worst."

"You have no idea."

"I have some idea," she says.

"Yeah, okay." I smile weakly. "I guess your friends are a *little* dramatic."

Sophie doesn't say anything.

I turn to face her. "Everything okay with the group? The squad isn't fighting, is it?"

"No, not squad drama." Sophie pauses. "It's Tessa."

"Oh, right. With the sketchy boyfriend. Ugh." I make a face. "Sorry, Soph. That has to suck. I don't know what I'd do if Drew or Felipe dated someone awful."

"Oh my God, Jamie." Sophie presses her hands to her face. "You are missing the point in, like, fifty billion ways right now."

"I'm missing . . ." I shoot a fuzzy glance at Sophie, who's now staring pointedly at her knees. And then it hits me.

"Tessa. *Oh*. Sophie."

Her cheeks flush. "Don't tell Mom, okay?"

"Of course not. Soph." I sit up straight, scooting closer. "So . . . you and Tessa. Are you guys—"

"No!" She winces. "It's just a stupid crush."

"It's not stupid." I peer at her profile. "Does she know?"

"No one knows."

"Okay." I nod. "Wow. So this is like . . . is this . . . you're coming out?"

"I don't have, like, a label or anything. I don't know." Sophie shrugs uncomfortably. "It's not a big deal. I'm just saying, maybe I kind of get the Maya thing—"

"Sophie. This is a big deal." I wrap my arms around her, hugging her tightly. "I'm really glad you told me."

"Okay." She squirms out of the hug. "Just don't be weird about it."

"I love you so much."

"Jamie! I said don't be weird."

Suddenly, she bursts into tears.

"Soph." I hug her again, and this time she buries her face in my chest. "Shh. Hey. It's going to be fine."

"I know." Her voice is muffled. "I'm just relieved. And I feel ridiculous. Like I just made a big deal out of nothing."

"You're not ridiculous."

She draws back, wiping her eyes. "Listen. I can't promise I won't steal your girlfriends—"

"Okay, someone needs to have a serious talk with you and your friends about appropriate age gaps."

"I love you too, by the way." Sophie smiles tearfully. "You're my favorite person. That was a rock solid coming-out talk. Ten out of ten."

"Ooh, good call. There should be Yelp ratings for this—"

"Hey. I have something to show you," Sophie says, reaching down into the stroopwafel box. She roots around for a moment before pulling out a manila envelope.

"Should I be worried?" I narrow my eyes. "It's not from Maddie, right?"

She laughs, pinching the clasp open. "Nope. Well, sort of. It's from everyone." She upturns the envelope, dumping a pile of postcards onto the bed. "You kind of inspired us."

I pick one up, examining it. It's addressed to Congressman Holden. *Hi, my name is Andrea Jacobs, I'm an almost eighth grader at Riverview Middle School, and I'm writing to say please vote no on H.B. 28. It is an unfair discriminatory bill and it is racist and cruel. Please vote no or I will remember and vote against you in five years which is when I am old enough to vote. Thank you for your time. Sincerely, Andrea Jacobs.*

I look at Sophie. "Andrea wrote this?"

"I know Holden's not going to vote against his own bill," Sophie says. "But a bunch of Hebrew school people live in other districts, so maybe their Congress guys will listen? I don't know. Maybe it's pointless—"

"It's not pointless." I shake my head. "Sophie, this is amazing."

"Everyone wrote one. Every single person," she says, nudging me sideways. "See, my friends aren't scary. Well, except Tessa. She's terrifying." She pulls Tessa's postcard out of the stack to show me.

Dear Congressman Holden, My name is Tessa Andrews and I'm thirteen, I go to Riverview Middle School. I am writing this postcard to tell you to vote against Racist H.B. 28 or I will tell my parents not to vote for you. Discrimination is not okay!!!!! Yours truly, Tessa Andrews.

"I can't believe you got everyone to do this. Sophie." I look at her. "During your bat mitzvah reception."

"In the teen room." She shrugs.

"I legit thought you guys were going to use that room to make out with each other."

Sophie stares at Tessa's postcard and sighs. "Yeah. I wish."

CHAPTER THIRTY-TWO
MAYA

The clock blinks 12:45 p.m. when I finally sit up in bed.

I didn't sleep all night. My chest constricts now, thinking of Jamie's face—the way his eyes widened when I told him we couldn't date. How he yanked his hand away from me. Tears spring to my eyes again. You'd think a person has only so many tears in their head—I know better now.

I pick up my phone from the nightstand. The texts keep coming. I even have a missed call from Shelby. I let her know I'm not up for talking, but appreciate her checking in. Thumbing through my messages, I land on my last exchange with Jamie. We'd been at the bat mitzvah reception when I sent it.

You'll see this text when you finish the toast—but you're

killing it! My cake smash trick is genius. I'm going to write a book about it and make millions.

And then, two minutes later, I'd added—

Oh! Remind me to tell you about Drew and Rachel.

I blink back more tears. Such casual messages—like I had no doubt there'd be a million more texts to follow.

I think back to the parking lot outside the temple, overlooking skyscrapers and oak trees. I always thought those parts in the movies where two people grew silent and leaned forward to kiss seemed so unrealistic. But in that moment with Jamie, kissing him seemed like the most natural thing in the world.

But we didn't kiss. We almost kissed. And an almost kiss isn't a kiss.

I wonder what Jamie's doing. The look on his face, the tear trailing down his cheek as the car pulled away—my stomach hurts. I should have let him drop me off at home. Maybe we could have talked. Sorted things out.

I can't imagine how upset he must be right now.

I open Instagram. I was so upset last night, I soft blocked Jamie and InstaGramm—but searching now, I find Jamie's profile. It's the same four photos from when he opened the account, plus the one of the Rabbi Rothschild quote he snapped yesterday. But nothing since then. No record of everything falling apart. I can look at these photos and almost pretend yesterday never happened.

I wish so badly it was true.

Rossum's official campaign account pops into my feed. I hesitate, before scrolling down to the video. Our video. I brace myself for the comments. I know I shouldn't do it— this is like picking a scab—but I need to know. As soon as I dip into the first few, I remember, yet again, you can't brace yourself for things like that.

They're the cutest.

Maya's got the most kissable lips.

She's not that hot.

He could do better.

How much you want to bet they're doing it?

There are twenty-seven nested replies to that one.

It feels like I got dipped in an ice bath. I drop the phone on the bed. I understand why Jamie didn't read the comments to me. But I don't know how I'll be able to look him in the face again.

I exhale and stand up. I throw a sweatshirt on over my pajamas. When I step into the hallway, a glass clinks in the distance. My mother. I don't want to talk to her about this. She tapped on my bedroom door late last night and peeked in at me. I did my best to look asleep. But I live here. I can only hold her off for so long.

I take my time brushing my teeth and washing up, but when I step into the kitchen, I freeze. I must be having an official nervous breakdown, because my brain just conjured

395

up both the most bizarre and most ordinary figment possible: My mother brewing tea in the kitchen. My dad on the
love seat, feet kicked up on the coffee table, watching soccer
in the family room.

"Maya." My father looks over at me and sits up.

It's real. He's really here. He's sitting on our couch,
watching television like he always does on Sundays.
They're hanging out together in this house—under the
same roof—like on a regular weekend. A jolt of sunshine
kicks in. As randomly and suddenly as they announced
their separation, it's over.

My mother turns off the stove and hurries to me as my
father strides over.

"You're back?" I whisper to my dad. "I knew you'd get
back together. I knew it."

"Oh, honey, no . . ." My mother glances at me and then
at my father. "It's still . . . it's a work in progress."

"I came over as soon as I heard what happened. We wanted
to talk to you. Together," my father says. "About . . ."

Oh.

I sink onto a kitchen stool.

My mother puts a hand gently on my shoulder.

"Holding up okay?" she asks.

I shrug. I want to say I'm fine, so we can get through
this conversation as quickly as possible. But the words are
stuck in my mouth. Because the truth is, everything is not

fucking fine. I am not okay. Tears spill down my cheeks.

In an instant they're hugging me. My parents on either side and me in the middle. If you told me twenty-four hours ago I'd be having a group hug with my parents under one roof, I'd have melted into a puddle of relief.

But today everything aches.

We walk over to the family room. I settle onto the ottoman and tuck my feet under; Willow hops into my lap and nuzzles me. My parents sit across from me on the love seat. Both watch me with concern.

"I'm okay," I manage to say. "I'm sorry for melting down like that."

"It's okay to be upset. The photo going viral. That'd be rough for anyone."

For a split second, I'm confused. And then it hits me all over again. The photo. The news sites and magazines and comments. They don't know about my fight with Jamie. They don't know the rest of it. And how the rest of it hurts so much more.

"I don't really want to talk about this right now," I whisper.

"But we need to," my mother says. "That's why we're having this family meeting. So we can all discuss together."

"Think you have to be a family to have a family meeting," I mutter.

My father leans forward.

"We are still a family, Maya," he says. "It's been a rough

few weeks, but no matter what happens, the three of us are forever connected. And you are always our top priority. That never changes."

I look down at my lap and blink back tears.

"I had no idea anyone was taking photos. One minute everything was great, and then all of a sudden, people are staring and talking and laughing." I blink back tears again. "It was mortifying."

"It'll blow over," my father reassures me. "A few bigger sites caught it, but most of it's just local stuff."

"I live locally," I say.

"And, well." My mother shifts and glances at my father, before looking at me. "Well, we also wanted to talk to you about . . ."

"Oh God." I look up at them both. "Is everyone talking? My phone has been buzzing off the hook. I'm so sorry. Serene and Rania texted me too, and . . ."

"Don't worry about any of that." My mother shakes her head. "This is between us. This is about our family. That's it. And, well, we need to talk about the kiss. Jamie is such a sweet boy—he always has been. Cute too. And, well, I understand why you'd want to kiss him, but . . ."

"We didn't kiss." I flush. "I swear. It's the angle that stupid photo was taken with, but we didn't. You have to trust me—"

"We believe you," my father says. "If you say you didn't, you didn't."

"Are you mad?" I ask in a small voice.

"We're not mad," my mother says. "It's natural to have feelings for someone. But." She glances at my father. "Even if you haven't kissed . . . you have been spending lots of time together."

"Trust me." I bite my lip to keep it from trembling. "You don't have to worry about Jamie and me."

"Dating in high school is incredibly complicated," my mother says. "That's why we've always cautioned you against it."

"Because my brain cells grow in after next year, right?"

"Not exactly." My mother smiles a little. "Like we said, there's so much already on your plate with high school, and college applications are around the corner, and . . ." She hesitates. "With Jamie, it'd be even more complicated. He's not Muslim. That opens up so many other questions. How will you reconcile your different identities and faith? How will you raise your children? Religious traditions and practices . . . It's a lot to consider."

"Um, first of all, I'm not in a relationship with Jamie, much less planning kids." My face burns. "And second of all, what about Auntie Jameela?"

"Uncle Scott converted," my mother says. "And my kid

sister is a good example of what I'm saying. She had your cousin Reem just after high school graduation. They're doing okay enough now, but trust me, they had major growing pains. Relationships are complicated when they start out so young."

"Apparently they're complicated at any age." I glance at both of them.

My mother's eyes get moist. My father looks down at his lap. Suddenly, I feel awful.

"I think what we're trying to say," my father says, "is that we all know how hard uncertainty is for you. And that's part of entering into a relationship. You go in not knowing what the future holds, and take a leap of faith anyway into the great unknown. You have to ask yourself if you're ready to add one more complication and uncertainty onto your plate—if you're ready to deal with the emotional fallout that can happen."

I don't want to admit it. I don't. But that makes sense.

I can't handle any more what-ifs.

"We're not here to dictate what you can and can't do," my mother says. "You're too old for that. This time next year, you'll be packing up for college."

"You're your own person." My father nods. "But we're also going to be here to tell you our opinions and thoughts—part of the gig when you sign up to be parents."

"I didn't mean to lash out," I say. "But I promise, there's

nothing to think about. Jamie and me . . . there's nothing happening."

And it's probably for the best.

We're quiet for a few seconds, and then my father clears his throat.

"There's also one more reason for the family meeting," he says.

My mother smiles at this. Both of them stand up.

"What is it?" I ask them.

"Come along and see." My father nods to the front door. We slip on our sandals and walk onto the driveway.

There's my dad's Toyota Highlander. Next to it is a Jetta.

"Whose car is that?" I ask.

"Yours," my mother says.

"What?" I glance at them and back at the car. "Are you serious right now? You're not pranking me? *That* is my car?"

"It's been waiting in my apartment garage for a week now." My dad smiles. "Thought we'd surprise you with it after the election, but today felt like a good time."

"Hopefully you like it," my mother says.

"It's certified pre-owned. And it's only got twelve thousand miles," my dad says. He continues to rattle off the features as I walk over and trace a hand over the metal exterior. I peek inside. Black seats. Car mats. A pink bow on the steering wheel.

"Thank you so much," I whisper. I pull them both into a group hug.

My father hands me the keys. He's getting in the passenger seat. We're going to take it for a spin.

I turn on the engine. I'm happy about this, but sadness seeps in too—because part of happiness is sharing things with the people you care about most.

And the one person I want to share this with more than anyone else is Jamie.

CHAPTER THIRTY-THREE
JAMIE

Gabe has been avoiding me since Saturday, and I guess I've let him. But I can't put this off any longer.

I park and walk in through the Fawkes and Horntail side entrance, stomach churning.

Hardly anyone's here—I guess everyone's at the Dunwoody office. It's just Hannah and Alison, yawning at their desks under the fluorescent lights of the annex. But a moment later, Gabe rolls his chair into view, iced coffee in hand. He pauses a few feet from Hannah's desk, laptop resting on his crossed legs.

I feel like puking. I'm not even kidding. My breakfast may not make it out of here with me.

Of course, Gabe grins when he sees me, like everything's totally normal. "Big J! You here for poll observer training?"

I glare down at him. "What's wrong with you?"

"Uh. Whoa."

"I'm not kidding. What the hell is wrong with you?"

Gabe sets his laptop on the floor and takes a sip of his drink. "If this is about the picture—"

"Of course it's about the picture!"

Hannah and Alison exchange glances, eyebrows halfway to the ceiling. "We're gonna just . . ." Hannah's already halfway to the annex door; moments later, Alison clicks it shut behind them.

"Dude," Gabe says. "Chill. I took it down."

"Yeah, from Rossum's site." I step toward him. "Great. What about BuzzFeed, Upworthy, Hypable—"

"Mashable now too." Gabe pokes his finger up cheerfully. "And Bustle and the HuffPo. You guys are more popular than Fifi! Who knew?"

"*You* knew! This was completely calculated!"

Gabe leans back, calmly gripping his cup. "Did I think it could potentially drive a little traffic to the campaign at a critical time? Sure. But did I know it would go viral—"

"You've been obsessed with going viral! All summer! Don't act like this wasn't your endgame."

"Look. Does it help the campaign? Yeah. More enthusiasm means more people actually showing up to vote. That's how this works."

The look on Gabe's face right now. The way his lips tug

casually upward. Like me losing my temper is just a funny little Monday morning distraction.

"I swear to God—"

"Look, Big J, don't hate the player—"

"Are you even hearing yourself? You used us. You put a really private moment up on the internet without our consent." My fists clench as I stare at him. "And thanks to you, Maya's not speaking to me."

"Oh, so it's my fault she overreacted—"

"She didn't overreact!" My entire body floods with heat. "Maya's not allowed to date, and you put up a picture that basically looks like we're making out. In public! You think that's how Maya wanted her parents to find out about us? From BuzzFeed?"

Us. One tiny syllable. The word feels like an open wound.

There's no *us* anymore for Maya's parents to find out about.

"Dude, how they find out isn't the dealbreaker here," Gabe says. "If they're freaking out, they would have freaked out anyway."

"How could you possibly know that?"

"Okay, you know what?" Gabe sets his coffee down, then stands abruptly. "How about you stop being selfish for one minute. Are you forgetting the election is tomorrow? Tomorrow! We have a red-as-hell district, and this is the first time we've *ever* had a real shot at flipping it. And with a supermajority at stake? Big J. If you're so worried about

Maya's family, you should be on your knees, thanking me for pulling out all the stops. We both know this hijab ban is moving forward if Newton wins—"

"Okay, *fuck you*," I yell.

"Whoa." He gapes at me. "I'm on your side—"

"No you're not. You don't give a shit about the hijab ban. You want Rossum to win so you can win. Full stop. So stop pretending you care. Of course I want Rossum to win! But I'm not going to exploit people to get there. Because that's what you're doing! You exploited me. You exploited Maya. Have you even looked at the comments? They're not all fun and heart eyes, Gabe. You think the comment sections are kind to women? To Muslim women?"

Gabe rolls his eyes. "That's a few people. Stop blowing this up. Ninety-nine percent of them think you're adorable. You're going to have adorable babies together—"

"Right, that's your narrative, isn't it? You saw the first comments and decided to keep fanning the flames. Does Rossum know what you're willing to do to win?"

"Jordan doesn't know shit about this." Gabe's face heats up. "You think this is just about winning? My ego?"

"That's *exactly* what I think."

"Do you even read the local news?" Gabe slams his hand down on Hannah's desk. "Do you even get what's at stake? H.B. 28 is the tip of the fucking iceberg, dude. Representative Karpenter from deep red fucking north Georgia's got one in the pipeline to remove discrimination protections in public schools. In the name of religious freedoms. We all fucking know what that means. Maybe think about your pals Felipe and Nolan before you come after me."

Gabe's words knock the wind out of me. A discrimination bill. Here in Georgia. I've seen them pass in other states, but our economy's so tied up with the film industry, Governor Doyle's never wanted to risk stirring up a boycott. But if Newton wins, and there's a Republican supermajority . . .

I think of Felipe and Nolan. Thank God they're graduating in a year. But what about all the kids who aren't graduating yet?

What about *Sophie*?

My heart slams around my rib cage, pressure building behind my eyes. I don't know if I'm about to burst into tears or detonate.

I whirl on Gabe. "That doesn't make what you did okay."

"Well, I'm sorry, Jamie, if my main fucking concern *the day before the election* is winning the goddamn election. I'm sorry Maya freaked out on you, dude. I am. But last I checked, Maya's not the only girl on earth—"

"Okay, that's—"

"Your comments are full of girls who think you're hot," Gabe continues, completely unfazed. "Dude. You want a girlfriend so badly? Make it happen, Big J. Go slide into some DMs. You know you've got, like, three thousand new followers since Saturday."

I just look at him.

"So, you're welcome," he adds.

"I'm . . ." I open Instagram, head spinning. Random girls think I'm hot. Not that I care, but that's, like, bizarro-world, alternate-universe levels of unexpected. *Me?* And three thousand followers? From the kiss picture? I wasn't even tagged. . . .

I tap over to Maya's profile, almost without realizing I'm doing it. But it doesn't load her usual feed.

It loads a picture of a lock in a circle. *This Account is Private.*

I can't catch my breath. It's like someone scraped me out from the inside.

This Account is Private.

"She." I blink. "I think she blocked me."

I sink back against Hannah's desk, legs suddenly weak.

Gabe's expression softens. "Oh, man. I'm sorry, bro. That's rough."

He reaches out to pat my shoulder, but I flinch away from him, voice choked. "Oh, now you're sorry?"

"If I'd known, I wouldn't have done it. Look, man. I'm trying to pull out an impossible win. I don't even know what I'm doing half the time. This is my first rodeo. I'm just stumbling around in the dark here."

I stare dumbly at my phone.

Gabe keeps talking. "Want to know the truth? I'm really fucking scared. This—all of this—could be for nothing. It rains? Boom. Low turnout."

I shake my head dazedly. "The weather's supposed to be—"

"That's just an example! I mean, you can do everything, *every single thing* right. Knock on every door. Organize the fuck out of everything and everyone. Stay on top of every media opportunity." He scrapes his hands through his hair. "And it could all go to shit tomorrow for literally no reason."

I look at him. "Then why do you do it?"

"Well, what's the alternative?" Gabe laughs, but it's strained and panicked. "Hand these fuckers the election? Believe it or not, cuz, I care about this shit. You think they're paying me well for this? You think I have a fancy job lined up in DC if this goes well? Look, 2016 fucking *wrecked* me. Turned my world upside down. And I'm just another white Jew. Not even close to the worst off." He exhales. "I can't fix this mess, but I want to fix a part of it. And this election? Jamie, it's so fucking small. You know, in the grand scheme of things. We win this? Nobody cares. It will be in the news cycle for a day or two, maybe, and that's literally just because of the Fifi story—"

"And me and Maya," I say.

"At least you put us on the map." He sighs defeatedly.

"Even if we win tomorrow, it's the puniest, most nothing victory. But it's my whole life right now. And it all comes down to the numbers—"

"No it doesn't," I say, and Gabe snorts. "It doesn't! It's not about the numbers. It's not even about the end result. Not entirely."

Gabe smiles sadly. "Oh, to have your shiny-eyed optimism—"

"I mean, the numbers are important. Really important. But that's *now*." I clutch the edge of Hannah's desk. "Yeah, in this moment, the numbers are everything. But when you step back from it, it's just another point on the timeline. History's a long game. It's the longest long game."

"That's bullshit," Gabe says. "Frankly, I don't give a shit if the world rights itself in a thousand years. That's not good enough."

"But I'm not talking about the world righting itself. I'm talking about us righting the world."

Gabe looks unmoved, but I keep going.

And it's the weirdest thing. I feel so messy and heartsick and completely off-kilter. But my mouth is saying exactly what I want it to say.

"It's not about waiting for the good parts of history. We're the ones who have to make them happen. We have to draw the timeline ourselves."

"Yeah, well. Right now, that just feels like a fuckton of pointless work."

"But the work itself is the point. You keep doing it, because otherwise, how do you keep from feeling helpless? It's like those sharks that keep swimming or they die," I say. "It's about the act of resisting. Waking up every day and deciding not to give up."

I peer down at my phone screen. Maya's locked profile, with its tiny circular profile picture. The soft brown of her skin. Her hair. Her smile, in miniature.

This girl who hates change, but wants to change the world. This girl who never holds back when it matters.

I didn't even know I could miss someone like this after two days.

"Hey." I glance up at Gabe. "You know, even if we lose, your work matters. All of this. It all counts."

"Yeah, well—"

"It matters," I say again. "Not that I think we're going to lose. No way. But I'm just saying."

Gabe snorts, but he's smiling. "You're pretty inspiring, Big J. You're going to be quite the politician one day."

I smile back. "I know."

CHAPTER THIRTY-FOUR
MAYA

I'm driving my car to the polling station. It still feels weird. Not standing in my driveway waiting for a friend or a ride. This is my car. I made a list last night of all the places I want to apply to for a job, now that I can actually hold one down. Barnes & Noble and Starbucks are both high on my "want" list.

Target would've been there too, but I'm not sure how Kevin would feel about hooking me up with a job, after what went down between us. And, well. There's the matter of Jamie too. Taking a job at his favorite place feels like a nonstarter.

My throat constricts, thinking of him. We spent nearly a month knocking on doors, handing out flyers, putting up signs. Now it's election day. And we aren't even speaking.

I park at the polling station, and pause to look at the

Instagram photo I posted this morning. A selfie of me with a Rossum button, encouraging all fifteen of my followers to get out the vote. I glance at the other pictures from this summer. The Eid brunch, a selfie with Boomer from last week. I look like I'm having the best summer ever. Insta-Maya and real Maya don't even live on the same planet.

I click over to Sara's feed. I'd thought she'd have texted me after the post went viral. But she's not following the election stuff, so it probably didn't even fly by her radar. It's strange how something can be someone's entire universe, but not even register as a blip for someone else.

Her most recent photos make me smile. You'd honestly think she works for the University of Georgia's marketing team. There are filtered photos of the campus, a selfie with a Georgia bulldog in full red-and-white gear. I pause at one from four days ago. She's posing with my favorite author on the planet—Angie Freaking Thomas. They're both smiling and Sara's holding up her latest book. I look down at the caption: *Standing room only for the one and only Angie Freaking Thomas.*

I laugh a little at that. Even in our estrangement, we manage to think the same thoughts. I hesitate before texting her.

Hope college is great. I hate how things ended with us. I miss you.

There are no three ellipses bubbling back to me. And that's okay. I love Sara, and even if I don't get back what I had, it was a beautiful friendship while it was mine. I don't regret telling her how I feel.

I feel a little silly about it now, but I'd built up election day so big in my mind, I almost expected bells to toll and confetti to spray on my head when I stepped into the polling precinct. But the Briarwood recreational gymnasium is definitely anticlimactic this late afternoon. For one thing, it's completely silent. Electronic voting booths line one end of the wall, and folding tables are set up on the other side of the room, with registration volunteers drumming their fingers. Some are reclined so far back in their seats, I swear they might be asleep. A police officer sits by the front door. Hannah is also here. She hands me my poll observer vest, and I sign in on the log. One woman in a business suit is punching in her vote, but otherwise, no one else is here.

My phone buzzes. I pull it out as a news alert flashes onscreen. H.B. 28 passed in the Georgia State House. I click open the article. I'm not supposed to be on my phone, but this has to be a mistake. They weren't voting on this until after the election.

But it's no mistake.

H.B. 28 passed. Evidently, the GOP is so confident Newton will win, they've begun the first step in making my mother's existence a crime.

The front door chimes. An elderly woman is struggling

to get through the door with her walker.

Get with the program, Maya. I shove my phone into my pocket. I'm here to help the elections run smoothly. This is what I signed up for. I hurry over and open the door for her.

"Thank you, sweetheart," the woman tells me. "You are absolutely wonderful."

While the woman fills out her information, Hannah walks over to me.

"It was sweet of you to open the door," she says, "but as poll observers we can't interact directly with voters, even if it's to be helpful."

"Oh," I say. "Sorry. Got it."

The woman finishes voting and heads to the exit.

"Thank you, again, dear," she says.

"Of course," I tell her. "Have a nice day."

"You know, you have the prettiest smile." She pauses by the door and turns to look at me. "It's the kind that makes you know the world is a beautiful place."

"Um, thanks."

"Hope you have a blessed day."

I watch her amble toward her car. It didn't escape my notice that she was wearing a Newton button. Neither did I miss the red hat she had on. I think of Kristin from Dickers's office. She was just like this lady, full of sugar and sunshine, saying the nicest things. And yet this woman. Kristin. They can look at someone like me—grin at Hannah—and still vote for Newton.

The lines pick up as the afternoon progresses. Some people coming through are walking advertisements of which way they're leaning, but I can't read most of the voters. I watch now as a couple in line whisper intensely to each other. The guy keeps raising his hands high up in the air every so often.

"I bet he's telling her he can bench-press her," I tell Hannah. "He totally looks like the type of guy to do that. She's like, 'Stop being obnoxious,' but he's like, 'I totally can!' I mean, why else is he putting his hands up like that?"

"Maybe." Hannah smiles politely at me, and then looks back at the crowd.

My smile fades. This is one thing I'm trying not to focus on. Hannah is great. She's wonderful. But she's not Jamie.

I clock out of my shift at five and pull out my phone. I click over to Jamie's page. I scroll down past the photo of the poster at the temple, and the handful of photos from our Jordan Rossum meet-up. I look at the one with us and Rossum. Then the selfie with just Jamie and me. And the next one. Where I'm grinning into the camera like meeting Jordan is the best thing that's ever happened to me.

I stare at my expression.

Suddenly—it all hits me at once. Like my life is a movie, flashing by at warp speed. Jamie and me in his car. The gift bag of Goldfish. Chocolate cake at Intermezzo. Sitting in the patio section together. Curled on his couch. The way my head fits so perfectly in the crook of his neck. How I get shy when he looks at me just so. The way he holds my worries and fears and happiness, and cradles them as though they are his own. And—I look down at the photo—the way he makes me happier than anyone I've ever known. Suddenly I miss Jamie so much I physically ache. I'm not heart eyes for Rossum. That goofy, lovesick grin isn't about him. It's about the boy I'm looking at. The one taking the picture.

I don't just want to kiss Jamie.

I'm in love with him.

My body bursts with adrenaline.

I need to see him.

Right now.

The last photo he posted is from this morning. A table with "I voted" peach stickers fanned out on a desk, with the caption: *Today's the day! Get out the vote! Unplugging and unwinding now. Fingers crossed for good news tonight.*

Unplug. Unwind.

I know exactly where he is.

I park my car in the Target parking lot and hurry inside. Past the Starbucks and video game consoles, past the magazine racks and shelves of DVDs. I swing by the clearance outfits. And there it is. The patio section.

And there's Jamie.

He's sitting in the wicker egg-shaped seat, thumbing

through a magazine.

Suddenly, my confidence wavers, thinking of how we left things. How he yanked his hand from me. What if the things we said to each other are things we can't move on from? He said he loved me.

But what if he doesn't anymore?

Just then, he glances up—he sees me. His eyes widen.

"Maya," he says.

Don't think. Just go.

"Jamie." I hurry over to him. I sit down next to him. Our knees brush against each other.

"I'm so sorry, Jamie. For what I said . . . the things—"

"No," he says in a rush. "I'm sorry. I should never have spoken that way. I was insensitive and off base. But I get it now. Your parents have their view on how this should go. And if you share their view, that's fine. More than fine. I know your religion and faith are important to you. I get that." He looks at me. His green eyes meet mine. "If we can't date, we can't. I respect that. But I don't want to lose you, Maya. That's what matters most to me. And I just—"

But I don't let him finish. I don't let him say another word.

I lean forward and kiss him.

He startles, and then he wraps his arms around me and kisses me back.

His lips are gentle and warm.

He is mint and lemons.

CHAPTER THIRTY-FIVE
JAMIE

Oh. Dear. God.

Maya just kissed me. I mean, she's kissing me. Present tense. My first kiss is happening right here, right now, in Target, of all places, which, okay, feels weirdly appropriate. Maya's hands cup my cheeks, and her lips taste like vanilla ChapStick.

My brain exits the station completely. I can barely breathe, my head's so foggy.

We move tentatively at first, but then we sort of find our rhythm. Her lips make space, and I fill it. I was so sure I'd be hopeless. I've never gotten anything right the first time. Not anything. Not ever. But somehow, this clicks. My lips just know how this works. At least with Maya, they know.

Pretty sure we were born for this. Pretty sure kissing didn't exist until we tried it.

Maya draws back, just barely, resting her forehead against mine. She's still cupping my cheeks. "I love you." Her voice breaks. "I'm in love with you. I'm so sorry it took me—"

I lean forward, kissing her harder. Her breath hitches, and that alone sends my heart into overdrive. Her arms fall past my shoulders. She's pressed up so close, her knees are almost tucked up into my lap. I would freeze history if I could. Right here. This exact moment. This is my favorite dot on the timeline.

"I love you." It comes out breathless. "I missed you so much."

"Me too. I can't believe this is happening."

"No kidding." I exhale. "Wow."

I glance up in time to see a store employee pointedly looking away from the patio section. "Um." I clear my throat. "Should we . . . go somewhere?"

I swear, I'm barely coherent.

Maya smiles. "Probably."

"I don't want to stop kissing."

"Dressing room?" she suggests.

"Wow. Yes." I kiss her again. "Good idea."

Of course, deciding to kiss in the dressing room is one thing. Making it there is another. Turns out, you can be so giddy that walking is a challenge. We can't stop bumping into each other, like magnets. And we keep sneaking behind displays and into aisles when no one's looking.

Someone walks by, just as I'm about to kiss Maya in the entertainment section. I shift gears. "Quick, pretend we're looking at the DVDs."

Maya nods solemnly. "*Emoji Movie*. On sale. Looks romantic."

"Oh, you want to see heart eyes?" I say. "Wait till we get to the kissing room." I blush. "Dressing room."

Maya laughs, taking my hand. "I'm so happy."

I can't even look at her. "Me too. God. Maya. You have no idea how much—"

"Hey, guys."

It's Kevin. Out of nowhere. He's scratching his head, looking nervously from Maya to me. There's a Georgia voter sticker affixed to his red polo shirt.

Wow. Worst timing ever. There should be an award for this. Called the Kevin Go Away Award. Presented to the Kevin who appears out of thin air to block you from kissing Maya Rehman in dressing rooms.

Maya doesn't let go of my hand.

"Hey," she says.

He smiles tentatively. "I'm really glad I ran into you guys. I feel so bad about how I left things last week."

"No, it's fine," Maya says. "I'm sorry I yelled—"

"Don't be. I needed the wake-up call. Maya. Listen. I

can't begin to understand what all of this must feel like for you. I don't know if I ever will. But I'm going to do a better job listening from now on. I promise." He taps his peach sticker. "Don't you want to know who I voted for?"

Maya's eyes widen.

Kevin shrugs. "You won me over. I don't love the guy, but he's way better than Newton, and he deserved my vote."

Maya looks dumbstruck. "Thank you."

Kevin grins down at her, and then up at me. "Anyway, I don't want to interrupt anything—"

"What?" I stutter. "Uh. Not at all."

"I'm just gonna . . ." Kevin points vaguely in the direction of the produce section. "Cleanup on aisle seven. Tangelo explosion."

The moment he's gone, Maya stands on tiptoe to kiss me in the middle of the aisle. Then she grabs both my hands. "Come on!"

We practically bolt past the electronics.

Thank God the dressing room's empty—not even an attendant. Maya tugs me into one of the family stalls, locking it.

"Hey, look at that," she says. "We're alone."

My heart pounds. "We are."

She sinks onto the bench, and I follow—kissing her forehead, her cheeks, her lips. But then she hugs me, shifting backward, until I'm almost on top of her. I rest my hand behind her head before it hits the bench. Our legs tangle together, sneakered feet dangling off the edge.

This time, when we kiss, it's more urgent. Her hands fall to the back of my neck, gently threading my hair. My fingers trail down her bare arms, and she smiles against my lips. "Now I have goose bumps."

She's so close I can feel the heat of her breath.

"Goose bumps in a good way?"

She laughs. "Yes, Jamie."

"This is—is this okay?"

"It's okay." She kisses me. "Very okay."

"I just want you to know, it's fine if we can't date. If this has to be a thing that happened once in Target." Maya laughs softly, and I tuck a strand of hair behind her cheek. "Seriously. Whatever you need this to be—"

"I want to be your girlfriend."

"Okay." I kiss her. "And your parents? Do you think they'll be okay with . . . us?"

"I don't know." Maya gazes up at me. "I'll figure it out. Can we take it slow?"

"We can take it any way," I say.

She pulls me closer, kissing me again. And again.

Her phone buzzes loudly, startling us apart.

"Okay." She sits up, scooting next to me. "So, now I see the appeal of having no reception here."

I laugh. "You should check that."

She glances at the screen. "It's my mom. Oh my God. If she could see me now." I look at her, half expecting her to look panicked. But she's beaming at me. "The polls just closed. She's at Scavino's doing interviews with Imam Jackson about the impact the election may have on the bill. Returns should be coming in pretty soon. I guess we should head over there." She rests her head on my shoulder. "Except I'm not ready to stop kissing you."

"I'll drive you. We can kiss at red lights."

"I have a better idea," she says.

So now I know: the only thing better than driving Maya is watching Maya drive. She hasn't stopped grinning since we left Target. And I can't stop staring at her profile.

Her dimple flickers. "What?"

"Nothing. You're just pretty."

Maya makes a *pshh* sound, wrinkling her nose.

"And a good driver," I add. "A responsible driver."

The lot at Scavino's is so full, we have to park in the grass—and it's even more packed inside the restaurant. The owners have draped the entire bar area in blue, with cardboard cutouts of Rossum's head mounted on crepe medallion centerpieces. It's more than a little jarring, seeing as Rossum's full body is here too. I mean, actual Jordan Rossum, in the flesh. He's at the bar with Gabe and Hannah.

Gabe slow claps when Maya and I walk in. So now my cheeks are supernovas.

There's no way Gabe could know about all the kissing. Maya and I aren't even holding hands right now. I mean, yeah, it feels like there are tangible sparks shooting between us. And no, I haven't been able to unglue my eyes from Maya's face since we left Target.

But maybe it's just an I-told-you-she'd-speak-to-you-again slow clap?

Probably better if Gabe doesn't know how little speaking we did at Target.

Rossum grins at us and waves, but suddenly Imam Jackson appears. Maya introduces me, and I try to act normal—but it seems I've used up my last shred of chill. My voice comes out high, almost squeaky. "I loved your WPBA segment with Tammy Adrian!"

"Why, thank you."

Grandma drifts toward us, shaking Imam Jackson's hand and hugging Maya and me. "More returns in from DeKalb County," she says, almost singing. "Maya, your neighborhood went sixty-five percent for Rossum."

"Oh my God. Really?"

"Mmm-hmm." Grandma smiles. "So far, so good! At this rate, Boomer will get his celebratory walk by ten."

"Boomer?" asks Imam Jackson—and the next thing I know, he and Grandma are absorbed in looking at puppy pictures on Grandma's phone. Maya watches them for a minute, and turns back to me smiling. But before she can even open her mouth to speak, Sophie sidles up.

"You guys look like you're having a good day," she says.

I tug her ponytail. "Shut up."

"I'm just *saying*." She beams. "Hey, have you seen Hannah?"

"Don't look now," Maya says as soon as Sophie wanders off toward the bar. "But our moms are huddled together."

"Is that a good thing?" I ask.

"I don't know. I can't see my mom's face."

"I mean." I lower my voice. "As long as she hasn't been watching the security cameras at Target . . ."

Maya steps closer, pressing the backs of our hands together. "I really think she'll come around."

I raise my eyebrows. "Really?"

"She'll have to. She will. I mean, it's *you*—" Suddenly, her hand falls to her pocket. "Yet another text." She pulls her phone out, looks at it, and looks up at me.

Her mouth hangs open.

My stomach drops. "Everything okay?"

"It's Sara." She peers up at me. "She says she's here. She's right outside."

CHAPTER THIRTY-SIX
MAYA

There she is. There's Sara. She's standing under the restaurant awning and tapping a finger against her leg nervously. There's an oval sticker on her dress with the words *I voted*.

"You drove all the way down here to vote?" I ask her.

She shrugs and smiles a little.

"Looked into Newton, and he's the ultimate troll. The chance to say fuck you to him was worth the gas money."

"Thanks for voting," I tell her. "And for coming here."

"Your mom told me where you were." She bites her lip. "Maya, I'm sorry. This was our last summer. I messed up. I really did."

"I'm sorry too." I embrace her.

"It kills me that you were going through so much, and you felt like you couldn't talk to me."

"I should have told you how I was feeling instead of bottling it up," I tell her. "And you were right. About me being privileged. I am. You had a ton of stuff on your plate, and I'm sorry I wasn't as understanding as I could've been."

We hug each other again.

"How've you been?" I ask her. "How's the dorm? Jenna? I want to know everything I've missed."

"The dorm is great, Jenna is good." Sara nods. "My summer class is okay. Work is fine. Busy. I love it there. But it gets kind of lonely sometimes too."

"Lonely?" I glance at her. "I thought you'd have five hundred friends by now."

"Maybe I do." She laughs. "But still, it's not the same. They can't get me in the way someone can who's known me since the Elmo days, you know?"

"I still have some of your fanfiction somewhere."

"Shut up." She laughs. "You do not have my 'tickle me' fanfic saved up."

"Just the drawings," I concede. "I could blackmail you for real."

"Where do you think you'll be applying next year?" she asks. "Deadlines for college are around the corner."

"Haven't thought about it much," I tell her.

"You'll at least apply to UGA, right?" She smiles.

"You've been brainwashing me about it since we were in

middle school, so maybe."

"Oh!" Her eyes light up. "I almost forgot. I got something for you!"

She opens up her purse, digs through, and pulls out a book.

"Is that . . . ?" My eyes widen.

"Yep." She grins. "Angie Thomas's newest book, and surprise! It's personalized to you."

I open the copy. Sure enough, there's my name in gold Sharpie.

"I can't believe it!" I hug her. She was thinking of me. Even when we weren't speaking—she had missed me too.

The restaurant front door swings open just then, and Jamie pops out.

"Hey," he says.

"Hi." I grin back.

We both smile at each other until Sara clears her throat.

"Oh." Jamie blushes. "Hi. And, um, sorry to interrupt, but Cobb and Fulton County are both about to report their results," he says. "Figured you might want to watch it?"

"We'll be right there," I tell him.

He grins at me. I flush a little.

"Whoa," Sara says, when the door shuts behind him. "What was that?"

"The results are in."

429

"That's not what I was talking about. Spill it."

"Yeah." I shrug. "So, we, um, kissed today."

"You what?" She breaks into a huge grin. "Is it too obnoxious to say I told you so?"

"It really is. And you did *not* tell me so!"

"Basically I did! I totally did!" She pokes my shoulder.

I can't even put into words how nice it is to share this with her. To tell her about Jamie. To see her so happy for us. I don't know what our friendship will look like going forward, now that we live two hours apart. But I'm so glad she's back in my life again.

When we step back into the restaurant, the mood is noticeably different. Reporters are pacing. The cameraman is biting his nails. Everyone is murmuring quietly. The television news anchor's voice echoes through the restaurant. I settle into a high-back chair next to Jamie, and Sara takes the one next to me.

DeKalb County is still colored in deep blue.

"Why is everyone looking so nervous?" I ask Jamie. "I mean . . . we're winning."

"Yeah, but the margin is shrinking."

"It's still in the double digits. I'm telling you—the KKK Grand Wizard endorsement is a fatal flaw. There's no way Newton is winning."

But then Fulton County results start pouring in. The

double-digit lead trickles.

"He's still got the upper hand," I tell Jamie.

"Yeah . . . ," he says. "I think these are the more conservative polling places reporting anyway."

Even though he nods supportively, I can tell in his eyes—he's worried. And I can't deny the knot that's settled in my stomach.

When the Cobb County precincts start reporting, the race tightens down to the single digits. Rossum has the lead in some polling precincts, but Newton is catching up. Quickly. Most of the wins and losses in each polling station are literally by one or two percent.

Jamie reaches for my hand under the table. It's going to shift, I tell myself. It has to. There's no way they're letting that Koopa Troopa win.

But then the northern districts start reporting.

It's like a kid tipped a red paint bucket over the entire upper portion of the map.

"It's a mistake," Jamie says slowly. "It has to be."

But it's not. It's real. The map is shifting red, and suddenly I feel like I'm in one of those cartoons, where Wile E. Coyote thinks he's standing on the edge of a solid cliff—except when he glances down, there's only the nothingness of air.

Because that's what we have now. Nothing.

The next forty-five minutes pass in a haze as everything

shifts. Then the final numbers flash on the screen: fifty-one point eight percent for Newton. Forty-eight percent for Rossum.

All those doors we knocked on. Every flyer we handed out. Every sign we put it up. It doesn't matter. We lost.

The restaurant is silent. Sara slides over and hugs me. Gabe leans forward, staring at the screen, as if he's willing it to change the results by the force of his expression. Jordan Rossum . . . he looks as devastated as I feel.

Jamie squeezes my hand. I fight back tears. I glance over at Imam Jackson and my mother—they're whispering to each other by the back wall. Lauren's on the phone talking to someone in a hushed voice.

It's like someone died.

Rossum heads outside with his team. Journalists hurry behind him. The people on the television are dancing in red T-shirts and fist pumping. It settles in me like a sinking brick—H.B. 28 is going to pass in the senate. It's going to become law.

My stomach feels like there's quicksand inside—my heart spiraling down.

After some time passes, Jordan returns. He stands in front of the restaurant. And then he concedes the election. Tears fill my eyes. I glance at Jamie—he looks shattered.

Rossum is eloquent and charming. He thanks all of us volunteers for everything we've done. Hannah's mother,

Lucia Adams, gets a shout-out for her election protection work and her fight to keep polling stations in minority areas from closing. There's a smattering of applause from the audience.

But I don't feel like clapping.

"I just don't get it," Jamie says quietly.

"Sorry, guys," Sara says gently. "I know you both put your hearts and souls into this."

I shrug, but yeah—we really did. And for what? We got close. But we lost.

"Hey, sweetie." It's my mother.

I drop Jamie's hand from under the table and straighten. Did she see us? If she did, she's got a complete poker face about it.

"You both doing okay?" she asks Jamie and me.

"Not really," Jamie says.

"Not sure how to feel okay when everything we worked for blew up in flames," I tell her.

"It's normal to feel disappointed right now," she says as Lauren joins us.

I don't know if *my* mom has figured anything out, but judging from Lauren's huge smile as she glances from Jamie to me, she *definitely* can tell.

"I just don't get it," I say. "How could they do this? How could they want him to represent us after everything he's said and done?"

"I know. But we came close," my mother says. "The closest anyone came in this district in almost thirty years, actually."

"Close isn't winning. He lost."

"You're right. But don't forget, this was a special election—this seat will be up for grabs again in sixteen months. Now we know it's winnable."

"And you see that woman over there?" Lauren nods to Hannah's mother, who's talking to a reporter right now. "There's quite a bit of buzz about her. She might run."

"But in the meantime, H.B. 28 passed in the House this morning." I sigh. "And there's a supermajority in the state congress now. So it'll become law."

"Oh yes." Lauren nods. "About that. There's a group of lawyers from Austin and Byrne who are teaming up with the ACLU to get ahead of that constitutional mess."

"Austin and Byrne?" Jamie tilts his head. He picks up a glass of water. "The one with the billboard up by The Temple?"

"The one and only." Lauren smiles slightly. "Our family friend Mark Plummons said he found information about it in a bathroom at Sophie's bat mitzvah. Isn't that the strangest thing?"

Jamie spits out water.

"Really?" I ask her. "They're already planning to fight the bill?"

"Hoping to scare them off before it goes any further, but no matter what happens, they're going to fight it to the end."

I glance at Jamie. He looks back at me and smiles a little. There's a team of lawyers working to squash this bill. We played a part in that. It's not much—hardly anything, to be honest—but it's something to hold on to. It gives me hope.

Imam Jackson approaches my mother just then—a few journalists want some comments from the masjid. Once she leaves, Jamie and I use the opportunity to slip into the back of the restaurant.

"Feeling any better?" I ask him.

"Still hurts like I got run over by a train," he replies.

"Same here. All that work . . ."

"For nothing."

I look at Jamie's crestfallen face. I take a step closer to him.

"I mean, I guess it wasn't for nothing," I slowly say. "Like our moms said, we got really close. Next time we'll get closer. Next time we'll win."

"But we could do it all over again and have the same result."

"Next election, there'll be more of us. You and I can vote by then. So will Drew, Felipe, Nolan, and Shelby."

"Yeah," he says. "Still . . ."

He's right. We don't know what will happen. We could get back out there next year. Knock on doors and put up signs, hand out water bottles to thirsty canvassers. Vote.

And we could still lose.

"We might give it our all and crash and burn." I take a step closer to him. "But we might win. We might actually change things. And *maybe* that makes it still worth going for, don't you think?"

I lace my fingers in his as he looks down at me.

"You've really thought this whole thing through, haven't you?" he says with a small smile.

But I don't reply. I kiss him instead.

AUTHORS' NOTE

In November of 2016, we watched in horror and panic as Donald Trump was elected president of the United States. Like many people, we were anxious about the type of world our children would now grow up in. Trump's hatred had given full license to others who shared his racist and bigoted views, in a way that felt very personal to us as Muslim and Jewish women. Antisemitism and Islamophobia rose sharply and vandalism of mosques and synagogues grew commonplace. In our home state of Georgia, a state representative proposed a bill that would have effectively banned Muslim women from wearing hijab in public. Days later, a high school in the Atlanta suburbs was graffitied with Trump's name, a swastika, and several racist and homophobic slurs. The bad news was relentless—and here in Georgia, it felt like we were drowning in it.

But then we stumbled upon a bright spot: a special election for a newly vacant seat in our district for the US House of Representatives. Georgia's Sixth District had been firmly Republican for as long as we could remember, but now an Atlanta man named Jon Ossoff hoped to change that. He demanded accountability and vowed to stand up against bigotry and hateful rhetoric. After weeks of feeling helpless against an onslaught of national horrors, this was exactly what we needed. His announcement was a raft in a sea of bad news.

We immediately threw ourselves into the campaign. Neither of us had knocked on doors for a political candidate before, and we were nervous—but it felt like something tangible we could do. The process was strange, sometimes tedious, and often thankless, but it was also uplifting and rewarding. And it was the first time we truly grasped the power of local activism. Ultimately, Ossoff lost his race— but the results in our deep-red Georgia district were remarkably close.

For us, these moments felt like the beginning of a story— one about joy, heartache, resistance, and hope. Maya, Jamie, and *Yes No Maybe So* were born from our belief that activism and love can heal and connect us, even in the most difficult times.

As for Georgia's Sixth District? Less than eighteen months after Ossoff's narrow defeat, Democrat Lucy McBath defeated the Republican incumbent in the 2018 midterm elections. She's the first Democrat to represent our district in forty years.

There is hope. Hold it tight, and keep fighting.

ACKNOWLEDGMENTS

Just like a political campaign, *Yes No Maybe So* wouldn't be possible without the team of passionate people who believed in this story and made magic happen behind the scenes. We're filled to the brim with gratitude for the many people in our corner, including:

Our brilliant editor, Donna Bray, who is changing history one book at a time.

Our phenomenal team at HarperCollins and Balzer + Bray, including Tiara Kittrell; Suzanne Murphy; Jean McGinley; Andrea Pappenheimer and team; Nellie Kurtzman, Audrey Diestelkamp, and team; Sari Murray; Patty Rosati and team; Alison Donalty and Chris Kwon; and Alessandra Balzer.

Soumbal Qureshi for the gorgeous cover art.

Our squad of rock star agents: Taylor Martindale Kean, Brooks Sherman, Wendi Gu, Stephanie Koven, Mary Pender, Kim Yau, and our teams at Full Circle, Janklow & Nesbit, UTA, and Paradigm.

Lucy Rogers and our incredible team from Simon &

Schuster UK, Leonel Teti and his fellow superstars at Puck, and the rest of our amazing international publishers, who took a chance on a book about US local elections.

Stacey Abrams, for literally everything.

The booksellers, librarians, teachers, Instagrammers, bloggers, and YouTubers, who help our books find their readers. You deserve the world.

Our expert readers, who made this book so much better with their thoughtful feedback: Mike Reitzes, Celeste Pewter, and Jennifer Dugan—and a special shout-out to Amie Herbert for bar mitzvah consultation!

The friends who offered their wisdom, talked us through titles and covers, and kept our heads on straight: S. K. Ali, Sakib Qureshi and Sameera Fazili, Adam Silvera, Jasmine Warga, David Arnold, Angie Thomas, Emily X.R. Pan, Nic Stone, Mackenzi Lee, Meg Medina, Rose Brock, Dahlia Adler, and so many more.

Matthew Eppard, Diana Sousa, and Sharon Morse, as well as both Phil Bildner and Cristin Terrill at the Author Village, who keep the world spinning.

Our biggest champions: Kalsoom and Anwar Saeed, Eileen Thomas, Jim and Candy Goldstein, Ali Saeed, Aamir Saeed, Caroline Goldstein, Sam Goldstein, and the Albertallis—with next-level, holy-fork gratitude to Kashif Iqbal and Brian Albertalli, who held down the fort during all the hours at Intermezzo and the Target patio session.

The kiddos who make the whole fight worthwhile: Waleed, Owen, Musa, Henry, and Zayn.

The volunteers, staffers, canvassers, protesters, resisters, voters, and all of you who have your representatives' numbers on speed dial. We see you, and we appreciate your efforts with all our hearts.

The organizations who have been fighting the good fight all along. There are far too many great ones to mention, but here are a few of our favorites. Check out their websites to learn more about them, and consider donating if you can.

American Civil Liberties Union: www.aclu.org
Southern Poverty Law Center: www.splcenter.org
Refugee and Immigrant Center for Education and Legal
   Services: www.raicestexas.org
Rock the Vote: www.rockthevote.org
Fair Fight: www.fairfight.com

Turn the page for a sneak peek at *Kate in Waiting*

OVERTURE

It really feels like an ending, in every way possible. With the curtains pulled closed, the stage might as well be another planet. A well-lit planet full of giant foam set pieces, inhabited only by Andy and me—and Matt.

Coke-Ad Matt.

"It's now or never," whispers Andy. He doesn't move an inch.

Neither do I.

We just sort of stand there, in the shadow of a papier-mâché Audrey 2.

There's nothing sadder than the end of a crush. And it's not like this was one of those distant-stranger crushes. Andy and I have actually talked to this boy. Tons of words, on multiple glorious occasions. No small feat, since Matt's the kind of gorgeous that usually renders us speechless. He's got one of those old-timey faces, with blond hair and pink cheeks. Our friend Brandie collects Coca-Cola merch, and I swear the vintage ad in her bathroom looks exactly like Matt. Thus the nickname. The ad says, "Thirst stops here." But in our case, the thirst doesn't stop.

It's basic Avril Lavigne math. We were the junior theater counselors. He was our cute townie vocal consultant. You truly could not make it any more obvious. And for a full six weeks, he's been the sun in our solar system. But he lives up the road from camp, in Mentone, Alabama.

Which is just about a hundred miles away from Roswell, Georgia.

So Andy's right. Now or never.

Deep breath. "Hey. Uh, Matt."

I swear I can feel Anderson's surprised approval. Damn, Garfield. Just going for it. Get yours.

I clear my throat. "So. We wanted to say goodbye. And. Um. Thank you."

Matt slides a sheet of music into his tote bag and smiles. "Thank me?"

"For the vocal consultation," I say. "And everything."

Andy nods fervently, adjusting his glasses.

"Aww, Kate! You too. So cool meeting you guys." Matt hoists his tote bag over his shoulder, shifting his weight toward the door, just barely. Exit posture. Crap. I'm just going to—

"Can we take a selfie?" I blurt. I'm already cringing. You know what would be cool? If my voice would stop shaking. Also, Anderson. My dude. Anytime you want to step up, be my guest.

"Oh, sure," Matt says. "Let's do it."

Well then.

We squeeze into the frame, curtain tickling our backs, and I stretch my arm out at the up angle, just like Anderson trained me. And we smile. I mean, I'm trying to. But I'm so flustered, my lips are trembling.

It's worth it. Even if I come out looking like a dazed fangirl, it's worth it. Raina and Brandie have been begging for photographic evidence of Coke-Ad Matt's cuteness, and God knows Instagram's yielded nothing.

But this picture isn't for the squad. Not really. Honestly, they're both just going to make fun of us for having yet another communal crush. According to Raina, Anderson and I are enmeshed, which basically means we're codependent. Apparently some people believe falling in love is a thing you're supposed to do on your own.

And yeah, Raina aced AP Psych so hard, she's practically a licensed psychologist already. But here's the thing she doesn't get. It's not about Matt. Or Josh from last summer, who had very strong opinions about breakfast. Or Alexander from the summer before, who was really into being from Michigan. It has nothing to do with any of them.

It's about Anderson and me. It's about scheming in the prop closet and reading way too much into every flicker of eye contact. It's about brushing our teeth six times a day, always prepared for the unexpected makeout scenario. And in the end, when the makeout scenarios never materialized, it hardly mattered. It didn't matter. Because the makeouts weren't the point.

The giddiness was the point.

And I feel like this all sounds like a Bit Much, but that's just Andy and me. We bring it out in each other. And truthfully, summer crushes make for a surprisingly fun and robust team activity.

Less fun now that summer's over. Now it's just that sinking-boat feeling of a crush lost too soon. A crush cut down in its prime.

But that boat's so much less lonely when your best friend's on board.

SCENE 1

Five minutes into junior year, and I'm done. No, seriously. Let's burn this whole year to the ground.

For one thing, I can barely keep my eyes open. Which doesn't bode well, seeing as I haven't even entered the building yet. Or left the school parking lot. Or even unbuckled my seat belt.

And it's Anderson's fault.

Because Anderson Walker knows I need seven hours of sleep to not be a zombie demon on Xanax, and yet. And yet! This mess of a boy let himself into my house, into my room, and turned on my lights at five thirty a.m. Because he needed my input on his first-day-back cardigan choice. Navy blue with brown buttons, or navy with navy buttons. "Just give me your gut reaction," he'd said.

My gut reaction was hurling a pillow at his face.

Now, almost three hours later—right on schedule—he's spiraling again in the parking lot.

"You're sure the navy's okay?"

"Andy. It's fine."

"Just fine?"

"More than fine. You look perfect."

And he does. He always does. Anderson's honestly too cute for this earth. Smooth brown skin, dimples, and a short, tapered Afro, not to mention big brown eyes behind plastic-framed glasses. And he's got that nautical schoolboy aesthetic down to a science: crisp button-downs and cardigans and rolled-up pants.

He rubs his cheeks. "I just don't want to look like trash. It's the first day of—"

But he's drowned out by trap music blasting out of a Jeep. Make way for the fuckboys.

Unfortunately, Roswell Hill High School is fuckboy ground zero. Mostly the suburban athletic subtype. *Fuckboius jockus*. No joke. Just stand in the hallway and put your arm out for two seconds, and you'll hit a fuckboy, right in his mesh athletic shorts. They're everywhere, armies of them, all in RHHS team gear. So prolific we had to give them a not-so-secret code name. F-boys. Which doesn't exactly obscure the meaning, but at least it keeps Brandie's innocent ears from exploding.

I glare at the Jeep through Anderson's passenger window. The driver keeps cupping his hands around his mouth, megaphone-style, to holler at groups of girls who walk by. The f-boy mating call. But his car door's flung wide open and is therefore blocking my door.

The sheer audacity of f-boys.

6

"Kate." Anderson pokes me with his keys, but I snatch them. I love his Funko Rapunzel keychain so much, it almost makes me want to learn to drive. Almost.

Our phones buzz simultaneously. Text from Raina or Brandie, no doubt.

Andy glances at his screen. "Come on, they're already down there."

Okay, that gets me moving. We've seen Raina a few times since camp ended, but Brandie left for Mexico the day before we got back. Which means it's been over six weeks since the full squad's been together.

Anderson grabs my hand to help me over the gear shift, and then we cut through the parking lot, bypassing the front entrance entirely. Instead, we head for the side door, which has direct access to the theater hall. Straight to Ms. Zhao's room, where all the usual suspects have gathered.

Honestly, we theater kids are as instantly recognizable as f-boys. Though it's not so much about the clothes in our case. It's more like an aura. My brother said once that theater kids walk around like we're each under our own tiny spotlight. Pretty sure it wasn't a compliment.

It's true, though. Like, there's none of that forced nonchalance people have about the first day of school. Instead, we have Margaret Daskin and Emma McLeod near the accessibility elevator, butchering *Newsies*, and Lindsay Ward gasping into her phone, and Colin Nakamura using Pierra Embry's head as a drum. And of course, Lana Bennett's delivering an urgent lecture to Kelly Matthews, who I can only assume made the mistake of referring to the school musical as a play. There is literally nothing Lana Bennett loves more than explaining the difference between musicals and plays to people who . . . clearly know the difference between musicals and plays.

Brandie and Raina are relatively chill, though, just leaning against the back wall, reading their phones. I think it's generally understood that, out of our squad, they're the ones who mostly have their lives together. I used to go back and forth in my head about which one of them was the mom friend, but the truth is, they're both the mom friend. They're just the mom friend in different ways. Raina's the bossy mom who makes everyone stay healthy and hydrated and on top of their schoolwork. Brandie's the soft mom who'll let you cry all over her cardigan when your crush starts dating an f-girl from the volleyball team.

Today they're so distracted, we're practically nose-to-nose before they notice us.

"Boo," I say.

They both look up with a start, and Raina's eyes go straight to Anderson's keys in my hand. "Kate, did you drive?"

I laugh, tossing the keys back to Andy. "Yeah, no."

"Didn't you say you were going to—"

"Yup. And I will."

Raina narrows her eyes.

"I will! Really soon."

I mean, technically, I could take the driver's test

8

tomorrow—I've had my permit for almost a year and a half. But I haven't taken the plunge. And I'm not exactly dying to, either.

At the end of the day, I'm really a passenger seat kind of person.

Brandie hugs me. "Your hair looks so cute!"

So maybe Anderson's five-thirty wake-up call paid off. Normally, my hair's a notorious mess. It's that halfway point between blond and brown, and left to its own devices, it's almost recklessly wavy. But right now, it's what Anderson calls white-girl-on-YouTube wavy. I do think it's worth the effort every now and then, given that I'm a person whose overall attractiveness is highly hair-correlated. But now I feel like I'm broadcasting to the whole world how hard I'm trying.

"How was Mexico?" I brush the ruffled sleeve of Brandie's dress. "I love this."

She smiles. "It was great. Really hot, though. How was camp?"

"I mean, none of our campers died."

"Well done," Raina says.

"And." I press my hand to my heart. "Matt knows our names."

"Cokehead Matt?" Raina grins.

"Okay, that's blasphemy." I scrunch my nose at her. "I'm serious, he's like an old-timey dreamboat—"

"Which they'd already know if someone was capable of taking group selfies without decapitating people."

"Um, it's not my fault Matt's six feet tall," I say. "Did I mention he's six feet tall?"

"Literally ten times," says Raina.

Anderson turns to Brandie and Raina. "Did I tell you he knew how to pronounce Aeschylus? On the first try?"

"Sounds like boyfriend material," says Brandie.

"God yes," says Anderson. "Don't you want to just, like . . . wear his letterman jacket and let him pin you—"

"—to a bed?" Raina asks.

Anderson bites back a smile, and then shakes his head quickly. "Anyway." His eyes flick back to Ms. Zhao's door. "No updates?"

"Nothing," Raina says. "Not even a clue. Harold thinks it's going to be *A Chorus Line*."

Anderson whirls to face her head-on. "Why?"

"Gut feeling?" Raina shrugs. "Ginger intuition?"

"Is ginger intuition a thing?"

"I mean, according to Harold."

Harold MacCallum: world-class jellybean. Sunshine in boy form. Raina's boyfriend. They met about a year ago in this online trans support group Raina moderates. Harold's cis, but his twin sibling is nonbinary, and he actually lives pretty close to us. He's super shy, and kind of wonderfully awkward. Raina gets this smile in her voice whenever she talks about him.

"Okay, well I have a theory," Anderson says. "It's a medieval year."

"What?"

"Hear me out. Last year was *West Side Story*. Freshman year was *Into the Woods*. And they did *Bye Bye Birdie* when we were in eighth grade."

"I don't get it," says Brandie.

"I'm just saying. The PTA is super cheap, right? So we're just cycling through two sets of costumes. We've got the fifties costumes and the medieval costumes, and they alternate them so no one catches on. Just watch. Any minute, Zhao's coming out with the sign-up sheet." Andy's enjoying this now—drawing out the info, dimples activating. "And you'll see. It's a medieval year. Mark my words. *Cinderella, Camelot*—"

"Or it's going to be *A Chorus Line*," I say, "and you're going to feel like such a dumbass."

"Yeah, but." He lifts a finger. "*A Chorus Line* in medieval clothes. Follow the money, Garfield. Follow the money."

Raina and I snort at the exact same moment. But before either of us can make the requisite wiseass remark, Ms. Zhao's door creaks open.

And the whole corridor goes silent.

Anderson grabs my hand, and my heart's in my throat. Which makes zero sense, since there's no suspense here. It's the same every year. Ms. Zhao announces the fall musical on the first day of school. Then I spend a week or two freaking out for no reason, playing the soundtrack on repeat, letting my daydreams run wild. It's that same nonsensical thought every time.

11

Maybe this is the year. Maybe this is when the switch flips. But the truth is, I always know exactly where I'll find myself when the cast list gets posted.

Bottom of the page. Nameless part in the ensemble. I'm an absolute legend in the category of Nameless Parts in the Ensemble.

But somehow this moment gets me every time. The way everyone freezes when Ms. Zhao steps out of the theater room. The way she keeps her face impassive and doesn't make eye contact with anyone until the sign-up sheet's officially on the door.

At least that's how it's supposed to go.

But when the door flings open at last, it isn't Ms. Zhao there at all.

BECKY ALBERTALLI

returns with a crush-worthy new novel
about love, friendship, and theater

KATE
IN
WAITING

...IS ON HER WAY!

BALZER + BRAY

An Imprint of HarperCollinsPublishers

www.epicreads.com